EMERGENCY LIFTOFF!

"Portmaster, this is Warhammer. Request permission to lift ship."

"Negative, Warhammer. Permission to lift denied. Report with your entire crew to the Portmaster's office."

"Unable to comply. Request permis—"

The sudden tug of a tractor beam cut him off midword. The 'Hammer began to lurch and sway as the beam kept on pulling the ship downward.

LeSoit could feel the strength members of the 'Hammer's frame vibrating. He reached for the console and pulled on the forward nullgravs. Nothing happened—only the steady throb of overstressed metal.

LeSoit hit the console again. With a tremendous deep-throated roar, the heavy realspace engines came on. Power that should have driven Warhammer's mass up to near-lightspeed poured out of the ship's engines, turning the deckplates of the bay to slag beneath them. All over the console, warning lights burned red. "This is it—either we shake apart fighting their beam, or we burn it out and break free...."

**Tor Books by
Debra Doyle and James D. Macdonald**

*The Price of the Stars
Starpilot's Grave
By Honor Betray'd*

BY HONOR BETRAY'D

BOOK THREE OF MAGEWORLDS

DEBRA DOYLE AND
JAMES D. MACDONALD

A TOM DOHERTY ASSOCIATES BOOK
NEW YORK

This is a work of fiction. All the characters and events portrayed in this book are fictitious, and any resemblance to real people or events is purely coincidental.

BY HONOR BETRAY'D

Copyright © 1994 by Debra Doyle & James D. Macdonald

All rights reserved, including the right to reproduce this book, or portions thereof, in any form.

Cover art by Romas

A Tor Book
Published by Tom Doherty Associates, Inc.
175 Fifth Avenue
New York, N.Y. 10010

Tor® is a registered trademark of Tom Doherty Associates, Inc.

ISBN: 0-812-51706-7

First edition: July 1994

Printed in the United States of America

0 9 8 7 6 5 4 3 2 1

For Margaret Esterl Macdonald
"Art in the blood, Watson."

ACKNOWLEDGMENTS

Thanks, as usual, are owed to a lot of people: to Katie and Sherwood, for constant encouragement; to Nancy and Elric, for friendship and hospitality above and beyond the call of duty; to Andrew, for commentary and helpful suggestions. We would also like to thank our agent, Valerie Smith, and our editor, Patrick Nielsen Hayden, for their enthusiasm, patience, and support.

Prologue
Galcen Nearspace: *Sword-of-the-Dawn*

T HE HEARTWORLD of the Republic hung against the darkness of space like an enormous, glittering opal, swirled with bright green and deep blue and white streaks of cloud. Looking out from the observation deck of his flagship, Grand Admiral Theio syn-Ricte sus-Airaalin knew that he had accomplished the impossible. He had brought a warfleet through hyperspace to strike without warning, and all the enemy's inmost citadels lay under his hand. He called the roll of them in his mind: Galcen Prime Base; Galcen South Polar; the Grand Council of the Republic; the Adepts' Retreat.

Knowledge of his victory brought sus-Airaalin no special pleasure. Now, and not the long years of preparations or the desperate battle just past, was the period of greatest danger. Having done the impossible, he would have to do more— hold what he had gained, and bring the outlying sectors of the Republic securely under control.

We can do it, he thought. *With luck, and with the aid of the Circles. If we don't lose too much of the fleet in any one action, or if we can augment our forces somehow . . . we've spent too much already, in ships and in lives, when we had little enough to begin with.*

The commander of the Resurgency's warfleet was a realist, or as much a realist as any man could be and hope to bring back the old ways and the old knowledge. sus-Airaalin had understood from the beginning that his only chance for success lay in throwing massive strength into a single unexpected blow, crushing the head of the serpent while it slept. But the broken pieces of this particular serpent could still fight; and if they should rejoin, like the braidworm of legend that made one beast out of many, then what the Adept-worlds had done to the Circles thirty years before would pale beside their vengeance now.

He would stop that, if he could, for the sake of a generation not yet born when the Old War ended in crushing defeat and systematic, relentless destruction. The young men and women who crewed the ships of sus-Airaalin's fleet and worked in his new-formed Mage-Circles were children of poverty and repression. They had never known the former days of power and vainglory, when Eraasian warfleets raided the Adept-worlds at will and broke whole planets for daring to resist. For them—and not for the Resurgency—sus-Airaalin would do whatever must be done.

Even now, he thought. *Even to this.*

Straightening his shoulders, he turned from the viewport and left the *Sword*'s observation deck, making his way through the narrow passageways to the detention area at the heart of the ship. Outside the door of the deepest cell, he paused for a moment to gather his resolve, then laid his hand on the lockplate. The door opened. He stepped inside, and the door closed again behind him.

There was no light in the cell. sus-Airaalin touched a control near the door, and the ceiling panels began to emit a pale, dingy glow. The man who lay on the narrow metal bunk stirred briefly and opened his eyes; then, with an effort, he sat up, although his hands were manacled and chained to the wall behind him.

The prisoner was not a fearsome man to look at. He was scarcely taller than sus-Airaalin, without the Grand Admiral's compact sturdiness; his black hair hung lank around features made haggard by captivity. Not, one might think, a particularly threatening figure, but sus-Airaalin knew better. This was Errec Ransome, Master of the Adepts' Guild: the Breaker of Circles.

He regarded his visitor without surprise.

"My lord sus-Airaalin," he said.

The Grand Admiral inclined his head in the barest shadow of a formal bow. "Master Ransome."

"Your personal attention . . . honors me."

Although dried blood stained the pale skin around Ransome's mouth, still the Adept Master seemed amused. sus-Airaalin let the faint mockery go past unremarked. He had his own reasons for not giving Errec Ransome into the hands of the Resurgency's intelligence wing, reasons that had nothing to do with either Ransome's honor or sus-Airaalin's pleasure.

I ought to kill him now, sus-Airaalin thought. *The longer he's a prisoner, the greater the danger to all of us.*

"I know too much for you to kill me," said Ransome, as if he had read the unspoken thought—as perhaps he had. He was the Adept Master, and powerful enough that not even manacles wrought for that purpose could render him entirely harmless. "What you want, Magelord, you'll have to gain through your own strength. There's no Circle standing behind you here."

"No," agreed sus-Airaalin. The Mages of his Circle had given themselves into his control and his protection; he would not repay their faith by using them so. He unclipped the silver-and-ebony rod that hung from his belt and, stooping, laid it on the dull metal floor. "Nor will I forget myself and make this into a contest for lordship."

"You spoke differently at Prime Base."

"I offered you challenge then according to our way," sus-Airaalin told him. "And you refused. There is never a second challenge. That, also, is according to our way."

Irony flickered in the Adept Master's dark eyes. "And is this?"

sus-Airaalin didn't answer. Instead he drew in all his

strength—like a man preparing for some physical exertion, though no part of his body moved—and struck at the gates of Errec Ransome's mind.

It was like battering his fists against the barred and metal-bound doors of some massive citadel—like trying to break down the portal of the great Retreat itself. Wall upon wall it rose above him, tower upon tower, secret upon secret.

A cold wind tore the air about him, keening among the mountain crags. Black clouds spread out like ragged banners across the sky overhead. sus-Airaalin was alone. He longed to call upon the strength of his Circle, but he did not dare. He had laid his staff aside to keep that temptation from him.

Whatever happens, I will not give over those who have trusted me into the hands of the enemy.

He struck again at the ironwood gates. His knuckles split and bled with the force of the blow. He struck a third time, and the great gate splintered and fell open. sus-Airaalin stepped through the gap and entered into the citadel of the Breaker of Circles.

Within was desolation: courtyards empty of everything but blowing dust; rooms that held only sticks of broken furniture; dark halls leading nowhere except to doors locked strongly against further passage. One by one, sus-Airaalin smashed the doorways open, forcing his way into deserted chambers where nothing lived besides an echo of voices.

Is this all there is? He fought against a surge of bitter, irrational anger. *The Master of the Guild should have more to guard than dirt and rubble.*

He suppressed the thought and went on, searching always further down and inward. At last he came to a door that swung open easily when he put his hand against it. Inside, he found another barren space, this one empty except for the man who knelt there in meditation, with his back to a solid wooden door.

The man lifted his head. sus-Airaalin realized that he was facing Errec Ransome, as the Master of the Adepts' Guild might look if he lived another three decades or more. The sleek black hair was dulled with grey; the dark eyes were deep-set and shadowed in a worn and furrowed face. He followed sus-Airaalin's gaze past him to the locked door.

"Yes," he said. "What you look for is there."

"How do you know?"

The old man laughed. There was an edge of madness in the sound. "How could I not, my lord sus-Airaalin? You told me yourself with every lock and barrier you broke."

"Master Ransome," sus-Airaalin said. "Open the door. Or I will break it and you together."

The old man looked at him. sus-Airaalin heard the ghost of laughter in his breath. "Very well, my lord. It isn't locked. Open it yourself, if you want."

"I will," sus-Airaalin told the old man. He strode forward and swung open the door. There was nothing behind it but a blank wall of grey stone. Again sus-Airaalin heard the faint sound of Errec Ransome's voiceless laughter.

"You have your answer," Ransome said. "What you look for, you will not find. This place will crumble before it yields up anything more to you. Now go."

sus-Airaalin shook his head. "No. I *will* have it."

He put his hands against the blank wall and pushed with all the strength in his shoulders.

Wood and stone cried out under the strain, but nothing moved. The ground shifted underneath his feet in a queasy sideways slide, and an upward glance showed him that the plaster ceiling had broken into a thousand tiny cracks. White dust fell onto his hair and shoulders in a powdery rain, and the walls began sliding and tilting against one another at odd angles like paper cards.

sus-Airaalin abandoned his efforts and ran. Behind him in the swaying, ransacked fortress, the old man kept on laughing.

With a desperate surge of effort, the Grand Admiral pulled himself away from the treacherous architecture of Ransome's mind. When his vision cleared, he was back in the physical reality of the flagship's detention level, still standing where he had planted his feet at the beginning of the struggle. His staff lay untouched on the floor.

Across from him, Errec Ransome slumped against the wall of the cell. Fresh blood trickled from the Adept Master's nostrils, and from the corners of his eyes. But when he straightened and met sus-Airaalin's gaze, there was a dark triumph on his face.

"Not yet, my lord sus-Airaalin," he said. "Not yet."

PART ONE

I. Gyfferan Farspace: *Night's-Beautiful-Daughter*
   Suivi Point: Entiboran Resistance
      Headquarters; *Warhammer*
   Nammerin: Namport

Out on the farthest edge of Gyfferan-controlled space, the texture of the universe stretched and altered. Like a shadow against the stars, the flattened black teardrop shape of a Deathwing raider emerged from hyperspace. Minutes later a second ship appeared. This one displayed the bright colors and needle-sharp outline of a Space Force surface-to-hyperspace courier. Together, the mismatched pair began their realspace run toward the heart of the Gyfferan system.

On board *Night's-Beautiful-Daughter*—for so the Deathwing's log recordings had named the Magebuilt vessel—Mistress Llannat Hyfid wandered about the empty corridors, trying in vain to escape her own increasing inner tension.

Llannat was a small woman, dark-haired and brown-skinned, and her appearance these days implied enough contradictions to make anyone tense. She wore the black broadcloth tunic and trousers that were an Adept's formal garb; but her boots were Space Force standard issue, and instead of an Adept's plain wooden staff she carried the short, silver-bound ebony rod that was a Magelord's weapon and badge of rank. The crew members on board the Deathwing avoided her as much as possible, out of a respect that verged on superstitious awe.

The clothes and the staff don't help even a little with the main problem, she thought glumly. Her wanderings had taken her to the ship's galley, where the smell of fresh cha'a emanated from a bulky, squarish urn. *We've got to make it to Gyffer without getting blown up by system defenses programmed to fire on "nervous."*

Llannat had given the order for the hyperspace transit herself. At least, everybody else on board the Deathwing said that she had given it. She didn't recall doing any such thing; she'd been deep in a trance at the time, observing the structure of the universe through a Magelord's eyes.

And now I've got the whole damned crew looking at me like they expect me to go crazy or work a miracle, or maybe both at once. . . .

She abandoned her search for a mug and pressed the heels of her hands against her temples.

"I have a headache," she said aloud.

Her words sounded flat and dull against the echo-absorbent walls of the Deathwing's galley. She saw a movement in the doorway: Lieutenant Vinhalyn, Space Force reservist and scholar of Mageworlds language and culture, the acting captain of *Night's-Beautiful-Daughter.*

"We brought the emergency medikit over from *Naversey,*" Vinhalyn said. "There may be something in there that can help you out."

"I don't think so. It's not that kind of an ache."

"If you're sure . . ."

"I'm sure," she told him. "I'm a medic, remember?"

The expression on his face made it plain that he hadn't, in fact, remembered. Llannat shook her head, resigned.

"Never mind," she said. "I have trouble remembering it myself sometimes. Believe me, life was a whole lot easier when I was just Ensign Hyfid of the Space Force Medical Service."

Of course, that was before I started hearing voices that

*weren't there and seeing things that hadn't happened yet
and coming loose from my body while I was drifting off to
sleep at night. Nobody asked me if I wanted all of that, but
I got it anyway . . . and the next thing I knew, there I was
on a mountaintop on Galcen, with Master Ransome himself
asking me if I wanted to join the Guild and be an Adept.*

Llannat sighed. *And like a fool, I said yes.*

Vinhalyn looked at her. The scholar-reservist was an older
man whose active service dated back to the end of the First
Magewar, and he deferred to Llannat as he had to the
Adepts of those earlier days. "If there's anything I can do to
help . . ."

"Not really," she said. "But thanks. Let me know when
we make contact with Gyfferan Inspace Control."

Vinhalyn nodded and left.

Llannat watched him go, then went back to looking for a
cup. When she found one, on a shelf where a half-dozen of
the standard-issue plastic mugs from *Naversey* stood among
the Deathwing's shorter, rounder ones, she poured herself
some cha'a from the galley urn. What sort of hot drink the
Mageworlders had brewed in the big metal pot she didn't
know—maybe Vinhalyn did; she'd have to ask him about it
sometime—but the *Daughter*'s current crew had managed to
adapt the filtration setup to produce cha'a of hair-curling
strength.

She sipped at the steaming liquid. *The Professor would
have known what they used to brew on board the old
Deathwings,* she thought. *He probably drank enough of it in
his day.*

"What's this 'probably' nonsense?" she muttered to herself. "The Prof *owned* this ship, galley and all."

He hadn't just owned it; that was the problem. The
Professor—whose true name she had never learned, and
doubted that anyone living had ever heard—had been a
Magelord himself before he abandoned sorcery and gave his
oath to the ruling House of Entibor. What kept Llannat
Hyfid awake during the night and made her pace the ship's
corridors during the day was knowing that the Professor had
intended *Night's-Beautiful-Daughter* for her.

First his staff, she thought. *Then his ship. What other little bequests does he have for me. that I haven't found yet?*

The original legacy had come to Llannat blamelessly enough. She'd lost her own staff in the fighting on Darvell, the same day the Professor had died,. and Beka Rosselin-Metadi—in an impatient, almost unthinking gesture—had given her the dead man's staff as a replacement. Master Ransome, who hated the Magelords as he hated nothing else in the civilized galaxy, wasn't likely to be pleased with Llannat if he ever found out. In the end, however, an Adept's choice of staff was a personal decision. Not even the Master of the Guild could force her to alter it.

The ship was something else again. The Professor had emptied *Night's-Beautiful-Daughter* to vacuum and left her to drift. When the derelict raider turned up in the Mageworlds Border Zone, the pilot and copilot were still on board—five hundred years after the Professor had cut their throats and left Llannat Hyfid a message written in their blood.

"Adept from the forest world: bring this message to She-who-leads. . . ."

Those were the words as Llannat remembered them, from the waking dream in which she had relived the Professor's deed. Lieutenant Vinhalyn, however, had translated the blood-scrawled characters somewhat differently: *"Find the Domina."*

But the Domina was dead.

"Domina of Entibor," said Beka Rosselin-Metadi. She jerked the twisted iron tiara out of her hair and threw it across the room onto the rumpled bedsheets. On Suivi Point appearances were everything; the acting government of Entibor-in-Exile kept its front office ready for official visitors, even early and unexpected ones, by throwing all the clutter into the living quarters at the back. "Leader of the Second Resistance. Hope of the Galaxy. It stinks like a load of rotten fish guts."

"Gently, Captain," Nyls Jessan advised. Beka's copilot and number-one gunner was lean and fair-haired, with grey eyes and pleasant, if ordinary, features. He smiled at her. "Gently. When did you ever smell rotten fish guts, anyway?"

"Sapne, in the main port-market. I told you the place was a pestilential sinkhole, remember?"

"I remember." Jessan moved up behind her and began taking the pins out of her long yellow hair. "If you're thinking about Tarveet of Pleyver, the comparison is certainly apt. But you don't have to like him—"

"I know, I know," said Beka, as the intertwined plaits came free and fell down one by one. " 'Just work with him.' Mother used to say the same thing."

Jessan kept on unbraiding her hair; his fingers moved warmly against her neck, making it hard for her to concentrate. With an effort, she gathered her thoughts and went on.

"How did Tarveet get to Suivi Point, anyway? Why the hell couldn't the Mages have snapped him up on Galcen along with the rest of the Grand Council?"

"That would have been nice," agreed Jessan. "I suspect that the esteemed councillor was already here visiting his money when everything fell apart."

"Taking some cash out for a walk, more likely." Beka frowned. "I wonder who he was planning to buy with it."

"Before the Mageworlds invaded? He could have been after almost anybody." Jessan paused, and his hands came to rest lightly on Beka's shoulders. She leaned back against him; his breath caught for a second before he continued, "At least now he's willing to give some of it to us."

"And we can't afford to be choosy." She sighed. "I know. Tarveet needs a Resistance fleet to protect his investments for him, and we need all the backers we can get. But a fleet's the only thing his money is going to buy; I hope he isn't expecting me to come along with it."

She felt Jessan's grip tighten and then relax. "If the esteemed councillor from Pleyver makes that particular mistake," her copilot said, his High Khesatan accent more marked than usual, "then I will disabuse him of the notion."

"Poor Nyls." She shook her head. "I do believe that Tarveet managed to get under your skin."

"Well . . . somewhat."

" 'Somewhat.' " Beka turned to face Jessan. In spite of herself, she smiled. "You do a really good look of exquisite disdain, did you know that?"

"Just one of my many talents," he said.

"Ah." She regarded him thoughtfully. "You have others?"

"So I'm told."

"That's nice." Her finger traveled down his shirtfront, teasing open the fasteners along the way. "Tell me about them."

"I play an excellent hand of cards," he said. He reached out and undid the top button of the quilted jacket Beka wore to keep out the chilly air of the Suivan domes. "I'm a passable shot with a blaster . . . a fair pilot . . . and a good enough medic in most cases to keep my patients breathing."

He undid the other buttons one by one as he spoke. Beka shivered. She had dressed in haste that morning—after Tarveet's comm call had pulled her out of bed cursing—and wore nothing beneath the jacket except her bare skin.

"You never learned all those on Khesat," she said.

"Only the cards," he told her. "My acquaintances back home considered me a shamefully unaccomplished fellow."

"Foolish of them." She took a step closer, and rested one hand on his chest where the shirt fell open. "Didn't you learn anything else on Khesat?"

He slipped his hands around her waist under the open jacket, and bent his head to lick gently at the hollow of her throat. "One or two things, before I left."

Beka laughed again, and pressed harder against him. "I thought so," she said. "Tell me."

"Oh, flute-playing, flower arrangement . . ." His mouth traveled further downward. ". . . frivolous versification . . . and the finer points of . . ."

The comm link on the bedside table sounded—a piercing squeal, far different from its usual restrained beeping. Jessan didn't look up. The comm link sounded again.

"Hell." Beka pulled a hand free and picked up the link. "That's *Warhammer*'s private signal. Something's wrong at the spacedocks." She keyed on the link. "Rosselin-Metadi here."

"LeSoit here, Captain." *Warhammer*'s number-two gunner sounded agitated about something. "I think you'd better come out to the ship."

By now Jessan had worked his way down past her collarbone. She mastered her breathing with some difficulty and said over the link, "Can it wait?"

"I don't really think it can, Captain."

She bit her lip. "All right. I'll be there in a few minutes. Rosselin-Metadi, out."

Beka keyed off the link. Jessan stopped his downward explorations and stood for a moment with his head pressed against her neck.

Then he sighed and stepped away. "Duty calls."

"Duty has a rotten sense of humor." Beka was already buttoning up the quilted jacket. That done, she pulled a fastener out of one pocket and gathered her hair into a loose tail down her back. Redoing the formal braids would take more time than she wanted to spare. "Hand me that damned tiara, and let's go see what's got Ignac' buzzing us on the private code."

In Namport, in a windowless room above Freling's Bar, a young woman slept with her back against a locked door. She moved restlessly in her sleep, then lay still for a few seconds, opened her eyes, and sat up.

Klea Santreny was thin and small-boned, with a tangle of curly, light brown hair; she would have seemed more girl than woman still, at twenty Standard years, except that working for Freling was no way to stay young. Her grey eyes had shadows under them like bruises, and cheap bangle bracelets on her left wrist hid the old, pale scars beneath.

She had fallen asleep on the coarse-piled carpet, with her day-pack tucked underneath her head for a pillow. Her Adept's staff, a piece of iron-hard *grrch* wood that had begun its career as a broomstick, lay on the floor beside her. A few feet away, in the center of the room, a tawny-haired young man in a beige coverall was moving through the sequences of what looked at first sight to be a slow, graceful dance. He held a plain staff of blond wood in both hands.

Klea drew her knees up and sat for a while watching him. The last time she'd seen Owen—that was all the name she had for him, though she knew he had a family somewhere on Mage-occupied Galcen—he'd been lying on the room's only bed. His body had been bruised and swollen, and there had been blood on his face and his clothes. But now the marks of ill-usage were gone, and he moved easily, without flinching.

She wondered where he'd been and what he'd done. And how he'd done it; he hadn't brought the staff into the locked room with him, any more than he'd brought those transitory bruises. "Going out of body," Owen had called it, when he first told her what he needed to do. As far as she could tell, he hadn't left the room to do it.

He finished the sequence and turned toward her, his attention seeming to come back from concentration on something not visible in the here-and-now. Hazel eyes regarded Klea with a thoughtful, measuring expression.

"I should have thanked you before," he said.

She looked down and away, toward the corner of the room where the ugly carpet met the peeling mirror on the long wall opposite the bed. "You don't need to do that. The room's yours until morning—you paid for it."

"I'd never have gotten in here if you hadn't brought me." He frowned. "And this is not a place you should have had to come back to."

"It's not so bad," Klea said. Gratitude wasn't something she'd encountered much of, and she wasn't certain how she felt about it.

"Don't lie," Owen said. "You're not one of Freling's hookers any longer. You're an apprentice to the Guild."

She snorted. "And your teacher's going to have fits when he finds out what sort of riffraff you've let in."

His expression changed from faint reproof to something she couldn't name. "Master Ransome doesn't have anything to say about it anymore."

"He's dead?"

"No," said Owen. "I'm no longer bound to him."

"What happened?"

"I asked him for an end to my apprenticeship."

Getting straight facts out of Owen, Klea reflected, was worse than pulling out mud-thorns. Persistence was the one tactic that sometimes worked. "So—did he give it to you?"

"He said I already had it. What he gave me . . ." Owen paused. "He gave me Mastery over the whole Guild."

Klea jerked her head up, startled. "He did *what*?"

"He can't fight the Magelords any longer," Owen said. "They have him prisoner—on one of their ships, I think, orbiting Galcen. When I came to him there—"

She stared at him. "You went . . . 'out of body,' did you call it . . . all the way to Galcen?"

Owen nodded. "It was necessary. When I found Master Ransome, he told me that if I wanted to serve the Guild, I would have to claim the Mastery of it."

"So you did."

"Yes." The corners of his mouth quirked briefly upward. "Granted, nobody knows about the change except for Master Ransome and me—and you, of course—which is going to make asserting my authority somewhat difficult."

"Uh . . . yeah." Klea shook her head, bemused. "So what are you supposed to do with this authority once you assert it?"

"Defeat the Magelords," he said. "Restore the Guild."

"All by yourself?"

"No," he said. "You're going to help."

Suivi Point proper—the original settlement, and not the myriad smaller habitats strung out along the Suivan Belt—spread across its main asteroid beneath a series of transparent domes. Over the years, full climate control and artificial gravity had come to most of the residential and business areas, though not to the low-rent districts on the fringes or to the warren of interconnected tunnels and caverns hollowed out of Suivi's inner depths.

The spacedocks were located well away from the better part of town, behind an impressive series of airtight checkpoints, partly to lessen the risk of accidents from ships coming in and leaving—"but mostly," Beka said to Jessan as they walked along one of the dockbound glidewalks, "they want to keep the scum and riffraff confined to the port quarter as much as possible. The first thing a free-spacer learns about Suivi Point is that the people who keep their money here don't want anything to do with the folks who help them make it."

The glidewalk slid into an interchange where several of the routes peeled away and others joined the main stem. Overhead, a lighted holosign flashed its crimson letters on and off: DINING AND ENTERTAINMENT/PORT ALLEY–SECOND STREET/NEXT LEFT; MAIN DOCKING/NEXT RIGHT; LAST EXITS/FORWARD THIS WALK.

Jessan glanced up at the sign. " 'Last Exits'? What have we got there—mortuary services?"

"Not exactly," Beka said.

"What do you mean, 'not exactly'?"

"Well . . . some of the higher-class firms do include final disposition in their package deals."

"Package deals," said Jessan. "Packages of what?"

Beka's lips twitched in a humorless smile. "Executions. Formal, semiformal, or impromptu, all nice and legal."

"How charming."

"This is Suivi Point, remember—if you can't buy it here, it's not for sale anywhere."

Jessan looked curious. "I suppose you have to buy a trial and a conviction first?"

"It helps."

A little farther on, the glidewalk for Main Docking split off the primary track. The stores alongside changed from gaudy souvenir shops to cheap eating establishments and grim-looking transient hotels. Sealed airlocks broke the graffiti-stained walls at irregular intervals.

Beka pointed at one of the locks. It had a sign stenciled on the hatch: CAUTION! P-SUIT AREA. NO GRAVITY OR ATMOSPHERE BEYOND THIS POINT.

"You have to watch those. Sometimes the portside kids take the warning signs down for laughs."

"I'll bear that in mind," Jessan told her. "Along with all the other quaint local customs."

Beka chuckled. "Not the sort of place the group tours from Khesat make a habit of visiting, I suppose."

"I have never," said Jessan, "traveled anywhere with a group tour. And while the Space Force, in its infinite wisdom, sent me to a number of fascinating places, Suivi Point wasn't one of them."

"Lucky you. *I* got Suivi Point for my very first port call after I left home. It was a real eye-opener, let me tell you—if Ignac' hadn't been looking after me that time, I might never have made it back to the ship."

"Then I owe Gentlesir LeSoit a debt of gratitude," Jessan said with a marked lack of enthusiasm, as they followed a smaller glidewalk off the main branch. "Remind me to pay it back to him someday."

They stopped in front of an airlock door with a security palmplate set into the hatch. Beka put her hand on the plate; it beeped, and the synthesized voice of the door's annunciator said, "ID scan confirmed. Docking bay atmospheric integrity confirmed."

"Good," said Beka. "I'd hate to think that somebody had let all our air out while we were gone. That happened to the *Claw Hard* once, while I was crewing on her," she went on while the lock cycled them through. "Captain Osa didn't want to put up the nonrefundable one-week deposit on the docking fee when we were only going to be here for two days. So the Port Authority depressurized our bay until he handed over the money."

"Somehow I'm not surprised," murmured Jessan.

Inside the docking bay, *Warhammer* rested on landing legs beneath the transparent dome. On the far side of the enclosed space another airlock, this one with its NO GRAVITY OR ATMOSPHERE warning still fresh and clean, led out to the asteroid's surface.

The *'Hammer*'s ramp was down, but the force field was up. It took Beka's hand on another ID panel to turn off the field so that she and Jessan could pass through.

An unfamiliar p-suit hung in the open locker inside the *'Hammer*'s door. Beka and Jessan glanced at each other.

"Looks like our problem is a visitor," Jessan said.

"Not to mention somebody Ignac' doesn't think he can handle all on his lonesome," Beka said. "Which means that shooting him, her, or it won't be an option for us, either."

"It's always possible that they mean us no ill will."

"Hah. Legit business shows up at the place in town, like our old buddy damn-him-for-interrupting-breakfast Tarveet. We might as well go on into the common room and see who's there."

As she spoke, Beka checked the knife up her left sleeve. Maybe the Domina of Entibor-in-Exile couldn't get away with a tied-down blaster, but she was damned if she was going to walk around Suivi Point without a weapon or two for backup. And Jessan, for all his Khesatan elegance, had a single-shot needler concealed somewhere about his person, along with various other lethal surprises. If matters did come down to violence, they'd be ready.

She straightened the heavy tiara—without the formal structure of braids to anchor it, the famous Iron Crown of Entibor tended to slip askew—and stepped through the door into the common room. Jessan followed her, a step or two behind.

Two people waited at the common-room table. Ignaceu LeSoit, dark and wiry, with his thin mustache and his well-worn blaster, was a familiar sight. The woman was a stranger, dark-haired, her face creased with worry lines, but she wore the uniform of the Republic's Space Force and the insignia of a full captain. She rose and bowed when Beka entered.

"My lady," she said. "Please forgive this irregular method of securing an audience—but I needed to meet with you, away from the eyes and ears of the local authorities."

Oh, wonderful, thought Beka. *More politics, and it isn't even lunch yet.* "I haven't got the time for diplomatic games. What do you need?"

The Space Force captain glanced from Beka to Jessan and back. "I have reason to believe," she said, "that the

Steering Committee of Suivi Point wishes to commandeer my forces. In fact, I suspect that the committee's messenger is looking for me right now. Regardless of the situation on Galcen, I don't want to swear allegiance to Suivi Point, or to have my ships taken from my command."

I don't blame her one little bit, Beka thought. *Let those bastards on the committee get a fleet of their own, and it'll be hurray for Suivi Point and to hell with the rest of us.*

She did her best to keep her features schooled to an expression of mild interest, as if they were discussing nothing more pressing than the allocation of tax levies for glidewalk repair. "So what do you want from me?"

The captain paused. This was not, it seemed, a decision she had come to easily. "Domina," she said, "we—myself and those under me—wish to swear ourselves formally to you. . . ."

I don't believe this, Beka thought. *Nobody's bothered with all that oath-of-fealty nonsense since before I was born.*

She kept her face impassive. The Space Force captain was still talking.

". . . with the understanding that you not require us to oppose the Republic's Space Force or to act against the Republic's interests, and that you will release us from our oath once the present situation normalizes."

Beka drew a deep breath. "Is that all?"

"Yes, Domina," said the captain. "All I ask is that you put me and my detachment under your protection."

"All?" she asked. "Sounds like a great deal for you with not much in it for me."

"I'm afraid so, my lady. I can only hope that you'll be generous."

"Generous," said Beka. "Right. Hang on for a moment while I confer with my advisors."

She didn't wait for the captain's reply, but nodded to LeSoit and Jessan and swept out of the common room in her most regal manner. The Iron Crown, fortunately, didn't slip until she was out of sight around the bend in the passageway that led to the engineering spaces.

"Well," she said, as soon as they had a solid bulkhead

and a closed door between them and the Space Force captain. "What do you think?"

"It *is* a chance to increase the size of the fleet," LeSoit pointed out.

"To more than one vessel. Yes, that's a start. Jessan, what's the Space Force got here?"

Jessan sighed. "Small stuff . . . space-only, no ground presence . . . I don't know anything more specific than that. I've been out of the loop for over a year now, remember?"

"Then get back into it," she told him. "I want to know what's in port, what's coming in, what's going out. This is important. Find out. I'll wait."

LeSoit was looking smug. "Captain Yevil's detachment consists of one destroyer, two fast couriers, a hyperspace-capable transport, and a half-dozen local defense single-seat fighters. Of those six, only three are fully operational."

The 'Hammer's number-two gunner leaned back against the bulkhead and favored Jessan with a bland smile. The Khesatan's lips tightened, but he didn't reply.

Beka took a deep breath and ignored the byplay. "Opinions on the cost to us of taking the captain up on her offer?"

Jessan shrugged. "We might annoy the local authorities."

"I can live with that. How about her conditions?"

"Not unreasonable, considering the situation."

She nodded. "Fine. Jessan, you're now officially the General of the Armies of Entibor. She's under your command. Don't disappoint me."

Beka looked at her little group. "Well, let's go back in there and accept the captain's oath. This is starting to shape up into an interesting day."

II. Galcen Nearspace: Sword-of-the-Dawn
Suivi Point: Entertainment District; Warhammer
Gyfferan Farspace: Night's-Beautiful-Daughter

GRAND ADMIRAL sus-Airaalin was, reluctantly, at work in his office when the messenger arrived. Reluctantly, because he disliked the office's cramped space—back on Eraasi, he'd worked out-of-doors whenever he could, seeking out the high mountains and the desolate places as a defense against spies and eavesdroppers. Now that he didn't need such measures, he found the confinement of shipboard life oppressive. His preferred station on the *Sword*'s observation deck gave him a view of the stars and enough room to pace back and forth, but some of his duties as admiral could only be carried out in the room assigned to their performance.

Correspondence, for one thing—letter after letter from the leaders of the Resurgency. They hadn't been able to reach the Grand Admiral for several weeks by Eraasian reckoning, while the Mage-Circles had suppressed all hyperspace communications in order to maintain secrecy for the attack on Galcen. The gradual return of the hi-comms network, however, had put an end to the Resurgency's silence.

He called up the first message in the morning's traffic and read it, frowning slightly.

> "With regard to the possibly replicant body of Rosel Quetaya, flag aide to General Jos Metadi, sent to us from the morgue at Prime Base Hospital: extensive testing will be necessary to determine whether the deceased is ours or the original. syn-Tavaite has been summoned. If you could tell us by whose agency the death occurred . . ."

sus-Airaalin sighed and switched on the autoscribe pinned to his collar. "Be aware, as I believe I told you when I sent you the body, that the Space Force authorities at Prime Base were exercising their minds over the same question. Since General Metadi himself was not at Prime when the attack occurred, he may well be at large in the galaxy in the company of one of our own. Please do your best to expedite your findings in this matter."

He clicked off the autoscribe and brought up the next item in the queue—fulsome congratulations, this time, from sus-Ieleen syn-Arvont, who had fought sus-Airaalin and his plans for the Circles ever since the beginning. Now, predictably, syn-Arvont was trying to curry favor. sus-Airaalin was about to switch on the autoscribe again to dictate a response when the office door beeped at him.

"Come," he said, with relief.

The door opened and a trooper entered. "My lord sus-Airaalin," he said, and saluted. "We have an intercept, one of high interest."

"What is it, Criaal?"

"This, my lord," the runner said, handing over a message tablet.

sus-Airaalin glanced at the display, noting that the style of the intercept was that of the Republic's Space Force, with an indicator in the header showing a point of origin in the Gyfferan system. The message itself was written in the Standard Galcenian that the Adept-worlders used in their dealings with one another:

View all traffic from COMREPSPAFOR INFABEDE with suspicion. Ari Rosselin-Metadi, LCDR, SFMS, sends.

"The sender is on the watch list," said Criaal.

"I know," sus-Airaalin said. "I put him there. Please summon Mid-Commander Taleion."

The trooper departed, and sus-Airaalin looked again at the tablet. According to the intercept log, this particular message had been acquired by the force sent to secure Cashel, found there in hardcopy at the General Delivery transshipment point.

"My lord sus-Airaalin."

The Grand Admiral looked up. Mid-Commander Mael Taleion stood in the open doorway. sus-Airaalin's aide, and the Second of his Circle, was a small, unremarkable man of common Eraasian stock. Like Trooper Criaal, he carried neither the lesser nor the greater honorifics in either mother-line or father-line, and in the old days would have been fortunate to rise any higher in the officer corps than under-lieutenant.

To the shame of our ancestors, sus-Airaalin thought. *How much talent did we waste that way, over the years? In one thing, at least, our defeat forced us to change for the better.*

He gestured at the office's other chair. "Enter and sit, Mael. We have something here which disturbs me greatly."

Taleion sat, and regarded the message tablet curiously. "Is that it?"

"It is." sus-Airaalin pushed the tablet across the desktop for closer inspection. "What do you make of it?"

The mid-commander picked up the tablet and studied the message, his lips moving as he worked to translate the Galcenian text. After a minute, he looked up.

"The obvious conclusion, my lord, is that General Metadi's eldest son is somewhere on Gyffer."

sus-Airaalin nodded. "Exactly. And I distrust obvious conclusions. Consider the date this message was sent—three days, perhaps four, after the earliest on which a courier ship fleeing the attack on Galcen could have brought word to Gyffer of our success."

"I . . . see." But Taleion still looked doubtful.

"*Think*, Mael," sus-Airaalin urged. "The Adept-worlders are not fools; they'll be expecting us to intercept and scan their message traffic. So when a system—a conveniently nearby system—lets slip in plain text that one of the persons we are most likely to be seeking is there . . . then, Mael, I begin to suspect we're looking at a trap."

"A trap. Maybe you're right, my lord—but whose?"

"Metadi," said sus-Airaalin at once. "It has to be. Who else in the Adept-worlds would dare use their commanding general's children like counters on a gaming board? And Metadi was not on Galcen when it fell."

"True, my lord. But we've also heard from the daughter, the one that was supposed to be dead—this could be her work."

"I don't think so," sus-Airaalin said. "From what we know of Beka Rosselin-Metadi, she'd never attempt anything this indirect." He smiled in spite of the gravity of the situation. "From that one, I'd expect nothing short of a frontal assault."

"Assuming it's Metadi we're dealing with," said Taleion, "what do we do?"

The Grand Admiral rose to his feet. The tiny office, with its mountains and snowdrifts of paperwork, felt more confining than ever. In spite of himself, he began to pace.

"Our orders from the Resurgency are clear," he said. "We must break the Space Force. We must be sure that Commanding General Jos Metadi is dead. We must be doubly sure that all his children are dead. Now that we have come this far, complete victory is our only safety."

"You'll get no argument from me on that, my lord."

"Good. Consider, then. We have here a message all but inviting us to Gyffer—a rich target in its own right, with its shipyards and its weapons merchants and its planetary fleet. I believe, Mael, that if we take the warfleet to Gyffer we'll find General Metadi already there waiting for us."

"Most people," said Taleion, "would avoid Gyffer like a soul-bane if they thought that was going to happen."

"True enough," the Grand Admiral said. "But there's a big difference between the man who steps ignorantly into a snare, and the one who walks into it with his eyes wide open. The first man is caught; but the second has baited a trap for the hunter."

Nyls Jessan smiled as he matched Captain Rosselin-Metadi's quick strides along the glidewalk back to their storefront quarters. The morning's diversions so far had been varied enough to provide amusement: first Tarveet of Pleyver dropping by to issue veiled threats before breakfast, then LeSoit's call for assistance. Accepting the fealty of the Space Force CO had been ... well, interesting. Beka had kept a straight face throughout, and the Iron Crown hadn't slipped askew until the ceremony was almost over.

The hastily formalized relationship had something in it for all concerned: the CO kept her warships out of the hands of the Suivans, whose loyalty to the Republic had never impressed anybody; the Resistance got the nucleus of a fighting fleet; and Jessan, somewhat to his own surprise, had a new title.

General of the Armies of Entibor, he thought, and shook his head. *What* would *they say on Khesat if they knew?*

"Did you mean it?" he asked curiously.

Beka glanced over at him. The events of the morning so far had left her in a brittle and unchancy mood: her blue eyes were brighter than usual, and her pale skin was flushed along the cheekbones. "Mean what?"

"The 'General of the Armies' bit." He laughed quietly. "My relatives will have heart palpitations if they ever find out."

She raised an eyebrow. "Why? Isn't the Domina of Lost Entibor good enough for them?"

"I'm afraid they'd say just the opposite," he told her. "The Iron Crown is too good for my branch of the family. We're supposed to stay out of galactic politics, marry into the minor aristocracy, and keep on adding to the stable of extra heirs."

"Too bad," she said. "You can apologize later. But right now I need you to run the fleet—I don't want *my* ships coopted by the Space Force any more than our friend back there wants her vessels taken over by the committee."

"Understandable," Jessan said. "Not that we've currently got any ships for the Space Force to coopt. Except for *Warhammer*, of course, and I don't think they'd try that."

"Don't worry; we'll get ships. As soon as word spreads around. And if that doesn't work—"

He frowned. "You can't take on the entire Mage warfleet with your bare hands."

"No." She halted, facing him, so that they both stood still while the glidewalk carried them past the taverns and amusement centers of the upper Strip. "Look. I thought about this a lot before I made up my mind to do it. We both know that the whole Space Force couldn't have gone down when the Mages took Galcen. Whoever's running things on the Mages' side has to know that, too—and the more time the Magelords take up with worrying about me, the less time they've got to spend hunting for the rest of the fleet."

Jessan sighed. He hadn't forgotten his first meeting with Beka Rosselin-Metadi, when he'd seen her step out into the range of a dozen blasters for the sake of a clear line of fire. She'd been in disguise that time, as the one-eyed and slightly homicidal starpilot Tarnekep Portree, but the line between her proper and her alternate personae had never been very thick.

"If you're going to make a target of yourself," he began, "you could at least—"

"Excuse me, my lady," came a voice from off on the stationary border of the glidewalk.

Beka turned. "Yes?"

The Domina was on her best behavior—Jessan recognized the cant of her head and the polite-but-distant tone of her voice as a good imitation of the late Perada Rosselin—but she still looked edgy. She took one glance at the speaker, a heavy-set man in the uniform of a Suivan Contract Security operative, and her hand came up to straighten a button of her quilted jacket.

Jessan felt a stirring of disquiet. That button was one of the Professor's little toys from their asteroid base; the concealed audio pickup would transmit directly to *Warhammer*'s comm console and main ship's memory.

Something's not right, he thought. *She wants to save this conversation for the record.*

The ConSec officer faced Beka and Jessan a pace or two ahead. "Are you the woman identified as Beka Rosselin-Metadi, who styles herself Domina of Entibor?"

Beka's lips tightened at the "styles herself"; her hand fell away from the jacket buttons as she looked down her nose at the officer. "I am. What is—"

Two more ConSec officers stepped onto the glidewalk, taking her one by each arm, pulling her from the glidewalk and shoving her face-first into the wall on the right.

The first man pulled a blaster and took a step back. "You're under arrest. Submit yourself quietly."

Jessan paused. Though it might be acceptable Suivan etiquette to abandon a shipmate under these circumstances, Khesat and the Space Force had higher standards. He thought about going for the needler in his right-hand coat pocket, or the small sharp knife in his boot top—but in close quarters against so many, neither one was good enough for anything besides a last-ditch attempt. Especially not when Beka looked like playing this one as Domina of Lost Entibor all the way to the end.

Follow her lead, he told himself. *Do what you can.*

By now a fourth ConSec had joined the other three, and was busy searching Beka for concealed weapons. The captain's opinion of Suivi Point being what it was, he was finding them—first tearing the seam of her left sleeve from cuff to elbow as he took away the long double-edged knife, then reaching to scrabble around inside the front of her quilted jacket.

Jessan heard the sound of ripping cloth, and the ConSec pulled out a small chunk of glittering metal.

"Needler," he said. "Oh, naughty, naughty lady."

Beka stiffened.

"You're quite mistaken," she said. "Everything here is perfectly fine." Her Galcenian accent was even more marked than usual, and the words were pitched to carry. The comm link in her jacket button should be picking them up with ease. "Everything here is perfectly fine."

That's the signal, thought Jessan, as the two ConSecs pinning Beka against the wall brought her arms up higher between her shoulder blades. *Time for a distraction, I think.*

He took a step forward.

"Excuse me," he said to the first ConSec, who still had his weapon trained on Beka while the others did the search. "May I ask your authority for this intrusion?"

The ConSec hit Jessan across the face with the blaster. "*There's* my authority."

Jessan had expected a reaction of that sort, and rolled his head with the blow. All the same, the impact raised a welt along his jaw. Warm blood started trickling from his cheekbone. He ignored it; there would be enough time for first aid later.

"Oh, dear," he said—his High Khesatan accent more pronounced than ever. If the ConSecs thought they were dealing with a Central Worlds prettyboy straight out of the comedy holovids, so much the better. "In that case, I must insist that you take me into custody as well."

The ConSec shook his head. "Sorry, buddy, but I don't have arrest orders for you."

Jessan glanced over at Beka. The officer searching her was taking his own good time in checking for weapons around her hips and groin. So far, though, he hadn't found the comm link hidden in the jacket button, still activated and relaying everything back to the '*Hammer* and Ignac' LeSoit.

I don't like depending on that man, Jessan thought. *He thinks too highly of the captain for his own good. But one makes use of the tools to hand.*

He looked back at the ConSec with the blaster. "You might consider taking me in for resisting arrest."

"No good. I'm not arresting you, so you can't resist."

"I see," Jessan said. He took a step closer—*I'm going to regret doing this, I can tell that already*—and laid a hand on the ConSec's arm. "But I do believe that you can arrest me for interfering with a security officer in the lawful perform-ance of his duty."

Before Jessan could brace himself, the ConSec swung his fist and connected with Jessan's midsection. It was a short, powerful blow; the man knew what he was doing. Jessan felt the remains of his breakfast coming back up in a wave of nausea as he crumpled onto the glidewalk margin.

The ConSec grinned and kicked him once, perfunctorily, in the face. "Sorry, buddy—you haven't been any interfer-ence at all." He turned to the others. "Let's take her in."

They bound Beka's hands behind her back. Two of the ConSecs pulled her from the bulkhead. One at each elbow, they started to walk her down the passageway toward the main glidewalk.

The head ConSec looked over at her tattered clothing and tight-lipped expression. "Sorry about that, lady," he said. "If you didn't want to show your titties to all of Suivi you shouldn't have carried a needler under there."

He scooped up the Iron Crown from where it had fallen during the body search. "Get her down to detention. Move out."

Ignaceu LeSoit watched Beka and Jessan go down the *'Hammer*'s ramp, heading back out to the docking bay and thence to Suivi's administrative district—better quarters for planetary royalty than a battle-scarred starship, even if Cap-tain Rosselin-Metadi did fret at having to bunk portside.

Nyls Jessan had been right, though, LeSoit conceded grudgingly. The Domina of Entibor couldn't set up head-quarters right here on the ship. Not as long as it was the only ship her Resistance had.

Well, that isn't the problem anymore.

He turned back to Captain Yevil of the Space Force with an inward sigh. "Right, then, Captain. We're going to have to get comms and such straightened out now, and work on command and control matters later. Chain of command for your units is the Domina Beka, General Nyls Jessan, then you."

"And what is your position in the chain of command?"

"Acting commander of this vessel in the Domina's absence." *And fair enough,* he added to himself, *when that damned Khesatan has got everything else.*

Yevil nodded in comprehension. "A second task unit. Very well."

For the next few minutes, she and LeSoit were busy exchanging frequency and phase information for ship-to-ship communications, in both lightspeed and hyperspace environments. LeSoit handed over a set of crypto chips for standard transceivers; Yevil sealed them into the breast pocket of her uniform tunic with a nod of thanks.

"We'll be sending ours over as soon as I'm back on board my ship," she said. "I'm sorry we can't give you everything, but some of it is classified at a level so high there's no way I can justify giving it out."

"Don't worry about it. The Domina isn't handing over everything either."

"I see," said Yevil, without visible surprise, and they moved on to the next item on the agenda, the compilation of a master list of crews, armament, and power plants for all the vessels in the Domina's newly expanded fleet. As a solitary raider back in her fighting days, *Warhammer* wasn't fitted out with many of the comms needed for multivessel coordination—no main battle tank, for example; LeSoit wasn't even certain whether the Republic had used such things during the Old War—so getting *Warhammer* fitted out as a flagship looked like it would take some time.

Several minutes later, the buzz of the *'Hammer*'s entry alarm broke into their work. LeSoit glanced up from his clipboard.

"Sounds like we've got a visitor," he said. "I'd better go check it out."

Still holding the clipboard in one hand, he hurried to the main door. A man was standing at the top of the ramp. The force field was up, but even through the blurring effect LeSoit could make out the newcomer's ConSec uniform.

He frowned. If somebody had hired the law on Beka and her crew, things might get expensive. You could buy anything on Suivi Point, including justice, but some varieties would cost you a great deal more than others—under the circumstances, LeSoit decided, he wasn't going to let down the field.

"What can we do for you, officer?"

The ConSec cleared his throat. "I have a message for the master of this vessel."

"She isn't here. I'm afraid I'll have to do. Now, what's the problem?"

"I'm here to escort you."

LeSoit took an automatic step backward in spite of the protective force field. "Escort me where?"

The ConSec man opened his mouth to say something, but LeSoit's clipboard gave him an answer first. Its tiny onboard speaker emitted the sharp beep that meant an override-priority message on the *'Hammer*'s main communications system, followed by an unfamiliar voice: "All personnel aboard RSF *Warhammer*, please report to the portmaster's office immediately. All personnel aboard *Warhammer* . . ."

"I don't like the sound of that," LeSoit said to the ConSec. "Can you tell me what it's all about?"

The ConSec shrugged. "Portmaster needs to verify your registry, is all I know."

"Sounds like a paperwork drill. Can't it wait?"

Over the clipboard speaker the voice was still droning on: "All personnel aboard RSF *Warhammer*, please report to the portmaster's office immediately. All personnel . . ."

The ConSec officer shook his head. "I'm afraid not. You'll lose your berthing assignment unless you verify your registry."

"Port officials," said LeSoit in disgust. "Nobody's ever going to convince them that something might be more important than filling in line seven on page two of form one-twenty-eight-A. I've got some urgent business here on board, officer—why not tell the portmaster you couldn't find me when you buzzed at the door? I'll be along as soon as I'm done."

"Please accompany me now," the ConSec said.

Then the clipboard beeped again—louder this time, in the nerve-quickening double rhythm that heralded one of the Domina's own direct-to-ship universal-override transmissions—and disembodied voices began to speak.

A Suivan voice first, with the coarse accent of the outer belt: *"Are you the woman identified as Beka Rosselin-Metadi, who styles herself Domina of Entibor?"*

Then Beka's voice, a precise, carefully educated light tenor that, heard in isolation, could have belonged to either a man or a woman—but, at the same time, could never have belonged to anyone else but her: *"I am. What is—"*

"You're under arrest. Submit yourself quietly."

LeSoit looked at the ConSec officer. "Registry check," he said. "Sure. Try another one."

The voices over the clipboard speaker continued: *"Needler. Oh, naughty, naughty lady."*

Then Beka again, distinct and forceful: *"You're quite mistaken. Everything here is perfectly fine."* A pause, and then the last phrase again, very clearly. *"Everything here is perfectly fine."*

"Right," said LeSoit, and turned his back on the ConSec officer. He hit first the Close Door button and then the Raise Ramp lever, and was headed for the 'Hammer's cockpit before the ConSec finished scrambling away to safety.

He passed through the common room at a dead run. Captain Yevil caught up with him at the cockpit door.

"What's going on?"

"The Domina's emergency lift-ship signal," LeSoit said, palming the lockplate. "We're out of here."

Llannat finished her cha'a in the galley of *Night's-Beautiful-Daughter* and put the cup aside.

It's time, she told herself sternly. *You can't put it off any longer.*

She left the galley and made her way through the Deathwing's corridors toward the heart of the ship.

Magebuilt and alien though the raider was, most of the divisions within its hull were recognizable to the *Daughter*'s current crew. Bridge, engine room, galley, berthing spaces ... throughout the ship the familiar compartments housed the things that were necessary to move a handful of planetbound creatures from star to star.

One chamber, however, had no counterpart on any Space Force vessel: a small room lined all in black tile, save for a stark white circle in the middle of the empty floor.

The meditation chamber, Lieutenant Vinhalyn had named it when she'd asked him. The long-ago assassin who'd turned *Night's-Beautiful-Daughter* into a starpilot's grave had been part of a Mage-Circle, and a Magelord as well.

One of the Great Magelords, Llannat thought. *As if I needed any more proof.*

Only someone that powerful, and that arrogant, would have dared attempt what the Professor had done: reach out across half a millennium to grasp the threads of the universe and work with them according to his own designs. And only a Great Magelord would have stayed alive all the years afterward, through sheer force of will—

Until he found a student who could finish his work.

Llannat sighed. That was where thinking about the Professor always took her—to the knowledge that something unfinished was waiting for her, something she had to find or learn or do, and that she had but one place and one way to go asking about it.

The door of the meditation chamber slid open at Llannat's approach. She entered, and the door closed again behind her. She still wasn't sure how the mechanism functioned. At first the door had opened and shut for everyone on board, like the door in a fashionable shop; now it only worked for her.

For a moment the room was dark. Then light came from diffuse and concealed sources to fill the chamber with a dim underwater glow. Llannat went to the center of the white circle and knelt there, breathing slowly and letting her awareness go loose to float into darkness.

Power.

It moved strongly here, in the complex artificial patterns that betrayed the presence of Magework. *Sorcery*, the Adepts called such uses of power—their own strength came from riding the flow of the universe, rather than from manipulating it. Llannat had found the room oppressive enough at first to make her physically ill.

Time had changed all that. Now she moved with ease among the wrought and knotted threads of the Professor's long-ago workings. Sometimes she seemed to glimpse fragments of a greater—and still unfinished—design.

Silver cords, she thought. *Underneath everything, the silver cords tie it all together. If you dare, you can reach out and touch them. Work with them. Change the way things are, and the way that things might be.*

The moment of insight frightened her. If Master Ransome knew what she was doing these days, and how she was doing it, he would surely declare her a sorcerer and a traitor and an enemy of the Guild.

He's wrong. I know I haven't done anything to betray the Republic, and I don't think I'm working against the Guild. . . .

In her mind Llannat seemed to hear her own voice reciting the Adept's vows, as she had spoken them before Master Ransome himself at the Retreat.

". . . to speak truth, to do right, to seek always the greater good. . . ."

She shook her head. *Nothing in there about loyalty to anything. In the healer's oath, yes; in my commissioning oath, oh yes; but I haven't broken either one of those.*

Magework, on the other hand . . .

Llannat forced the thought aside. Gradually, her mind grew still again, and she waited, not thinking, until she became the question she had come to this place to ask.

As soon as LeSoit reached the '*Hammer*'s cockpit—with Captain Yevil close behind him—he started working the safety webbing of the pilot's seat into place with one hand. With the other hand he snatched up the comm and flipped it to the Port Control link.

"Portmaster, this is *Warhammer*. Berthing assignment no longer required. Request permission to lift ship."

"Negative, *Warhammer*. Permission to lift denied. Report with your entire crew to the portmaster's office."

"Unable to comply. Request permiss—"

The sudden tug of a tractor beam cut him off in midword. The *'Hammer* began to lurch and sway on her landing legs as the beam—normally used to assist a vessel into its assigned berth—kept on pulling the ship downward.

On the other side of the cockpit, Yevil was already strapping herself down into the copilot's seat. "Guess they don't want us to leave."

"We knew that already," LeSoit said. He picked up the comm link again. "Portmaster, this is *Warhammer*. Release your tractor beam and open the bay. I'm leaving."

"Negative, *Warhammer*. Come to the office."

LeSoit could feel the strength members of the *'Hammer*'s frame vibrating under the tractor beam's relentless pull. He keyed on the link again.

"Portmaster, *Warhammer*. You have five seconds to release me. Four. Three. Two. One. Out."

He reached for the main control console and pulled on the forward nullgravs. The *'Hammer* should have tilted toward the vertical in preparation for lift-off, but nothing happened—only the steady throb of overstressed metal, hovering just below the threshold of audibility.

"They have the entire Suivan grid to draw on," said Yevil. "All we've got is ship's power."

"I'll give them ship's power, all right." LeSoit hit the console again—first main power, and then, with a tremendous deep-throated roar, the heavy realspace engines. Power that should have driven *Warhammer*'s mass up to near-lightspeed from the bottom of a gravity well poured out of the ship's engines into the confined space, turning the deckplates of the bay to slag beneath them. All over the console, warning lights burned red. "This is it—either we shake apart fighting their beam, or we burn it out and break free."

"Energy guns!" Yevil shouted at him over the racket of

the engines. "That's what they'll do. They'll bring in energy guns and take us out right here."

"Not if they don't want to lose half of Suivi when we blow," LeSoit shouted back. "The hell with all of them. Max power, override."

The noise of the *'Hammer*'s engines rose in a bellowing, many-voiced crescendo. Yevil swore.

"Are you trying to kill us both?"

"The Domina gave me the signal to lift ship. We're lifting."

"What about the goddamn *dome*?"

"Hell with the dome. We mass more than it does. Let Suivi worry about it after we're gone."

Then the docking bay tractors went off. *Warhammer* tilted back on her nullgravs with neck-snapping speed, hurtling upward and smashing through the closed dome of the docking bay. Loss-of-pressure alarms shrilled and whurrped, and the damage-control panel lit up in a matrix of red and amber lights. *Warhammer* kept on driving upward.

"Lost integrity in number-one hold," LeSoit recited as he turned switches all over the panel. "Lost integrity in number two. Closing airtight doors to maintain pressure in critical areas. Commencing jump run *now*."

III. Infabede Sector: RSF *Selsyn-bilai*; UDC *Veratina*
Gyfferan Farspace: *Night's-Beautiful-Daughter*
Suivi Point: Entertainment District; Resistance Headquarters
Nammerin: Namport

RSF *SELSYN-BILAI* waited in the darkness between the stars. With hyperspace communications down hard all over the galaxy, and Admiral Vallant claiming Infabede Sector in defiance of the Republic, no word had come out of Galcen Prime for over two weeks—no instructions from headquarters to continue prosecuting the war, or to surrender.

Not that Jos Metadi intended the latter. Chance might have brought the Commanding General of the Space Force to this remote area of space; but chance had also provided him with a ship. The *Selsyn* was only a glorified cargo vessel that in better days had spent her time ferrying supplies from Prime Base to Infabede, but at the time of the war's outbreak she had been the temporary home of a fully-armed company of Planetary Infantry and a pair of long-range reconnaissance craft.

"Damn, but it gripes me to leave you on this one," General Metadi said to the commander of the infantry detachment.

"There's no help for it," Captain Tyche said. The Planetary Infantry officer checked the charge on his blaster and slipped it into the molded-plastic holster of his light battle armor. His troopers, already boarding their recon craft in the docking bay, would be wearing heavier gear, hardshell p-suits with integral weaponry that could take out vehicles and knock down walls. "If you get killed, then it's all over for us. But as long as you're safe, even if we lose the battle—"

"—the war goes on," Metadi finished for him. The General, his aide, and the det commander had gathered in the office of the *Selsyn*'s late CO for a final conference before the ship dropped out of hyperspace. "I know. I agree. It was my idea. But I don't have to like it."

"Console yourself, sir," said Commander Quetaya. Rosel Quetaya was a trimly built woman with a loose cap of black curls and dramatic rose-and-ivory coloring—but Metadi had chosen his aide for other reasons than her looks. "You could still die bloody in hand-to-hand. No guarantees."

"That thought will have to keep me warm," Metadi said. He began to pace about the cramped compartment. "All right, Tyche, we're going to drop out at the rendezvous point in less than an hour. Keep those recons inside our sensor shadow for as long as you can. If there's anything out there waiting for us, assume it's one of Vallant's pickup ships and commence your attack. Meanwhile, I will remove this vessel to a safe location and await your signal. If you don't make it ... well, that'll be my problem, not yours."

"Too true, General. I wouldn't want to trade you for it, either." Tyche looked thoughtful. "What about any loyalists that might be mixed in with Vallant's people? It'd be a pity to lose them."

Quetaya nodded. "If we want to make up a fleet, we'll need all the crews we can get."

"Don't worry about it right now," said Metadi. "Concentrate on taking that first ship. After the smoke clears, we can think about sorting out the survivors."

"I'd sure like to have an Adept on hand for that part," Quetaya said. "For the sorting, I mean."

"No you don't," Metadi told her. "Every time I've had to work with Adepts, it's complicated things beyond belief."

Quetaya looked curious. "I thought your copilot on the old *Warhammer* was an Adept."

"He was," said Metadi. "Trust me, Commander. I'm speaking from experience."

The *Selsyn*'s intraship comm system clicked on. "Dropout from hyperspace in ten minutes," a voice blared. "I say again, dropout from hyperspace in ten minutes. All hands take your assigned positions."

"That's me, sir," Tyche said. "I have to get down to the docking bay and join my troopers."

The infantry captain saluted, turned, and headed off at something close to a run. Metadi and Quetaya watched him leave.

"There goes a good man," the General said after a moment. "I hope we see him again."

Llannat Hyfid knelt within the white circle in the black room. All around her the air system hummed, and the thousand tiny sounds of a living ship filled the darkened chamber.

At length she sighed and rose to her feet. Meditating had eased her tension, but the question she had brought with her into the black-walled chamber remained unanswered. Perhaps something waiting for her on the *Daughter*'s bridge would have meaning, if there was, indeed, any meaning to be found at all.

The door to the corridor opened as she approached. Llannat stepped through it, and into a room that she had never seen before.

She was standing in a Space Force office; she'd been in enough of those to recognize the layout and the furnishings. The battered metal desk: stock issue. The integrated wall calendar, with planetary days in black and Galcenian days superimposed in red: stock issue. The clock on the wall, also a Standard-and-Local: yet more stock issue. Even the floor wax smelled like the kind used in every Space Force installation from Galcen to Spiral's End.

But the office wasn't any one of the dozens that she'd used or visited in the course of her career in the Med Service. The window behind the desk opened on an unfamiliar vista—a landing field where the late-afternoon sun glanced off the tall spires of grounded ships—and the man behind the desk wasn't a Space Force officer. He was a lean, tawny-haired young man in a dockworker's shapeless coverall, sitting back with his feet up on the careful stacks of Space Force standard-issue forms and documents.

She knew him. Beka Rosselin-Metadi's brother had been a senior apprentice and a teacher at the Retreat during her time there, though he'd never claimed Mastery or taken Adept's vows.

"Owen!" she said.

He didn't seem surprised by her arrival. He nodded toward a door in the far wall—an old-style wooden door with a latch and hinges, out of place in the familiar office setting. "What you're after is in through there."

Llannat hesitated for a moment. Then she walked across the room and put her hand on the latch.

"We'll meet again," Owen's voice came from behind her. "And then—who can say?"

She turned the latch and pushed the door open. This time, no standard Space Force room awaited her, nor the deckplates and bulkheads of *Night's-Beautiful-Daughter.* Instead, a narrow hallway stretched out ahead of her into the dark.

And behind her, as well. The office room was gone now, leaving her alone in the impenetrable blackness.

Light, she thought. *I need light.*

She unclipped the staff from her belt and let the power of the universe flow and focus through its ebony length. There was a moment of warmth, and then she stood in the center of a nimbus of emerald light. She looked about her, and saw that she stood on a rough pavement of dry-laid flagstone, with walls of cut and fitted stone to either side.

Llannat walked on. The narrow passage began to turn through a series of corners and bends, until at last she stood before another door, this one even older than the first, of rough wood with hinges of wrought metal. No latch or doorknob, either; nothing but a heavy ring of twisted iron. She lifted the ring and pulled.

The door opened, and she was in another room—one that had a floor of blond wood in elaborate parquetry, and for its far wall a row of windows, tall and casemented, like a curtain of glass. Beyond the windowpanes the sun was rising over distant hills, filling the whole space with a ruddy light. From the forest outside the chamber came a clamor of birds.

A long table of carved openwork in the center of the room held a tray of bright fruit in colors that echoed the flowers on the trees outside. A man sat on one of the delicately made chairs at the table, a decanter and a single goblet of amber fluid standing before him on a silver tray.

He rose, and turned. It was the Professor, dressed in severe black, holding in his hand a silver-bound ebony staff—the same one that Llannat carried now. She saw his gaze move from her hand up to her face.

"Greetings," he said. "So you were the one, after all."

"But you're dead!" Llannat exclaimed before she could help herself, and felt her skin grow warm with embarrassment.

"A fate we all share, one day or another," the Professor replied with his gentle smile. Llannat realized, belatedly, that they were both speaking Court Entiboran—a language she had never taken the trouble to learn.

Somewhere in the near distance an alarm began to shrill, breaking up the golden morning with its high, incessant clamor. The Professor looked over his shoulder toward the perfect blue of the sky beyond the window.

"For some," he said, "the day will arrive sooner than they expected. It has begun. Come with me."

He walked past her, through the door by which she had entered. This time, when she followed him, the door led to yet a third room, as rich and sumptuous as the one before. This one had a dark wood floor, and paneled walls hung with heavy tapestries. A massive stone fireplace filled most of the far end of the room, but the hearth was clean-swept and empty.

The Professor went to the fireplace and pointed with his staff at one of the stones of the hearth. It was not rough-finished like the others, but polished, and carved with the arms of House Rosselin and of Entibor.

"Look and remember," he said. "All times and places meet where the power of the universe does not extend. Some have called me a traitor. Others may call you the same. But you and I, we will know the truth."

All through his speech, the distant alarm bell continued to ring. Llannat opened her mouth to ask what it meant—

—and found herself once more in the black room of *Night's-Beautiful-Daughter*, kneeling in the center of the white circle, with the Professor's last words finding somber echoes within her own mind, and the warning bell for final approach into Gyffer sounding in the corridor outside.

The answer she had been seeking came to her, late and—now that she'd found it—unwelcome.

Sorcery, she thought. *That's what I did when I gave the order to jump for Gyfferan space: I reached out like a Magelord and changed a part of the universe, because there's something waiting for me on Gyffer that I need to find, if I'm going to make the future turn out like it ought to. . . .*

Her breath caught.

Or maybe like the Professor thought that it ought to, five hundred years ago.

Captain Amyas Faramon—until recently of the Space Force, now of the Infabede Unified Defense Command under Admiral Vallant—was inspecting one of the starboard gun nacelles on the *Veratina* when his recognition signal sounded.

He left the gunnery officer and the junior supply officer in whose company he had been making the inspection and keyed on the bulkhead-mounted comm link. "Captain."

"Pickets report contact exiting hyper," the voice at the other end said. "TAO requests your presence."

Faramon clicked the key twice by way of acknowledgment and turned to his inspecting party. "Carry on without me, gentles. I expect your report at midday."

The gunnery officer gave a quick nod. "Sir."

By the time the captain had reached *Veratina*'s Combat Information Center, the track of the unknown had already been laid in and plotted. Faramon joined the tactical action officer at the main battle tank.

"What do you have?" he asked.

The big holovid display in the middle of CIC would normally be showing a three-dimensional representation of whatever action was going on. At the moment, though, hi-comms remained erratic all over the Infabede sector, limiting real-time updates to what the *'Tina*'s own sensors could pick up. Lightspeed communications from the picket ships provided the rest of the necessary data—all of it, however, subject to time lag.

The TAO pointed at a blue dot in the tank, one of several representing small UDC vessels doing picket duty in the area. "*Fleyde*, here, reported the dropout, and got us the initial track via lightspeed comms. Current position of the unknown extrapolated to here."

The red dot that marked an Unknown/Hostile vessel was flashing on and off to indicate a projection not yet confirmed in real time. Faramon studied the display for a few seconds.

"Very well," he said. "Take your position to intercept and inform me of your progress."

As he spoke, one of the enlisted crew members looked up from a monitor screen. "Uneven trace on active sensors."

"Very well," the TAO said. "Continue tracking."

Faramon took his seat in the command chair and began to scan the clipboard full of printout flimsies already waiting for him. Perhaps he'd become a desperate space mutineer, he mused, but the paperwork never stopped. The details of running a ship remained the same, whether he took his orders from Admiral Vallant in Infabede or from General Metadi on Galcen.

Though perhaps advancement in rank would move a little faster—somebody, after all, would have to take over the Defense Command once Admiral Vallant reentered civilian life as Coordinating Director of the Infabede sector. Vallant had all but promised . . .

"It won't be just the overdue promotions, Faramon. Mark my words, any number of things are going to start moving again once the Infabede worlds aren't being held back by the dead weight of the rest of the Republic."

The voice of another crew member broke in on the captain's pleasant speculations. "ID on unknown—RSF *Selsyn-bilai*. Negative on special recognition signal."

"Understand *Selsyn-bilai*," the TAO replied. "Reserve retrofit stores ship." He turned to Faramon. "Damn. Here I was hoping for a warship."

"Cheer up—maybe you'll get one next time," Faramon told him. "And remember, right now supplies are equally important."

Colonel DeMayt, the commander of the *Veratina*'s Planetary Infantry detachment, left her position near the main battle tank and spoke to the crew member in charge of passing orders to the detachment's ready room. "Prepare the boarding party. Vessel has not been secured."

"Lightspeed transmission from *Selsyn-bilai*," called a crew member from the comms panel. "Reports mechanical breakdown, requests assistance."

The TAO shook his head. "This isn't even going to be a challenge," he said to Faramon. "Request permission to let the junior officer of the watch take this one for training."

"Permission granted," Faramon said without looking up from his paperwork.

"Active sensors report target tumbling," the crew member at the monitor called out.

The junior officer of the watch turned to the lightspeed comms tech. "Transmit to *Selsyn-bilai*, 'Interrogative: are you able to maneuver?' "

There was the usual delay as the lightspeed message went out and the reply came back. Then the comms tech said, "*Selsyn* reports horizontal stabilization system malfunction. Negative on able to maneuver."

"Time of closest point of approach five minutes," said the

comptech at the main battle tank. Now that *Veratina* had the unknown on active sensors, the red dot no longer blinked, but glowed steadily, and the small blue dots of the picket craft had been joined by a bright blue triangle representing the *'Tina* herself.

"*Selsyn* on visual," called out the sensor tech.

"Put him on screen," the JOOW said. "Stand by rescue and assistance detail."

Over on the sensor panel, an external visual screen lit up. The long, cylindrical shape of a deep-space stores ship appeared on the screen in enhanced-lowlight. The ship was revolving around its horizontal axis, nose and tail tumbling end over end.

"That's one sick bird," the TAO muttered, and Faramon had to agree. The *Selsyn* must have run into the Mage warfleet on her way to the rendezvous point, to get shot up that badly.

"Transmission from *Selsyn*," said the comms tech. "Request permission to transfer all personnel except skeleton engineering crew."

The junior officer of the watch looked over at the TAO, who nodded. "Permission granted," said the JOOW.

"Boarding party muster in the docking bay," Faramon said to Colonel DeMayt. "Process them through as they arrive."

"Closest point of approach in one minute," reported the comptech at the main tank.

"Two contacts inbound," called out the sensor tech. "Both squawking lifeboat identifiers."

"Very well," said the JOOW.

"Wait a minute," the TAO said suddenly. The change in his voice made Faramon look up from his paperwork and lean forward in the command seat. "Those aren't lifeboats. Those are—"

The low-light screen washed out into a dazzle and went dark.

"—recons."

Jessan lay curled and immobile on the glidewalk margin, watching Beka recede into the distance through a pain-filled haze. She wasn't resisting—not typical of her, but a good thing under the circumstances. Suivan Contract Security wasn't being any gentler than it had to.

I don't know where that guy learned his stuff, but he knows his pressure points like an expert.

The Khesatan groaned, tried to stand up, and failed. *He's also got a fist like a rock.*

A second attempt brought Jessan upright, leaning his back against the wall. Glidewalk traffic began to resume its normal flow. Nobody looked at him, and he wondered how long ago the Suivans had burned out on watching incidents like the last one.

The ConSecs hadn't taken his comm link; he took it out of his pocket and tried *Warhammer*'s code.

No response.

He transmitted the code again. Still no answer.

Jessan switched to LeSoit's private code, the one guaranteed to bring the *'Hammer*'s number-two gunner out of a dead sleep and straight up to attention in a single move. No response again.

All right. He drew a long, careful breath. *Looks like Gentlesir LeSoit picked up the signal and lifted. So* Warhammer*'s probably safe.*

That just leaves the captain.

Jessan pushed himself away from the wall. Moving slowly and cautiously, he made his way through the glidewalk system to the storefront headquarters of the Entiboran Resistance. He'd been half-afraid of finding more ConSecs guarding the door when he arrived, but everything looked normal—no uniforms in sight, and the door opened to his ID-scan.

He stepped over the threshold. Inside, the rooms were empty and undisturbed. Even the rumpled bedsheets and the covered warming-trays from the food shop around the corner remained as he and Beka had left them earlier. It looked very much as if whoever was behind the arrest didn't want to break up the Resistance.

For the moment, it seemed, they didn't want Nyls Jessan

either. He wondered if his diligently cultivated air of ineffectuality had done the trick—so many people in the outplanets thought that all Central Worlders were effete and foolish that it didn't take much work to convey the impression.

Or maybe we've got somebody here who's focused on Beka and no one else. Which could be very, very bad.

Time to put myself back in order and pay a visit to the local lockup.

Jessan spent the next half-hour in the refresher cubicle, patching up his injuries as best he could. Given an extensive medical kit and his own first-class training, the results were more than adequate. By the time he was done, all the visible marks of ill-use had vanished. The associated aches and pains—which hadn't—were throbbing discreetly out of public view.

He selected a long-sleeved Khesatan shirt of white spidersilk shot through with fine gold thread, added a loose velvet day coat of subdued russet, and transferred most of the contents of the front-office cashbox into an inside pocket. When a last call to *Warhammer* went without an answer, Jessan was ready to make his way back out into the domes of Suivi Main.

"You're going to save the universe and I'm going to help you," said Klea. Behind her words, the room's climate-control system wheezed and rattled. "I don't believe it."

Owen shook his head. "The universe exists whether we help it or not. But the Guild and the Republic need all the help they can get."

"But why us?"

He looked at her. "Why did you pick me up and drag me home, that time when the local Mage-Circle caught me snooping and left me for dead?"

"I don't know," she said. She remembered the back alley where she'd found him lying unconscious. There'd been blood on his face that day, and thick Namport mud in his tawny hair, and she'd been half-drunk from the aqua vitae she'd poured into herself to blot out the sound of other people's thoughts. "I was there, is all. Somebody had to be."

"Exactly," he said. "Somebody has to be."

Klea grimaced. "And guess who it is this time." With a sigh, she picked up her day pack and shrugged it onto her shoulders. "How do we start?"

"By walking out of here. After that, it depends."

"Depends on what?"

"On what happens outside," he said. "When we see which way the currents of the universe are flowing, then we'll know."

"You'll know, maybe. I'm not that good."

"All you need is practice." He smiled briefly. "The way things look right now, you'll get plenty before we're done."

Shifting his staff into his left hand, he moved past her and reached out to open the door. His fingers brushed the panel; he froze for an instant, then drew his hand away.

"The door," he said. "Did it feel like this when you touched it before?"

"I don't know." She took a step forward and laid an experimental hand against the surface. The door looked the same, but the metal seemed to bend and deform itself inward against her palm, as if some cold, viscous liquid had filled the hallway outside to the bulging point. "No. When I was leaning against it, it felt like a door."

"Then we'd better open it carefully." He pointed with his staff. "Stand there. And let me go through first."

Klea took the position he indicated and gripped her staff with both hands. Her mouth was dry, and her pulse thudded underneath the skin of her throat. Owen touched the lockplate and the door slid open.

The lights were all out in the hallway, even the dim blue safety glows along the baseboards. In the darkness a darker figure stood, robed and hooded in black, with a molded black plastic mask over its features and a short ebony staff gripped in one black-gloved hand. Light that was not light hung around the figure in a scarlet nimbus, and the staff it carried burned with a cold crimson fire.

The Mage-Circle . . . they've found us again.

Owen was already moving, gripping his staff near one end with both hands and bringing it around to smash across the Mage's throat. He leaped over the blackrobe's body as it crumpled. A second Mage loomed up out of the darkness beyond the open doorway, staff swinging toward Owen in a blaze of gory light.

Klea—shocked at last into action—brought up the *grrch*-wood broomstick that Owen had made into her apprentice's staff, and thrust forward with the butt end into the Mage's face. The wood smashed against the mask so hard that her palms stung and the black plastic caved in beneath the impact. The blow that the Mage had aimed at Owen missed by a handsbreadth as the Mage fell backward into the dark.

Then she and Owen were out in the corridor, and the blue safety glows were back on again—the Mages had put them out, she supposed, though she wasn't sure how. The two blackrobes lay motionless on the hall carpet. Owen picked up the ebony staves and broke them one at a time.

When he had finished he straightened and looked at Klea. "Now we can go."

"What about . . . ?" She indicated the Mages.

"They're dead."

She'd expected that. "So we just leave them here? Let Freling get rid of them?"

"Why not?" He looked at the bodies for a moment, then glanced back at her with a curious expression. "Of course, you could always burn the whole place down on top of them—it might be tidier, in the long run, and I think you'd enjoy doing it."

"I could . . ."

"If you wanted to. It's easy enough."

She stared at him, tongue-tied. Part of her remained appalled at the suggestion, but another, deep-buried part of herself stirred to life in response, so that she was filled with a sudden overwhelming awareness of fire. Owen was right, she realized; she *could* do it, letting that part of Klea Santreny rise up and stretch out nonmaterial hands and pull in as much heat as her heart's anger could hold.

Drag it in, she thought, *and twist it all together, and then*

... leave it someplace. With the cleaning rags in the back closet, or the grease in the kitchen, or the loose wires in the climate-control. Leave it, and walk away. And before long, something will start to burn. ...

She swallowed hard, fighting down the image of Freling in his dirty white apron—Freling with his "business proposition" and his "fair split of the take"—Freling with his hot breath and his big, hairy hands—trapped and cooking in the fire of her anger until his skin cracked open and the melted fat ran out like blood.

"No." Her voice was a thread of sound, nothing more. "I don't want to."

He looked at her, and his expression was distant and forbidding. "Speak the truth. Falsehood is for sorcerers and stage-magicians, not for someone who wants to be an Adept."

"All right," she said. "I do want to. And it'd be easy, as much as I've hated this place. But I'm not going to do it. Knowing I can—"

"Is enough?" There was no warmth in the question, only a boundless disbelief. "The truth, Klea."

"No, blast you, it's *not* enough!" She was starting to shake; she took a deep breath and waited until her heartbeat steadied. "But someday it will be, and I'm damned if I'm going to screw all that up just to make myself happy now."

All the coldness left his face then, and he smiled.

"Truth spoken truly," he said. "Let's get out of here and see about getting off Nammerin before they close the port."

IV. Infabede Sector: UDC *Veratina*
Suivi Point: Main Detention
Galcen Farspace: *Sword-of-the-Dawn*
Warhammer: Hyperspace Transit

THERE WAS an instant of frozen disbelief in *Veratina*'s Combat Information Center as the officers stared at the blackened screen. Then the sensor tech's voice cut across the silence.

"Two targets speed up-Doppler. *Selsyn* has stopped tumbling."

Captain Faramon dropped his clipboard and leapt to his feet. "I have the watch! Shields up!"

"Recon craft still on constant bearing decreasing range."

The collision alert began to sound, its steady tocsin beating like a pulse underneath the antiphony of orders and response. Vacuum-tight doors hissed closed all around, and he could feel the slight increase in air pressure.

"Condition red, weapons free," Faramon said. "Take those scouts under fire."

"Under fire with energy guns," replied the TAO. "Inside minimum range for missiles."

"They aren't slowing down," said the sensor tech. Her voice sounded tight, as if she were fighting to keep tension from sending the pitch upward.

"Impact in five seconds," said the comptech at the main tank. "Four. Three. Two. One."

The impact came without sound, but a shudder ran through the deckplates under Faramon's boots. His ears twinged with a sudden change in pressure.

"You wanted a warship," he snarled at the TAO, as a second, smaller impact rattled underfoot a moment after the first, and the damage-control board began lighting up with red and amber loss-of-pressure lights. "Set general quarters! Damage control—where did those craft hit us?"

"In the docking bay," the crew member at the board replied.

"Scratch our boarding party," Faramon said to no one in particular. The collision alarm changed to the signal for general quarters.

"Get me a report," he said to the damage-control talker. "Investigators out."

"Damage reports coming in now," the talker replied. "Two impacts. One at speed, second made a braked landing."

Faramon knew what that meant. "We've been boarded. Colonel DeMayt, security alert!"

A moment later, the intraship comm link gave a pop and a hiss, and began to speak. "Crew of RSF *Veratina*," said the voice. "This is General Metadi."

"Hell and damnation," Faramon said. Whoever was talking had the General's distinctive accent and delivery, that was for sure—Faramon had heard the man speak often enough at the Space Force Staff School in Galcen Prime. Not even three decades of association with the powerful and well-bred had managed to clean the dockyards of Gyffer out of Metadi's voice.

"Your officers are in open rebellion against the Republic," the voice on the link went on. "Their mutiny has failed. Put down your weapons. Don't resist and you won't be harmed."

"Shut that thing off!" Faramon snapped.

"Trying, sir," said the comms tech. "It seems to be coming from Internal Communications Central."

"Crew of RSF *Veratina*," the voice began again, "this is General Metadi. . . ."

"He was supposed to be on Galcen," said the TAO. He had to raise his voice to make himself heard over the combined noise of the general quarters signal and the voice—recorded? live? Faramon couldn't tell—of the Commanding General. "Do you think it's really him?"

"It's him all right," Faramon said. "Either here or on the *Selsyn*. I don't know how he got here, but—"

"No comms with C or D decks," the damage-control talker said. "Compartment 02-33-277 reports sounds of blaster fire."

"Display ship's status," Faramon ordered the comptech at the main battle tank.

We have to win this one, the captain thought, as the blue and red dots in the tank winked out and were replaced by a wireframe model of the *'Tina*. Compartment 02-33-277 showed up as bright red, and C and D decks in amber, while the rest of the ship glowed blue. *Or else Vallant has Metadi loose at his back.*

The TAO nodded toward the tank display. "Doesn't look too bad so far. If all they've got is ship's crew off *Selsyn*, we're about matched in skill, and we have more people."

"Stores ships don't carry long-range recon craft," said Colonel DeMayt. "I'd say Metadi brought along some infantry."

"That could make things a bit more difficult," Faramon admitted. He turned to the active-sensor tech. Of the crew members in CIC, she was closest to the sealed bulkhead compartment where the small arms were kept. He passed over the keycard. "Open the weapons locker. Hand out arms to all officers in CIC."

"Aye, aye, sir."

The sensor tech was already moving as she spoke, inserting the keycard and sliding the locker door aside. A moment later she was standing with her back braced against the bulkhead, a blaster clasped in both hands.

Colonel DeMayt reached for her sidearm—she was Planetary Infantry of the old school, and always went armed. It didn't do her any good this time, though; the sensor tech shot her before she could bring the weapon to bear. DeMayt collapsed backward across a worthless hi-comms panel. The tech swung the muzzle of her own weapon back to point at Faramon's head.

"Nobody asked *me* if I wanted to join a mutiny," she said. Her voice had risen several notes in the stress of the moment, but her grip on the blaster, Faramon noted with an odd feeling of detachment, was quite steady. "Put your hands up."

"Five—four—three—two—" Ignaceu LeSoit counted off the seconds in hyperspace as the digits flicked by on the navicomp chronometer. "—one, dropout!"

His hand stabbed down on the console to initiate the dropout sequence. The grey pseudosubstance of hyperspace, which had swirled briefly outside the cockpit viewscreens, gave way again to the diamond-studded blackness of a starfield.

LeSoit sat back in the pilot's chair with an explosive sigh of relief. Blind-jumping from a shortened run-up was tricky stuff; tricky enough that he didn't care what the Space Force captain thought about his piloting. The fact that they were still alive—and that no new alarm lights had joined the ones already flashing—was the only testimonial he needed.

A few seconds of relaxation were all he granted himself, however, before leaning forward again to check their position. The navicomp had already finished cross-referencing beacons and starfields and assorted other aids to galactic navigation, and the result put them safely beyond the range of anything on Suivi that didn't have hyperspace engines.

He turned to the woman in the copilot's seat. "Captain Yevil, it's time for you to signal your ships. Let them know that you've sworn to the Domina, and tell them not to make a move until they hear from you—or from her, or the General of the Armies, directly. Anyone else gives them orders, they say no, and shoot if they have to."

Yevil reached out for the comm link handset. Then she paused. "We will be joining up with them, won't we?"

"Not immediately," LeSoit said. "First I have to check things out and see how badly we're hurt. And I'm going to do some repairs."

"I can read a status board, even on a merch, and this isn't a p-suit job. You're looking at spacedock work."

"So I'll get the *'Hammer* into a spacedock."

"Where?" asked Yevil. "You sure as hell can't go back to Suivi Point. And the way things are right now, there's no guarantee that anywhere else will take you either."

"I know," LeSoit said. "Don't worry. I've got a place I can take us."

"Gyffer?"

LeSoit shook his head. "Not Gyffer," he said. "Someplace where they owe me—you don't need to know where."

"Ah," said Yevil, looking knowledgeable. "That kind of place."

"Right," said LeSoit, not entirely truthfully. He didn't think the Space Force captain would consider even the outbreak of war a sufficient excuse to ignore some things—and what he intended to do was certainly one of them. "But first, let me go see if we're in shape to get anywhere at all."

They were, it turned out, but just barely. LeSoit's walk through the ship—those areas that weren't sealed because of pressure loss—showed him that conditions were fully as bad as he'd expected. The hyperspatial reference block had shaken itself out of alignment during the *'Hammer*'s fight against the tractor beam, and their breakout from the docking bay had left gaping wounds in the freighter's hull.

But the old *Libra*-class freighters were built tough, LeSoit reflected, designed for long-haul runs with high-risk cargo back when the civilized galaxy was a lot less civilized than it was now. And this particular *Libra*-class had been modified until she was even tougher. She had the strength and the heart for one more jump, and then—

Then Ignac' LeSoit would see what kind of credit he had these days.

Beka told me to lift ship, he thought. *She didn't tell me where to go.*

All the same, LeSoit took his time putting the reference

block back in synch. He checked again to make sure that the airtight doors and bulkheads were keeping what remained of the *'Hammer*'s atmosphere inside the ship where it belonged. When he couldn't put it off any longer, he headed back to the cockpit, where Yevil was waiting.

"Can we make it?" the Space Force captain asked.

"As long as we don't try anything fancy. You have your signal ready to transmit?"

"I'm ready," Yevil said. "How long is our little side trip going to take, anyway? I have some people who need to know."

"They don't need to know that bad," said LeSoit. "They can wait until we show up again. Besides, I won't know how long the repairs will take until I get there."

"I see," Yevil said. She picked up the handset again. "Hi-comms or lightspeed, do you think?"

"Lightspeed." It was good to have an easy question for a change, LeSoit reflected. "It's the only sure means. Hi-comms are unreliable as hell right now; the Mages are probably jamming them wherever they can. With lightspeed, if the wrong people use the message to get a directional fix on us, we'll already be long gone."

Yevil shrugged. "On this vessel you're the captain."

"In the Domina's absence," LeSoit said. "Don't forget that part. If you've got your message ready, go ahead and transmit."

"Sending," Yevil said. She began to speak code groups over the lightspeed link. "All vessels in Suivi Space Force Detachment, this is Suivi SF Det, I transmit in the blind, immediate execute, Link, Alfa Echo, Two Mike, Echo Five, Delta Sierra, Niner Six. . . ."

A few moments later she finished, saying, "Unlink, standby, execute," and keying off the link. "That's it, then," she said to LeSoit. "They aren't going anywhere without orders from either me or the Domina. And the Steering Committee of Suivi Point can go straight to hell."

"Sounds like a good idea to me," said LeSoit. He fed power to the *'Hammer*'s realspace engines and put the freighter onto a straight-line course. "Commencing run-to-jump."

Warhammer made her run-up without setting off any more alarms. The stars blazed beyond the cockpit windows, then gave way to the swirling iridescence of hyperspace. LeSoit set the autopilot, unbuckled his safety webbing, and stood. He stretched, feeling his shoulder joints cracking from the tension of the past hour. "Well, we're in. All we have to do now is stay on course."

"Without probing too deeply into embarrassing specifics," Yevil said, " 'stay on course' to where?"

"A place I know of. If it still exists."

"Beka Rosselin-Metadi," said Jessan patiently. "Domina of Lost Entibor, of Entibor-in-Exile, and of the Colonies Beyond. Also master of record for the armed merchantman *Warhammer*, Suivi registry."

He waited on the other side of the armor-glass barrier while the clerk on the fifth level of Suivi Main Detention checked his request against the records of the desk comp. Getting this far had exhausted a good part of the petty cash supply in his day-robe pocket, and had gone a long way toward explaining why no motion in Council to throw Suivi Point out of the Republic had ever failed to find a seconding voice. Most worlds in the civilized galaxy at least theoretically offered equal justice under the law; here on Suivi, nobody even bothered pretending. Jessan hoped he hadn't been working under a false assumption in coming here first. Real Contract Security officers would have turned Beka over to Detention Services, but if those four thugs back on the glidewalk hadn't been the genuine articles she could be almost anywhere in the Belt by now. On the other hand, Mages or Mageworlds agents would have taken him as well, instead of leaving him free and essentially unharmed.

Finally the clerk looked up from her comp screen and once again recognized his presence. "Gentlesir Jessan—we do indeed have an indefinite holding contract on your associate."

Jessan tried to remember what the Academy's crash

course in galactic law for medics had said about contract
justice, Suivan style. *I think the "indefinite" means they'll
hold on to someone forever if the contractor keeps on paying their fees.*

He laid a ten-credit chit on the counter top, next to the
hatch in the armor-glass barrier. "What are the charges?"

At least on Suivi Point nobody had to slip bribe money
under the table—the "suggested gratuities" list was posted
in the first-level lobby. The clerk pulled the ten-chit through
the barrier without blinking, and punched up another screen
on the desk comp.

Her eyes widened. "Picked up on—my goodness, it's a
murder complaint, ten-year-old warrant."

Ten years. Jessan did some quick arithmetic in his head.
*The captain's first port call after leaving Galcen—the one
where she almost didn't make it back to the ship ... someday I'll have to ask her what she really did.*

He remembered something else she'd told him about that
first visit to Suivi. "Is there anybody else named in the original complaint?"

"An off-worlder named LeSoit," the clerk said. "Listed as
a crew member on the *Sidh*, no home of record given."

"Is he in custody as well?"

"He wasn't on the invoice when we got her," the clerk
said. "You'll have to take it up with Contract Security."

Jessan laid another couple of ten-chits on the counter.
"Thanks anyway. Do you have a date-of-release or a price-
to-match on Captain Rosselin-Metadi? I have the authority
to release funds if necessary."

"Sorry, this contract is coded Non-Negotiable."

Jessan raised an eyebrow. "For a simple murder complaint? On Suivi Point?"

"Yes ... well. The contractor has filed new charges since
turning over the subject."

Jessan laid down several more credit chits, and watched
them slide across the counter. "May I ask for an enumera-
tion?"

"Sure." The clerk punched up another screen on the desk
comp. "Let's see ... 'endangering the defense of Suivi

Point, trafficking with the Mageworlds, and impersonating a planetary ruler' . . . plus assorted minor charges for concealed weapons, resisting arrest, and indecent exposure."

"Indecent exposure?" Jessan shook his head. "I'll never understand some people." He put another ten-chit on the counter. "I need to speak with Captain Rosselin-Metadi before I leave."

"Sorry," the clerk said. "The subject's being held incommunicado right now, with a transfer scheduled to max-pri."

"Isn't that a bit extreme, even for the new charges?"

The clerk shrugged. "It's not my fault that the Mageworlds situation has everybody nervous. The max-pri, though . . . that's customary whenever a contractor asks the committee for a summary termination order."

"I see," Jessan said. He took out the last of his credit chits and slid it under the barrier. "And who is the contractor that wants a summary termination on Beka Rosselin-Metadi?"

"A corporation called Tri-Worlds Holding," the clerk said. "From Pleyver."

"Ah," said Jessan. "I see."

Brigadier General Perrin Ochemet—Space Force Planetary Infantry, formerly commander of Prime Base on Galcen—lay awake in his darkened cell. He wasn't certain how long he had been a prisoner of the Mageworlders; food and water came to the cell at regular intervals, and enough dim light to eat and drink by, but he had no idea how many meals a day his captors thought fit to give him.

They weren't starving him; the meals were adequate though not lavish. He had been questioned, of course—it would have surprised him not to be—but the interrogation had been cursory enough to be insulting, as if the CO of Prime Base had nothing of importance to tell them. The one question in which they displayed genuine interest was the one for which he didn't have an answer:

"Where is General Metadi?"

He hadn't even bothered lying. *"I don't know."*

They hadn't believed him at first—had asked him the

same questions several times over, with varying degrees of emphasis. In the end they'd brought in one of their Mages, a masked figure in a black cloak who'd listened to him saying *"I don't know"* yet another time.

The Mage had done nothing except look at Ochemet from behind the black plastic mask. Then he—or she; Ochemet couldn't tell which—had said something in the Mageworlds tongue, and the questioners had left him alone ever since.

Now, however, the faint noise of his cell door sliding open told Ochemet that his period of grace had ended. *I should have known they wouldn't forget about me for very long.* He closed his eyes and prepared himself for renewed questioning.

"Get up and come with me."

The voice didn't belong to any of the Mageworlders. The tone was all wrong—low-pitched and urgent, almost ragged, and without a victor's self-assurance. The accent was wrong, too. Ochemet opened his eyes again.

The greyish illumination that accompanied his meals had returned to the cell. In the dim light, Ochemet saw a shadowy figure standing next to his bunk, and recognized the face above the ragged clothing.

"Master Ransome!"

"I'm flattered that you remember me," said the Adept. "But time is short. We must be going."

Ochemet sat up and swung his feet down onto the floor of the cell. He looked closer, and saw that the Guild Master's wrists were torn, the dark blood running down freely across the palms of Ransome's hands.

"You're hurt."

"Not badly. Follow me."

Ochemet stood. "I hope you've got a good idea this time. The last time I followed you someplace, I ended up in here."

"What needs to happen, happens," said Ransome.

Out in the narrow corridor, they turned to the right; always before, when being led away for a questioning session, Ochemet had gone to the left, and this new route was strange to him. In silence, he and Ransome threaded their way through a maze of low, narrow passages, heading from the core of the ship toward its outer skin, where the lifeboat pods waited in bay after bay.

There, beside one of the open pods, Ransome halted. "This one will do."

Ochemet shook his head. "They'll shoot us out of the sky."

"And take a chance on killing one of their own people by mistake? No—watch."

Ransome lifted away an access plate in the bulkhead, revealing a series of switches marked in yellow script. He pulled sharply on one of them; it came out of the socket and dangled at the end of a bundle of colored wires, so that the bare terminals on the reverse were plainly visible. Moving with a deftness that surprised Ochemet—Adepts weren't supposed to know about tricks like that—Ransome laid the edge of the access plate across two of the terminals.

All up and down the corridor Ochemet heard a series of snaps and whooshes as vacuum-tight doors slid shut. The deckplates under his feet vibrated with the serial percussion of explosive bolts pushing lifeboats away from the ship. He felt Ransome's hand pressing against his shoulder blades.

"Inside!"

He half-stepped, half-tumbled into the pod with Ransome close on his heels as the door snapped closed. There was the sharp crack of the ejection bolts, thunderous in the enclosed space, and the pod tumbled free. Ochemet lurched sideways, grunting as one of the zero-g handholds slammed into his rib cage, and stumbled into one of the padded seats.

Automatically, he groped for safety webbing—found it—and worked to fasten it around him while his mind tried to make sense of everything that had happened. In the seat beside him, Master Ransome looked tired but satisfied.

Ochemet drew a deep breath. "It looks like we've escaped," he said. "Now tell me something—what's going to keep the Mageworlders from catching us all over again?"

"The Mageworlders have other problems at the moment," Ransome said. "They've already begun moving their main fleet out of Galcen orbit."

"If you say so. But there isn't anything wrong with their shipboard holding cells, I know that much. So how *did* you manage to get loose?"

There was a pause. "It is a cardinal mistake," said the Adept finally, "to confuse the name of a thing with its essence, and another mistake to think that the power lies in the name."

"I suppose you're going to explain that?"

"It's simple enough," Ransome said. "The Magelords created chains and manacles to hold the Master of the Guild, but in their fear of him they forgot about Errec Ransome."

Ochemet stared at him. "But you *are* the Master of the Guild!"

Ransome smiled. Ochemet found the expression disquieting on the Guild Master's bruised and bloodstained face.

"So the Magelords thought," said the Adept. "And it will prove their downfall in the end."

In *Veratina*'s Combat Information Center, nobody said anything, or moved. The sensor tech's aim was unwavering, and Colonel DeMayt's body lay across the console as a testimony to her resolve. She was still holding Faramon at blaster-point when the doors at both ends of CIC blew inward and troopers in armored p-suits swarmed through, energy lances at the ready.

One of the troopers relieved the sensor tech with the blaster, keeping Faramon pinned in the command chair, while the others took over the watch stations in CIC without resistance. The officer in charge, a young man with infantry captain's pips on his collar, wore an armored suit like the rest of his troopers. Somewhere along the way to *Veratina*'s CIC he'd abandoned the bulky helmet and the gloves. Now he paced back and forth, frowning slightly, as reports came in over the intraship comm system: "Engineering secured." "Comms secured." "Weapons stations secured."

Eventually a sergeant appeared in one of the broken doors and saluted. "All secure, sir."

The infantry captain's frown eased slightly. "Very well.

You may stand easy on station. Signal to *Selsyn*: All secure. Tyche sends."

"Aye, aye."

There was silence for a moment, while Tyche continued to pace the area. Then one of the PI troopers called out, "*Selsyn* rogers for signal."

"Pass to *Selsyn*, ready to receive visitor."

More time passed—enough time for a shuttle to cross between the two ships—while Faramon sat in his command chair and felt the cold sweat trickling down his back. Then General Metadi himself strode into CIC, flanked by a pair of troopers with energy lances at the ready and followed by a flag aide with a miniature blaster in one hand and a loop of gold braid on her shoulder.

The General didn't bother looking at Faramon. "Captain Tyche," he said. "Report."

The infantry officer saluted. "Sir. RSF *Veratina* is in Republic control, mutineers captured. Five casualties among our troops. Still working to determine how many the mutineers lost. Sorting out who actually mutinied and who just got press-ganged into going along with them is going to take even longer."

"Very well. Have you located the commanding officer of this vessel?"

"Yes, sir." Tyche gestured toward the command seat, and for the first time Metadi looked in that direction.

"Captain Faramon," the General said. "You were on Galcen for Staff School, what, three years ago?"

Faramon managed to nod.

Metadi glanced around the Combat Information Center—looking for something, it seemed to Faramon. Then the General's gaze lit on the body of Colonel DeMayt, still sprawled across the hi-comms console. Metadi went over to the corpse and pulled the insignia from DeMayt's uniform collar.

He turned back to the infantry officer. "Captain Tyche, front and center."'

The officer stepped forward. "Sir."

The General took a step forward in his turn, reached out

with his free hand, and removed the captain's pips from Tyche's collar. Then he pinned the colonel's insignia in their place.

"Captain Tyche," he said, "I'm promoting you to the rank of Colonel, Space Force Planetary Infantry, effective immediately."

"Yes, sir," said the infantry officer. "Thank you, sir."

"Don't thank me yet, Colonel," Metadi told him. "I'm convening a special court-martial. And you, I'm afraid, are the only officer available who is either equal or superior in rank to Captain Faramon. You are, therefore, the entire board. And the charge is mutiny."

"Yes, sir," Tyche said. He turned and looked at Faramon for a moment, while Faramon tried not to flinch from the infantry officer's regard. Finally General Metadi spoke again.

"Colonel Tyche, what is your verdict?"

"Guilty," said Tyche at once.

"Very well, Colonel. I accept your verdict."

The General turned again to Faramon. The entire proceeding had taken, Faramon realized with a shiver, somewhat less than a full minute.

"Captain Faramon," Metadi said, "you have been found guilty of mutiny, for which the penalty is death or such other sentence as a court-martial may direct. Sentencing is delayed upon the pleasure of the court. In the meantime, Captain—I have a few questions for you."

Grand Admiral sus-Airaalin threw the manacles down onto the bunk. The cuffs were stained red-brown with drying blood, but they were unbroken, and the chain was fixed to the wall of the detention cell.

"He's done it, Mael."

"I fear so, my lord."

"Continue searching."

"Yes, my lord." Mid-Commander Taleion hesitated for a moment before continuing. "It would appear, my lord, that Master Ransome departed the *Sword* with the jettisoned lifepods."

sus-Airaalin had been frowning at the empty restraints;

now he lifted his head and regarded Taleion somberly. "You think that, do you?"

"Ransome's mind is too well guarded for us to touch it directly," Taleion said, "but the Circle has been able to tap into the scene that General Ochemet sees. He is, in fact, inside one of our lifepods, and Master Ransome is with him."

"Continue searching the ship anyway," sus-Airaalin said. "If we lose them, the Resurgency will have us flayed alive—and with good reason. Errec Ransome is dangerous."

"Perhaps we should have killed him in the first place."

The Grand Admiral shook his head. "No, Mael. Ransome is too strong, too focused—kill somebody like that without breaking him first, and he'll barely notice that he's dead."

Taleion paled slightly. *"Ekkannikh,"* he said, using the old backcountry term for an unpropitiated ghost.

"Just so," said sus-Airaalin. "And not the sort that you can buy off with a bit of wine at Year's End, either." He frowned again at the manacles. "These restraints should have held the Guild Master, no matter how great his will to escape might have been. They were Circle-forged for that purpose, and more than one life was spent to strengthen them."

"Then how—?"

sus-Airaalin's mouth twisted. "We've been caught in the web of our own cleverness, Mael. It was the Master of the Adepts' Guild we feared, the Breaker of Circles who was our scourge and our constant enemy; and we made these chains to his measure. If our prisoner was able to break free of them, it can mean only one thing: Errec Ransome is no longer the Master of the Guild—and the vows and obligations that bound him, bind him no longer."

V. Suivi Point: Main Detention
Gyffer: Port of Telabryk

THE SHORT-TERM holding cells in Suivi Point Main Detention were made out of cheap plast-block and painted an unlovely beige. Beka had seen them before, when *Claw Hard*'s chief engineer had gotten himself contracted-in for drunk and disorderly, and she'd been the one who brought down the money to buy him out. Her own brush with what passed for law on Suivi Point had come much earlier, and hadn't gotten that far.

She'd anticipated staying in the holding area indefinitely, stretched out yawning on the cell bunk and reading the graffiti scratched into the walls—an extensive and informative collection of obscenities in various languages. Instead, she hadn't been in short-term holding for fifteen Standard minutes before another deputation of armed ConSecs showed up to escort her down several levels to an area she had never seen.

The new cell block had a force field over a cipher lock on a blastproof door. Inside, everything was dull black metal, under a pitiless unshaded light from recessed panels protected by armor-glass. Under the measured impact of her escort's booted feet, the metal floor plates gave back only the dead, anechoic notes of ultra-heavy soundproofing.

She didn't need to ask where she was now; Main Detention's max-pri cell block had been legendary all over the space lanes back when she was a green kid fresh out of a Galcenian finishing school. The narrow corridor was lined with solid metal doors; the ConSecs opened the third one they came to, and pushed her through it. The door slid shut behind her with the solid noise of panels meeting in a blastproof seal.

Beka stood for a moment in the center of the tiny room—no bigger than one of the holding cells up above, and furnished with the same bare essentials—before falling onto the thin mattress in the metal bunk and preparing again to wait until somebody showed up to talk.

Somebody would, eventually. Main Detention charged by the hour, and top security was expensive; if she was in here on a max-pri contract, she had to be worth a lot of money to one of ConSec's richer clients. Worth it alive, not dead; murder was cheap on Suivi Point.

A longer time went by than she'd expected—several days, counting by the regular arrival of bland but nourishing meals on flimsy trays. She didn't see anyone, and began to fear that her isolation was the point all by itself.

What the hell is going on out there? she wondered, and was hard put to keep from pacing back and forth in frustration. But a max-pri cell would have both visual and audio pickups, and she was damned if she'd give the ConSecs a free show. *Why do they need me out of sight if they don't need me dead?*

I hope Ignac' got the signal. The last thing I need is for Main Detention to seize the 'Hammer for payment of cell fees.

She sat up, hugging her knees to keep from breaking into frantic, random motion. *And Nyls. I really, really hope he isn't in the next cell over, waiting for that damned family of his to come up with a matching sum.*

Cheer up. Security didn't have a contract to bring him in before; he tried his damnedest to get himself arrested and

*they wouldn't do it. He may not know much about how
things work on Suivi, but he does know a lot about money.
And I don't think I've ever seen him scared.*

More time passed, and no one came. She was starting to
wonder if Jessan's murder had been a line item in somebody's budget after all—*he could be dead already and I'd
never even know it*—by the time a force field shimmered
into place at the entrance to her cell, and the heavy
blastproof door slid open.

Ari Rosselin-Metadi yawned and swallowed the dregs of
his cha'a. Last night had been a hard night in the Pilot's Joy,
with a restless, short-tempered crowd; the fights he'd broken up had been vicious affairs, a matter of sudden deep
grudges settled not just with boots and fists but with knives.
He'd long since ushered out those customers who were capable of getting to their feet, and had removed a number of
limp and oblivious drunks to the back alley.

Now he sat, slumping, in a corner by the bar—a big,
dark-haired man with the quiet manner of someone who has
spent most of his life trying to disguise his own strength.
Ari had joined the Space Force to stay out of politics, and
the Medical Service because most of the time he preferred
mending things to breaking them. He disliked the fact that
his appearance intimidated some people. They tended to eye
him sidelong, as if wondering whether they could trust him
not to break the furniture, or the good porcelain, or their
bones. Because he disapproved on principle of unequal
combat, he disliked even more the fact that his obvious size
and strength made other people try to start trouble.

On a shelf behind the bar, a miniature holoset was showing a repeat of last night's episode of *The Innocence of
Ternia*. After everything that had happened to and around
Ternia, Ari decided, the fact that she was still innocent
proved that she was touched in the head. Ari watched the
shifting images for a while, then shook his head.

"The whole thing," he said finally, "comes down to who
gets nervous first—the Mageworlders or Admiral Vallant."

"Vallant," the bartender said. He was picking up the dirty

glasses and stacking them for the kitchen crew. "You missed him on the news a little while ago—some kind of hi-pri feed straight out of the Infabede sector. Wanted us to surrender to him right away before the Mageworlders got around to asking us first. Is he really as short as he looks in a holovid tank?"

"Shorter," said Ari, who had served under the admiral on RSF *Fezrisond* for a brief but memorable period, before Vallant's plans for mutiny had prompted him to make an abrupt departure. "Do you think the Citizen-Assembly's going to listen to him?"

"Doesn't look like it."

"Good," Ari said. "If you beat Vallant, you can take his ships and use them to fight the Mageworlders when *they* show up. The crews, too, some of them. Not everybody in Vallant's fleet likes the thought of giving away most of the Republic."

"Mmph." The bartender sounded dubious. "Not everybody on Gyffer thinks that fighting is such a good idea, either. Better the admiral than the Magelords."

Ari shook his head. "It won't work. The timing on all this is too neat for coincidence—Admiral Vallant's going to be running the Infabede sector as a wholly owned subsidiary of Mageworlds, Incorporated."

"Is that so bad?"

"Depends on how you feel about making ships and weapons to help the Magelords take over the rest of the civilized galaxy."

"Yeah . . . but if we fight, what's to stop the Mageworlders from slagging us like they did Entibor?"

"Time," said Ari. "The Siege of Entibor lasted for three solid years. If what's left of the Space Force can pull itself back together, and if the other worlds don't roll over and play dead at the first sight of a Magebuilt ship—"

He broke the speculation off unfinished. The miniature viewing tank behind the bar was showing a stylized Gyfferan sphere with the words "Special Newsbreak" orbiting in bright orange letters around the equator, and a flashing montage of images layered behind it: the golden dome of the Gyfferan State House; the abandoned Space Force installation at Telabryk Field; the orbiting docks where the big merchant ships, seized a few days earlier by the Assembly, waited to be fitted out for war.

"They just broke into the regular programming," said the bartender nervously. "Something's going on."

The news service's logo glowed for a few seconds longer before fading to an image of Telabryk Field in the early dawn. Against the dark sky—the sun wasn't above the horizon yet—a set of contrails showed gold as they caught the light. The picture in the globe expanded as the magnification increased, and Ari saw that the holocams were tracking a black spaceship, a sleek and deadly craft with a silhouette like a bird's wing or a flattened obsidian teardrop.

It was a picture out of the history books, or out of decimal-credit popular romances about the old days before the First Magewar—a Magebuilt Deathwing raider. Four local defense fighters surrounded the alien craft, flying top, bottom, right, and left, swinging in formation onto the landing path for Telabryk Field.

The bartender stared. "What the hell do they think they're doing, letting that thing in?"

"Maybe it didn't give them a choice."

The holocam relaying the picture moved through an arc of clear sky to show another ship, a Republic Space Force courier, following the Deathwing. Belated, the bartender turned up the sound, and the polished, orotund voice of Telabryk's most popular news broadcaster filled the room.

". . . ETA ten minutes. That is, time of arrival will be six-eleven Telabryk local time. Defense forces identify the vessel as a Mage warship. No word so far on the purpose of this visit. Speculation among knowledgeable sources concerns a peace parley or diplomatic mission. Sources at the Citizen-Assembly give an official statement of 'No comment,' but repeat that the public has no cause for alarm."

"Right," said the bartender. "Tell that to the folks in the port. Tonight's going to be worse than last night."

"Just what we needed."

"Yeah. What do you think—is it legit?"

Ari shrugged. "Who the hell knows?"

They watched the holoset in silence for a while. Inside the tiny globe, the Deathwing and the Space Force courier settled onto Telabryk landing field. The four Gyfferan fighters circled above the port like watchful, predatory birds.

Another few minutes passed. The broadcaster's voice rose and fell in practiced inanities that Ari had no trouble recognizing as meaningless time-filler. He ignored them, and waited. At last the metal side of the Magebuilt craft opened, and a ramp swung down to the pavement. A moment later, two people appeared in the open door—a thin man in Space Force uniform, and a small, dark woman in an Adept's formal blacks.

Ari felt the hair rise on the back of his neck. *I don't believe it. The universe does not work like that.*

Then the holocam recording the events moved in for a close-up of the newcomers' faces. The man was nobody Ari recognized—a reserve lieutenant from the last war by his insignia and ribbons—but the young woman was Mistress Llannat Hyfid.

He shook his head. *What do you know about it, Rosselin-Metadi? Maybe for Adepts the universe does work that way.*

"Are you all right?" asked the bartender. "You look like somebody hit you over the head with a brick."

"The Adept," Ari said. "I know her."

"Right. And I'm the head of the Grand Council."

"No, really. We served together on Nammerin . . . she's Medical Service too, or at least she used to be. . . ."

He realized that he was babbling, and fell silent before the bartender could get interested enough to start asking him inconvenient questions. In the holoset, Llannat Hyfid and the reserve lieutenant were entering a sleek hovercar marked with the insignia of the Gyfferan Foreign Ministry. The door of the hovercar slid closed behind them, and the vehicle sped away from the landing field.

Ari stood up.

"I have to find her," he said. "The two of us need to talk."

* * *

The blastproof door slid closed, but the force field stayed up, making a waver and a shimmer like the ghost of a hot day in the chill air of Beka's cell.

She could see through the field well enough. "You," she said. "I should have known."

Tarveet of Pleyver looked aggrieved. He was a thin man, with a sagging face and watery grey eyes and a tight, puckered mouth. When he spoke, his lips came loose enough to show the wet pink lining. "You don't seem very happy to see me, my lady."

"I'm not your lady," she said. "Unless Pleyver is planning to swear allegiance to Entibor."

"That wouldn't be workable, I'm afraid." Tarveet licked his lips. "Actually, I had another sort of proposition in mind."

Beka sat motionless on the edge of the bunk, her hands flat on her thighs. *Here it comes. This is where he tries to buy me.*

"Talk," she said. "But don't expect me to feel very positive about anything under the circumstances."

He didn't even pretend to look ashamed. "I felt that you would do better for having some time alone to think things over."

"Considerate of you." She paused. "You said you had a proposition. Let's hear it."

"Ah," he said. "Yes. Well . . . there are a number of charges laid against you in the arrest and detention contract, beginning with an incident some ten years back at a portside eating and drinking establishment—"

"It was self-defense. A cheap buyout, if there's anybody on Suivi who misses the son of a bitch."

Tarveet shook his head regretfully. "I never knew him, alas, but I find myself concerned over his untimely demise. So much so that I consider the usual blood price in such cases to be almost an insult to my integrity."

"I'm glad there's something around that can insult it," she said. "So—what else?"

"We can't just pass over the matter of your presumed death on Artat without an adequate investigation. Under the present circumstances, the civilized galaxy doesn't need a pretender to the throne of Entibor."

"Gene scan," she countered. "Dahl&Dahl keeps the family records; you can do a check, no problem. Besides—if I'm not me, then I didn't shoot that guy ten years ago, either."

"A quibble. These things do require sorting out, you know. But the most immediate and urgent matter is the possibility of treason—"

"What?" She was on her feet and halfway across the cell before she remembered the force field and brought herself up short, fists clenched and body trembling with rage. "How *dare* you—"

"Treason," he said again. "And deliberate endangerment of the Suivan settlements."

Oh, damn. She fought to keep her face from showing her dismay. *That last one is bad.*

Because it's true.

She swallowed hard and made her voice stay as before, calm and slightly insolent. "Purely out of idle curiosity— what are you calling treason these days?"

"According to your ship's official log as transmitted to Suivan officials, your last recorded port of call was Ninglin in the Mageworlds; scant days before the current outbreak of hostilities. This requires investigation."

"I was picking up some money hauling intersystem freight," she said. "All clean and legal."

"But the suspicion remains—particularly in light of your subsequent actions."

"Now we come to it." She crossed her arms over her chest and faced him squarely. "Which of my subsequent actions do you want to talk about?"

"We can begin," Tarveet said, "with that singularly ill-advised hyperspace transmission of yours—tantamount to issuing an open invitation to the Mageworlds Warfleet."

She bit her lip. *Damn. I wish he'd let well enough alone.* "I had my reasons. And I *am* the Domina of Entibor. It's none of Pleyver's business how I conduct my world's affairs."

"Perhaps not. But unless something can be done, your current legal difficulties will make it hard for you to conduct those affairs at all."

"Aha," she said. "Now we're back at that 'proposition' of yours, aren't we? What's the deal?"

Tarveet smiled primly. "I can take care of all the outstanding fines and assessments, and see to it that all contracts for your arrest and detention are withdrawn. In return, my lady, you can make me your consort and General of the Armies of Entibor."

She stared at him, her gorge rising. "Consort? *You?* I wouldn't let you in the same bed with me if I was dead and laid out for burning!"

His pale face colored. "The arrangement need not be formalized in the old style, my lady. The title position alone will be sufficient."

"Sorry." She was clenching and unclenching her fists. *If it wasn't for the force field I'd kill the bastard with my bare hands.* "The position is already filled."

"Oh, yes. That charming gentleman at the office. Such things can change, you know."

"I wouldn't if I were you, Tarveet. He's one of the Khesatan Jessans. Think of this as a friendly reminder."

"I didn't have in mind trying anything that clumsy, my lady. You can release him yourself any time you choose."

"I don't choose," she said, tight-lipped. "Understand this, Tarveet: Nyls Jessan is satisfactory on all counts as General and consort."

Tarveet smiled. "Then given your continued obduracy, and the threat your plans present to the Suivan settlements, I have no choice but to remove myself from the discussion before the Steering Committee of Suivi Point concerning your summary termination." He paused. "Do you wish to reconsider?"

Beka closed her eyes. *Oh, Nyls. I hope you're alive to get me out of this.*

"No," she said. "I don't. Now get the hell out of here before you make me sick."

* * *

The Gyfferan Foreign Ministry's hovercar moved with ease through the crowded streets outside the spaceport. Telabryk Field on Gyffer wasn't as big as the port complex of Galcen Prime, but as far as Llannat Hyfid was concerned, once the industrialization and urban sprawl reached a certain point she couldn't tell the difference. She liked her cities small—Namport was about her upper limit, or the Galcenian village of Treslin in the shadow of the Adepts' Retreat. Nothing on her homeworld of Maraghai was bigger than either of those.

Country girl, she thought. *At least* that *hasn't changed.*

She found the idea comforting. This morning's sessions at the Ministry—a debriefing, really, with voice-stress analyzers and other verification equipment set up and running—had made it clear that a number of other things about her had altered beyond recovery. The very young Llannat Hyfid who'd left Maraghai to join the Space Force would never have noticed the equipment in the first place; and the older Llannat who'd come back to the Space Force from the Adepts' Retreat would never have evaded its detection.

I had to do it. If I told the Ministry about everything that happened on board Night's-Beautiful-Daughter, *they'd lock me up and wipe out the keycode.*

At least they still consider me Space Force. If I had to stay at the local Guildhouse, I'd wind up spilling my secrets to somebody before long. The Prof's staff raised enough eyebrows around there the last time I was on Gyffer, with Ari and the rest of the 'Hammer's *crew.*

The hovercar paused at the main gate to the Field proper. A heavy-duty force field made the air in front of the entrance waver and ripple like a mirage on a hot day. A guard in the uniform of the Gyfferan local defense forces stepped out of the field's generating kiosk; when the Ministry driver flashed an ID at him, he waved at his partner inside the kiosk and the field went down long enough for the hovercar to pass through.

In spite of the inconvenience—not to mention the outright distrust with which she and Lieutenant Vinhalyn had at first been received—she was glad to see that Gyffer was taking its resistance to the Mageworlders seriously. The *Daughter* and RSF *Naversey* had been met in force by in-system ships almost as soon as they crossed the planet's nearspace threshold; if it hadn't been for the presence of the Space Force courier, Llannat suspected, the Gyfferans might well have destroyed the Magebuilt raider without bothering to ask questions.

So the war isn't lost yet. If Gyffer holds firm, the rest of the Republic still has a chance.

Of course, if a medic from the backwoods can figure that much out, then so can the experts. Which means that the whole enemy fleet is going to show up on our doorstep any day now.

"Welcome to the war," she muttered under her breath.

Next to her in the back seat of the hovercar, Vinhalyn nodded. "Just so."

The hovercar glided on across the vast plain of the landing field. Compared with the first time she'd been in Telabryk, the place was almost empty. After what she'd learned during the conference at the Defense Ministry, Llannat wasn't surprised. Most of Gyffer's usual merchant traffic would have cleared out as soon as word hit the planet about the fall of Galcen Prime. The ships that had stayed behind—either voluntarily, or caught by the Citizen-Assembly's closing of the port—would be up in the orbital yards, getting fitted out with shields and weaponry.

The dark wing-shape of *Night's-Beautiful-Daughter* loomed up over the tarmac ahead, and beside it the thin bright needle that was RSF *Naversey*. The low, blocky buildings of the Space Force installation stood nearby, their abandoned state made more obvious by the presence of the two vessels. Llannat grimaced. The Gyfferans at the Ministry had not been happy about the way the Space Force had left Telabryk, even though they'd conceded the possibility of standing orders that had to be obeyed.

"Somewhere out there," she'd said, with as much persuasion behind the words as she dared to use, *"the Republic's fleet is regrouping. All we have to do is hold out until they come back."*

That had brought a skeptical look to the face of the Ministry rep who'd been asking most of the questions, but his manner had softened a little afterward. Whatever the Gyfferan's feelings about the local Space Force contingent, at least Llannat and Vinhalyn—surprised themselves by the outbreak of war—weren't being held personally responsible.

The hovercar came to a halt outside the main building of the Space Force installation. Llannat and Vinhalyn got out, the lieutenant thanked the driver, and the hovercar sped back toward the gate.

Llannat let out her breath in an explosive sigh. "Well. At least *that's* over."

"Temporarily, at least," said Vinhalyn. He glanced over at the sleek black hull of the Magebuilt ship. "Some of our hosts are certain to find the *Daughter* as fascinating as I do—there are one or two academics on Gyffer with an interest in Old Eraasian artifacts. But the preparations for war will keep them occupied for a while, I hope."

"Until you've got enough notes to publish something first?"

The lieutenant smiled, a bit grimly. "I may be fated to end my scholarly career the way I began it—as a lieutenant in the Republic's service—but the full report on *Night's-Beautiful-Daughter* will keep my name alive in the archives all the same."

"Worse things could happen," said Llannat. "And we may see a few of them, if we're not careful. Let's go on in and tell the others what the Ministry's going to do with us."

Vinhalyn nodded, and led the way into the main building, where they'd left the rest of the crew. The courier ship's original complement had been augmented by the four crew members of a *Pari*-class scout that had been docked with the Deathwing raider when the Mageworlds warfleet broke through the Net. That brought the crew up to twelve people, counting Llannat and Vinhalyn; not much of a Space Force presence on a planet facing imminent attack.

The interior of the building was dim after the sun glare over the landing field. Llannat stood for a moment just inside the tinted armor-glass of the door, letting her eyes—and her other, nonphysical senses—adjust to the change.

The Space Force installation hadn't yet lost all traces of its previous inhabitants. She could sense the residual shock and tension of their hurried departure, overlaid by the auras of the building's new occupants. After their time aboard the Deathwing, all of them were known to her. She relaxed a bit in their familiarity. With relaxation came a sudden awareness of another presence, one whose strength and steadiness had almost lulled her into accepting it as a part of the pattern.

She caught her breath in surprise. *That's not one of the* Daughter's *crew! That's—*

"Ari?" she said, and heard her voice quaver on the edge of a shaky laugh. "What in the name of everything in the civilized galaxy are you doing *here*?"

He stood up. As usual, he'd found the lowest chair in the most inconspicuous corner of the room, and had occupied it with a stillness that even some Adepts never managed to learn. It was a hunter's stillness, that he'd learned from the Selvaurs who controlled Llannat's homeworld. Ari had been fostered among the big saurians—he and they were built to the same scale—and the nonhuman training showed in the way he held himself. Most big men were awkward and clumsy, or at least to Llannat they seemed to be, but Ari moved with the easy grace of the Forest Lords.

The bow of respect he gave Llannat had never been learned on Maraghai, however, and his Galcenian had the pure native accent.

"I've been waiting for you," he said. "I thought about going to the Defense Ministry, but decided that coming here would be easier."

She took a step closer, putting out a hand to touch the fabric of his sleeve and feel the muscular solidity of the arm beneath it.

"No, no," she said, struggling against laughter. "I mean, what are you doing on Gyffer? The last I heard, you were headed for RSF *Fezrisond*—we had a bet, remember, that

she wouldn't get out of the Infabede sector while you were
on her?"

"I remember," he said, smiling down at her. "You lose,
I'm afraid. The *Fezzy* hasn't left Infabede yet that I've heard
of." His smile faded. "She's Admiral Vallant's flagship, you
know. When Vallant declared his mutiny, I decided it was
time for me to leave."

"Leave how?"

"The *Fezzy* carries a fighter detachment on board. So I
stole one of the long-range craft and brought it here." He
shrugged, looking unhappy. "Gyffer was the only place in
range that looked safe. I didn't know about the Magefleet
then."

"Nobody did," she said. She let her hand slide away from
his arm; at the last moment, his fingers caught hers, and
held them. "We knew there was trouble coming—but we all
thought that we'd have more time."

VI. Innish-Kyl: Waycross
Gyffer: Port of Telabryk
Lady LeRoi: Hyperspace Transit to Pleyver

BACK IN the days of the First Magewar, Waycross on Innish-Kyl had been one of the gaudiest and most riotous ports in the civilized galaxy. The privateers who preyed on the Mageworlds supply fleets had made Innish-Kyl their base, returning to Waycross between forays to sell off their stolen cargo and refit their battered ships. Three decades of peace and prosperity, however, had turned the onetime pirates' haven into an ordinary third-rank trading nexus, a bit rough around the edges but rich in historical associations.

That, at least, was how things had stood a few weeks ago, before the Mageworlders took Galcen. Now Innish-Kyl had a fighting fleet in orbit again—*Karipavo, Shaja*, and *Lachiel*, three capital ships from the former Space Force Net Patrol. The portside Strip was thronged with free-spending spacers, all with money in their pockets and full of the urge to party away the strain of combat. Captain Jervas Gil, commanding officer of the *'Pavo* and commodore of the three-ship force, wasn't surprised at how fast Waycross had snapped back into its old shape.

"The changes never did go that deep," he said to his aide, Lieutenant Bretyn Jhunnei.

The two officers sat in one of the far back tables in the Blue Sun Cantina, nursing tumblers of the bad local brandy and making conversation as best they could over the gabble of voices. Gil and his aide were both in civilian clothing, as were most of the dirtside crews. Since coming to Waycross, the commodore had also resumed styling himself "Baronet D'Rugier"—a title he'd seldom bothered with since leaving his homeworld of Ovredis and going into the service. But now that he'd be associating with and commanding civilians . . .

"The last time I was in Waycross," he continued, "I lost count of how many laws I wound up breaking."

"All in a good cause, sir, I'm sure," Jhunnei said. "Any leftover legal problems that we need to worry about?"

"There shouldn't be. We falsified the records and deep-spaced the body."

She didn't blink. "Sounds like an interesting evening."

The lieutenant was a dark-haired woman with a sallow, bony face and an air of unobtrusive competence. In peacetime, she would have been on the fast track for advancement—Gil's last promotion had come after his successful completion of a similar tour of duty as aide to General Metadi. These days, Gil wasn't sure that there was a Space Force left for advancing in, outside of his own three ships and the handful of smaller craft that had survived the battle at the Outer Net.

If only hi-comms weren't still so damned spotty . . .

The Mageworlders had pulled off their surprise attack by suppressing the hyperspace communications network upon which so much of the Space Force's strategy and tactics depended. It wasn't supposed to be possible, not with a multiply-redundant and self-healing system, but the Mages had done it. Even now, with the network slowly coming back on-line, outsector comms were erratic and subject to time lag.

Several minutes passed. The crowd in the Blue Sun grew denser and rowdier. The dim air was streaked with the blue-grey fumes of incense and smoking herbs, and the mingled sweet and bitter smells warred with the odor of sweat and spilled beer. The Blue Sun's climate-control system, already overburdened, tried to compensate by drawing power from the light panels and the emergency glows. The system's efforts gave the cantina's illumination an irregular and unsettling flicker.

"So what do you think, sir?" Jhunnei said at last. "Is this 'Captain Merro' person going to show up or not?"

"I hope so," Gil said. "Having him throw in with us will make it easier to get the rest." He took another sip of the atrocious brandy. "Unfortunately, the sort of people we need right now are the sort of people who under happier circumstances would be right at the top of our stop-and-search list, and don't think they don't know it."

"Merchant-captains with fast mean ships that are a bit faster and meaner than they ought to be" was how Gil had phrased it to the Blue Sun's bartender when he was first putting out the word. The bartender had understood him well enough: *"You'll want to talk with Cap'n Merro, then. If you can get Merro's Luck of the Draw on your side, most of the others'll follow."*

Another few minutes passed. Just as Gil was about to give up and call it a night, a tall figure loomed over the table, blocking most of the light.

I'm Merrolakk. Are you the Baronet D'Rugier they said was looking for me?

The language wasn't Standard Galcenian, but a hooting, rumbling speech that most human voices found uncongenial. Gil was not one of the few who could speak it; he wouldn't have understood it, either, without the crash-tutoring he'd undergone during his stint as General Metadi's aide. The General had negotiated the first firm alliance between the Republic and the Selvaurs, and was bound to the big saurians by complex ties of sworn-brotherhood and child-fosterage. Learning to "hear" the Forest Speech wasn't an official requirement for working with Metadi, but Gil sometimes thought it should have been.

Captain Merro wore a vest full of pockets, most of them

sealed and bulging, and a holstered blaster on a weapons belt. No knife, though; the Forest Lords regarded edged weapons as fang-and-claw substitutes permissible only for infants or for those made feeble by age. Gil also noted Merro's bright green scales and uncrested skull, the former marking the captain as belonging to one of the minor Selvauran subraces, and the latter marking him—marking *her*—as a female. The bartender hadn't mentioned that last detail; perhaps he hadn't known the difference, or hadn't cared.

Gil nodded courteously. "I'm D'Rugier, yes. Sit down, please, Captain. Would you care for some brandy?"

The Selvaur took a chair on the other side of the table. *No, thanks. You say you've got a business proposal for me?*

"Of sorts. Are you interested?"

It depends. Is it going to be profitable?

Gil shrugged. "As you said yourself, it depends. But with luck, yes. And the more ships who participate, the better."

Merrolakk's yellow eyes dilated with interest. *What kind of job are you thinking about?*

"A simple one, really," said Gil. "I intend to enter the Magezone, find whatever merchant ships might be there, and transfer their cargos to mine."

The Selvauran captain hooted under her breath—with amusement, as far as Gil could tell. *Pirate, eh?*

Gil shook his head. "No. Privateer. I'm carrying letters of marque and reprisal."

Whose?

Before Gil could answer, he spotted a new arrival in the Blue Sun. The newcomer, a young Space Force trooper in an awkward mixture of uniform and civilian clothing, looked around the room, wide-eyed, before shouldering a way through the crowd to their table.

"My lord Baronet," he began—hesitating a bit on the title. "A word with you."

"Of course," said Gil. He turned to Merrolakk. "Excuse me for a moment."

The Selvaur laughed again with the breathy *hoo-hoo*

sounds of her species. *He brings word that more of your fleet has gathered, twenty-seven vessels of various classes, coming in from the Net.*

The messenger clearly didn't understand the Forest Speech. He gave Merrolakk a curious look, then leaned closer to Gil's ear and whispered, "We've found twenty-seven undamaged units in the Net. They'll be making orbit later tonight or early tomorrow."

Was I right?

Gil ignored the Selvaur. "When did you get the word?" he asked the messenger in an undertone.

"We picked up lightspeed comms with them a couple of minutes ago. I came right over."

"Thank you," said Gil. "Prepare to receive them; refuel, rearm, refit as necessary."

"Yes, sir."

Gil nodded the messenger on his way, and turned back to Merro. "I believe we were discussing a business proposition."

You could call it that, said Merro. She still sounded amused. *Assuming it's successful—what kind of prize fees are you talking about?*

"You take half," said Gil. He'd done some research on the subject before coming down to the Blue Sun this evening, and the cut he'd proposed had been a standard one in the old days, whenever an eager or ambitious captain brought together more than one ship for a privateering foray. "Divide it with your crew as you see fit. The other half goes to me—for the good of everyone under my flag."

What happens if I hit a run of bad luck?

"You'll be taken care of, don't worry. I have some long-term investors backing the project."

Gil paused. The next bit would be tricky, even with the sweetening of that bad-luck guarantee. "I will also direct you as to the general area of your operations, the rules of engagement, and your treatment of prisoners, if any."

The captain smiled—an almost-human expression, except for the flash of predatory fangs. Gil knew enough Selvauran physiognomy to recognize that she wasn't entirely pleased by his last statement. *I see. You keep tight control and you take half my profits. What have you got for me that's worth it?*

"Well," said Gil. "For one thing . . . when the Republic is restored, I won't have to hunt you down myself."

This time Merro did show her teeth. *Brave words for a man who's lost his fleet.*

Jhunnei spoke up for the first time. "If you think the Magelords can give you something better, you can go ask them."

I might.

She's bluffing, Gil reassured himself. *The Selvaurs were allies of the Republic in the last war; the Mages won't be eager to make deals with them now.*

"When can I expect your answer, Captain?"

Soon, Merro said. *After I've spoken with my associates.*

Gil nodded. "Call on me when you have something—but I can't wait on your answer forever. I'll be taking my fleet out of orbit before very long."

I understand. Can you tell me when?

"It depends. As soon as possible."

So.

Merrolakk regarded him for a moment longer without saying anything, then rose and walked away—but no farther than the bar, where she ordered up a mug of something green. Jhunnei looked after the Selvauran captain with a curious expression.

"Do you think she's going to go for it?"

"I hope so," said Gil. "Because it's the only way we can get enough ships."

"We have a slight problem here," Lieutenant Vinhalyn said to Ari. The two of them were conferring in what had once been the CO's office at Telabryk Field. The Space Force evacuation had left the room as bare as the rest of the installation; even the files on the desk comp had been wiped. "I'm the senior line officer on-planet, and you're technically a deserter—which raises the inconvenient question of what I'm supposed to do with you now that I've got you."

"I know," Ari said. "If it's any help, I can plead extenuating circumstances. I didn't think I ought to stick around on *Fezrisond* and let Admiral Vallant drag me into mutiny."

Vinhalyn nodded. "True. Your family name alone would make you far too valuable as a potential hostage. But we still have to account for that fighter you appropriated for the journey."

"I was going to turn it over to the base CO as soon as I reached Gyffer," Ari said. "So I suppose it's yours."

"Thus augmenting our little squadron to three ships; or two and a fraction, anyhow."

Ari smiled briefly at the mild witticism: Eldan dual-seaters were high on armament, and had considerable hyperspace range, but they weren't very big.

Vinhalyn continued, looking thoughtful. "Rather than putting you in the medical department with Captain Lury, I'm going to assign you to general duty and keep you as our one-man fighter squadron. As for your alleged desertion . . . I'll fill out all the proper forms. Under the circumstances, though, it wouldn't surprise me if the paperwork never made it all the way to Galcen."

"Thank you, sir."

"Don't thank me," Vinhalyn said. "There's a fight coming—Gyffer couldn't get away with rolling over and playing dead even if the locals wanted to—and we'll be right in the middle of it. I made a point, this morning, of offering our help to the Defense Ministry before anybody in the room could work up the initiative to commandeer us."

Ari followed his reasoning. Relations between the Space Force and the local defense fleets were a delicate matter, even in peacetime, and it was better to volunteer for trouble than to set a bad precedent. "What about that Deathwing raider you brought in?"

"An armed ship is an armed ship," Vinhalyn said, with a sigh. "I'd prefer to study *Night's-Beautiful-Daughter* at more length, naturally; a perfectly preserved Deathwing raider from the early days of the Eraasian Hegemony is a scholar's treasure beyond all price. But we do what we must."

"And Llannat—Mistress Hyfid?"

"She stays with us, she says; but Adepts choose their own paths." Vinhalyn looked at Ari curiously. "Mistress Hyfid is a friend of yours?"

"We were stationed together on Nammerin," Ari said. "She saved my life."

"I see," said Vinhalyn. "Well, if you're interested in renewing old acquaintance, I wouldn't dally. Once the fighting starts, none of us are likely to have much time."

By the time Commodore Gil and Lieutenant Jhunnei abandoned their table in the Blue Sun Cantina, local midnight had already come and gone without any new word from Merrolakk. The Selvauran captain had left the bar not long after their conversation, and Gil and Jhunnei had waited on her return for as long as they dared. They couldn't hold down a table forever, though, without appearing anxious, and therefore weak—always a bad idea when dealing with one of the Forest Lords. At last Gil pushed his empty glass away from him with a sigh.

"Time to go, Lieutenant," he said. "We'll see if our friend Merro is any more helpful in the morning."

He left a couple of ten-credit chits on the table to cover their tab, and worked his way through the close-packed tables to the door. Lieutenant Jhunnei followed close behind him.

Outside, the night air felt cool and dry after the sweaty congestion of the cantina. *Karipavo*'s shuttle was in docking bay 358-A, several minutes of brisk walking away from the crowded activity of the Strip. As soon as they were free of the noise, Gil pulled a comm link out of his coat pocket and keyed it on.

"Commodore Gil here. Status on the new arrivals?"

The voice of the shuttle pilot came back over the link with a tinny clicking sound. "Word from the *'Pavo* is that the entire flotilla is up there in high orbit, awaiting orders."

"Good," said Gil. "How soon can they be ready to make a hyperspace jump?"

"They report they're ready right now."

"Even better. Anything else to report?"

"Nothing, sir."

"Very well. Get ready to lift for orbit; we'll be with you in about ten minutes."

He clicked off the link and pocketed it again. "Let's get moving," he said to Jhunnei. "I want to be out of orbit and heading for hyper by local dawn—if Merrolakk hasn't gotten in touch with us before then, she'll have to wait until we come back into town."

"Yes, sir," said Jhunnei.

Her voice sounded oddly absent and detached, and she hadn't moved since Gil started his conversation with the shuttle pilot. The patchy light from a nearby holosign shone down on her face. Her eyes were half-shut, and she held her head at an angle, as if listening.

Gil regarded her anxiously. "Is something wrong?"

"Maybe," she said. She hesitated for a moment, and then appeared to make up her mind. "Commodore, I don't think we should walk any further along this street. Something very bad is going to happen if we do."

Ari found Llannat Hyfid out back by the skipsled loading platform, in a secluded corner where the bulk of two adjoining buildings cast a patch of cooler shadow on the hot tarmac. She still wore the black trousers and the plain white shirt of her formal Adept's gear; the stiff broadcloth tunic hung, neatly folded, over the handrail of the loading platform nearby. She had her staff, the short ebony one that she'd brought back from the raid on Darvell, and she was practicing the movements of the ShadowDance, alone.

Ari had seen the Dance before. Given a younger brother who'd seemed destined for the Guild from toddlerhood, he didn't think he could have avoided seeing it. But he knew that the movements as Llannat did them were not in the customary form, any more than was the staff she carried.

If I were an Adept, he thought, *I'd probably be all bent out of shape about the changes.*

But he wasn't an Adept, so he could lean against the loading platform and enjoy watching Llannat work through the postures and sequences, first slowly and then with a sharp, decisive edge. She was sweating in the warm midday sun, so that her brown skin glistened, and her black hair was coming down in loose, curling tendrils from its knot at the back of her neck.

He waited there as a hunter would, not calling attention to himself until she had finished. When she was done, she nodded a greeting in his direction, then clipped her staff back onto her belt and came over to the loading platform.

"I saw you come out here," she said as she retrieved her tunic from the safety railing. "I stopped the sequence as soon as I came to a good spot."

"You could have kept on. I don't mind watching."

It was hard to tell, with her dark complexion, but he thought she blushed. "I don't mind having you watch me. But you came out here to talk, I think, and I haven't had much friendly conversation lately."

"Lieutenant Vinhalyn seems to regard you highly enough," Ari said. He frowned. "Is there a problem with one of the others?"

She shook her head. "Not unless you call too much awe and respect a problem. Which I do, when I'm on the receiving end of it, but there's no polite way to make them stop."

"I suppose not. Isn't there anything I can do to help?"

"Don't start respecting me so much we can't talk anymore. And whatever you do—no, whatever *I* do—don't get scared of me. I don't think I could stand that."

Ari felt a stirring of apprehension, like a fist closing on something just behind his rib cage. He took a deep breath and willed the tightness away. "I won't do it, then."

"Thanks." She was quiet for a moment; then she reached out and laid her fingertips against the back of his wrist. He felt his skin warming under her touch. "I missed that, you know—having somebody treat me like a regular person, instead of like some kind of miracle-working oracle."

What did you see for them? he wanted to demand of her; *what did you say?*

But he knew better than to ask.

Commodore Gil glanced down the street. Most of the groundcar traffic had gone home for the night, and the heavy null-grav cargo transports wouldn't be making an appearance until the grey hours just before dawn. Waycross at this hour belonged to the free-spacers who made their way on foot—sometimes strolling and sometimes staggering—from one gaudily illuminated place of entertainment to another.

"I don't see any problems," Gil said. "Everything looks about the same as usual."

"That's what I don't like."

"You're starting to sound like an Adept."

"I do a great imitation at parties." She nodded toward a narrow side-street branching off to their right. "Humor me, please, Commodore. Let's go that way instead."

Gil looked at his aide for a moment longer, then shrugged. "No reason we shouldn't, I suppose. This is Waycross, after all—sneaking around in dark alleys is practically the national sport."

With Gil in the lead, they left the main thoroughfare and started down the alley. Their new route wasn't much more than a murky service passage between two rows of buildings, dimly lit by occasional blue safety glows marking back entrances and garbage bins. The night sky was a paler stripe of darkness overhead. Halfway down the alley, an access ladder of some kind ran up the wall on Gil's left.

Jhunnei halted. "That's it," she said. "Look."

Gil bent and examined the ladder. There was enough light for him to see a thin crust of mud clinging to the iron rungs. He touched it, and felt the coolness of residual moisture. The dirt was only half-dry.

"Looks like somebody climbed up the ladder recently," he said. "Probably a maintenance worker."

"That track isn't more than half an hour old," Jhunnei

pointed out. "And midnight's an odd time for anyone to be doing maintenance, even in Waycross."

She paused. "Call it a hunch, Commodore—but I think it's time we split up. You check out whatever's going on up on the roof, and I'll take a little walk down the main street and see if anyone shows an inordinate interest in me."

Gil looked at Jhunnei for a moment, considering. What she proposed could be dangerous—though more so for her, as the one to draw fire, than for him. On the other hand, there *was* the muddy footprint on the ladder.

If she's right about that, Gil thought, *then her proposal's a sound one. And if she's wrong, and it was some environmental-systems tech doing a bit of emergency repair work . . . well, we won't hurt anyone by checking out the situation.*

"Good idea," he said aloud. "Let's do it, Lieutenant. If nothing happens, we'll meet back here in fifteen minutes."

Jhunnei nodded. "Yes, sir." She faded away toward the mouth of the alley.

Gil set his foot onto the bottom rung of the ladder—the caked dirt fell away when his boot sole touched it—and climbed up until he came to the low brick wall that ran around the flat roof of the building. Keeping his feet planted on the top rung of the ladder, he raised his head a few inches above the edge of the parapet and looked about.

His caution didn't do him much good. The big e-c housings in the middle of the roof cut off his view, and cast their shadows everywhere. He swung himself up onto the roof, and pulled out the miniature hand-blaster he'd carried up his sleeve ever since his tour as an aide, when he'd picked up the habit from General Metadi. Keeping his head low, he made his way around three sides of the roof until he could look down at the main street.

There she was, Lieutenant Bretyn Jhunnei, five stories below—and not alone. She was walking beside someone who seemed eerily familiar; who was, in fact, Gil's double, from the nondescript brown hair down to the combination of uniform trousers with the formal pleats and tucks of a white spidersilk evening shirt.

She shouldn't be able to do that!

Gil shook his head. *It doesn't matter right now. She is doing it, so make use of it while you can.*

Lady LeRoi wasn't carrying cargo to Pleyver this trip. Nothing produced on Nammerin, the freighter's previous port of call, would pay as much to reach the Pleyveran system as had the passengers crowded into every cubic inch of the *Lady*'s free space. Her captain had hooked up life support in the holds and stacked the cargo bays three deep with jury-rigged acceleration bunks.

The ship's environmental systems labored noisily under the added load of so many extra bodies. The air smelled like sweat and stale urine, even with the scrubbers cycling overtime, and the drinking water was flat from repeated distillation—and so bitter with purifiers that nobody ever forgot its origins. The food was, by official definition on the side of the package, sufficient to sustain life under emergency conditions.

"This is the first emergency I've ever seen that was mostly boredom," said Klea. "And I never thought that a person could get tired of eating water-grain."

She and Owen were in crew berthing, a relative luxury Owen had secured for them back at Namport by methods about which Klea still wasn't sure. He was doing some kind of work in return, down in the maintenance sections of the ship, but the *Lady* had turned away a dozen passengers for every one she took aboard, and Klea didn't think Owen could have bought their tickets with labor and money alone.

"Be grateful that Nammerin-to-Pleyver isn't one of your longer jumps," he told her. "The *Lady* isn't exactly a demon for speed. Now ... the ShadowDance."

Klea looked about the cramped cabin. The only light came from a blue low-power glow set into the bulkhead near the door. Sleeping crew members occupied all four of the regular bunks, and two more crew members—thrown out of their own quarters to make room for paying passengers—found places as Owen and Klea did, in sleepsacks on the deck.

"Here?" she said. "There isn't an extra inch to Dance in."

"One must learn accommodation."

"If I kick somebody and wake them up, they're liable to accommodate me straight out an airlock."

"I don't think so," said Owen after a moment's consideration. "They're more likely to throw you in with the hold passengers. You shouldn't let the prospect disturb you."

"That's easy for you to say," Klea grumbled.

Nevertheless she folded the sleepsack and stood up, grasping her broomstick staff in both hands. She placed her feet in the beginning position and began to Dance.

It was difficult, working in such a small area. She felt as if invisible barriers surrounded her, circumscribing her movements—forcing her to scale everything down, to take smaller steps and move more slowly and always, always return to the center point she had established when she began. But she persisted—and between one awkward motion and the next the essence of the ShadowDance asserted itself, transcending her dogged endeavors and flowing into her like bright water.

Owen had said once, back on Nammerin, that the ShadowDance was as much a meditation as it was a combat skill or a means of acquiring self-discipline. She'd come close once or twice to understanding through experience what he had meant, but never as close as now, when the small patch of clear deck that was her Dancing-ground seemed in that moment to stretch out toward infinity, as if her movements themselves were creating it around her out of nothingness.

The door and the bulkhead were gone; they had receded with everything else into the infinite distance she was creating with her Dance. Only the low-power glow remained, suffusing everything with a blue, sourceless light.

This is no-place, she thought—not stopping the steps of the Dance, keeping the Dancing-ground in being around her. *This is no-time. This is nowhere I have ever been.*

This is important.

She kept on Dancing. Phantoms and illusions began to take shape around her in the blue light.

These are what I came here to see.
She Danced, and watched.

The inchoate forms drew together into a single clear vision—and she was no longer all by herself on the Dancing-ground. Somewhere in the blue infinity ahead of her, too far away for her to touch but so close she could see the finest detail, another Dancer worked as she did to keep the nothingness at bay.

Who are you? What are you doing here inside my Dance?

She flung the questions out into the universe of blue light, but the other did not answer, or even seem to hear. A slight man, far from young, with grey hair and a worn, lined face, he moved in a Dance that was at once like and not like the one that Owen had taught her. The staff he worked with was not an Adept's, meant to be grasped in both hands, but a shorter rod, of ebony bound with silver, that he held in a loose one-handed grip.

She couldn't fail to recognize the weapon. The Circle-Mages on Nammerin had carried rods like that one.

But the man she was watching didn't act like a Mage, didn't wear the black robe and gloves and the immobile mask of black plastic that made all the members of a Circle look alike. And he was alone ... no shared strength of his fellows to draw on when his own powers began to fail. Only himself.

Wait. He isn't alone after all.

Now she could make out another form, half-obscured by the blue shadows behind the old man. It was a woman this time, fair-skinned and taller than the man who guarded her, swathed from head to foot in a hooded cloak of some rough-textured white fabric.

Are you the one I came here to see?

This time, her question seemed to reach its target. The hooded woman turned her head and looked directly at Klea. The woman's eyes were a deep, brilliant blue, sharp and penetrating, but beyond the sharpness was a fear too profound for words.

Have I failed again? Have you come too late?

The thought struck Klea like a blow from a knife; she

drew a sharp breath, and stumbled. The infinite blue Dancing-ground contracted around her like a skin tightening, and she fell down and away, out of the trance and back into the tiny, crowded cabin aboard *Lady LeRoi.*

She swayed and almost fell. Owen caught her, lowering her with strong hands down to the deckplates. She was shivering; he opened the sleepsack and wrapped it around her shoulders.

"You saw something," he said.

She didn't bother asking how he knew. "A man," she said. "And a woman. I think—I think he was guarding her. From the nothing. Keeping it away."

"These people. What did they look like?"

"Strangers," Klea said. "A fair woman, and a man with grey hair. And a staff like a Magelord's, but no mask. And they were waiting for something."

She paused, remembering the fearful question in the woman's deep blue eyes. "Or someone."

VII. Innish-Kyl: Waycross
Warhammer: Hyperspace Transit to Base
Pleyver: High Station

GIL CONTINUED his circuit of the roof, pacing his aide and her phantom companion, until he came to the corner where the road to the docking bays split off the main street. He peered around the turning, and drew his head back in haste.

A man—a free-spacer by his garments, though not a prosperous one—crouched a few feet away behind the shelter of the parapet. The spacer clutched an energy lance in his hands, and he was watching Jhunnei's progress along the street beneath. She passed beneath him, Gil's uncanny doppelgänger still walking by her side. The man raised his weapon and sighted down toward the street.

Gil flicked his hand-blaster to "stun," and fired. The sniper collapsed against the stone parapet. A bolt from the energy lance struck the holosign for the Hundred Blossoms Cabaret and disintegrated its waltzing flowers into an explosion of colored sparks. In the street below, Jhunnei glanced upward, and Gil's double winked out of existence with considerably less fuss than had the Hundred Blossoms' sign.

Gil collected the fallen energy lance, then moved away

from the unconscious sniper to wait for his aide. A few minutes later she joined him on the rooftop.

"Good shooting, Commodore."

"Thank you, Lieutenant." Gil looked at her for a moment without saying anything, then sighed. "Tell me something, Jhunnei. Did you know he was waiting up here? Or did you make a lucky guess?"

Jhunnei paused. "I . . . suspected. Strongly."

"Suspected," said Gil. There was another stretched-out silence, broken only by the background racket of the port and the nearby fizzing and popping of the broken holosign. Jhunnei seemed pale and nervous in the scant light. "Lieutenant, tell me something straight out. Are you an Adept?"

"Adepts can't hold rank, sir. Everybody knows that."

"Do they?" Gil regarded his aide thoughtfully. "Errec Ransome used to say as much to everybody who asked, and the handful of known Adepts in the service used to make a big point of not wearing any kind of insignia. It strikes me now that if I were Errec Ransome, and wanted to place an observer or two in the Space Force, I'd say the same."

Jhunnei remained silent.

"Well?" Gil prompted.

"With respect, Commodore, I can't answer your question."

"That's insubordination, you know."

"Yes, sir."

Gil paused again, considering. "I don't want to lose a perfectly good aide," he said finally. "Can we agree to take your silence as an affirmative?"

"Take it as you please. Sir."

"Don't get so stiff," Gil said. "As far as Waycross is concerned, we're both civilians anyway."

"Yes, sir. If you feel you can trust me, sir."

"Very much so, Lieutenant."

She seemed to relax then—until he saw the change, Gil had not appreciated the depth of her previous unease—and glanced over at the still-unconscious sniper for the first time since her initial greeting.

"What about him?" she said. "Do we take him home with us and ask him lots of interesting questions?"

Gil shook his head. "He's not important. Somebody hired him to take a shot at us, is all."

"Well, yes—but don't we want to find out who?"

"I don't think we need to bother. Unless I miss my guess, we'll find whoever hired him waiting for us at the docking bay."

"Now you're the one who's being mysterious, Commodore."

Gil smiled. "This is wartime, Lieutenant. A man has to take his pleasures as he can find them."

By the time *Lady LeRoi* docked at High Station Pleyver, Klea was more tired of dried, reconstituted water-grain than she would ever have believed possible. To her chagrin, Owen insisted that they wait a day to disembark.

"We'll leave ship when the crew does," he said. "No sense in getting ourselves shunted off to transient quarters with all the other refugees."

"I suppose not," she said. Until now, she hadn't thought about what might happen if Pleyver didn't want all the people the *Lady* was bringing. Not everybody who'd left Nammerin was going to be better off in a new place.

It wasn't until the next morning that she collected her belongings—the ancient daypack and the *grrch*-wood staff—and followed Owen down the *Lady*'s ramp to the landing-bay deck. The great echoing cave of the bay, with only the shimmer of a force field at the open end to keep hard vacuum where it belonged, looked like nothing she'd ever seen outside of a holovid show. Owen seemed unimpressed, as if he'd seen and done such things enough times to make them commonplace, but Klea stared about like any other tourist.

She'd thought that the *Lady* looked big when the ship stood on landing legs in the middle of Namport's otherwise empty field. But that was before she'd had a chance to see what a freighter looked like when it rested in a nullgrav cradle at an orbital dock. The metal side of the ship curved up and away from her as she descended the ramp, seeming to stretch as far as the horizon of a small world. Then she looked out in front of her, and saw the ranks of larger and smaller ships in their cradles, and the moving pinpoints that were the spacers, port laborers, and officials who worked in this part of High Station.

"I hadn't realized a spacedock was so big," she said.

Owen glanced back at Klea over his shoulder. "This is one of the smaller bays," he told her. "Independent merchant craft, mostly—vessels that can do surface landings if they have to. If you want to see something really big, you need to check out the docks on the Space Force side. The cradles over there can handle anything the Republic's got."

"I'll take your word for it."

Nervously, she looked away from the long vista and back to the foot of the *Lady*'s ramp. There was a distortion in the air down there, too, one that she traced without much trouble to the semicircle of portable force-field generators set out on the deckplates. Two people in uniforms of some kind sat at a folding table just outside the field.

"Customs inspection," said Owen, before she could ask. "Immigrant processing. High Station's an artificial environment and they like to keep things orderly."

"That's why you waited?"

He nodded. "Yesterday would have been a mob scene. Anybody looking the least bit strange would have gotten shoved up the ladder for somebody more important to decide on, and from there it might take days to get out. Today they're bored."

She and Owen were both wearing spacer's coveralls from the *Lady*'s clothes locker, courtesy of Owen's work down in the engine room, and she wasn't surprised when the inspectors waved them past with nothing more than a cursory glance at their papers—which, in fact, did not exist as anything more than imaginary constructs. She'd known for quite a while now that Owen was good at making people see things that weren't there.

"All right," she said, after the thick armor-glass doors had shut between them and the docking bay. "We got off

Nammerin, and we got off the *Lady*. Where do we go next?"

"We find a bar," he said. "And buy a drink."

She shook her head. "I don't think I want—"

"Then drink tap water with ice in it," he said. "But we need to hear all the hot gossip, and hear it fast."

For such a tense confrontation, the encounter with the sniper had taken very little time. Gil and Jhunnei reached docking bay 358-A, and *Karipavo*'s shuttle, only a few minutes later than Gil had originally planned. The craft's ramp was still down but the entry force field was up, with a crew member standing guard down below.

The trooper saluted. "Commodore. There's a visitor waiting for you inside the shuttle, sir."

"I rather thought there would be," said Gil, returning the salute. "Did our visitor say what was wanted?"

"No, sir. Only that he—that it—that you were the only person it was going to talk to. At least, that's what the chief *says* that it said."

"She," Gil said, as he palmed the security lockplate at the top of the ramp. The force field dissolved to let him and Jhunnei pass through. "If it's who I think it is."

It was. Merrolakk the Selvaur sat on one of the acceleration couches in the main body of the shuttle, with the nervous crew members giving her plenty of room. The slit pupils of her yellow eyes narrowed when she saw him.

D'Rugier.

Gil thought he detected a note of surprise in the hooting, rumbling voice. "Captain," he said. "Have you conferred with your associates, then?"

My associates. It wasn't surprise, now, in the Selvaur's voice, but amusement. *Oh, yes. We conferred.*

"And have you made up your mind about our business deal?"

I had a few doubts, Merro said. *But not anymore. I'm throwing in with you, Commodore—my ships, your terms.* She held out a big, green-scaled hand. *Done?*

The Selvaur's switch to his military title wasn't lost on

Gil. He met her grip to seal the contract in free-spacer fashion. "Done."

Good enough, said Merro. *When do you launch?*

"As soon as possible. You'll be informed. See Chief Bertyn about codes and comm frequencies; you can pass them around to your own people as you see fit."

Merro stood, stretching. *I'll see that everybody's up to speed before we lift,* she promised. *What's our first target?*

"I'll let everyone know after the fleet is formed up," Gil said. "Spacers in port talk more than they should, and I don't want the Mageworlders to listen."

Fair enough, said Merro.

The Selvauran captain headed off in the direction of the shuttle's cockpit, presumably to consult with Chief Bertyn. Gil and Lieutenant Jhunnei looked at each other. Gil was the first to speak.

"Well," he said. "Between those twenty-seven ships from the Net, and Merrolakk's irregulars, it looks like we have a fleet."

"Merrolakk," said Jhunnei thoughtfully. "She's the one who set up that ambush, you know."

"I know. I didn't think you did, though."

"I didn't—not until we got here. But *you* knew."

"I met a lot of Selvaurs when I was with General Metadi," Gil said. "It's the way they think. Merro wasn't about to join forces with someone she hadn't checked out first. So she arranged for a test."

"That's arrogance for you," said Jhunnei. "Auditioning the commodore of the Mageworlds Fleet like a—like a cabaret act."

Gil shrugged. "It's the way they think, is all. If it turned out that I was clever enough, or lucky enough—or in my case, Lieutenant, well-advised enough—to evade Merrolakk's ambush, she'd be here waiting to make a deal. If I didn't make it . . . well, she'd have an amusing time watching a bunch of thin-skins run around getting hysterical."

"Not for very long," said Jhunnei.

Gil looked at his aide—who was, it seemed, probably an

Adept and probably one of Errec Ransome's deep-cover operatives as well—and shook his head. "I think our Captain Merro is luckier than she knows."

"There's no such thing as luck, sir. Not really."

"Too bad," said Gil. "Because from now on, we're going to need a lot of it."

Portside on High Station was cleaner and better behaved than Klea had expected. The bars all had OPEN 33 HOURS signs on them, and they all came fully staffed with the usual complement of hookers and joyboys, but nobody seemed to be offering anything more exotic than the standard services. The dancers in the zero-g bubbles at the Web-Runners' Grill looked like only that—dancers—and when one of the free-spacers drinking at the bar pointed at the nearest bubble and asked the bartender a question, the bartender shook his head. The free-spacer shrugged and went back to his drink.

Owen must have seen Klea's change of expression. "This is High Station," he said. "Nobody comes here for the night life. Any lonesome spacer who wants some real entertainment can take a shuttle dirtside to Flatlands Portcity."

"You sound like you've been here before."

"I worked in Flatlands for a while."

She looked at him. "Like you did in Namport?"

"Yes."

"You've gone a lot of places—"

"—and done a lot of things," he finished for her. "All for the sake of the Guild. At least, I thought so at the time."

"Did you like it?"

" 'Like' isn't the right word. But I was good at my work, and it gave me satisfaction to do it well."

"Don't you like it anymore?"

"Times have changed," he said, "and not just because the Mages took Galcen. But don't worry about it. You're a free-spacer on port leave. Lean back, enjoy yourself, and listen for two things: what's happening on Pleyver, and what ship is leaving next for Suivi Point."

Klea leaned back obediently, and tried to open her ears, but in spite of its cleanliness and good order the bar reminded her too much of Freling's place for her to relax. Instead, she found herself growing fearful that if she let down her guard she'd once again start seeing and hearing other people's thoughts. That way was madness, and she'd barely escaped falling into it back on Nammerin.

"I'm sorry," she said finally. "I'm not going to be any good at listening for stuff in here."

He didn't look surprised. "Go walk around for a while, then, and pick up what news you can that way."

"Is it safe?"

"This is High Station," he said. "As long as you stick to the docking bays and the main concourse you'll do fine. I'll meet you at the free-spacers' hostel on this level."

Klea left the Web-Runners' Grill and walked for a while through the big portside concourse—only one of many, if the holomaps in the information kiosks could be believed. It was a new experience, looking at the licensed establishments as an off-worlder and a possible customer, instead of as part of the merchandise. After a while, though, exploration palled—even with the holomaps she didn't dare to go very far—and she headed back toward the docking bay.

Another ship had come in while she was with Owen, a much-battered freighter that lay in the next cradle to *Lady LeRoi*. The massive doors of the ship's cargo hold stood open, and crew members and dockside workers were loading cargo on nullgrav pallets.

Klea felt a sudden intense interest in the freighter's comings and goings, a sensation like the thoughts of others impinging on her own, but without the associations of pain and fear. She wandered closer to the new arrival, trying to imitate Owen's trick of looking like someone who always belonged wherever he happened to be.

"What ship?" she asked the nearest crew member.

"*Claw Hard*, out of Kiin-Aloq," said the spacer. "Just in, and going to be out again as soon as we get her unloaded." He looked at Klea speculatively. "All we need's a couple of hands for the engineering watches. You ever stood realspace control?"

"My partner has," Klea said truthfully. "I'm training."

She made haste to divert the conversation before she had to tell an outright lie. "Where are you going from here?"

"The outplanets, probably—as far from the fighting as we can get. Accardi is where the cargo's bound."

"Thanks," she said. She'd never heard of Accardi—didn't know whether it was a sector, a planet, or just a port—but the same inner prompting that had pulled her over to the ship was urging her to action again. "Listen, my partner and I are looking for a ship out of here ourselves. I've got to go tell him."

"Don't let the deckplates rust under your boots," the spacer advised. "If we're still here when you get back, talk to Captain Osa about a berth—you can say that Ragen sent you."

Klea headed for the free-spacer's hostel almost at a run. Owen was there as he'd said he would be, sitting on one of the lobby couches and paging through the flatscreen newsreader that a trusting management had bolted to the end table. He looked up as she hurried in.

"There's a ship about to depart," she said. "For Accardi. And they need a couple of hands in the engine room."

"Accardi. Damn. That's a long way from anywhere. But we can't stay." He tapped the screen of the newsreader with one finger. "The Pleyveran Senate declared for the Mageworlds at 3200 yesterday, Flatlands local time. At 0425 Standard, which is 3251 Flatlands local, High Station proclaimed itself a separate—and loyal—member of the Republic. Qualified oddsmakers are giving the standoff a fifty-fifty chance of turning into open warfare before the Magefleet even shows up."

Ochemet was no longer certain how much time had passed since he had entered the lifepod with Errec Ransome.

There was no viewscreen in the tiny survival craft, only what looked like a rudimentary monitor of some sort, and a few equally rudimentary controls, all labeled in what Ochemet presumed was the Mageworlds alphabet. Ransome wasn't touching any of them. The Master of the Guild—the *former* Master of the Guild, Ochemet reminded himself—sat with his eyes closed and his head thrown back against the padding of the acceleration couch. His face was pale under the streaks of dried blood.

Finally, Ochemet broke the silence. "I hope you're expecting somebody to retrieve us."

"No," said Ransome.

"I see." Ochemet looked at the control panel. Its handful of buttons and readouts meant nothing to him. He was Planetary Infantry, not a starpilot; he'd only worked in atmosphere, and never with anything more complicated than a scoutcar. Ransome, though, had flown with General Metadi in the *'Hammer*, during times almost as bad as these. "If that's the case, hadn't you better start trying to figure out the instrumentation on this thing?"

Ransome didn't open his eyes. "No. Be silent."

Ochemet gritted his teeth to keep from demanding a better answer. The Adept—Ochemet supposed Ransome was still an Adept, even if he was no longer the Master—was clearly doing something that required intense concentration, even if he wasn't ready to explain what it was.

More time went by; Ochemet didn't know how much more. The Mages had taken his chronometer from him when they captured him, and in the tiny lifepod there was nothing that could be used to measure the passage of hours, or even of days. Finally Ransome gave a long, shuddering sigh and opened his eyes.

"There," he said. "It's done."

"What's done?"

"Making us safe," Ransome said. "Hiding us from the eyes of the Magelords and the prying of their Circles."

Ochemet took a deep breath. "That's very good," he said carefully. "But where, exactly, are we going?"

Ransome gave another of his unsettling smiles. "Nowhere."

"I thought you were planning on escape," Ochemet said. "If I'd known it was suicide you had in mind, I'd have stayed put and let the Mages waste their energy on keeping me."

"An admirable devotion to duty," said the Adept. "But unnecessary. We have not, in fact, left the ship—though it pleases our former captors to believe that we have done so."

Ochemet stared at him. "I saw you launch the pods!"

"The launch was a necessary diversion. Actually entering one was never a requirement. Nor are we in one now."

"But we're in a pod right now. I felt this one cutting loose. I've got a bruise coming on my ribs from not getting strapped down in time."

"A simple illusion," said Ransome. He made a waving-away gesture with one hand. "If Lord sus-Airaalin or any of his minions probed your mind during our escape, they saw as truth what you believed to be true. By now, they count us as long gone, drifting somewhere in Galcenian space and waiting in vain for a rescue."

"I see," Ochemet said. He was angry again. If Ransome hadn't been the only other citizen of the Republic within range of lightspeed comms, he would have struck the older man. "I suppose you have a plan ready for what we do next?"

"We wait. And when it's time for us to leave, we go."

"In a lifepod?"

"No," said Ransome. "That's why we're waiting: we're going to need a ship. Sooner or later the Mages will give us one."

Captain Gretza Yevil had been through worse months than the one just past—there'd been a few weeks during her thirteenth year that could still reduce her to bloody-minded despair if she dwelt on them for too long at a stretch—but nothing lately.

Interplanetary war ... Mageworlders holding Galcen Prime ... the Domina under arrest and Suivi Point a milli-meter away from switching sides ... and now this. Stuck on board a crippled ship bound for an unknown destination. I might as well have been kidnapped for all the say I had in anything.

And I hate playing cards.

Nevertheless, the games of kingnote and double tammani

she'd played with Ignac' LeSoit had been the only distractions available during the time that *Warhammer* spent in hyperspace. LeSoit had resisted all her efforts to find out where they were going—when, in desperation, she'd made that information the kingnote forfeit, he had responded by cheating so blatantly that she gave up in disgust. They went back to playing double tammani for pocket change instead.

Finally there came a ship's-morning when LeSoit told her to strap down on one of the common-room couches and get ready for hyperspace dropout.

"Time for us to meet your mysterious buddies?" she asked.

"If we're lucky. But trust me, Captain—you don't want to take official cognizance of these people."

"So you keep telling me."

LeSoit just shrugged and headed for the 'Hammer's cockpit. Yevil found a place on one of the couches and strapped the safety webbing in place.

The dropout wasn't as smooth as it could have been; the queasy sense of dislocation lasted for several seconds. But for an old ship with bad structural damage it wasn't bad, and Yevil had to give Ignac' LeSoit several grudging points for his skill at shiphandling.

The 'Hammer continued its run in realspace, but not for long. Soon Captain Yevil felt the vessel settling down into a landing—beam-assisted, which usually meant a small enclosed bay like the one they'd broken out of on Suivi.

Not an orbital yard, then, she thought, *and probably not a major field like Prime or Telabryk.*

Ship's gravity went off a few minutes later, confirming her guess. Wherever this place was, it had a pull only about half of the Galcen-based Space Force standard.

A moon of some kind, or an asteroid.

She unstrapped from the safety webbing, but didn't bother going in search of LeSoit. The Domina's number-two gunner was certain to show up with new instructions before long. When he did, his expression was an odd mix of relief and worry; relief that the place was still here, Yevil guessed, mixed with worry about his reception.

"Captain Yevil," he said. "We've reached our destination. The repairs won't be a problem, but I have to leave the ship for a while, and I have to request that you not leave the ship or enter the cockpit. It wouldn't be safe for either of us."

"Understood. Where are we, anyway?"

LeSoit shook his head. "I can't tell you that."

"I'm not surprised," said Yevil. She tried again. "Is this some kind of criminals' haven, or a pirate base?"

"You know I can't answer that either."

Yevil shrugged. "It was worth a try. But there's one thing I have to know before I put on the blinders. Will what you're doing here touch either the Domina's honor or mine?"

"No," said LeSoit. "My word on it. I'd never harm Beka—the Domina; and if you stay where I told you to, nothing's going to compromise you either."

"I won't lie," Yevil said. "There's a funny smell to all this stuff about secrecy and looking the other way. But not so funny I can't live with it."

LeSoit went off on his mysterious errand. Yevil played a game and a half of solitaire kingnote during his absence. Then the Domina's gunner returned, still looking nervous. They spent another week or so playing double tammani while *Warhammer*'s hull and deckplates resounded with the noise of heavy repairs.

The clanging and the vibrations finally stopped, but LeSoit made no preparations for getting underway. Instead he grew steadily more restless and uneasy—almost, Yevil thought, as if he were waiting for someone—until after several more days there came a ship's-morning when she woke up and found the door to her berthing space sealed from the outside.

The air in the docking bay was thin and cold. Ignaceu LeSoit shivered a little where he stood at the top of *Warhammer*'s ramp. He had already sealed the cockpit doors and locked Captain Yevil into her cabin; now he toggled on the entry force field behind him and looked about.

The size of the bay continued to impress him, even after the weeks the *'Hammer* had already spent there undergoing repairs. Off in the shadowy distance, low-power glows illuminated arched doorways in the bay's metal walls; closer by, the worklights cast harsh white circles on the blast-scarred deckplates. Away to the right, amid a fountain of blue and pink electric sparks, a welder was working on a battered scoutcraft.

Coming here had represented a serious risk, especially with Yevil on board, but with the Domina's money out of reach on Suivi Point, this place had been the only choice. LeSoit could get the necessary work done here without monetary charges, something which was both good and bad—good, for the obvious reasons; bad, because the people here usually wanted payment anyway.

How many repair bases and stores depots like this one there were in the civilized galaxy, LeSoit didn't know. He suspected that there might be others, but he knew that he'd never find out for sure. This base was the only one for which he knew the coordinates. He had memorized them long ago, and then had hidden them so deeply by the techniques he had been taught that not even a mind-scan could have brought them forth against his will.

A messenger waited for him at the foot of the ramp—a short, dark-haired woman in scuffed boots and plain brown fatigues. She spoke to him in badly accented Galcenian.

"Come. You're wanted."

"He's here?"

"Yes."

She didn't say anything more. LeSoit wondered if she was just naturally taciturn. Or was he listed as dangerous to talk to these days, because of the company he kept?

He followed the woman across the open deck—through the tangle of ships, power lines, gas cylinders, and crates of supplies—to one of the arched doors leading out of the bay. They went on down the plain metal corridor, past the sickbay and through a maze of narrow passages where more men and women in brown fatigues hurried about their business. At length they came to a large room, empty except for a table and two chairs.

"Wait here," the guide said, and left him.

A moment later the inner door opened, and another man entered. LeSoit went down on one knee.

"My lord sus-Airaalin," he said.

PART TWO

I. Republic Space: Eraasian Base Suivi Point: Administrative District; Main Detention

"IEKKENAT," SAID sus-Airaalin. To LeSoit's relief, the Grand Admiral smiled as he said the name; and he spoke in Eraasian, the proper language of trust and fellowship. "Iekkenat Lisaiet. Until I heard the message I hadn't dared to hope. Stand up, man—it's a good omen, seeing you again after so long a time."

LeSoit rose. "I feared that I had failed you, my lord."

"Not so. You've done honorable service, these past ten years and more."

"My heart is glad to hear it," LeSoit said. It felt good to use his birth-tongue again, after a decade and a half spent in speaking and thinking Standard Galcenian. "When I learned that the young Domina was dead on Artat, I thought I could do nothing further, except to settle my personal debts in the matter."

"But she lives, Iekkenat, and the reports I have received show that you were in no little way responsible." sus-Airaalin smiled again. "Others may not commend you for that, but their thoughts are not necessarily mine."

LeSoit bowed his head. "I'm honored by your trust, my

lord." He paused, gathering his thoughts. "I must confess that under the present circumstances, I'm not certain what I ought to do next."

"Return to the Domina," sus-Airaalin told him, without hesitation. "Serve her as you would serve me; report to me—and me alone—those things which I might find of interest; and above all, keep her alive."

"Still?" LeSoit didn't bother to hide the relief he felt. Orders to protect could become orders to destroy, if it served the Resurgency's purpose; years ago he had left the *Sidh*, and Beka Rosselin-Metadi, because he feared that he would no longer carry out such an order if it came.

sus-Airaalin nodded. "At all cost. If the Domina lives, Iekkenat, then whatever else may happen, some of us at least will have accomplished what we set out to do."

"You've seen it, my lord?" LeSoit asked eagerly. Grand Admiral Theio syn-Ricte sus-Airaalin was a great personage among the Masked Ones—and like all those who worked in the Circles, he could speak, if he chose, with the force of prophecy. "Is it truly so?"

"I desire it," sus-Airaalin said. "And what I desire, I will bring to pass, in spite of all opposition." The words fell with the absolute certainty of stones; for a moment even the Grand Admiral seemed oppressed by their weight. Then he let out a long breath and straightened his shoulders. "Now go quickly—there is much to do. You have business at Suivi Point."

"My lord," said LeSoit, and bowed again.

He kept his eyes lowered until the closing of the inner door told him that the Grand Admiral had left. Turning, he palmed the lockplate for the outer door. It slid open. Outside in the passage the messenger who had brought him waited to guide him back to the ship.

Warhammer was still there, balanced on landing legs in an open part of the big docking bay. The clutter of lines and scaffolding that had surrounded the ship during most of her stay had vanished sometime during LeSoit's talk with the Grand Admiral. With the ship's hull clear, the finished repair work showed up plainly. LeSoit noted with satisfaction that the base's technicians had done as good a job as those in any Republic yard outside of Gyffer or the Central Worlds.

We have the stars again, he thought, and let himself remember, for a moment, the long years spent in reclaiming the lost knowledge and technology—stealing it back, part by part and manual by manual, from the ones who had destroyed it.

He went up the *'Hammer*'s ramp and palmed the security lockplate to bring down the force field. Inside, the ship appeared quiet and undisturbed. He brought up the ramp and sealed the entry, then went through the common room to the cockpit and unsealed that area as well. Once the ship was in hyper, he decided, would be the right time to unlock Captain Yevil's cabin; less chance that way of having her notice things that nobody—Yevil included—really wanted her to see.

He strapped himself into the pilot's seat. A red light was flashing on the comms panel; keying on the link brought up a crackly voice speaking again in bad Galcenian.

"*Warhammer*, prepare to depart."

He replied in the same tongue, though with a considerably better accent. "*Warhammer*, departing."

Nullgravs hummed and hydraulic systems sighed as the *'Hammer* lifted from the deckplates and brought her landing legs back up into their housings. LeSoit touched the controls again, putting the ship into a slow turn to the launch path. As the cockpit swung around, a glance through the viewscreens showed him Lord sus-Airaalin watching from the rear of the bay.

The Grand Admiral raised a hand in salute Then *Warhammer* finished her turn, and all that LeSoit could see was the straight empty deck of the launch path, with the blackness of open space at the end.

He took *Warhammer* out on a long run-to-jump, then put the ship through a series of short jumps in random directions—enough, he hoped, to confuse anyone who might try to backtrack him from his final dropout—before putting the ship into hyper one more time for the long run to Suivi Point.

The shifting grey pseudosubstance of hyperspace filled the cockpit viewscreens. LeSoit watched it for a few moments. The swirls and flashes of iridescence always gave him a headache, but at the same time they held an odd fascination. Then he stood, stretched, and slid back the cockpit door. Time to go let Yevil out of her locked cabin, and hope for the Domina's sake that the Space Force officer was disposed to forgive the insult.

Nyls Jessan had lost patience with Suivi Point.

Beka's arrest on trumped-up charges had come as a surprise to him—although the captain herself, who'd been on Suivi before, had seemingly half-expected something of that nature. *"Turn over enough flat wet rocks,"* she'd said, *"and you'll find out which one the slime is under."* If the Suivans had kept on playing by their usual rules, the knowledge gained would have been worth most of the indignity and expense.

But something more was going on here than the usual games of bribery and harassment that made up justice in the Suivan mode. Under normal circumstances, an arrested party could buy out of all charges by matching or topping Contract Security's fee. A direct petition to the Steering Committee for someone's summary execution was not, however, considered normal circumstances. Only a member of the committee could make such a petition, and only a committee member could lodge a counterpetition to block the process.

Membership on the Steering Committee, unfortunately, appeared to be the only thing on Suivi Point that *wasn't* for sale to the highest bidder.

After meeting over the course of several weeks with a long series of Contract Security representatives and committee officials, and dispensing a surprising amount of money in tips, honoraria, and bald-faced bribes, Jessan was forced in the end to admit defeat. He tightened his lips on one of Beka Rosselin-Metadi's favorite oaths, then turned to the clothes locker at the Entiboran Resistance Headquarters and dressed himself in a Khesatan afternoon coat of subdued black with a charcoal-grey lining. He put a single-shot needler in one pocket and a miniature blaster in the other, in addition to the knife in his boot, and went to ask the favor of a counterpetition from the banking firm of Dahl&Dahl.

In her initial off-the-record assessment of various local companies, Beka had rated Dahl&Dahl as a moderately dependable ally. The firm had cared for the remaining scraps of House Rosselin's private treasure—including the original and genuine Iron Crown of Entibor—and had also handled the late Professor's much greater personal fortune. When Ebenra D'Caer and his masters on the other side of the Net had arranged the assassination of Domina Perada, they'd tried to put the blame on Dahl&Dahl, which should have given the firm and the Resistance an enemy or two in common.

Which is a hell of a big assumption, Jessan thought, as he finished his speech to the company's underpresident in charge of listening to strangers. *These people are barely going to admit that they know her name.*

The underpresident leaned back in his cushioned chair. "We will examine your claims, of course. And if it makes good business sense . . . then we will make a decision on that basis."

Jessan didn't like the sound of that. In his experience, when you heard people talking about how sound and businesslike their decisions were, it usually meant that somebody's partner was about to get sold out.

He suppressed a sigh. Caring too much—even the appearance of caring too much—could be deadly. His best chance now was a studied disinterest. "May I know when the decision is likely to be made?"

The underpresident nodded. "We will inform you."

Jessan rose. "I'll call on you again, if I may. One must keep current with these things."

The man from Dahl&Dahl inclined his head. "Of course."

Jessan bowed, and allowed himself to be escorted back to the outer offices, and thence to the lobby. A jowly, heavyset man dressed like a free-spacer pushed himself up from one of the reception area chairs and followed him out onto the glidewalk. Several minutes later, with the man still trailing him just outside of vocal range, Jessan decided to force the issue. He stepped off the glidewalk into a brightly lit restaurant that appeared to specialize in sweet and savory pastries, and took a seat where he could see the front door.

His new shadow followed him in and slid into the other side of the booth. Jessan nodded a pleasant greeting—this was, in fact, the sort of establishment where strangers might find themselves sharing a table during a busy hour—and put his left hand into his coat pocket underneath the table. The miniature blaster was charged and ready in case of need, and at close range the lack of a chance to aim wouldn't matter.

He smiled politely at the heavyset man, taking note of the free-spacer's droopy brown mustache and the shadow of stubble along his jaw.

"Is there some way I can be of assistance?" he asked.

"Maybe," said the other. "Folks portside tell me you're the one who can find Beka."

Jessan kept his features schooled to amiable good will. "Do they? That's nice."

"Yeah." The free-spacer didn't seem impressed by Jessan's efforts. "Carry a message to her, okay?"

"What kind of message?"

"Tell her that I've come 'cause I saw her announcement—picked it up on hi-comms while I was running the Web out of Pleyver—and I want to join her."

Finally, thought Jessan. *Somebody.* "In that case, it would help if you let me know your name."

"She'll know who I am."

"No doubt," Jessan said. "But I don't, I'm afraid. And she'll want me to tell her."

The free-spacer hesitated for a moment, as if struggling with his own suspicions, and then said, "Tell her that Frizzt is here. Frizzt Osa. I've got *Claw Hard* in waiting station. No Point berths open, they say. I took the local shuttle down as soon as we got here."

"Ah." Jessan settled back. "Yes. Are you willing to swear to Beka Rosselin-Metadi, Domina of Lost Entibor, of Entibor-in-Exile, and of the Colonies Beyond?"

Osa's mustache twitched. "She's been putting on airs since I saw her last. But I'm here because she was the best damn shiphandler I've ever seen, and that's a fact. And when someone crews for me, they're family, even if they do jump ship and leave an old man to do his own steering."

"Since you put it that way," Jessan said, "I'll accept your oath to the Domina as a given. Are you ready to accept an assignment on her behalf?"

"Wouldn't have come looking for you if I wasn't."

"Excellent. In that case, Gentlesir Osa, I need you to take word to every Space Force unit in Suivi nearspace that their commanding officer has sworn to the Domina. Tell them that they're not to make contact with Suivi Point for any reason. They should go to Condition II, Wartime Cruising, and await further orders. Now—are you armed?"

"Me? Or my ship?"

"Your ship."

"*Claw Hard*'s got a couple of guns on her," Osa admitted. "You can't work the outplanets naked. Pirates, you know."

"Pirates. Right." Jessan was silent a moment, thinking. "Since you're throwing in with us, Captain, I'd like to ask for the loan of a couple of your crew members. This is Suivi, after all, and one or two obvious bodyguards might discourage some of the rougher elements."

"Not a problem. I'll send down a couple of my people on the next shuttle. Got an address they should report to?"

"Here," said Jessan. He glanced at the booth's menu pad. "The, ah, Merry Dumpling Pastry Shop, on Central across from the Suivi Mercantile Building. I'll find them."

"I'll tell 'em to wait," Osa said. He stood up. "And you can tell Beka that I want to hoist a few with her in memory of good times past. I might even forgive her for jumping ship if she'll come pilot for me again. Never saw a hand like hers on the controls—she was better than me and that's a fact."

"I'll let her know," Jessan said.

After Frizzt Osa had left, Jessan ordered a cup of cha'a and sat for a while, thinking. The good captain wasn't a very prepossessing sort, but he was still the first volunteer brought in by Beka's hi-comms message, not counting the local Space Force contingent who would have picked up the signal live. If someone like that could be moved to respond, then others would certainly come to Suivi as well.

And just as certainly, Jessan reflected, there would be a Mageworlds sympathizer among them, or an agent, or someone else who intended to do Beka harm.

Beka Rosselin-Metadi lay on her bunk in Suivi Main Detention's max-pri cell block. She was beginning to suspect that Contract Security put drugs of some sort in the food packets—she'd started losing her sense of time not long after Tarveet's first visit.

The councillor had come back at least twice since then, maybe three times. She was losing track of that, too; she couldn't tell whether some of the visits were real, or just highly detailed dream sequences. This time, however, she'd slept so deeply she hadn't dreamed; when she woke up, her prison coverall was disarrayed and smelled of sweat, and she felt bruises coming where she hadn't had any before.

Beka didn't like the implications of that.

You pay enough on Suivi, and you can get anything. They've been questioning me under chemicals. What do I know to betray? How weak we are?

The true name of Tarnekep Portree. The numbers, locations, and balances of all the bank accounts. How the 'Hammer got her speed. The coordinates of the asteroid base.

When I get out of here, I am going to kill Tarveet. Slowly.

She shook her head. The motion made her feel sick to her stomach; more evidence that the ConSecs were slipping something into the food—or maybe it was the water, or the air.

Face it, girl. You're not going to get out of this one. You gave the Domina business your best shot, and it didn't work. Somebody else will have to save the civilized galaxy, be-

cause you're going to be dead. Or the next best thing to dead, anyway.

I wonder how long it takes to go insane down here?

It struck her that she was likely to find out eventually, if she wasn't finding out already. She moved restlessly on the narrow bunk. Her body complained at the change in position.

I wish I could talk to Nyls. Tell him to kill Tarveet for me someday. Tarveet . . .

Maybe I should have taken the bastard's offer while I had the chance. Nyls wouldn't have liked it very much, but he could have lived with it for a day or two. Long enough for me to get out of here, and for Tarveet to have a brief encounter with a very sharp knife.

Beka sighed. It was a good thought, and one that warmed her blood a little here in the chilly detention block, but she knew that she couldn't have gotten away with it. Tarveet already knew her far too well, all the way back to that dinner party, the year that she was just-turned-six and her brother Owen was barely seven, and her mother was sponsoring High Station Pleyver for separate representation on the Grand Council. . . .

Tarveet had been younger then, too, his limp brown hair not yet gone to grey, and the flesh on his long lantern jaws not quite so loose and sagging. He'd always had clammy hands, though, and the habit of pursuing his lips and wetting them before he said anything. The six-year-old Domina-in-Waiting—well-scrubbed and best-gowned for her introduction to the important visitors—had loathed him almost on sight.

"He patted me on the face," she said to Owen, after the grownups had gone off to talk and she'd made her escape to the rooftop terrace. Owen had found her in their private hiding place among the box-planters at the sunny end a few minutes later. The tall fronds of salad fern and ruffled whipgrass arched over both of them like a green tunnel, shading them and speckling their skin with shifting dots of light. "It felt like a bunch of fat worms touching me."

"He's a bad man." Owen spoke with absolute conviction.

Beka just nodded. She'd known for as long as she could remember that her brother was never wrong about such things. "People say he was a hero in the war, though. Mamma likes him."

"No, she doesn't."

"She smiled at him," Beka said. The feeling of betrayal was still strong. "And he said that I'd be a fine Domina someday, and to—and to let him know when I was old enough to look for a consort—and she laughed and told him that she would!"

"Maybe," said Owen. "It doesn't mean she likes him. She smiles and makes promises to lots of people she doesn't like."

"That's lying."

"Only if she doesn't keep the promises. And the smiling's just good manners."

Beka made a face. "Then I don't like having good manners." She paused, remembering something else. "What's it mean, anyway, a 'consort'? I was afraid they'd all laugh at me if I asked."

"A consort's a Domina's husband, like Dadda."

"No," she said at once. "Tarveet isn't. Not even a little bit. And I won't take him, no matter what Mamma says when I'm grown up."

"You won't have to," Owen said. "Mamma knows that."

"Then why did she *say* it?"

"Politics," he said, in the tone of voice that told Beka he was quoting what somebody else had said—or maybe, had thought without saying. Owen could do that, too. "She wants to keep him sweet until High Station's petition goes through Council."

"Mamma can sweeten him by herself, then. I don't want to." She pulled up her knees and hugged them tightly. "I'm supposed to sit next to him at dinner, too. I hope he gets sick."

"He won't."

"I know." She scowled. "I wish I could make him get sick."

"That's not very nice."

"I don't care. I don't like him."

Owen didn't say anything. She sat and brooded on the unfairness of the world, until a shift in the wind made the ferns and whipgrass bend down and brush against her skin. Distracted, she turned her attention from her list of grievances to the ecosystem-in-miniature of the box-planters. Maybe if she got dirty enough she wouldn't have to sit at the big table after all. . . .

"Hey," she said a minute later. "Owen, look."

Her brother looked where she was pointing. "That's a big one, all right."

Oblivious to their interest, the garden slug continued eating its way along the frond of salad fern. The slug was, as Owen had said, a big one, almost a finger in length, and a bright, almost yellow, green, exactly the color of a fresh sugar-pepper. Beka felt an idea growing inside her head—a truly marvelous piece of naughtiness, something that would pay back Tarveet for patting her face with those damp, wormy fingers, and pay back Mamma, too, for laughing and making Tarveet promises she didn't mean to keep.

"You know what, Owen? I bet I can *so* make Councillor Tarveet sick. I bet if he eats a slug for dinner he'll be sick all over the table."

"He won't eat it, though."

"There's going to be sugar-peppers in the salad. There's *always* sugar-peppers in the salad."

"Nobody's going to mistake a slug for a sugar-pepper."

"They will if you help me," Beka said. She looked at her brother. "Please?"

Owen never had been able to refuse her anything. Dinner that night had been a memorable experience for everybody present—even now, in Main Detention's max-pri cell block, Beka smiled at the memory.

I don't care what happened afterward. It was all worth it.

Jessan made his way back to the Merry Dumpling Pastry Shop nearly twelve frustrating hours later, having carefully stayed in the public areas of the Suivan business district during the interval. Dahl&Dahl hadn't contacted him so far, which after the earlier conference didn't really surprise him. He was getting the feeling that Beka wasn't going to come out of Main Detention legally.

His latest round of visits along Embassy Row, made after talking with Frizzt Osa, hadn't done anything to change his mind. The Galcenian Interests Section was shut down tight, the doors locked and the windows darkened. The Khesatan Interests Section was still open, but with a drastically reduced staff; the sympathetic woman left minding the office hadn't been able to promise anything more than sending a message to Khesat as soon as the spotty hi-comms allowed it. And there was no Entiboran Interests Section, unless Jessan wanted to count the storefront office he'd shared with Beka until her arrest.

Jessan's final stop had been the Gyfferan Interests Section. Beka was half-Gyfferan, after all—not to mention being the daughter of a planetary hero. Maybe that would be enough to get her diplomatic immunity, or at least enough official backing to make her a risky target for intrigue. But the Gyfferan Interests Section, though full of obvious activity, had been locked and guarded. A sign on the front door read: ALL CITIZENS OF GYFFER ARE ADVISED TO LEAVE SUIVI POINT AT ONCE.

Disheartened, Jessan returned to the pastry shop. Down back, in the booth he had shared before with Frizzt Osa, a pair of spacers in faded, much-washed coveralls sat nursing half-empty cups of cha'a. The one facing his way was a young woman with brown curls and worried eyes. Her companion, a man by the set of his shoulders, had tawny hair grown shaggy enough to skim his collar in the back.

Jessan purchased a steamed vegetable bun and a cup of cha'a at the front counter. Carrying his purchases, he slid carefully into the booth across the shop's narrow central aisle from the pair. From this close he could see that the man and the woman both wore *Claw Hard* shoulder patches.

They also carried the long, polished wooden staves that proclaimed them as Adepts to anybody with an eye to notice them, and which left Jessan in no doubt as to why Osa had picked this particular pair of crew members to lend him for the duration. Right now the staves were propped inconspicuously against the wall of the shop, and the two spacers seemed interested in nothing but their cha'a; but Jessan had seen what even a quiet and respectable Space Force medic like Llannat Hyfid could do with such a weapon if she felt the need.

He ate his steamed bun without undue haste and wiped his fingers on the disposable napkin before looking into the dregs of his cha'a and murmuring, "Osa sent you?"

The man turned toward Jessan. "Are you the gentlesir who's been sleeping with my sister?"

The accent was pure Galcenian, and uncannily familiar, as was the expression in the man's hazel eyes.

Jessan sighed. "Since I don't have the honor of your name, I really can't say."

"Osa says that you're the General of the Armies of Entibor," the man said. "If that means what it used to, then you're sleeping with my sister. I'm Owen Rosselin-Metadi." He nodded toward the woman across from him. "And that's Klea Santreny. Osa asked for volunteers, and we're them."

"Ah," said Jessan, unsurprised. "I thought the eyes looked familiar. I suppose I shouldn't ask how you happened to show up on Suivi Point now that the galaxy's fallen apart?"

"Not here," Owen said. "No."

The young woman—a girl, really; she couldn't be much over twenty in spite of the lines around her eyes and at the corners of her mouth—was looking at Beka's brother with an expression that Jessan couldn't quite place.

"You never told me your name was Rosselin-Metadi," she said to Owen. Her accent was another one Jessan recognized, strong Nammerinish backwater-talk this time. "You never told me your last name at all."

Owen glanced back in her direction and his fair skin reddened slightly. "I'm sorry. I forgot."

"Forgot." She drew a deep breath, and Jessan got the impression that only strength of will kept her voice from rising to a shriek. "You belong to one of the most famous families in the civilized galaxy, and you ... just ... forgot?"

"I'm sorry," Owen said again. "I really don't think about it very much. I'd have told you if you asked."

She closed her eyes and let out a sigh. Jessan smiled in spite of himself.

"Now I see why Ari used to say that his younger brother only connected to reality at a few widely divergent points."

"Ari wouldn't know reality if—" Owen shut his mouth on whatever else he'd been going to say. After a few moments of silence he went on. "I'm many things, Gentlesir Jessan, but I'm not a mind reader in any sense that you'd find immediately useful. Is there somewhere safe we can go while you fill me in on what's happening? I've been—out of touch—for a while."

"Right," said Jessan. "Walking around is best. Finish your cha'a, and I'll give you two the galactic diplomat's decimal-credit tour of downtown Suivi Point. We have a lot to discuss."

II. Gyffer: Telabryk Local Defense Base; Space Force HQ Building
Suivi Point: Administrative District
RSF *Karipavo*: Mageworlds Space

THE GYFFERAN Local Defense Force was one of the handful of planetary fleets that hadn't merged into the Space Force at the end of the First Magewar. That independence had caused a great deal of comment at the time. Gyffer's unswerving loyalty to the Resistance—and the fact that even after a long and devastating conflict the planet remained self-sufficient enough to opt for neutrality if pushed too hard—eventually silenced the opposition. Gyffer kept its own fleet, and policed its own system space, with only a minimal Space Force presence.

Since the fall of Galcen, even that much of the Republic's protection was gone. Gyfferan scoutships patrolled the distant reaches of local space, out beyond the sensor range of the farthest unmanned watch stations, relaying their messages back to Telabryk via the local links once hi-comms had returned.

So far, the reports had all been the same: *No activity in this sector. Continuing patrol.*

"What everyone's hoping they'll run into," Ari said to Llannat, "is at least some of the Space Force."

Llannat shook her head. "Don't count on it."

The two of them were in the officers' club at the Gyfferan LDF's Telabryk base. They'd been extended privileges along with the rest of the people off *Naversey* and the *Daughter*, and the club's dining room at least provided hot meals made from actual ingredients, instead of reconstituted and reheated space rations.

Under normal circumstances, the Telabryk club would probably have been a cheerful, gossipy place, with cold buffet and salad tables every day at lunch, half-price bar from local twilight until full dark, and live entertainment every LastDay night. These days, the circumstances were anything but normal. Tense, harried-looking men and women in LDF uniforms ate their meals too fast, talked too much or not at all, and didn't look at the flatscreen monitor set into the wall beside the dining-room door.

Until recently, Ari suspected, the screen would have displayed the Telabryk base's Plan of the Day, or the club's list of upcoming social events. Since the fall of Galcen, though, and the Citizen-Assembly's decision to resist both the Mages and Admiral Vallant, the dining-room screen and others like it had changed their displays. Now the screen showed a continuously updated roster of the LDF's long-range scoutships, by mission status: in the launch queue, on patrol, and safely home to Gyfferan nearspace. According to the local newscasts, a roving scoutship would detect the approaching enemy—whether Vallant's mutinous forces out of Infabede or the Mageworlds warfleet fresh from the conquest of Galcen—and warn Gyffer of the impending attack.

None of the people in the Telabryk officer's club expected real life to be anything like the newscasts predicted. Sooner or later, one of the scouts would fail to make its scheduled report. That failure might be all the warning the LDF would ever get.

"*Naversey*'s headed back in," Ari said. "I checked."

"Good." Llannat poked at her salad with her fork. "I was worried. It's hard to tell, sometimes, what's true and what's just nerves."

"Can't you stop it?"

"Not the true stuff," she said. "And not the nerves either, mostly." She poked at the salad again, turning over the shreds of unfamiliar Gyfferan greenery as if she expected to find something crawling there. "I wish . . ."

"Wish what?"

She shook her head. "Nothing. It's just that seeing the future isn't enough, even when you can trust it. You can dodge things a little, take precautions here and there, but it's all too slippery. There's nothing solid that you can grab hold of—no way to reach out from where you are and make the change."

"Now you're starting to talk like my brother."

"It only sounds that way," she told him. "Owen wouldn't even *think* some of the things I just said—and I wouldn't be saying them if he was around. He works very closely with Master Ransome; everybody in the Guild knows it."

"What does that have to do with anything?" Ari demanded. "Seeing the future can't be against the rules; you told me once that Ransome does it himself sometimes."

Llannat was starting to look a bit tight around the mouth, as if she'd gone further into something than she'd intended to. Ari waited. Most people would keep on talking if you didn't say anything; and Llannat seemed to trust him, which was a warming thought all by itself.

"It isn't seeing the future that Master Ransome doesn't like," she said after a while. "It's the idea of doing something about it."

"That's stupid," said Ari. "Anybody can change the future. Everybody does. What we do now changes it all the time."

Llannat appeared doubtful. "Maybe. But what if, sometimes, what you do *now* is reach up ahead and do something *then* . . . what if you take what you've seen and make it over into what you want to happen?"

Adepts, he thought, and suppressed a sigh. Between having Owen for a brother, and Errec Ransome for an old family friend, he'd grown up listening to stuff like this. *Sooner or later, they all drift loose from reality.*

"Now is now," he said aloud, "as far as I could ever tell. And change is change."

"Oh, Ari." She reached across the table and caught his hands in her own. "That's what the Mages do, in their Circles. And the Guild calls it sorcery."

"Damned if I know why," he said. Her hands were cold. "Is that really all the difference there is?"

"There's other stuff. But that's the important one."

She seemed to know a great deal, Ari reflected, about things that Adepts were supposedly forbidden to deal with. Not that the knowledge was making her any happier, as far as he could tell. And Llannat Hyfid had been his friend on Nammerin, during a time when he had desperately needed friendship.

"If it isn't anything you can help," he said, still holding her hands, "then don't let it worry you."

"I wish things were that simple. But they aren't." She paused, then looked straight at him. "What if . . . what if the time comes when there *is* something I can do to help—only it's the wrong kind of thing?"

The answer to that one, he thought, was surprisingly easy; maybe it wasn't so easy if you were an Adept.

"Help first," he said. "Explain later. And if somebody tries to give you trouble, tell them to complain about it to me."

Klea Santreny didn't much care for Suivi Point. She'd thought at first, before she left *Claw Hard* with Owen, that a dome settlement on an asteroid would be something like High Station Pleyver—clean and well behaved and loyal to the Republic. She hadn't been portside for an hour before she figured out that if Suivi Point was any of those things, it was only up on top where it showed.

The "galactic diplomat's decimal-credit tour" that the man called Jessan had promised them didn't change her opinion. She stuck close to Owen—*Owen Rosselin-Metadi*, she told herself firmly; *if he won't remember it then somebody's going to have to remember it for him*—while

Gentlesir Nyls Jessan took them from one end of Suivi Point to the other.

She wasn't sure what to make of Gentlesir Nyls Jessan himself, for that matter. He dressed like a rich Khesatan do-nothing straight out of the midafternoon holodramas, and he certainly had the accent for the part, but his hands were all wrong. They looked like they knew things the rest of him didn't.

After listening for a while to his conversation with Owen, she felt inclined to believe what the hands were telling her.

"... being held in Suivi Main Detention on a max-pri contract," Jessan said, as he pointed out the ten-story-high mosaic depiction of the Spirit of Enlightened Mercantilism on the front wall of the Suivan headquarters of Dahl&Dahl, Ltd. "Notice, if you will, the particularly garish color scheme and the awkward poses of the main figures...."

Klea craned her neck up at the pictures. "It's part of the building," she said. "And the way that things feel ... I don't know much about art and all, but that picture is just right for the people here."

Jessan lifted an eyebrow. "A banker with a sense of irony? I suppose it's possible."

Owen said, "Is there some reason why you didn't attempt to buy her out? I realize that a max-pri contract would represent a considerable sum of money—"

"Indeed," said Jessan. He gestured gracefully at a multilevel shopping gallery on the other side of the concourse. "Observe, also, the renowned Crystal Arcade, a favorite picture-postcube subject all over the civilized galaxy ... considerable sums of money are not, in this case, the problem. The problem is that Tarveet of Pleyver has a seat on the Steering Committee of Suivi Point, and we do not."

Owen closed his eyes. "Tarveet. Oh, damn."

"Exactly. The esteemed councillor from Pleyver has petitioned the committee for your sister's summary termination."

"On what grounds?" Owen's voice and expression didn't change, but the surge of anger that came out from him

struck Klea like a physical blow. Jessan must have felt it as
well, because he shook his head.

"Calmly, Master Rosselin-Metadi. Calmly. On the
grounds that she deliberately and willfully endangered the
settlements of the Suivan Belt." He paused. "And we aren't
aided in the Steering Committee by the fact that, on the face
of it, the accusation is perfectly true."

Owen let his breath out slowly; Klea could feel him sub-
duing the anger, holding it in check. "Do we have any
friends on the committee?"

"This is Suivi Point," said Jessan. "There's not a lot of
friendship to go around. But there are certain individuals
and corporate entities with varying amounts of self-interest
which we can call upon. Dahl&Dahl"—he gestured again at
the Spirit of Enlightened Mercantilism—"being one of the
most prominent."

Owen glanced up at the mosaic without expression.
"What kind of help were you planning to ask them for?"

"I've already asked them for the favor of presenting a
counterpetition," Jessan said. "It remains to be seen whether
or not they will do so. However, if you and your apprentice
can convincingly portray a pair of off-planet bodyguards—"

"Easily," said Owen.

"—we can go into the office behind that extraordinarily
tasteless façade and make inquiries concerning their decision."

The life of a commerce raider, Commodore Jervas Gil reflected, would be considerably more fun if there were any
worthwhile commerce to raid. So far, the gold and dia-
monds of the Mageworlds trade had mostly turned out to be
medicinal herbs and small spacecraft parts. Nobody in his
hastily patched-together fleet was going to retire rich on
stuff like that; and the Mageworlds weren't likely to miss it.

It wasn't as if Gil hadn't tried. He'd used the classic raid-
ing tactics from the first Magewar, taught in the service
schools: either drop out well away from a world, lie there
silent and dark until a merchant ship lifted, then swoop in
and intercept before the merch could jump to hyper; or

watch the known dropout points and intercept vessels as soon as they appeared. Then—depending upon whether you intended to search ships and take prisoners, or just wanted to seize the major cargo and wreak general havoc—you had your choice of grappling with tractors and boarding, or taking the ship apart from a distance with guns and picking through the broken pieces at your leisure.

The first way was riskier, but realized more profit for the victors. The second method was a lot safer, at the price of all the uncontainerized cargo and small loose items that could be found on board an intact vessel, not to mention the salvage value of the ship itself. Both ways still worked. But the resistance in force that Gil was hoping for never materialized.

"Nothing," he said gloomily to Jhunnei, after several weeks of more-or-less fruitless endeavor. He and his aide had just spent a dispiriting two hours taking inventory of the spoils to date, and had come up with a probable resale value not quite equal to their current expenditures on fuel and supplies. "No armed response whatsoever. Do you suppose the Mageworlders came through the Net with every single warship that they had?"

"It's possible," said Jhunnei. "We've done all we could to draw them out, short of actually hitting dirtside targets, and that's probably our next step."

"I don't want to do that," Gil said. "There's no point in inflicting random damage if we can't take a world and hold on to it. And if blowing up their ships and stealing their cargoes isn't good enough to make the Mageworlders send a task force after us, I doubt that a planetary attack would do any better."

Jhunnei shook her head. "Not likely. Whoever's running the war from their side feels like a gambler and a real hard bastard. He's opted for the all-or-nothing win, and I don't think anything we can do is going to make him split his forces."

The comm link beeped. Gil set aside the clipboard with the spoils inventory and picked up the link. "Gil here."

"Communications, sir. We've just picked up a hi-comms message from *Luck of the Draw*."

"Good," said Gil. This sounded like promising news at last—a few days ago, Merrolakk had taken several of the privateers off on a hunting foray. Maybe her efforts had paid off where Gil's hadn't. "Where's the *Luck* now? And what's her message?"

"She's just entered the local system," reported the comms tech. "Captain Merrolakk requests permission to rendezvous with *Karipavo* for a direct conference. It seems that her latest raid netted her some important-looking papers—and a prisoner."

In the half-empty bachelor officers' quarters at the Space Force installation on Telabryk Field, Llannat Hyfid woke from an uneasy sleep. The conversation over dinner at the LDF officers' club had been disturbing; she'd said more than she'd intended, and far more than she should have. If she'd been talking to anyone besides Ari Rosselin-Metadi, and if the Mageworlders hadn't already broken up the civilized galaxy into convenient pieces, she would have been in serious trouble.

The Guild hunts down Mages wherever it can find them— "*for the common safety,*" *Master Ransome always told us, and under the circumstances I can't really say he was wrong.*

She turned over on the narrow bunk. A bar of light came in through the high window. Not moonlight, but the reflected skyglow off the port; so strong, even almost deserted as the Field was, that it made a pale streak slanting down across the darkness.

Face it, I don't look all that much like an Adept anymore. A Magelord's ship, a Magelord's staff . . . even my thoughts are turning strange.

When she looked at the night through half-closed eyes, she had to acknowledge the change. Her Adept-trained awareness of the flowing Power in the universe was still there; but these days, if she tried, she could dimly perceive something else as well: the silver cords that brought together the past and the future, weaving their patterns across the present.

That's what the masks are for. The knowledge slipped into the forefront of her mind like an old memory. It was one of the things the Professor had known, that had come to her somehow during her visionary trance back on the Deathwing. *They shut out the distractions of flesh and blood, and let you see.*

She couldn't sleep now; her thoughts had left her too restless for that. With a sigh she rose from her bed and dressed herself again in Adept's blacks. Then she picked up the Professor's ebony staff and clipped it onto her belt before slipping out into the night.

The few small buildings that made up the Space Force installation on Telabryk Field were dark. A light shone through the window of the main office—Vinhalyn, she supposed, working late, or whoever had the duty tonight. She went around back to the open area by the loading platform, where she had practiced the ShadowDance and Ari had come to watch.

When she got to the place, she wasn't really surprised to find him there before her. He stood leaning back against the side of the platform, looking up at the night sky. As always, the quietness of his posture would have let normal eyes pass over him without noticing. He turned his head at her approach—he had keen ears by any human standard, and the Selvaurs on Maraghai had trained him well enough to let him earn clan status among the Forest Lords.

"What brings you out walking at this hour?" he asked. His voice was a soft rumble.

Llannat took a place leaning against the platform next to him. "I couldn't sleep." She paused. "What's your excuse?"

He shrugged. In the dark, with his massive height and his broad shoulders, it was like watching a mountain shift position. "Same thing, more or less."

They stood for a while in companionable silence. Far off on the LDF side of the field, a returning scoutship settled onto the concrete in a streak of light and a roar of engines.

"That's another one back," she said. "So far, so good."

"The good luck can't last forever. Which do you think it's going to be, the Magefleet or Vallant?"

"We'd better hope it's Vallant," Llannat said. "The most he's got is going to be a sector fleet. Whatever the Mages have put together, it was big enough to break through the Net and take out the Home Fleet at Galcen."

She frowned upward at where the stars would have been, if she could have seen them through the skyglow. "If you're really looking for an answer, it's that I don't know which of them is going to get here first. But it's going to be soon, and it's going to be bad."

He nodded. "I thought so. . . . I wish that I could wish you were someplace else. But I'm too selfish for that. I'm glad you're here."

"So am I." She was silent for a few moments, remembering the silver cords the Professor had seen and drawn together five hundred years before—the work that she herself had finished, or had begun to finish, on board *Night's-Beautiful-Daughter*. "I think . . . I believe . . . that I came here because of you. Because I had to find you."

"Me?" He turned his head to look directly down at her, though she couldn't make out his expression in the dark. "What good would I be to an Adept? Owen always did say I was thicker than a two-meter stack of plast-block bricks."

"Your brother doesn't know everything."

Ari snorted. "Try telling *him* that."

"Don't worry. He'll learn." The words came unprompted, with the flat echo of certainty, and she shivered in spite of herself. "Oh, damn. I wish I could quit doing that."

"I can't help you there, either. I wish I could."

"You do help," she said. "By being here, and being you. I don't need another Adept—we're all crazy, you know; it comes from spending too much time looking at the inside of things—I need someone who doesn't have trouble remembering what's real."

Llannat heard his breath catch a little. "If you aren't telling me lies in order to be kind . . ."

"No."

"Then I'll stay. For as long as the Magelords and the Space Force let me. Longer, if you ask."

She laughed unsteadily. "Coming from you, Ari Rosselin-Metadi, that's practically a proposal of marriage."

"If you'd like to take it that way."

"Yes," she said. "And yes."

Klea had never impersonated a bodyguard before. The trick, she decided after watching Owen for a few minutes, was not to impersonate anything at all.

If I am one of Gentlesir Jessan's off-planet bodyguards, then what an off-planet bodyguard looks like ... is me.

In the office of Dahl&Dahl's executive vice-president for public affairs, she stood against the wall on one side of the door while Owen stood on the other. Jessan and the man from Dahl&Dahl ignored them both.

"I'm gratified," said Jessan, "that you were able to provide me with an answer so expeditiously."

The man from Dahl&Dahl pursed his lips and looked mournful. "Unfortunately, Gentlesir Jessan, the only answer that I'm able to give you is a negative one."

"Ah." If Jessan was angry, it didn't show. "I take it your superiors were unwilling to accommodate us in the matter."

"No, no. The firm of Dahl&Dahl still has the most earnest support for your cause, and for the cause of the Republic. However—"

"Yes?"

"—by our best projections, a counterpetition to block the Domina's termination could not muster enough votes in committee to override the original. Under the current circumstances, Dahl&Dahl can't possibly risk putting it forward."

Jessan nodded. "Understandable. You are, after all, men and women of business ... but is there something new about the current circumstances of which I ought to be aware?"

"Yes," said the man from Dahl&Dahl. "At its next meeting, the Steering Committee will declare Suivi Point to be an open port, not allied to either side in the present conflict."

Not even a little bit like High Station, thought Klea. *And High Station has a lot more to worry about if they lose.*

"I see." Jessan rose and bowed. "In that case, gentlesir, it's time I took my leave."

The man from Dahl&Dahl rose and bowed also. "Believe me, we do regret our inability to help you in the way you desired."

He reached into an inside pocket of his jacket and took out a slim folder—the printed cover carried a full-color reproduction of the mosaic out front. "A listing of our available banking and investment services," he explained. "In case you're interested in patronizing us again someday."

Jessan took the folder. "I shall certainly keep your firm in mind," he said. "In the meantime—good day, gentlesir, and please accept my best wishes for your future prosperity."

He bowed again and turned to leave. Klea wondered for a moment if bodyguards were supposed to bow or anything, and decided that somebody who wasn't officially there couldn't be expected to say goodbye. She and Owen followed Jessan out of the building without speaking.

Nobody said anything until they were back out in the middle of the main concourse. Jessan paused to look up at a statue made of welded metal augmented by shifting holovid displays; like good bodyguards, Klea and Owen paused also, a foot or so behind him.

"Mixed media," the Khesatan said appreciatively. "Quite good, actually—I wonder if the artist's local?"

Klea heard Owen sigh. "I don't know. It shouldn't be difficult to find out, though, if you think it's important."

Jessan looked surprised that anyone should have needed to ask. "The only halfway-decent piece of public statuary on Suivi Point? Of course it's important ... but not urgent. What I had in mind for the next few minutes, in fact, was a thorough perusal of the fascinating piece of informational literature our friend back there pressed upon on me at parting."

"So you noticed that."

"I could hardly miss it. Let's see, now . . ." Jessan took the folder out of his pocket and opened it. Several narrow sheets of stiff paper tried to fall out; he caught them, and riffled through them. His expression of mild interest never changed, but Klea could feel his excitement building as he read through the close-printed pages. "Yes. Yes, indeed. I shall *certainly* make it a point to invest with Dahl&Dahl."

Merrolakk the Selvaur hadn't changed her style when she brought *Luck of the Draw* to join Gil's fleet. She'd added a Space Force standard-issue comm link to the collection of weapons and small tools attached to, or stowed in, her gunbelt and vest; but that was all. *Karipavo*'s briefing room, already small and cramped, seemed even smaller after she'd entered.

She greeted Commodore Gil with a casual nod.

D'Rugier, she said—using his civilian name, probably to underscore the voluntary nature of their current association. After the manner of Maraghai, she'd left off the title. Taking orders wasn't something that the Forest Lords were particularly good at, and neither was working inside anybody's hierarchical system except their own.

"Merrolakk," Gil said. "I hear you've been lucky."

Not a whole lot going on out here. But I got a ship.

"We've been getting ships too," said Jhunnei. "All of them loaded with things like roots, berries, and cheap engine parts. Was yours any different?"

Hard to say. This one had shields and guns, and then the damned thing blew itself up on me.

"Warship," Gil said. No wonder Merro was looking so pleased with herself. "You said something about a prisoner?"

There was a lifepod. I grabbed it with a tractor beam— and look what I found inside.

The Selvaur unfastened one of the bulging pockets of her vest, and pulled out a paperbound notebook and a handful of what looked like some kind of datachips. *Files and hardcopy. The prisoner was carrying them.*

"Let's have a look," said Gil. He took the notebook and

opened it on the briefing-room table. "Hold on to the files; we can't read 'em without the right comps anyhow. The hardcopy, though . . . we're in luck. Flatpix."

"Maybe not so lucky," Jhunnei said quietly. "I don't like what I'm seeing here."

Gil didn't like it either. Interleaved with the pages of small neat handwriting in an unfamiliar script were pictures of a young woman in Space Force uniform, a commander by the insignia, shown full face and profile. The flatpix had more handwriting on the backs and in the margins, and some of this text was done in careful Galcenian lettering.

Names, carefully recorded in the original language for accuracy's sake: Jos Metadi; Rosel Quetaya. Place names, too: Galcen, Gyffer, Pleyver, Ophel.

Another flatpic showed pictures of the same woman at full length, nude this time, with the mark of a tight-focus blaster burn in the middle of her forehead.

"No," Gil said. "This isn't good. Whether it's something that matters any longer, I don't know. Merrolakk—you said there was a prisoner?"

Yes.

"Have you questioned him yet?"

Her. Wearing some kind of uniform. Haven't touched her.

"Good," said Gil. "Don't. Bring her over to the 'Pavo. If it turns out she's got any ransom value or suchlike, the profit's all yours. But whatever she knows, is mine."

III. RSF *Karipavo*: Mageworlds Space
Suivi Point: Main Detention
RSF *Veratina*: Infabede Sector

T HE PRISONER was stocky and dark-haired, with a square, snub-nosed face under a short mop of greying curls. She sat on the edge of her bunk in *Karipavo*'s brig, with the bearing and expression of someone who has been expecting the worst for some time already, and who hasn't yet been disappointed.

In the office of the *'Pavo*'s security chief, Commodore Gil regarded the prisoner's image in the flatscreen cell-block monitor and shook his head.

"I don't think she's going to crack without some kind of encouragement," he said to Lieutenant Jhunnei. "So far, we don't even know if she speaks Galcenian. If she doesn't, we'll have to find somebody on board who talks ... what *do* these people speak, anyway, Lieutenant?"

"Eraasian," his aide said. "Most of them. At least as a second language."

"How about you?"

Jhunnei shook her head. "Not enough to hold a conversation. I can read a bit of the script, but that's all."

"Not very helpful." Gil sat for a moment with his chin in

his hand, contemplating the image on the flatscreen. "So there she sits, unless she suddenly gets an overpowering urge to have a chat. Which I doubt will happen."

"Your restraint's all very noble, Commodore. But there's a war on—we can't afford to simply wait for answers."

Gil sighed. "Unfortunately, Lieutenant, I just happen to be noble. *A* noble, anyway. It says so right on my ID papers. Besides ... what's the point of winning a war if you become exactly like your enemy along the way?"

"What's the point, indeed?" Jhunnei's features took on a thoughtful but excited expression. "There could be advantages in becoming a little bit more like the enemy."

"I don't think so."

"Let me finish," she said. "What I mean is, don't treat her the way that *you'd* like to be treated—treat her the way that *she'd* like to be treated."

"So you do have something up your sleeve."

"Maybe," said Jhunnei. "For starters, I'm betting that she does in fact speak Galcenian. It isn't exactly unheard-of on the far side of the Net, especially for the educated and ambitious, and some of the notes on those papers were in Galcenian."

"Suppose she does have the language?"

Jhunnei looked grave. "Then, Commodore, there is a chance that you can induce her to cooperate voluntarily."

"Ah." Gil turned in his chair and looked at his aide, who was most certainly not an Adept and who had definitely not trained under Errec Ransome. "I suppose that you, Lieutenant, have by an odd coincidence studied the Mageworlders thoroughly enough to know how to gain that cooperation?"

"In preparation for my assignment, sir, I felt it best to review the available material on the society we'd be guarding." She looked back at him with a straight face. "The better to advise you, sir."

"And did that review happen to take place at the Retreat? No, no, you don't have to answer that. Advise me, then."

The lieutenant relaxed a little. "Yes, sir. The Mages—the Circle-Mages and the Magelords—have a distinct code of honor, though not necessarily one that our half of the galaxy finds congenial. Within their Circles, they offer up their lives and energies in ritual combat; succession in the Circles proceeds through formal duels.

"The society that the Mages live in takes its inspiration from their model. Dueling is part of their social interaction."

"I'm not following you," Gil said, though he suspected that he was following her all too well. "Spell it out."

"I mean, fight a duel with her. She's not a Mage—I don't think she is, anyway—but the tradition of stylized combat is one of those things that carries over. If you win, then she'll feel obligated to help you."

"If I win, she's likely to be dead."

"That's what keeps it honorable."

"And if she wins, I'll be dead."

"That's right," said Jhunnei. "Or if you yield, she'll expect you to take her orders afterward."

Gil looked back at the picture on the flatscreen. The woman in the cell didn't look like a combat trooper—more like a specialist or technician of some sort.

"I don't like the idea of taking on somebody who may not have the training to fight back," he said to Jhunnei. "Why don't you fight her?"

"No, thank you—I don't want to put a Mageworlder under obligation to me. It would set a bad precedent. And besides," Jhunnei went on, "why should you refuse her the honor of fighting the senior commander? She *is* the senior survivor from her ship."

Gil was still watching the flatscreen. The prisoner hadn't changed position or expression yet so far. "I suppose that if I challenge her she gets to choose the weapons?"

"You've been watching too many holovids," Jhunnei said with a smile. "You're the one in a position of strength here. You get to choose."

Gil frowned. "Well, I'm damned if I'll give her a blaster. Not on shipboard. Too easy to have accidents with one of those. How about a staff?"

"If she were a Mage, maybe. But she's not a Mage."

"Just as well. I'm not an Adept." Gil stared out into space for a few minutes and then nodded to himself. "Lieutenant—what do we have in the ship's armory by way of edged weapons?"

"Probably not much," said Jhunnei. "But I'll bet that the metals shop can run something up."

"Two sets of something," Gil said, reaching for the comm link. "Matched."

Beka woke from a thick, unnatural sleep.

For a moment, feeling the hard, narrow bunk underneath her, she thought that she was in crew berthing on the old *Sidh*, making her first long jump from Galcen to the Suivan Belt. Then her vision cleared and she saw the blank metal walls of the detention cell. Her skull pounded; her mouth felt scummy and dry. *Drugs again,* she thought.

A high-pitched buzzing noise broke the silence, sounding loud and unnatural in the confined space of the cell. A force field shimmered into place between her and the door. She made herself sit up on the bunk.

The cell door slid open, and a ConSec guard stepped inside. He was carrying a bundle of pale green cloth, some kind of shimmery rustling stuff that flowed over his arms in glistening folds. There was something hard wrapped up inside the bundle; when the ConSec dropped the armload of fabric onto the floor, it hit the metal plates with a muffled clunk.

She blinked at the pile of green cloth. "What's that?"

"Clothes," said the Consec. "Get dressed. By order of the Steering Committee of Suivi Point."

"I am dressed," she pointed out. "What do I need to change for—some kind of trial?"

The ConSec grinned. "Something like that."

"Screw the committee," she said. "The clothes I've got on suit me just fine."

"Committee says you wear these. Either you put them on yourself, or I'll fetch a couple of my buddies and we'll dress you ourselves."

"All right. If it makes the committee happy."

"Thought you'd see reason."

The ConSec stepped back outside the cell and the door closed. The force field went down.

Reluctantly, Beka got off of the bunk and picked up the green cloth. The lengths of slick imitation spidersilk unfolded into a formal gown—a quick-copy knockoff of the dress she had worn to make her holovid broadcast. A heavy object fell out of the cloth onto the metal floor.

Beka picked up the Iron Crown of Entibor and laid it on her bunk. She looked at the tiara of twisted black metal, and felt a sour taste of sickness rise and burn in the back of her throat. She clenched her fists and swallowed.

Damned ugly iron thing, she thought. *It killed my mother and I wasn't smart enough to get the message. I had to pick it up and wear it myself.*

She unfastened the prison coveralls to her waist and pulled the gown over her head as quickly as possible—the ConSecs were undoubtedly watching her on the security monitors. Recordings, she suspected, would be on sale all over Suivi by evening, to anyone with the interest and the cash. When she started to work on the traditional structure of multiple braids that went with the Iron Crown, a hidden speaker clicked on.

"Don't waste the committee's time. Put on the crown."

She bit her lip and pulled her long hair back into the loop-fastener that had been packed with the gown, a fastener like the one that she'd been wearing when the ConSecs arrested her. The force field shimmered back up as soon as she finished settling the Iron Crown into place.

Three ConSecs came in this time, two of them with blasters and the third—the one who'd brought in the dress—with a set of binders. The two with blasters stayed well back, out of each other's way. The third one came up to the force field.

"Turn around," he said. "Put your hands behind you. No tricks or we stun you and carry you down to the studio."

They would, too, the bastards.

She turned around and stood with her back to the ConSecs. "What kind of trial happens in a studio?"

She heard the faint buzz of the force field going off, and

felt the cold metal binders slipping around her wrists. The lock snicked shut.

"They already held the trial," said the ConSec. "This is the execution. You going to walk like a good girl, or do I have to stun you?"

Her mouth went dry. *A chance,* she thought. *All I want is a chance to fight back. But it's no good if they stun me.*

"Bastards," she said. "I'll walk."

The senior officers' wardroom aboard RSF *Veratina* boasted, among other luxuries, a miniature version of the main battle tank in the cruiser's Combat Information Center. Dots of blue light—some of them large enough to be seen as tiny wedge shapes, and others appearing only as glowing pinpricks—floated inside the tank in an orderly formation.

Jos Metadi poured himself more cha'a from the silver urn and carried the mug back to the wardroom table, a long, heavy piece of furniture made out of ironwood hand-rubbed to a mirror polish. *Captain Faramon never got all this stuff out of general issue,* he thought as he seated himself in the matching ironwood chair that had also belonged to Captain Faramon.

Commander Quetaya and Colonel—until recently, Captain—Tyche already sat in the chairs flanking him. Both of them had mugs of their own cooling in front of them, on silver coasters with heat-resistant bottoms. Metadi caught the officers' attention with a quick glance, and nodded toward the blue lights inside the wardroom battle tank.

"There you are," he said. "We've collected ourselves a fair-sized little fleet. The question now is, what are we going to do with it?" He looked at his aide. "Commander— summarize the choices for me, just in case I've forgotten or overlooked something."

His aide looked down at the clipboard she'd brought into the wardroom with her, and then at the dots in the tank. "We don't have much in the way of firepower," she said. "Circumspection is always an option."

"Not now it isn't," said Metadi. "We don't have the time to be cautious. I want live targets."

"Yes, sir. In that case, our choices are essentially two. We have the original Mageworlds warfleet; but its location, its intentions, and its true capabilities are all unknown. On the other hand, we have Admiral Vallant's mutinous force. We know Vallant's strength; we know, in general terms, his location; and we have a pretty clear idea—thanks to Captain Faramon—of his immediate intentions."

"That we do," Metadi said. "We'll have to fight Vallant eventually; the question is whether now is the best time to do it." He looked over at the Planetary Infantry officer. "Nat, what are your opinions?"

Colonel Tyche regarded the cha'a in his mug as if he expected to find an answer floating there. When he replied to Metadi, he spoke slowly and carefully. "Vallant is an option, certainly. And as you say, we'll have to do the job sometime. But if the question is whether fighting him would make the best use of our current resources . . . well, General, I'm not certain."

Metadi nodded. "Understood, Colonel. What would you recommend that we do instead?"

"Get a secure planetary base and pick up more units," Tyche said promptly. "Leave ourselves the option of hitting the Mages or Vallant whenever we want. Keep both of them off-balance."

"And how would you go about finding a base?"

"Jump to Gyffer," Tyche said, as promptly as before. "See if they're still in the fight. Ask them to join us if they are."

"I see. Assuming that Gyffer doesn't tell us to pack sand, or tell us to join them rather than the other way around." Metadi turned back to his aide. "Rosel, what about you?"

"As long as you don't want to lie low and keep quiet, I'd say go after Vallant."

"Ah," said Metadi. "And why is that?"

"Permission to speak frankly, sir?"

"Of course. If I wanted blind agreement, I'd go talk to the shaving mirror."

"Thank you, sir. The main reason we should fight Vallant is that we've got a fair chance of winning. Right now we aren't capable of defeating the Mageworlders in a stand-up fight."

"I see," said Metadi again. "Thank you, Commander—and you, Colonel." He picked up his cha'a and took a long swallow, then set the mug down again on the silver coaster. "But what I'm going to do—barring a convincing reason why I shouldn't—is take our little fleet here and go out hunting."

Tyche looked interested. "With those picket-scouts we took from Faramon, and the *Veratina* for a mothership, it might work. What are you planning to hunt?"

"Big game," Metadi said. "The Mageworlds commander. Whoever he is, they probably can't follow through on their plans once he's gone—I don't believe they have another commander to match him for long-range strategy."

"You think we can win the war with a single bold stroke?"

Metadi chuckled in spite of himself at Tyche's eagerness. "Well, Colonel, I certainly don't plan to fritter it away with too much caution."

Quetaya shook her head in protest. "But how do we find the Mageworlds commander? If he's all that valuable, he's certain to be well protected."

"The protection itself will be the clue to his location," Metadi told her. "Once we find the enemy fleet, we'll engage and destroy the best-protected target. Then the next-best. And so on, until we've destroyed him."

"There's a lot of space out there to look in," his aide pointed out. "And the Mages will be hunting us as well."

"That doesn't concern me too much. I want them to find us." Metadi smiled as an idea came to him. "In fact, I'm going to send them a message telling them where to come and look for me."

The *'Pavo*'s machine shop had done an excellent job, Gil decided. Given his old Ovredisan court-formal rapier and dagger set to use for a model, they'd produced a matched pair of serious dueling weapons—not much for ornamentation, to be sure, but possessed of genuinely wicked points and edges.

"I doubt that they'd impress a real Golden Age swordsmith," he admitted to Lieutenant Jhunnei as he fastened on the hastily crafted sword belt and stuck the sheathed dagger in his waistband. He and his aide stood outside the 'Pavo's main docking bay, which even doubled-up with fighter craft still had the largest open area on board ship. "But I think they'll do."

Jhunnei looked worried. "I hope so, Commodore. One thing you have to remember, though—"

"Yes, Lieutenant?"

"You'll have to do your best. If I'm right, she isn't going to be interested in fairness as we think of it. As long as you aren't trying your utmost to win, you're cheating, and any promises she makes to you afterward will be nothing more than empty words."

Gil weighed the second rapier and dagger set in his hands. "All or nothing, eh? Well, if that's their way—" He tucked the weapons under his left arm and palmed the lockplate. "Give me a moment alone with her, then signal the others to come in."

The door slid open. He stepped through, and heard it close again behind him.

The prisoner was already waiting inside the docking bay. She wore a brown tunic and trousers over plain leather boots, and a pair of binders caught her wrists together in front. Gil approached and laid the second rapier and dagger on the deck between them.

"I'm going to assume you understand Galcenian," he said, speaking slowly and distinctly. "My name is Jervas, Baronet D'Rugier. I have captured you under articles of confederation, letters of marque and reprisal, and a declaration of war."

He paused to look at her. She said nothing.

"You are my prisoner," he continued. "But I will give you a chance to win free. If you can defeat me, I have ordered my second-in-command to take you anywhere in the galaxy you wish to go, and to deliver you safe and un-harmed."

Gil pulled out the code key to the binders and laid it on the deck on top of the rapier and dagger. As he did so, the door opened again, and several other people entered the bay: Jhunnei, Merrolakk, the 'Pavo's chief medic, and a pair of ordinary troopers, the last two carrying blasters and blocking the exits.

Remember, Merrolakk called out across the echoing bay. *If you damage her, you still have to pay me.*

Gil raised his voice, directing it to the newcomers. "You'll get paid, Merro—my word on it. Everyone, you are my witnesses: stay out of the fight."

He turned his back on the prisoner and started walking toward the far bulkhead. Before he had gone ten paces, something—a disturbance in the air, or the sound of a foot-step on the deck—made him spin about in time to see the prisoner lunging at him, rapier outstretched.

Gil had bare hands, and no chance to sidestep. Instead, he dropped his right hand to his rapier hilt and pulled out enough of the blade to meet the incoming lunge and knock it aside. He finished drawing his blade as the prisoner recovered.

He came to a guard position, snaking the dagger from his waistband as he did so, and flicked away the sheath.

"Well," he said, "it seems my terms are agreeable to you."

He tapped his opponent's rapier lightly, testing her. She lifted her blade to point at his eyes. He raised his guard, then beat the prisoner's weapon aside, using his greater strength of wrist to push the blade away. In the same move-ment he straightened his arm and lunged.

The point of Gil's rapier took the prisoner high in the left shoulder, drawing blood.

"First blood to me, gentlelady," he said. "Will you yield?"

She still held the binders in her left hand. By way of an-swer she whipped her arm forward—though with her wound the sudden movement must have hurt considerably—threw the binders at his head, and lunged again.

That's the spirit! Merrolakk hooted from the sidelines, as Gil flinched away involuntarily from the hurtling binders. *Make him work for it!*

Gil dropped to one knee as the thrust passed over him, and caught the prisoner's weapon between his crossed and uplifted blades. He rose, still keeping her rapier trapped between his own rapier and his left-hand dagger, and forced their linked blades up above his head. When he could push them up no higher, he snapped his right foot forward into her stomach.

The prisoner bent over, gasping. Gil took a step back.

When she straightened up, her face was paler than before, and Gil could see blood staining the left sleeve of her brown tunic. *All or nothing,* Gil thought, and thrust again, taking her in the meaty part of her thigh. He recovered, but even as he did so, the prisoner threw herself forward in a flying lunge.

Gil parried—but before the motion was complete, he understood the truth. The prisoner had counted on his response. She was deliberately trying to run onto the point of his rapier.

"Like hell you will," he muttered. He pulled the point aside and turned slightly to let the prisoner's thrust slide past him. Then he punched her in the jaw with his rapier's solid metal pommel.

She stumbled and collapsed sprawling on the deck, her rapier flying away from her. Gil stood above her, his blade pointed downward at her throat.

"I believe I've won," he said.

The prisoner said nothing. Before he could speak further she snatched her dagger out of her belt and tried to stab herself in the belly.

Gil knocked the dagger away with a sweep of his blade. He pinked the prisoner in the right shoulder and left thigh with a quick one-two motion, to keep her from moving, and resumed his guard.

"Yield," he said.

For the first time, the prisoner spoke, in badly accented Galcenian. "Kill me."

"No."

The prisoner closed her eyes. "You have won," she said through clenched teeth. "I yield."

"Medic!" Gil called to the crew members who stood by the doors.

After the woman had been removed in a stretcher under guard, Lieutenant Jhunnei came forward. "You surprised me," his aide said. "I was expecting something a bit less one-sided."

"Several years ago," Gil said, as he wiped off the blade of his rapier, "I was a wet and green aide to the Commanding General. One day, when we were both off duty, I remarked that it seemed to me that students at the Academy lacked sufficient training in low-tech fighting techniques. 'I think so too, Commander,' the General said. 'As of now, you're in charge of devising the new curriculum.' And *that*," Gil finished, "was what cured me of making casual comments in front of senior officers."

He bent to pick up the dagger sheath.

"Fortunately, our prisoner had even less skill than I. Now I think we should visit her and see what kind of help she can render, since she's just become a part of my crew."

Beka followed the ConSec out of the cell into the narrow corridor. She didn't have a choice—the two other guards, the ones with blasters, were right behind her. The loose folds of her skirt swirled against her legs and ankles as she walked.

The ConSec ahead of her was still talking. "I don't know who hates you, sweetie, but he's bought himself a first-class show. This one's going to be holocast in real time all over Suivi Point—"

"Shut up," said Beka.

The ConSec snickered. "Temper, temper—and then sent out over all the working hi-comm nodes."

Beka felt despair settling into her stomach like a lump of dirty grey ice. *So Tarveet gets everything,* she thought.

Suivi, Pleyver . . . and peace with the Magelords, bought and paid for with blood. My blood.

A doorway slid open as they passed by along the corridor. Four more guards came out and joined the procession, taking station behind and ahead of Beka, after the ConSec who'd been doing all the talking. But the new arrivals weren't with Contract Security; instead of the familiar brown-and-yellow uniforms, they wore long scarlet robes with deep, face-concealing hoods.

Termination technicians, Beka thought. *Executioners. Mine.*

The red-robes didn't look armed, though. Beka drew back her lips from her teeth in an expression that wasn't a smile.

All right, my girl. If you're going to spoil Tarveet's little holodrama for him, it's got to be now or never.

She kicked out with the side of her heel toward the red-robe walking ahead on her right.

The blow should have connected—breaking bone, throwing the procession into disarray, maybe even angering the blastermen enough to burn her down cleanly ahead of schedule—but her hands pinioned behind her back threw her off balance, and the long, rustling skirt tangled in her legs and slowed her down. The red-robe turned, quicker than she could finish moving, caught her leg, and lifted it. She hit the floorplates hard, on her back.

The red-robe laughed, a chittering thread of sound. Under his hood, she could see round, staring orange eyes in a flat, feathery face. The creature's curved beak worked open and shut among the feathers as he spoke again, and an answering chitter came from beneath his partner's hood.

Rotis, Beka thought as the ConSecs dragged her back to her feet. *A long way from the home nest for a gang of beaky-boys.*

The Rotis were the main intelligent race on one of the minor neutral worlds; you didn't see many of them in space, however, since their digestive systems demanded a diet of fresh-killed meat. The few cosmopolitans among them usually carried a private stock of fast-breeding foodmice whenever necessity forced them to travel off-planet.

These guys don't look like scholars and gentlebeings to me, though, Beka thought as she limped on down the corridor. *They look like the sort of lowlife that takes a job with an execution company on Suivi Point.*

Her stomach did a slow, queasy roll as she realized just what sort of execution the company probably had in mind.

Oh, wonderful. Tarveet's hired the specialty act.

IV. WARHAMMER: SUIVI NEARSPACE; SUIVI MAIN SUIVI POINT: LAST EXITS, LTD. RSF KARIPAVO: MAGEWORLDS SPACE

THE OPALESCENT nothingness outside *Warhammer*'s viewscreens vanished as the freighter dropped out of hyper. The asteroids of the Suivan Belt shone in the darkness of normal space like a diamond necklace against black velvet—a beautiful sight, but one that Captain Yevil didn't have time, at the moment, to appreciate.

The Space Force CO was back in the copilot's chair, wearing the headphone link to the comms. She glanced uneasily at the *'Hammer*'s acting captain.

"Better take us in low and slow," she said. "Suivi isn't going to be happy with us—not after the mess we made on our way out. I wouldn't be surprised if they had us tagged for shoot-on-sight."

Ignaceu LeSoit kept most of his attention for the *'Hammer*'s control console. "We don't have all that much time to waste. You need to link back up with your units, and I need to get in contact with the Domina."

"No argument from me on that one," Yevil said. "Just be

careful, will you? I'll try to establish communications with my task force."

"Good." LeSoit picked up the auxiliary headphone link. "I'll hit the commercial nets under the—what do you think? The *Pride of Mandeyn* ID?"

"Sounds reasonable."

While she was talking, Yevil had already set the main lightspeed frequencies for the Space Force's ship-to-ship comm system. She keyed the handset and said, "All stations in Suivi Space Force Detachment, this is Suivi SF Det, comm check, over." Then she sat drumming her fingers on the console and waiting for someone to answer the hail. A few feet away on the other side of the cockpit, LeSoit was punching in yet more codes and leaning back, eyes closed, to listen.

Her own comm set came to life. "Space Force Suivi Detachment, this is *Lekinusa*, over."

"Roger, *Lekinusa*," Yevil said, forgetting about LeSoit for the moment. "Interrogative status, over."

"Maintaining orbit," *Lekinusa*'s talker responded, "condition II, systems normal, status normal. Three civilian vessels have requested protection. Protection granted."

Yevil frowned slightly. Condition II—wartime cruising—wasn't a bad idea given the circumstances, but it did constitute a change since she'd made her abrupt departure with the *'Hammer*.

"Interrogative condition II?"

"Condition II set per direction of the General of the Armies," *Lekinusa*'s talker responded.

Good, they got the word that we're sworn to the Domina, Yevil thought. *Makes sense, even. But it does look like things have been happening while I was gone.* She went on to the next question.

"Interrogative civilian vessels?"

"Republic Armed Merchant *Noonday Sun*," said *Lekinusa*'s talker. "Republic Armed Merchant *Claw Hard*. Republic Armed Merchant *Calthrop*. All of them responding to the Domina of Entibor's request for volunteers."

Yevil nodded to herself. *Still good . . . interfacing with ci-*

vilians isn't going to be easy, but if this goes on we might collect enough ships to be an effective fleet.

"All units in Suivi Space Force Detachment," she said over the link, "this is Suivi SF Det. Immediate execute. Form on modified location coordinates zero niner tack three seven tack zero five. I say again, form on modloc coordinates zero niner tack three seven tack zero five, standby, execute, over."

"*Lekinusa*, roger, out."

Yevil leaned back in the copilot's seat. Over the earphone link, voices came and went as the rest of the ships in the command acknowledged the order one by one in order of seniority.

"Okay," she said to LeSoit. "Looks like everything's in pretty good shape over on my side. I'm forming them up for fleet maneuvers."

But LeSoit no longer appeared casual. He was toggling on the comm board's Capture Transmission mode.

"What is it?" Yevil demanded.

LeSoit waved her to silence.

Yevil watched his face go steadily paler as he listened. *It can't be anything galactic,* she thought uneasily. *I'd have heard.* She turned back to her own comm link.

"All units in Suivi Space Force Detachment, this is Suivi SF Det. Report local news of interest."

"Negative news of interest," came *Lekinusa*'s prompt response. "All transmissions from Suivi remain normal."

She heard LeSoit curse under his breath—not at *Lekinusa*'s transmission; he couldn't have heard it—at something else then, part of the commercial stuff. The freespacer toggled off the capture and unstrapped from his safety webbing.

"Come aft with me," he said. "There's a commercial holovid broadcast coming up from Suivi. I've heard the sound already. Now I want to see the picture that went with it."

The two of them headed aft to the *'Hammer'*'s common room, LeSoit running and Yevil hurrying to keep up. LeSoit slapped the On switch for the crew's entertainment system as he entered. Yevil jacked her headphone link into the system's comm panel and patched it through to the main board—this was looking like a good time to maintain contact with her units.

The common-room holoset emerged from the bulkhead on its folding arm. The tank lit up, first showing a sunburst display, then dissolving to a blank room filled with technicians setting up lights and holovid cameras. A dot of light in one corner of the tank spun, sparkled, and grew into an inset cube holding a still picture taken—Yevil recognized it at once—from Beka Rosselin-Metadi's call to arms. The inset held the picture of the Domina while the main scene changed to a close-in view of a set of manacles bolted to metal floorplates.

An announcer's rich voice spoke over the background images:

". . . a special show you don't want to miss. You saw the traitor commit her treason—now you can see her pay the price. Live on holovid, an InfoTain Six exclusive! Don't fail to watch InfoTain Six starting at ten-time today to see the whole show! The execution will be performed by Last Exits, Limited, so you know it'll be great! Here's how to join the InfoTain Six Dead Domina betting pool. . . ."

The main picture dissolved again, this time into instructions on how to place a bet on the exact time of Beka Rosselin-Metadi's death—"death" being defined, for the occasion, as the endpoint of her heart's final contraction.

Yevil closed her eyes. "Damnation," she whispered, then keyed on the headphone link.

"*Lekinusa*," she said. "Report location and status of Domina of Entibor if known."

LeSoit still looked pale and grim. He'd already unfolded the comp unit out of its bulkhead niche, and was pulling what looked like Suivan commercial directories out of main ship's memory. " 'Last Exits,' " he muttered under his breath. " 'Last Exits.' If we can find out where the execution is going to take place, we can—"

"*Lekinusa* just reported a blank on the Domina's location," Yevil said. "And Suivi local ten-time is real soon now. We don't have time. . . .''

"I've got an address. I'm going to do it anyway."

"Wrong. *We're* going to do it." She keyed on the link again. "Any unit in Space Force Suivi Det, this is SF Suivi Det. Send me engineering plans showing location of Suivi InfoTain Six studios and all spaces owned by Last Exits, Limited."

The little procession continued down the hall—the guard in the lead, followed by the hooded, chittering Rotis, then Beka, and the two ConSecs with blasters at the ready. They turned another corner and the corridor dead-ended in a solid metal door closed with a heavy cipher lock.

The guard tapped out a sequence on the lock's keypad. The door slid open. The pressure of a blaster muzzle against her back urged Beka forward, into a square, unfurnished room with glassy, mirror-polished walls. The round, outcurving lenses of holovid recorders goggled at her like fish eyes from all eight of the room's corners.

There was a metal ringbolt in the center of the polished floor, and a set of ankle binders attached to it by a short chain. Beka felt the blaster pressing harder against her back.

"Don't even think about it," said the guard. "Or this will get a whole lot worse."

She felt binders snap around her ankles, so that she was chained to the floor, without enough slack in the binders to kick out, or to go further than one or two mincing, unbalanced steps in either direction.

Don't ask how it could be worse, Beka thought. *This is Suivi Point. They can always come up with something.*

The metal wall ahead of her wavered and went transparent. Behind it stood a grey-haired, slightly stooping figure. Beka recognized Tarveet of Pleyver.

Of course. No holovid newscast for him. If he paid for it, he gets to watch in person.

"Can't you take us down any faster?"

LeSoit fed a measured increment of power to the *'Ham-*

mer's realspace engines. "I don't like all this crawling either," he said to Captain Yevil, "but if I try anything suspicious Local Defense is likely to stop me on the way in."

"Suivan Local Defense is a joke," Yevil said. "It's all contracted out, like surface security. Give them a show of force and they'll back off."

She keyed on the Space Force ship-to-ship comms. "All units in Space Force Suivi Det, this is SF Suivi Det. Neutralize local defense forces. I say again, neutralize local defense forces. Cover Republic Armed Merchant *Pride of Mandeyn*. Over."

LeSoit fed in more power as the vessels in Yevil's force responded to the order. He looked at the cockpit chronometer and the navicomp, and shook his head.

"It's going to be close."

Yevil gazed off into the middle distance as she estimated times and distances—the navicomp would have done it for her, but setting up the problem would have taken more time than she currently had.

"Too close," she said. "Unless there's a last-minute hitch of some kind, we aren't going to make it."

"We're going to try."

She pressed her lips together. "Late is worse than never. And I have my oath of fealty to consider."

"So do I," he said. "What do you propose to do about it?"

"You're on your own with that one." She keyed on her comm link again. "All units in Space Force Suivi Det, this is Space Force Suivi Det. Unless countermanded by me personally, attack Suivi Point commencing at eleven-time local. Maximize damage to commercial and business property; maximize casualties. Out."

LeSoit glanced over at her. "I thought Suivi was part of what you guys in the Space Force were supposed to protect."

"Not anymore," said Yevil. "It was their idea to execute the Domina; they're the ones that can damned well bleed for it."

"You won't get any argument on that from me."

"Good." She looked down at the glowing comp screen on her side of the main console. "Ship's memory is giving us a fix on our position relative to InfoTain Six and the Last Exits facility—they're all a long way from the spacedocks and too close for comfort to Main Detention."

"Any surface maintenance locks nearby?"

"I'm looking . . . yes."

"Fine. You take the controls and get us as close to one as you can. I'm heading back for the airlock. Soon's all the motion's stopped, pop the lock on the outside."

"Got it." Yevil began switching over the 'Hammer's main control functions to her side of the board. "What am I supposed to be doing while you're gone?"

LeSoit checked the charge on his blaster. "Watch InfoTain Six," he said. "They might have more of a show than they expected."

In Karipavo's sickbay, the prisoner lay under a light blanket on one of the beds. Only the basic monitors were hooked up and running, and she hadn't required time in a healing pod—two facts that cheered Gil considerably. All his other fights with edged weapons had been sporting encounters, and he hadn't much cared for the experience of mauling someone about with serious intent.

The object of that intent was still a trifle pale and subdued, most likely from trauma and loss of blood. Her bearing, though, had none of the earlier desperation that had impelled her toward death on his rapier's blade. Gil sat down in the visitor's chair by the side of her bed.

"Hello," he said. "After the way we met yesterday, I suppose it's time we got acquainted. I am Baronet D'Rugier. Whom do I have the honor of addressing?"

The woman looked at him for a moment. Her eyes were pale grey, with a dark ring around the iris. Seen at close range she was somewhat younger than the silver in her hair had at first implied—about Gil's own age, as far as he could tell, and certainly no older. Was it worry and hardship that had marked her thus, he wondered, or merely some quirk of heredity? When she spoke, her Galcenian had the heavy accent Gil had noted before, but the words come out fluently enough—he'd heard worse on some of the Republic worlds.

"I am called Inesi syn-Tavaite, my lord." She paused, as if searching her mind for something. "In your language, I think I am Doctor Inesi syn-Tavaite."

"Doctor syn-Tavaite," Gil said. "I offer you a place in my crew."

When she heard the words, the prisoner's grey eyes seemed to widen and grow lighter. Gil wondered briefly at the change in the woman's expression—had she found the thought of being placeless so bad that even a niche among the enemy was better than nowhere at all?

"You'll take me on?" she asked.

"I will," he said. "Where I'll assign you depends on your skills, of course."

She nodded. She had more control of her features now; the flash of gratitude was gone. "Of course."

Gil looked at her for a few seconds, assessing her. "You mentioned that you might be called 'Doctor.' Does this make you a medical practitioner, or an academician?"

"Both," the woman said. "I know something of diseases and of the body's functions, but my work has been theoretical for some years."

"I understand," Gil said. He rose. "When you're back on your feet, I'll give you an assignment where your talents will be best utilized. Good day to you, Doctor syn-Tavaite."

He left the sickbay, and went out into the narrow corridor where Lieutenant Jhunnei was waiting.

"Any luck with the prisoner, sir?"

Gil shrugged. "Well, we know that she's some kind of medical theoretician . . . at least, she says she is, and that's the sort of thing we should be able to check out. For what it's worth, I don't think she was lying."

"Did you get anything beyond that, though?"

"A name," he said. "It might even be her real one. Nothing else just yet."

"Maybe you should have leaned on her a little."

"No," said Gil. "I don't want to scare her back into a suicidal fit. Slowly does it, I think."

"I suppose so, Commodore."

Gil laughed under his breath. "You don't think it's worth the effort of cultivating her, I take it."

"Well, sir . . . she *is* a Mageworlder."

"She is that," Gil said. "But I think I can trust her, now that I've caught her. And I'll remind you that I did so on your advice and with your suggestions."

"That's not—"

"I keep my bargains," he said. "I'll let Doctor syn-Tavaite have a chance to keep hers."

"What exactly has she agreed to, Commodore?"

"Nothing yet. But I think that she will, given time."

Jhunnei frowned a little. "Yes, sir. And speaking of time . . . I've heard that some of the other ships' crews are wondering when pay and prize money will be handed around."

"Merro's been dropping hints, you mean."

"That's about the shape of it, yes."

"I can't say that I blame her." Gil considered his options. "We've had slim pickings on this run so far. Nobody's ever gotten rich or won a war off a single prisoner and a hold full of engine parts. But we haven't taken any losses either, and I think we've pulled in enough loot to tease people's appetites."

"Back to Waycross, then, for a payout?"

"Looks like," said Gil. He smiled slightly. "And if anybody on Innish-Kyl was betting against us making it back to port in one piece, this should give them a healthy surprise."

As soon as the *'Hammer* was securely down, Yevil stood and walked back to the common room. The holovid set was still in place. She switched it on and started a recording sequence—when the war was over, if the Space Force won, she was morally certain that she'd have to write up a report on whatever happened today on Suivi Point.

The special program had already begun. Yevil glanced from the holovid—an excellent three-dimensional representation with beautiful color—to the array of ship's chronometers on the bulkhead. One displayed Suivi local time:

straight up on ten. Another showed elapsed minutes and seconds since the *'Hammer*'s outer airlock door had opened.

Not long enough, Yevil thought. *Hurry, LeSoit.*

The holovid tank showed the same bare metal cubicle that the advertisement had featured earlier. A fanfare sounded as a door in one wall slid open to admit four figures robed and hooded in scarlet, and a tall, thin woman in a pale green gown: Beka Rosselin-Metadi. A ConSec guard followed close behind her.

"Here she is," said the voice of an off-camera announcer. "The Domina of Entibor, tried and found guilty of treason! Last call for bets in the Dead Domina Pool!"

Yevil moved to the other side of the holovid tank. Yes, the ConSec had a blaster pressed against the Domina's back, and her hands were caught in binders. The room's glassy, mirror-polished walls repeated the image all around—probably so that watchers who had to pick up the vid flat would be able to see all the details.

A metal ringbolt was fastened in the center of the room's polished floor, with a set of ankle binders attached to it by a short chain. The guard's mouth started to move. Yevil turned up the sound to hear what he was saying:

"Don't even think about it. Or this will get a whole lot worse."

Two more guards entered the room and snapped the binders around the Domina's ankles, chaining her to the floor. The binders on her wrists were removed, and the guards left. Another fanfare sounded over the speakers in the holovid tank.

"That's it!" called the announcer. "No more bets! And here he is, with a final offer of mercy—Tarveet of Pleyver!"

In the holovid, the metal wall ahead of the Domina wavered and went transparent. Yevil had never seen the councillor from Pleyver, except in current-events stillpix and occasional clips on the holovid news, but the man on the other side of the wall matched the public images well enough. The Domina was looking at him with a disgusted expression, as if he were something she'd found on the bottom of her shoe.

"You really should have accepted my offer," he said.

Beka didn't change expression. "Maybe. Would it make any difference now if I said I wished I had?"

Tarveet looked regretful. "I'm afraid not, my dear. Matters have proceeded much too far for that."

"Just as well. I'd be lying anyway."

"Charming as always," Tarveet said. "So be it."

He gestured, and the clear glass wall in front of him wavered again, changing back into a mirrored surface. The creatures in scarlet threw off their robes. The claws on their hands and halfway up their arms shone golden in the light, making dazzles of reflection in the mirrored walls. They chittered back and forth in their own language and began to circle Beka where she stood chained to the bolt in the floor.

"Those are Rotis," the announcer said. "Fast, strong, sapient; some of Last Exits' most popular technicians. And they only eat living meat!"

"There's just the four of them, though," came the voice of a second announcer, unctuous with false concern. "Do you suppose they'll be sated before she's dead?"

"I doubt it. They look pretty hungry to me—and if they get careless and nip an artery, she'll die before they're done eating. That won't make them happy."

The sound switched again to the pickup from the execution chamber: chittering Rotis; the Domina's heartbeat, specially amplified for the people with money riding on it; and then, cutting through all those, the whine of a blaster and a man's cry of pain. An instant later the mirrored wall shattered inward with a tremendous explosion of sound.

Collapsor grenade, thought Yevil, as the Domina wavered and fell forward, the binders around her ankles pitching her facedown onto the floor. *Ignac' must have gotten himself one from the weapons locker.* Blaster bolts lanced in over the Domina's head as she fell, taking down the Rotis. Then a tall, fair-haired man stepped in through the wreckage of the mirrored wall.

Wait a minute, Yevil thought, *that isn't Ignac'!*

The man bent to lift the Domina onto her feet.

"Nyls Jessan," the Domina said. "You took your own sweet time about getting here."

Jessan raised her to her feet and kissed her quickly on the forehead. Then, using what Yevil noticed was a very good form and stance indeed, he began shooting out the holovid cameras one by one. The tank in *Warhammer*'s common room went dark, then lit up again with a TECHNICAL DIFFI-CULTIES notice.

Yevil looked back up at the chronometers. Only four minutes after ten. But where the hell was Ignaceu LeSoit?

Beka let herself rest against Jessan's shoulder for a moment longer. The smoke and dust in the execution studio had begun to settle, and she saw the Rotis lying motionless on the metal floor, as well as more bodies—dead or unconscious holovid technicians—lying in the larger room outside the mirrored cube. She didn't see Tarveet anywhere.

"How did you get here?" she asked.

Jessan set her carefully back onto her feet again, and bent down to wrap cutting charges around the ankle binders. The charges flashed, scorching the cheap fabric of her skirt, and the manacles fell away. He straightened.

"Dahl&Dahl," he said. "They couldn't help you in the committee—or wouldn't; they might not have wanted to push a political fight they were bound to lose—but they stuck by us just the same."

"You mean they bought off the guards for you?"

"And gave us maps and schedules."

"Good for Dahl&Dahl. Where's Tarveet?"

"He's still breathing. Your brother's got him."

Beka took one careful step, then another. Her knees were still shaky, and the binders had scraped her flesh. "Ari?"

"No—the other one."

"Owen's here?"

She caught sight of her brother as the last of the smoke dissipated. He wore spacer's coveralls as usual; these were cleaner than the ones he'd been wearing the last time they met, with a vaguely familiar ship's ID patch on the breast pocket. He carried Tarveet's gangling body draped over his

shoulders. A young woman, also in plain coveralls, followed close after him. Both of them carried Adepts' staves.

"Owen!" Beka called the name aloud. "What do you
need Tarveet for? We have to get out of here!"

"He's a souvenir," said the girl. She spoke Galcenian
with an accent that Beka didn't recognize. "High trade-in
value."

"Well, *I'm* not going to take a turn lugging him out
to—to wherever we're going."

Jessan handed Beka his blaster and unslung an energy
lance from across his back. "Shuttle bay two. I've bought us
passage the hell out of here and up to *Claw Hard.*"

"Osa's here too?" Beka closed her hand around the cool
plastic of the blaster's grip. Automatically, she checked the
setting and the charge—both showed up full. "What's the
son of a bitch charging you?"

"Nothing. He's a volunteer."

"I'll be damned."

"You'll be dead if you don't come on," her brother Owen
called from the main studio. He shifted Tarveet's weight on
his shoulders long enough to produce a blaster of his own
from somewhere about his person. Beka had never seen him
carrying a blaster before, but she didn't doubt for a second
that he could use one. "Not even Dahl&Dahl can buy every
ConSec on Suivi Point for more than a few minutes."

"Then let's get out of here," Beka said. "I've been
dirtside too damned long—I want ship's metal under my
feet."

They left the execution studio and ventured out into the
corridors beyond: Jessan in the lead with his energy lance;
then Beka, moving awkwardly in her long skirt and soft-
soled prison slippers; then the strange girl in spacer's clothing, holding her staff at the ready; and last of all her brother
Owen, with his staff slung across his back by a cord, Councillor Tarveet draped over his shoulders, and a blaster in his
hand.

They made their way through the labyrinthine halls in silence. After a while the quiet and the tension prompted
Beka into speech.

"Where's Ignac'?"

"Damned if I know," Jessan said. "He took the *'Hammer* off Suivi when you gave the word—smashed her right through the dome when Port Authority wouldn't let him go—and I haven't heard from him since."

"Good man, Ignac'—knows how to follow orders."

They continued through the maze of accessways and maintenance passages. Beka suspected that the route had been chosen for its low traffic and lack of surveillance gear, not for any convenience to the shuttle bay. A few minutes later, she spoke to Jessan again.

"How did you manage to avoid getting arrested with me?"

"Tarveet apparently had me tagged as the Domina's pet Khesatan and a harmless fribble," he told her. "So I took considerable pains to keep everyone thinking along those lines."

Beka smiled in spite of herself. "I'd love to have seen the act. You do such a convincing fribble."

"What *I'd* love to know," the young woman behind her said, "is whether our friends gave the guards at the shuttle bay enough money to make sure they stay bought."

"They didn't," said Owen. "That's what you're sensing, Klea—ConSecs moving into place up ahead. And behind."

"Oh, damn." Beka stopped smiling and sagged wearily against the nearest wall.

"Make whatever peace you can with the committee after I'm dead," she said to Jessan. "But I'm not letting them take me again."

V. Suivi Point: Portside Warrens
RSF *Veratina*: Galcen System Space; Galcen Nearspace
Gyffer: Space Force Installation, Telabryk Field

IN THE warren of tunnels and accessways that ran behind and beneath the main thoroughfares of Suivi Point, the local annunciator system switched on with an audible click.

"YOU ARE SURROUNDED. SURRENDER YOURSELVES AT ONCE."

"Like hell," Beka muttered. She turned to Jessan. "Remember what I said, though. If you can talk fast, you may still have a chance."

He smiled and shook his head. "Sorry. I'm afraid you're stuck with me."

"YOUR TIME IS LIMITED," said the annunciator. "IF YOU DO NOT SURRENDER THE AREA WILL BE FLOODED WITH TOXIC GAS."

Beka gathered up the loose fabric of her skirt in one hand and kicked off the hindering slippers. She lifted her blaster in her other hand. "I say we charge the ones up ahead, then. One . . . two . . ."

"Wait," said Owen. "Not yet."

She looked at her brother. "I hope you know what you're talking about."

"Trust me."

"If you weren't my own blood kin—"

"SURRENDER YOURSELVES AT ONCE. COUNT-DOWN COMMENCING. TEN ... NINE ... EIGH—"

The annunciator broke off in midword as the sound of a collapsor grenade rumbled through the passageways. A cloud of oily smoke rolled down the hall toward them, fading into thin mist as the environmental controls caught it and pulled it away.

"Beka!" called a familiar voice from out of the smoke. "My lady! Captain Rosselin-Metadi!"

Beka laughed, somewhat wildly, and lowered the blaster. "Pick one of those and stick with it, Ignac'—you'll get me confused if you keep switching them off like that."

"Captain, then." LeSoit came forward as the last of the smoke blew away. He wore a pressure suit without the helmet, and carried a blaster in one hand. The cargo pockets of the p-suit bulged with what looked to Beka like half the contents of the 'Hammer's small-arms locker. "This makes the second time I've pulled you out of a tight spot on Suivi Point."

"If we stay here much longer," Jessan said, "you may have a chance to go for three. Back the way you came?"

"That's right." He glanced past Beka at Owen and the young woman Owen had addressed as Klea. "Who's the rest of the army?"

"Introductions later," she said. "Let's go."

They went back through the broken wall. Beka stepped fastidiously over the bodies of several ConSecs, smashed and torn by the collapsor's explosion. A little beyond the carnage, the hallway forked again.

"This way," said LeSoit, pointing with his blaster.

Jessan halted. "Are you sure? The docking bays are in the other direction."

"Don't worry." There was a maintenance hatch set in the wall of the right-hand passage. LeSoit bent to undog it. "We aren't going down to the bays."

The hatch opened into a cramped tunnel full of lines for air and power, twisted together like fat, multicolored snakes. Tubing and ductwork ran along the ceiling of the tunnel, reminding Beka of tree roots inside a dirt cave.

"Through here," LeSoit said. He looked again at Owen. "You may want to leave the passenger behind—low overhead."

"He comes along," Owen said.

"Whatever you want. Let's go."

They hurried down the tunnel in single file, half-crouching to keep from hitting any of the pipes overhead. Beka listened to the sound of Tarveet thudding into first one hard metal excrescence and then another. Eventually LeSoit stopped at another hatch and began working it open.

"Here," he said. "External maintenance workers' p-suit locker. Surface lock's nearby."

The alcove held three pressure suits, hanging ready along the walls with their helmets and magnetic boots lined up on the shelves above. Beka recognized her p-suit from the 'Hammer laid out on a plast-block bench.

"Is this going to be a long hike?" she asked.

LeSoit had already retrieved his own helmet. "No."

"Good." She waved a hand at the suits along the wall. "All right, everybody—pick a suit and climb into it just as you are. Sooner or later the ConSecs are going to figure out where we went and when they show up we had better be gone."

She set her blaster down on the nearest bench long enough to follow her own orders. The skirt of the gown bunched up around her waist inside the bulky p-suit, but the closure sealed without a problem. She picked up her blaster and the Iron Crown, then glanced at the others. Jessan had worked in a suit before, and so, apparently, had Owen; her brother was helping the girl Klea into hers.

She caught her brother's eye—hard to do through the bubble helmet of a p-suit, but she managed—and asked, "How much time do we have?"

"Five minutes, three, maybe less." His voice sounded tinny over the suit's internal link. "They aren't stupid."

Tarveet still lay where Beka's brother had dropped him in order to claim a p-suit. Now LeSoit nudged him with a booted foot. "What do we do with this one now?"

"I'm not leaving him behind alive," said Beka.

LeSoit stooped and picked up the unconscious councillor. "A man can live in hard vacuum for two minutes. If we take him along with us he has a sporting chance."

In the Combat Information Center of RSF *Veratina*, Jos Metadi sat back in the command chair and regarded the cruiser's main battle tank with a skeptical and appraising eye. Blue dots winked on inside the tank and started moving toward the blue triangle that marked the *'Tina*'s approximate position.

Commander Quetaya spoke quietly from her place just behind his right shoulder. "Scouts coming in, sir."

"I see them," he said. "Reports?"

"Prelims," she told him. "Fast scan shows no major enemy warfleet in Galcen nearspace."

Tyche wandered up, a mug of cha'a in his hand. "Looks like they've all gone away somewhere."

"I think we can draw them out," Metadi said.

"How?"

Metadi looked at the younger man. "To start with, Colonel, we aren't going to overestimate them."

Tyche looked somewhat puzzled. " 'Over'?"

"That's right, son. Back in the last war, I got a good look at what these guys could do—and at what they couldn't, which a lot of people missed. They're a long way from home, and they haven't got our resources to draw on—"

"How do you figure that, sir?" Quetaya asked.

"Stands to reason," said Metadi. "Take it from an old pirate: stealing things is hard work. If the Mageworlders already had as much as they wanted of everything they needed, they'd never have bothered trying to get it from us."

"Mmh," said Tyche. He communed with his cha'a cup for a moment. "I hadn't thought of it that way."

"Try it for a while," Metadi advised him. "It'll expand

your options. The Mageworlders are working against limits, just like we are; and they can make mistakes and get confused, just like we do—especially if somebody pushes them a little. So we're going to give them a couple of quick shoves and see if anyone does something stupid."

"I see," said Quetaya. "Exactly what kind of shoving do you have in mind?"

Metadi looked again at the array of blue dots in the battle tank, and smiled grimly. "I'm going to attack Galcen."

Quetaya gasped. "But those are your own people!"

"No more than anybody else this side of the Net," said the General, "and less than some."

"I suppose . . . ." Quetaya still sounded dubious.

"It's like this," he said. "I'm betting that the Mageworlders took Galcen first thing out of the box, as soon as they broke through the Net. That's what I'd have done, anyway. I'm also betting that their fleet isn't very big—maybe three times the size of Galcen's Home Fleet, a little less than four at the absolute max. Which is still small. One of our best-kept secrets, though apparently not quite well kept enough, was the relatively small size of the Home Fleet."

Tyche looked up from his cha'a. "I'd say you had to be guessing," he commented, "but I think I know better by now."

"I'm guessing," Metadi told him. "A three-to-one advantage is the least I'd want to try, and about the most they could get away with. Much more and we'd have noticed it for sure."

He paused a moment and went on. "Now, if the Mageworlders took Galcen—and remember, we're betting that they did—they didn't leave any significant force behind to hold it. That tells us—it tells me, anyhow—that they don't dare break up their fleet. Are you with me so far?"

"I'm with you," said Tyche. Quetaya only nodded.

"Good," Metadi said. "Meanwhile, look at us. We're also a small force. But the Mages don't know that. Only a strong force would dare to attack Galcen. If we take Galcen . . . why, then, we must be strong."

"Respectfully, sir," put in Quetaya, "we *aren't* strong enough to take Galcen."

"Of course not. But the Mages don't know that."

His aide still looked troubled. "The Mages can tell the future and see what happens at a distance. Making plans based on what they don't know is foolish. Respectfully, of course. Sir."

"There weren't all that many Mages to start with," said Metadi, "and there's even fewer now: Errec Ransome made sure of that. And if Mages are anything like the Adepts I've known, they can't tell if what they're foreseeing will happen five minutes from now in the next room or fifty years ahead and a hundred light-years away."

"So what do you propose?" Tyche asked.

"I propose to attack Galcen with everything we've got," Metadi said. "We take out their communications first. Then we press the attack—making sure my name gets mentioned frequently and in the clear—until a courier ship leaves. It'll have to be a courier, because we took out the comms. We let that courier go, then we track him and see where he's gone. That'll tell us where to start hunting."

"That's the plan?" asked Quetaya.

"Yes."

"You're crazy, sir. Respectfully."

"Thanks." Metadi smiled a little, remembering. "You know, Errec used to tell me the same damned thing, every time I had an idea. Only without the respect."

The Gyfferan moons had set long ago over Telabryk Field, and the stars and planets had faded. The rising sun spread a line of golden fire all along the eastern horizon and turned the sky rose-colored halfway up to the zenith.

Ari Rosselin-Metadi shifted his position, stretched a little, and yawned. He had fallen asleep with his back against the side of the skipsled loading ramp, after watching the night sky over Gyffer with Llannat Hyfid for long hours ... watching and talking, until she had drifted off with her head on his shoulder. He'd thought of picking her up and carrying her inside, but that would have meant leaving her behind afterward. Instead he'd stayed where he was, holding her, while over on the LDF side of the Field some of the Gyfferan long-range scoutships lifted off on patrol and others returned, dividing the hours of darkness with their comings and goings.

Llannat stirred and opened her eyes. He bent his head down and kissed her gently.

"Good morning."

She smiled. "And good morning to you, too, Ari. I'll have to sleep close to you more often . . . I didn't have bad dreams."

"It can be arranged," he said. "If we talk to Lieutenant Vinhalyn right now before breakfast, he can get the paperwork out of the way by tonight."

"I think I'd like that."

He stood up and held out a hand to her. She took it—a touch, nothing more—and rose lightly to her feet.

"Let's go, then."

Together, they went back into the main building and down the hall to Vinhalyn's office. The light coming through the windows was deeply golden, and Ari was filled with an incongruous sense of well-being.

This isn't right. The Magelords have broken up the core of the civilized galaxy, the Space Force is in complete disarray, and Gyffer is first in line for everybody's next attack. I shouldn't feel like I want to break out singing. But I do.

His buoyant good cheer didn't last very long. In the CO's office, Lieutenant Vinhalyn had what looked to Ari like a holovid news feed frozen into the auxiliary battle tank.

"Rosselin-Metadi," he said, before Ari could speak. "I was just about to send for you."

Ari cast an apologetic glance toward Llannat: it appeared that paperwork requests would have to wait. "Trouble, sir?"

"I'm not quite certain what it is," Vinhalyn said. He nodded toward the image in the tank. "This just came in over the hi-comms net; they showed it with the morning news, and I grabbed a copy for the record. The original broadcast is several weeks old—it got backdoored into the local node via the links on Perpayne. The direct links on Galcen and in

the Infabede sector are suppressing it along with the rest of
the news."

He paused. "In fact, this message may be why those links
aren't yet fully operational."

Vinhalyn touched a control on the desktop, and the picture in the holovid tank came to life. The stylized planetary
globe of the news service faded into the image of a young
woman seated in a chair of state. Her pale yellow hair was
arranged in intricate braids underneath a tiara of twisted
black metal.

Ari's breath caught in his chest. *Beka?*

He didn't want to believe it—not after everything Bee
had done to avoid assuming such a role—but the voice in
the holovid was his sister's, and no mistake.

"People of the Republic! A Mageworlds warfleet has attacked Galcen. Singly we cannot stand against them; we
must work together if we are to survive. If you have a ship
that can fight, or a ship that can be made to fight, or the
knowledge and skills to work such a ship, come to Suivi
Point, where we will build a fleet such as can capture the
galaxy. To this goal I pledge my resources; to this goal I
pledge my name and sign myself:

"Beka Rosselin-Metadi, Domina of Lost Entibor, of
Entibor-in-Exile, and of the Colonies Beyond."

Vinhalyn touched the control again and the picture
winked out. "I'm not altogether certain what to make of
this," the acting CO said quietly. "I was hoping you could
provide me with enough data to reach a decision."

"If you want me to vouch for her identity," Ari said, "I
will. Barring a gene scan, of course, there's no way to be
absolutely certain, but the voice and the physical appearance
are my sister's, all right—and the announcement itself is
pure undiluted Beka."

Vinhalyn shook his head. "At the risk of stating the obvious, Commander, Beka Rosselin-Metadi died in a spaceship crash on Artat."

"That may be obvious," said Ari, "but it's not true. The
wreck was staged. I ought to know; I've seen her myself
since it happened."

"I understand. Rosselin-Metadi, you know your sibling far better than I do. What does she think she can do with such a proclamation?"

"Stir up trouble," Ari said at once.

"Seriously, Commander."

"I am serious. Bee was born wanting to make trouble. In this case, she's doing it for a good cause—and at considerable risk—but it's trouble all the same."

Llannat spoke up for the first time since entering the acting CO's office. "She's drawing fire. As long as she's alive, the Mages can't give anything their undivided attention."

"Like I said. Trouble."

Ari frowned at the image in the tank. *I used to wish that Bee would grow up and remember who she was supposed to be. I should have known she'd wait until being the Domina was a good way to get herself killed. . . .*

Vinhalyn was looking thoughtful. "Useful trouble, however," he said. "The old planetary royalties have a strong following in some segments of the population. A new Domina of Lost Entibor will provide them with an emotional center for their resistance."

"A new Domina." Llannat was barely whispering now; Ari glanced at her, and saw that she had gone as pale as her brown skin would permit. "But I thought the Domina was dead."

"Right, then," General Metadi said to the Tactical Action Officer in *Veratina*'s CIC. "Three-position attack, standard formation. Head it in."

"Heading in, aye."

The heavy cruiser—with its screen of destroyers, transports, and fast couriers—commenced a run-to-jump. At the end of the run, the vessels vanished completely from the normal universe, leaving only an empty starfield behind them. Five minutes later and a long way away, the flotilla dropped out of hyper in Galcen nearspace.

"Status on the hypercom relay nodes?" Metadi asked.

"In place and operational," responded the crew member at the sensor screen.

"Good," said Metadi. He turned to the TAO, a commander. "Take them out."

"Aye, aye, sir."

The TAO gave the orders, and *Veratina* began weaving its search-and-destroy pattern in the space around Galcen. One by one the orbital relays appeared within the main battle tank—as green dots for supposedly fixed and permanent structures—only to wink out when the *'Tina*'s missiles hit.

Commander Quetaya glanced over the crew member's shoulder at the primary sensor screen. "I don't see any couriers leaving."

"I'll lend 'em one of mine if I have to," Metadi said. "Give it time."

"Wait. . . ." Quetaya looked at the screen. "Launch flare from Galcen South Polar."

"Got it," said the sensor tech. "Tracking."

Metadi leaned forward in the command chair. "What do we have?"

"Courier," said the sensor tech. A red dot appeared in the main battle tank, a fast craft moving on a run-to-jump. "Unfamiliar signature. Evaluate Magebuilt."

"Take it under attack. But miss. I say again, miss."

"Miss it, aye, two mil offset dialed in," said the TAO.

"Second launch flare," the tech reported. Now two red dots shone inside the battle tank, moving fast. "Another courier."

"Take out the second one. And anything else that lifts."

The *'Tina*'s guns fired. One of the red dots vanished.

"Got him," said the sensor tech. "Still tracking the remaining courier. Got his course locked in . . . calculating systems along his track . . . he's jumped."

"Very good," Metadi said, and turned again to the TAO. "Ready all our atmosphere-capable fighters, and hit the dirtside launch facilities as hard as you can. Take out communications centers, spaceports, and spacecraft, then get out of here."

"We can only do superficial damage in the time we've got," Quetaya pointed out.

"It'll do for showing folks that the Mageworlders haven't

taken over the galaxy yet," said Metadi. He watched the swirl of blue dots in the main battle tank that meant the *'Tina* was dropping off the fighter squadron.

Time passed. No more ships, Magebuilt or otherwise, lifted from any of Galcen's ports. Eventually a cloud of blue dots rose up like a swarm in the battle tank: the fighter squadron was coming back home. A crew member looked up from the lightspeed communications console.

"Fighter detachment reports light resistance. Major objectives achieved."

"Tell them, 'Well done,' " Metadi said. "And sound the 'fallback' signal—I want to get out of here as soon as the fighters have docked. What's the track on that courier?"

Commander Quetaya had one of the CIC comp screens lit and working. "Gyffer's the first place on his line, sir."

"Gyffer," said Metadi. His expression was thoughtful but not surprised. "The best spacecraft in the civilized galaxy come from the Gyfferan yards. Our Mageborn commander wants to repair his damaged units and get more ships, and he wants them badly enough to risk everything."

Metadi turned to the TAO. "Set course for Gyfferan system space."

The flotilla made its run-to-jump, and vanished from the Galcenian system. In the quiet that it left behind, parts of the broken and silent remnants of the hi-comms relays began drifting planetward like falling stars. Half an hour, Standard, after all the ships had jumped, a third courier—this one Republic-built—lifted from the far side of one of the system's airless moons, and made its straight-line run into hyperspace unhindered by either Metadi or Mage.

VI.

Warhammer: Suivi Point
Gyffer: Space Force Installation,
Telabryk Field;
Night's-Beautiful-Daughter
Gyfferan Sector: *Sword-of-the-Dawn*

T HE NOISE of *Warhammer*'s airlock cycling shut behind her was the sweetest sound Beka had heard since coming to Suivi Point. As soon as the safety light showed green, she unsealed her helmet and took a deep breath of the familiar shipboard air.

Home, she thought. *Safe. Or at least, as safe as I'm going to get for a long, long time.*

She turned to Ignac' LeSoit. "How's Tarveet?"

"He made it."

"Too damned bad," she said. "If he hadn't, I could have cycled him back out the lock and let the trash pickers find him when their shift changed."

"Sorry I didn't run slower. You want him stowed somewhere?"

"Yeah. Nyls?"

"Captain?"

"Help Ignac' get Tarveet strapped down in crew berthing. I'll be up in the cockpit getting the *'Hammer* ready for lift-off."

Leaving Jessan and the others to sort out their own accommodations, she half-walked, half-ran to the cockpit. So far, Contract Security hadn't tried to keep her ship from leaving the surface, but she didn't feel like betting her life and safety on how long that situation would continue.

The cockpit wasn't empty when she got there. The CO of Suivi's Space Force contingent was occupying the copilot's seat and—from the look of things—monitoring Suivan comms over a headphone link.

"Welcome back, my lady," said the CO—Yevil, that was her name. Captain Yevil.

Beka slid into her own seat and fastened the safety webbing. "Thanks ... I suppose it's your ships that are keeping the ConSecs from swarming all over us right now."

"They had better be," Yevil said. "My people have orders to neutralize ConSec and start firing on Suivi Point in less than an hour unless I countermand it personally. They've been in position for the last fifteen minutes. We didn't have time to exchange codes, so everything was passed in the clear; the Suivis know what we're up to, and the Steering Committee has been having hysterics all up and down the comm frequencies. Contract Security has bigger problems to worry about right now than a Domina on the loose."

"I hope the ConSecs have nightmares for a month," said Beka. "They deserve it. Keep your ships ready until I tell you to pull back. I want to get us off this rock in one piece."

She started working her way through the lift-off checklist as quickly as she dared. Yevil was good; the Space Force CO replied as needed from the copilot's side without hesitation. As soon as the run-through was finished, Beka flipped on the internal comm to the 'Hammer's common room.

"Everybody ready back there?"

Nyls Jessan's voice came over the cockpit audio. "Tarveet's locked into the number-two berthing compartment, and we've got your brother and his apprentice in number-one."

"How about you and Ignac'?"

"We can strap down in the common room—or we can

ride it out in the gun bubbles, if you think that would be better."

"Never hurts to be ready. Take the guns."

"On our way."

"Good." She toggled on the warm-up sequence for the realspace engines, and brought up the ship's nullgravs. As soon as the ship's weight was no longer resting on the landing legs, she checked the engine status readout and increased the power.

"Ready at the guns?"

"Number One gun ready," came Jessan's reply; and, like an echo, from LeSoit: "Number Two gun ready."

She pushed the 'Hammer's forward nullgravs to max intensity, tilting the body of the ship up toward the zenith. The hum of the freighter's realspace engines grew to a massive roar. She could feel their eager vibration down in the marrow of her bones.

I'm free. I'm alive. I have my ship. What else is there that matters, after all?

"Lifting in ten seconds," she said. "Nine ... eight ... seven ... six ... five ... four ... three ... two ... *now!*"

Inertia pressed her back in her seat as the freighter's engines took them away. The stern monitors showed the surface of Suivi Main dropping away behind them.

"Sensors up," Yevil reported from the copilot's seat. "Comms on line. Where to, my lady?"

"Any damned place but here." Beka frowned, trying to call up the right term from her father's tales of the bad old days. "Is there a—do your people have a sortie rendezvous?"

Yevil looked mildly startled. "Of course. Regulations."

"My big brother always did claim the Space Force regs were good for something besides taking up file space," Beka said. "Looks like he was right. Give your ships their orders and let's get the hell out of Suivi."

"Roger, my lady." Yevil switched on the ship-to-ship lightspeed comms. "All units in Space Force Det Suivi, this is Space Force Det Suivi, negat previous orders, do not, I say again do not, attack Suivi Point. All units sortie, muster at point gridposit Oscar Whiskey. Standby, execute."

The position plotting indicator gave a beep. "Wait a minute, what's this?" Captain Yevil asked. A rank of yellow triangles showed up on the cockpit's flatscreen monitor—unevaluated contacts dropping out of hyper.

Beka bit her lip. "Looks like the Steering Committee was screaming all over the comm frequencies for a reason. Can your people make an ID on any of those?"

"Coming in now," Yevil said. The Space Force captain listened for a moment over the headphone link. When she spoke again, her voice was tight and level. "*Lekinusa* evaluates the contacts as Magebuilt destroyers, mothership, and fighter screen. We're in trouble."

In the CO's office, the holovid likeness of Beka Rosselin-Metadi remained frozen in the tank.

"We all thought the Domina was dead," said Ari. "Mother was, and Bee—well, she'd already told the family what we could do with the title and the Iron Crown and all the rest of it. But it looks like she changed her mind."

"If your sister really is the Domina," Llannat said, still frowning, "there's something I think I'm supposed to tell her."

"What sort of something?" Ari asked.

"That's the problem. I'm not quite sure."

"In any case," Vinhalyn said gently, "it's not likely to matter for some time. Nobody's going to grant jump permission out of Gyfferan space under the present circumstances."

Llannat gave an audible sigh. "I suppose not." Her look of vague unhappiness, however, did not change, even after Vinhalyn turned off the holovid.

Ari took one glance at Llannat's shadowed expression and said to the acting CO, "Actually, sir, we had another kind of permission in mind when we came in here."

Vinhalyn smiled. "I can guess."

Ari felt the blood rising in his face. "We—I didn't mean to be that obvious. All we need right now is the basic paperwork to make everything legal. The celebrations can wait for later."

"Nonsense," said Vinhalyn at once. "If there's anything I learned during the last war, it was that waiting for later was usually a bad idea. I'm sure the LDF won't begrudge us the use of their officers' club lounge for a small party . . . especially if their people can come to wish you happy as well."

"Tonight," Llannat said, and Ari felt a chill go through him at the quiet certainty in her voice. "Let it be tonight, then. Because they won't have much more time."

Grand Admiral sus-Airaalin rejoined *Sword-of-the-Dawn* at the warfleet's rendezvous point, a few minutes in hyper from the extreme boundaries of Gyfferan territorial space. In spite of the battle that lay ahead, he was in a good humor as he came aboard the immense, black-hulled battleship. His diversion to the repair and supply base—a surviving installation from the Old War, restored in secret—had proved worthwhile after all.

Those of his agents who worked outside the protection of the Circles lived always in danger, both from the Adept-worlders they spied upon and from the Lords of the Resurgency who nominally controlled them. When sus-Airaalin had heard that Iekkenat Lisaiet was back on Eraasi and working as a bodyguard for the turncoat Ebenra D'Caer, he'd feared the worst—but Lisaiet had survived the experience, and through daring and good fortune was now in the place sus-Airaalin had always intended for him.

The only question, thought the Grand Admiral, *is whether Lisaiet protects the young Domina because I ordered it, or for another reason altogether. Perada Rosselin had a gift for evoking loyalty from the most unlikely sources; the tales I hear of Beka Rosselin-Metadi suggest that she is like her mother in that respect at least.*

"What news, Mael?" he asked Mid-Commander Taleion, as they paced together along the *Sword's* observation deck.

"We've made no contact with the Gyfferans as yet, my lord," Taleion reported. "Our contacts in Admiral Vallant's fleet say that the Planetary Assembly has rebuffed all of his overtures."

"Just as well," sus-Airaalin said. "I have no desire to fight with Vallant over a prize that we never ceded to him." The Grand Admiral frowned slightly. "I mislike dealing with Vallant; he is ambitious, and will bear watching. See to it, Mael."

"Yes, my lord."

"Is there any other news?"

Taleion consulted his message tablet. "Admiral sus-Hasaaden reports that he has diverted elements of the reserve force to Suivi Point in response to a request from the local government for military aid against the Domina of Entibor."

The Grand Admiral's features darkened. "I had not taken sus-Hasaaden for a fool," he said. "Until now."

"How is that, my lord?"

"The young Domina has no more power than we choose to allow. She was living at Suivi Point on sufferance, Mael; the galaxy was on its way to forgetting about her. But now—thanks to sus-Hasaaden and a Suivan oligarch with more money than courage!—*now* she is important enough to frighten politicians and claim the attention of our fleet."

"Shall I instruct sus-Hasaaden to call back the ships?"

"No. Now that we have pledged our assistance, it would be fatal to withdraw. Let him handle the matter as expeditiously as possible, and return to his assigned position."

Mid-Commander Taleion made a note on his message tablet. Before he could speak again, however, an alarm sounded, and the light over the observation deck's voicelink pickup began flashing yellow. The Grand Admiral strode across to the pickup and keyed it on.

"This is sus-Airaalin," he said. "Report."

"We have a contact up-Doppler, my lord."

sus-Airaalin's heart began to beat more strongly. He had known that Gyffer would not be an easy fight—the Resurgency's agents had spoken with respect about the fleet that defended the groundside port and the huge orbital shipyards—but he had not expected them to be patrolling aggressively this far out of their main system space.

"Who?" he demanded. "And get a lock on it!"

"It vanished before we could get a fix, my lord. Just now."

"A scout," sus-Airaalin said. "Making a long-distance patrol in microjumps."

Taleion said, "Do you think we were detected, my lord?"

"Their sensors are as good as ours, or better," sus-Airaalin replied. "And the Gyfferans aren't fools. I hadn't thought that things would begin so soon—but this leaves us no choice."

He spoke again into the voicelink pickup. "All vessels, stand by to rotate the formation. Assume tetrahedral attack vertices around the Gyfferan system."

I wish, Llannat Hyfid thought unhappily, *that someone would tell me what I ought to do. "Find the Domina" . . . and tell her—tell her what? That I'm alive, and her brother's alive, and I'm turning into something as close to a Magelord as an Adept can get without switching sides completely?*

The morning passed by without any new trouble to break the tension, and noontime came. Ari's undisguised happiness during their shared lunch warmed her enough to push the doubts away; as soon as she was alone again, however, they returned in force. Her mother and sisters back on Maraghai would have called the mood nothing but worry over the marriage celebration yet to come—that is, once they'd gotten over their amazement that the Hyfid family's odd girl out was going to have a marriage at all—but Llannat knew better. In a galaxy that seemed to get more confusing by the hour, marrying Ari was almost the only thing that made sense.

Everything else remained obstinately unclear. The universe in general, which on more than one occasion had intervened to push her forcefully in one direction or another, said nothing.

By the time she came off duty in the late afternoon, her

nerves were thoroughly on edge. She wanted nothing so much as a few hours of peace and quiet before the evening, and she knew that under the current circumstances there was only one place in all of Telabryk where she was likely to get them.

Night's-Beautiful-Daughter was deserted when she went on board, except for a lone Space Force ensign—Tammas Cantrel, one of the survivors of the battle of the Net—at work with a clipboard and stylus in what had apparently been the crew's mess.

Cantrel glanced up as she entered, and smiled broadly. "Mistress Hyfid! I heard about you and Commander Rosselin-Metadi—it's sure nice to get some good news for a change."

"Thanks, Tammas," said Llannat. She nodded at the clipboard. "It looks like Vinhalyn is keeping you busy out here while we wait for the trouble to start. What's the job?"

"Inventory," Cantrel said. "Space by space. Damned if I know why."

"The advancement of galactic knowledge, I suppose. He did give you a list of all the 'don't touch this or it'll blow up in your face' symbols, didn't he?"

Cantrel nodded. "And the 'don't swallow this stuff, it's poison' labels, too. I found a bunch of those in the galley. Looked like drain cleaner to me, but I took the safe way out and catalogued it as 'toxic powder, purpose unknown.' "

She laughed in spite of herself. "You'll make a scholar yet. Listen, Tammas—I'm going off by myself to think for a while, and you didn't see me come through here. All right?"

"No problem, Mistress Hyfid. You never went by."

"Thanks," Llannat said again.

She left and made her way alone to the *Daughter*'s meditation chamber. The cool white tiles set in their circle on the black floor were calm and inviting. She knelt in the circle and let her mind go free, slipping by now almost effortlessly into that state which was neither dream nor memory.

A voice that was like and unlike her own seemed to speak in the interior silence.

I'm still confused about what to do. I need answers.

She knew the voice that replied. The Professor's antique Court Entiboran accent was unmistakable.

If you look for answers, Mistress, you'll have to take whatever you find. There's no picking and choosing here.

I know, she said. *I'm ready.*

Then come.

She stood, and felt the black cloth of a Magelord's long robes swirl around her booted ankles as she stepped forward. She held her staff in one gloved hand, and a black mask overlaid her features.

The mask shut out the distractions of everyday sight, the jarring colors and niggling details that kept her from seeing the fabric of the universe whole and unmarred. If she chose, she could look sidelong and see the silver destiny-threads that wove in and out of the grand design. With the power of a Circle behind her, she could seize the threads and reweave the pattern according to her own desire.

She looked downward at a puddle of light where the white tile floor had been earlier. The light shone from somewhere overhead onto a long narrow table of scarred and dented metal, the sort of plain utility furniture that anyone might use. Someone was lying on the table—someone robed and masked, like herself, all in black.

I've seen this before, she thought. *But the last time I came here I was the one who lay wounded, and there was no help for me . . .*

. . . and before that, when this was real, I was the one who fought against the Circle-Mage for Ari's life, and it was Ari who fired the blaster that ended the fight.

Llannat became aware that she no longer held a staff in her right hand, but a silver dagger. She spoke to the one who lay on the table, and her voice was deep and strangely accented.

"Did you succeed?"

"I don't know," came the reply, heavy and muffled with pain. "He was poisoned, as you ordered, but he had an Adept with him."

"An Adept!" came a voice from elsewhere in the meditation chamber. "How much does Ransome know?"

"Enough to make him wary, it seems," Llannat replied. She glanced over to the fair man who sat cross-legged against the wall of the chamber. Was he the one who had spoken? She couldn't be sure. "Very well; we can wait. Someone else can do our work for us—you know the ones I mean."

A harsh laugh sounded from someone else in the chamber. Everyone knew that the Lords of the Resurgency would sooner use the Circles than their own agents, and sooner the Adept-worlders than the native-born. "That's right," said the one who had laughed. "Let *them* take some risks for a change."

The wounded one who lay on the table stirred and tried to rise. "What about me? Can't you do something?"

Llannat could see the blaster burn, flesh blackened among the black cloth, the cloth further darkened with clotting blood. Ari's aim had held true; without a healing pod, this was a fatal injury, though not a fast one—and before the end the pain would be profound.

She shook her head.

"You have a point," she said, with genuine sorrow. "Failure must always draw its reward."

Lifting the silver knife, she stabbed it down—a clean stroke, sudden and merciful, granting a speedy death.

For a moment she paused, eyes closed and head lowered, before straightening again and looking about. The room was empty, except for the one who still sat cross-legged against the wall. He had a staff balanced across his lap, a long staff of plain wood like the ones the Adepts used. She recognized him now: Owen Rosselin-Metadi. He'd been haunting a lot of her visions lately. And those visions had been coming more frequently, lasting longer, and giving more detail than ever before, halfway between dream and remembrance.

"You're not dreaming," he said. "Or remembering. The time has come, just as I told you it would."

"What do you mean, 'the time has come'?" she asked. "We're outside of time here."

Owen stood, unfolding from his seated position with practiced grace. "Let's find a way out of here," he said. "The path is in this direction, I think."

He led the way and she followed, going out of the *Daughter*'s meditation room and into a long corridor all of stone that stretched off, full of closed doors, into the shadowy distance. He put his hand on one of the doors.

"Are you certain you wish to follow?" he asked.

"I'm certain," Llannat said, and followed him into the darkness.

The new corridor went on for a long way in the dark; Llannat stuck close behind Owen, keeping up with him by the rustle of his clothing and the tap of his bootheels on the stone floor. Then the stone walls opened out around them, and she was once again in the Summer Palace on Entibor—not as she had seen it in the Professor's holovid re-creation, but as it had appeared on the morning of the first attack. She had been there with the Professor, in her waking dream aboard *Night's-Beautiful-Daughter*. Soon, if she remained here, the alarms would go off, and the Lords of Eraasi would begin their three-years'-work of reducing the Domina Perada's planet to poisoned slag.

"Quickly," she said to Owen. "This way."

She led him through the arched doorway into the paneled room with the great stone fireplace.

"Here," she said, pointing to the inset stone with the arms of Rosselin and Entibor. "Behind here."

With Owen's help she pulled the stone from the wall. There was an empty space behind it. She pulled away another stone and another, until there was an opening wide enough to crawl through. She entered, and found a dark room.

Her staff began to glow with a green and vivid light, revealing that the room held a box of clear crystal and black wood. A stasis box, and within it a human figure: the dead and blasted body of Tarnekep Portree.

"Is this something that was?" Llannat asked Owen. "Or is it something that will be?"

For answer, Owen pointed to the far wall of the room.

What should have been cut and fitted stone was nothing but grey mist, swirling and opalescent like the pseudosubstance of hyperspace. Llannat recognized it at once—she'd been there, though not of her own will, when she fought against the Mage-Circle on Darvell.

"All times and all places," said Owen, "meet in the Void."

Llannat saw the grey blankness of the Void pressing nearer, crowding in. Then she seemed to fall away, back into her waking reality, and what had been the pale nothingness of the Void was only the white tile circle in the *Daughter*'s meditation room before her eyes as she lay facedown on the deck.

"Who the hell do the bastards think I am?" Beka demanded. "The entire Home Fleet?"

She was bringing up the *'Hammer*'s shields and flipping open the link to the gun bubbles as she spoke. "Nyls, Ignac'—we've got Mages dropping out of hyper. Don't worry about the big guys; just keep the fighters off us while we run to jump. Captain Yevil—pass the rendezvous coordinates to *Claw Hard*. I don't want Frizzt Osa stuck here explaining this mess to ConSec."

"Already done, my lady. *Claw Hard*, *Calthrop*, and *Noonday Sun* have RSF emergency coordinates and comm settings." Yevil went back to speaking over the headphone link. "All units in Suivi Det, change to tactical comms, standby, execute."

Beka watched the yellow dots on the flatscreen growing closer to the *'Hammer*'s position. A glance at the cockpit viewscreens showed nothing yet on visual—not that it mattered. Sensor eyes saw farther than organic ones, and it was the sensor eyes that aimed to kill.

Over in the copilot's seat, Yevil had finished punching in the new comm settings. "All units: condition red, weapons free. Offset guide on *Warhammer*. Muster at point Oscar Whiskey, clear the way with fire."

Beka hit the comm to the gun bubbles again. "Lock in targets as they come in range. Fire for effect."

"More trouble," said Yevil, with a sideways nod toward the flatscreen. "The Mages have our jump point figured. They're moving to block."

"If that's the way they want to play it . . . we'll save the rendezvous for later. Tell your people to jump when and as they can. I'm taking the first clear run-up that comes along."

Beka checked the monitor on the position plotting indicator. The yellow dot that was the mothership still moved across the flatscreen on a course that would put it right on top of her projected jump point.

I can't jump early; the damned mothership'll be too close by the time I get up enough speed . . . below, maybe?

She cross-checked the new line with the navicomp. *Hurry up*, she urged the red Working light. *Damn, I wish we had one of those battle tanks the Space Force uses.*

The Working light went off. *That line's clear. Good.*

"Putting in down vector," she said aloud. "Yevil, keep your people out of my way!"

She heard Yevil speaking over the link to the other ships, and a moment or so later Jessan's voice, from the Number One gun bubble: "Don't try that again. We almost ran into someone."

"I'll try not to. And he wasn't that close."

"He sure looked that close to me . . . watch it, fighters coming in."

"Whose?" That was LeSoit, at Number Two.

Beka glanced out the viewscreen. "I've got them on visual. Yevil—do we have an ID?"

"ID'ed as ConSecs," said the Space Force captain. "Coming out of Suivi."

"Fair game," said Beka. "Take them under fire with guns."

She heard Jessan's acknowledgment, then LeSoit's, and *Warhammer*'s energy guns lashed out. The ConSec fighters slowed and fell back toward the Suivan surface.

"No stomach for trouble there," said Beka. "Yevil— where are the Mages now?"

"Coming within range." The *'Hammer*'s viewscreens lit

up with crisscrossing rays of scarlet flame as the Space Force captain spoke, and a nearby explosion lit up the cockpit with glaring light. "All units: deploy countermeasures. My lady—how much longer to jump?"

Beka checked the PPI flatscreen again. "They've got a destroyer maneuvering to cut off the secondary jump point. We'll have to try another run."

She stole a quick look at the energy readouts from the gun bubbles. The weapons-system power indicators were flickering, indicating almost continuous fire. *Looks like Nyls and Ignac' are keeping the bad guys busy. Good.* She went back to looking for a jump path.

"Ah-hah," she said. "Got one. Coming high left." She put in the course correction as she spoke.

"Maneuver independently," Yevil was saying over the headphone link. "All units, maneuver independently."

The *'Hammer* drove onward. Beka watched the navicomp and the PPI screen. The Mages would spot the new jump point—they had sensors and navicomps, or something that worked just as well—but did they have a ship that could move to block it?

"Not this time," Beka muttered. "Not this time. Stand by for jump ... ready ... *now!*"

She pushed the realspace engines a fraction farther forward, and lit off the hyperdrives. The stars ahead blazed and vanished, then were replaced by the grey of hyperspace. She counted to ten, slowly, in Mandeynan, before dropping out.

"Right," she said, leaning back in the pilot's seat. "Gunners, stand easy on station."

She turned to Yevil. "Let's find out where we are. Then we can see about getting to your rendezvous."

VII. Gyffer: Local Defense Base, Telabryk Field
Warhammer: Hyperspace Transit
Gyfferan Sector: Sword-of-the-Dawn

ARI ROSSELIN-METADI had left RSF *Fezrisond* with only one uniform, and that one a regular shipboard coverall with the working minimum of insignia. Lacking anything better—and being, in any case, well outside the standard size range for programmed tailoring—he'd expected to get married in that uniform as well. He'd reckoned without the goodwill of the Gyfferan Local Defense Force and the fast service available in Telabryk's garment district: when he returned to his quarters at the end of the day, he found a proper dress uniform, its transparent wrapping still warm from the fabricator, waiting for him on his bunk.

He changed into the new clothing with some trepidation. *This is turning into more of a party than I bargained for,* he thought as he sealed the front of the tunic. *I thought we could just take care of the paperwork in Vinhalyn's office and go about our business. But people need something to take their minds off Vallant and the Mages, and we're all that's available.*

Lieutenant Vinhalyn and Ensign Cantrel were waiting for

him outside the building with a hovercar. He was glad; on foot in dress uniform was no way to cross the several miles of Telabryk Field that lay between the Space Force installation and the LDF Base.

"Where's Mistress Hyfid?" he asked. Except for Vinhalyn and Cantrel—and himself—the hovercar was empty.

"Gone on over to the officers' club," Cantrel said. "Everything there is all set up. The food and all that, I mean."

"I see," said Ari. "Thanks."

He didn't say anything more. Too much conversation would risk evoking all the traditional heavy-handed witticisms, even from the likes of Cantrel and the scholarly Vinhalyn.

The dress uniform was already having its usual effect on him, making him feel conspicuous and monumental, and as out of proportion among his more normally-sized surroundings as a menhir in a flower garden. At such times he tended to grow obsessed by the fear that a casual move on his part might have more speed, or more force, than he intended. In a universe filled with small breakable objects, he moved slowly, with all deliberate caution.

The sun had almost set by the time the hovercar glided into the parking area of the LDF officers' club, and the sky to the west of Telabryk was a deep orange-red. Nearer to the zenith, where the colors shaded to blue and purple, shone a steady dot of light—the gas giant that was one of the Gyfferan system's outer planets, and one of the brightest objects in Telabryk's nighttime sky. The parking area itself was full of hovercars, speederbikes, and other personal vehicles, far too many for an ordinary MidWeek evening.

Ari closed his eyes briefly. *This is absurd. I never . . .*

"Here we are," said Vinhalyn.

They left the hovercar and went into the club. Inside, the crowd was even larger than Ari had feared.

I don't know any of these people, he thought unhappily. *Somebody must have decided to open up the bar for free drinks.*

Somebody had also decorated the main dining area of the club with what looked like all the colored paper party

streamers available for sale within a day's trip in a fast shuttle. Fresh flowers in bowls and vases filled every niche and
every flat surface, making the club look and smell like a
greenhouse on a holiday. At the far end of the room was a
table with a white cloth on it, flanked by more, and longer,
tables holding a great deal of food—a lot of fruit, for some
reason Ari supposed was deeply symbolic, as well as the
usual cakes and sandwiches.

The central table, though, was empty, except for a plain
black-lacquered tray holding a ceramic pitcher, two cups,
and a loaf of flat bread. Llannat Hyfid stood near the table,
looking small and quiet in the midst of the noisy, cheerful
crowd. She wore an Adept's formal black, with her staff at
her belt, but it didn't look like anybody had come down
from the local Guildhouse to share the celebration.

When she saw Ari, she smiled. The change of expression
gave her plain, dark features a beauty that transcended mere
ordinary good looks. Ari thought he would happily endure
almost anything if she would only smile that way at him
forever.

He took her hands in his. "Believe me," he said, "I didn't
expect any of this . . . this stuff."

"Neither did I," she said. "But it doesn't matter. They
only want to wish us good luck. And themselves good luck,
too, but there's no way to do that."

Behind him, Lieutenant Vinhalyn cleared his throat
gently. Ari became aware that the whole room had fallen silent, leaving him standing with Llannat and Vinhalyn in the
midst of a circle of watchers. The acting Space Force CO
pulled a small bundle of folded printout flimsies out of his
tunic pocket and laid them on the stiff white tablecloth.

"The final copies of the domestic partnership forms,"
Vinhalyn said. He smoothed out the wrinkled flimsies and
weighted down the stack with a standard-issue stylus. "If
you could both sign in all the marked spaces . . ."

Reluctantly, Ari let go of Llannat's hands and picked up
the stylus. It felt even smaller and clumsier in his fingers
than such implements usually did, and there were a lot of
marked spaces. He made himself write carefully, so that the

characters didn't go sprawling and wavering all over the empty blocks.

When he was done he handed the stylus to Llannat. She took it and began signing her name in turn—the same firm, unhesitant lettering he'd seen every day back on Nammerin, on forms and reports and requisitions. She signed the last page, and handed the flimsies and the stylus back to Vinhalyn.

Ari had been expecting the room to break out in conversation and the clink of glassware as soon as she finished, but nobody spoke. The room stayed quiet, and the trays of food waited untouched on the side tables. He felt painfully awkward and outsized, standing there in the center of things, and he cast a desperate glance toward Lieutenant Vinhalyn.

The acting CO nodded toward the pitcher and cups, and the loaf of flat bread. "That's it as far as Space Force is concerned," he said, "but we're on Gyffer now, so we ought to follow Gyfferan custom. You're supposed to pour wine for each other, and break off pieces of the bread."

Ari nodded. "All right," he said. Somewhere in the back of his mind a memory surfaced, of his father saying, *"It was space biscuit and Innish-Kyl firewater, but that was good enough. . . ."*

He let the recollection slip back into the depths, and watched Llannat Hyfid pouring wine from the pitcher into the cup nearest to him. When she was done, she handed him the pitcher; it was fuller than he'd expected, and he had to concentrate on not letting it slide out of his grip. He filled her cup and set the pitcher back down on the tray.

The bread was dark and rough-textured. The piece he broke off and gave to Llannat shed brown crumbs on the tabletop like rain. Llannat broke off a piece in turn and gave it to him; the taste was rich and nutlike, with sweet bits of whole grain in it.

She was already sipping at her wine. At a nudge from Vinhalyn, Ari picked up his own cup, looked down uncertainly for a moment at the golden-tawny liquid, then tilted it back and drained it in a single swallow.

The silence broke then—in cheers and whistles and a few ribald comments that made his ears burn—and the strong native wine went straight to his head. Llannat Hyfid was grinning at him in pure amusement.

"So here we are," she said, under the noise of resumed conversation and the general rush toward drinks and sandwiches. "Married and everything. You do realize that since we're the guests of honor, none of these nice people can go anywhere until after we've left?"

Ari set his empty cup back down on the table. "In that case, we should probably leave here as soon as possible. Would now be a good time, do you think?"

"Now would be wonderful," she said.

For Klea Santreny, the lift-off from Suivi Point was the worst part. The fight at the execution studio had been vicious but exciting—the sort of thing she suspected she ought not to start liking too much—and the retreat through the portside warrens had gone too fast for her to become frightened. Then had come strapping herself into the padded bunk in crew berthing, and waiting for the pressure of acceleration to ease.

But this time the red Danger light over the cabin door had kept on burning. There had been strange shudders and rattlings in the frame of the ship, and a steady percussive noise that seemed at once too high for her ears to pick up all the notes, and too low. The sound vibrated in her teeth and bones like a repeated chord from a madman's orchestra, causing her to cry out in sudden fear.

"What is it? What's going on?"

Owen spoke from the other couch. His voice was tense but steady. "The *'Hammer* is firing her guns."

"We're in a battle?"

"Yes."

"Is there anything we can do?"

"Not here," said Owen. "Not now. Wait."

She had waited. In time—a short time, by the bulkhead chronometer, but it seemed long—she felt the queasiness that marked a jump into hyperspace, and the noises stopped.

A few minutes later, the green Safety light came on. They unbuckled the webbing that anchored them to their couches, and Owen said, "Well, we're here."

Klea stood, unsteadily, and stretched. She reached for her staff where she'd strapped it down on the couch beside her.

'Where's 'here,' though?" she said.

Owen shrugged. "Hyperspace somewhere, at a guess. Whoever was trying to stop us, didn't. Bee's a good shiphandler."

" 'Bee'?"

"Beka. My sister."

Klea thought for a moment about the yellow-haired woman who had so nearly gone to her death wearing the Iron Crown. "I thought you said she was the Domina."

"She is." He sighed. "But she wasn't, for a long time, except for the name. She's flown starships for a living since she was seventeen."

"Your family let her do that?"

"Well . . . no. But she did it anyhow."

She ran away, Klea translated mentally. *I'm glad somebody got a better deal out of that than I did.* But this didn't seem like the time to pursue the question further.

The wave of queasiness that marked a hyperspace dropout came; shortly afterward, the ship jumped to hyper again.

They left the berthing compartment and went into the starship's common room. The compartment was still empty when they came in, but it didn't stay empty long. Klea was still looking about uncertainly—there hadn't been time to get her bearings before lift-off—when the door leading to the cockpit snicked open. Beka Rosselin-Metadi stepped into the common room, followed by an older woman in Space Force uniform.

Owen's sister was still wearing the long green dress she'd had on for the execution; it was ripped at one shoulder, where a badly set-in sleeve hadn't withstood the scramble of their escape, and the full skirt was ragged and charred along the hem. Her face was pale except for a flush of bright red at the cheekbones, and shadows like bruises underneath her eyes.

Beka looked at Owen for a moment without saying anything, then turned her unnerving blue gaze onto Klea. "And what the hell are you?" she asked without preamble.

Klea relaxed a little. She'd been asked that question more than once aboard *Claw Hard* on the run to Suivi Point, and the words came easily by now. "Master Rosselin-Metadi's apprentice. Klea Santreny, from Nammerin."

"Apprentice, eh?"

"You have her to thank for my being here," Owen said. "She saw a blue-eyed, fair-haired woman being protected by an elderly gentleman, but needing more help. You're the only blonde I know, and the man sounded like your old co-pilot, the dead one. Since he's not around, I decided to check on you."

"Thanks, I suppose."

Klea wasn't sure what an apprentice Adept was supposed to call a Domina, and compromised by leaving off the formal address entirely. "You're welcome," she said.

Owen's sister didn't appear to take offense—or maybe, Klea thought, she had enough things to be offended at already. Before anybody else could say anything, however, footsteps sounded on the deckplates. Nyls Jessan and the dark man Beka had called Ignac' came into the common room together.

"That was good shooting, you two," said Beka as they entered. "Thanks."

Jessan bowed—an exaggeratedly formal gesture that made Owen's sister smile in spite of her obvious exhaustion. "We aim to please. We also aim. Occasionally."

"Idiot," Beka said, but there was a note of affectionate laughter in her voice, and the jangling, sharp-edged tension that was so much a part of her nonphysical presence eased off somewhat. "Is there any cha'a?"

"In the galley," said Ignac'. "It's cold, though."

"I don't care," Beka said. "And if somebody were to doctor up the mug with something a bit stronger, I don't think I'd care about that either."

Ignac' went off in what Klea supposed was the direction of the starship's galley, and Beka sat—collapsed, really; it was plain to Klea that the Domina was close to falling down from exhaustion—in one of the chairs by the common-room table.

"All right," she said. "We'll be coming out of hyper at Captain Yevil's rendezvous point real soon now, and everybody's going to want to know what we're doing next. Which is a good question, and I'm open to suggestions myself. Nyls?"

The Khesatan had taken a seat at the table while she was speaking. Now he shook his head. "I don't know. I've been—preoccupied with other things the past few days."

"You're forgiven," said Beka.

Ignac' came back from the galley with a mug of cha'a-and-something, mixed with a heavy enough hand that Klea could smell the sharp tang of the liquor. Beka took it, drained what looked like half of it in one gulp, and went on talking.

"Thanks. . . . Galcen's out, I know that. But I don't know the situation anywhere else."

"Bad," said the woman in the Space Force uniform—from her nametag, the Captain Yevil that Beka had mentioned earlier. "We haven't heard from any of the sector fleets yet except Infabede, and all the word we've gotten on that one says Vallant's gone rogue and taken the fleet with him."

"No welcome there, then." Beka sipped at her remaining cha'a. "I wish we had a few more ships; I'd try for Pleyver. Maybe send them their ex-councillor back home from high orbit without a lifepod while I was at it."

"Not a good idea," said Owen. He'd been leaning on his staff without saying anything during the talk so far; from the way the others reacted, it seemed that everyone except his sister had forgotten he was there. "They've got a civil war of their own going already. Pleyver's declared for the Mages, High Station's loyal."

"Three cheers for High Station," Beka said. She turned to Ignac'. "LeSoit—how about you? Ideas?"

"I don't know," he said. "Ophel, maybe. Or another one of the neutral worlds."

"Most of those are a long way from here," Captain Yevil pointed out, "and closer to the Mageworlds than civilization. There's a reason why they're neutral, after all. Unless you're planning to give up the resistance and settle down someplace—"

"Not yet," said Beka. "What other choices are there?"

LeSoit began counting on his fingers. "Entibor's dead, Sapne might as well be dead, Khesat and the rest of the Central Worlds are too close to Galcen, Nammerin's too far away—"

"Nammerin's got Mages on-planet already," said Jessan, somewhat to Klea's surprise. She wondered when the Khesatan had been on Nammerin, and what he'd been doing there.

"Not so many Mages as before," said Owen. "But you're right. We can't trust it."

"We can't trust *any* world," Beka said. Her eyes were brighter now, and she didn't look as tired as before. "Not without more information. The first step in getting more information is going where we can find it—and in this part of space, if it isn't Suivi then it's Innish-Kyl."

Emergencies can take many forms, so Space Force emergency supplies ranged from very high tech to very low. Now, in a small room at Space Force HQ Telabryk, a candle burned. Ari had pilfered the candle from emergency stores—an act of wild abandon for someone usually so matter-of-fact and painfully scrupulous—and had set it up in a saucer from the galley. Now the room was full of yellow-orange light and soft brown shadows.

Llannat was taking the pins out of her hair. When the heavy mass of it was freed, it would hang down below her shoulder blades almost to the small of her back. Keeping it up off her shoulders, as required by Space Force regulations and plain good sense, was a major undertaking.

"I keep thinking I ought to cut it," she said, breaking without preamble into the candlelit silence. Her voice sounded as if it belonged to a stranger. "But I never do."

"Don't ever. Please." Ari was still standing beside the

plast-block windowsill where he had placed the candle. She didn't think he'd moved since he'd put it there. He was halfway across the room, but she felt as if he were standing close enough to touch her.

"I won't if I can help it." She took out the last pin and laid it beside the others on the table, then shook out her hair and ran her fingers through it. "I usually braid it at night, because of the tangles. Shall I—?"

"Not tonight. No."

Ari's reply came quickly enough to embarrass him, it seemed; his usually pale skin had darkened in the golden light.

Llannat didn't say anything, but went on as though she hadn't noticed. She unfastened the black broadcloth tunic of her formal Adept's gear, and hung it carefully on the back of the chair. Shirt and undergarments followed, until she was bare to the waist, with her loose hair brushing against her skin.

She sat down on the edge of the narrow bed and bent over to unfasten the uniform boots. As she worked, she heard sounds of movement from over by the window; Ari had apparently broken free of his immobility enough to begin taking off his dress uniform. She took her time over the boots, carefully rolling up the black socks and placing them inside, then pushing the boots back side by side under the bed.

When she looked up again, Ari had taken off the uniform tunic and the shirt underneath. The candle threw highlights and shadows on the muscles of his torso, and the pale white lines of old scars stood out against his skin: deep punctures from massive teeth in the flesh of his forearm, and long, slashing claw marks along his back and ribs. Those would be the scars of his Long Hunt, back among the Selvaurs on Maraghai—proud marks, not to be erased.

He still held the white shirt in one hand; when she stood and came up next to him, his fingers twitched and loosened, and the shirt fell onto the tile floor. She put out a finger and touched the raised white scar that cut across one of Ari's ribs.

"Sigrikka?" she asked, naming the largest and most feared of Maraghai's great predators, excepting always the Forest Lords themselves. He would have killed it after the Selvauran fashion, without the use of any weapon other than his own body.

"Yes," he said. *"Sigrikka."*

She let her finger slide up the rib to his breastbone, and down the line of dark hair that ran to his navel. Ari shivered, eyes closed, at her touch.

"What's it like," she said, "being strong enough to do something like that?"

"Frightening," he said. His voice was barely above a whisper. "Everything breaks so very easily. . . ."

"Ah," she said. "Ari, put out the candle."

Obediently, he pinched out the wick. Except for the square of starlight that was the window, the room was dark.

Llannat reached into the currents of power and called up light. She held up the sphere of cool, bright green flame in her cupped hands for an instant, then let it go.

"Don't be afraid," she said. "Nothing we do tonight is going to hurt me. *Nothing.*"

Grand Admiral sus-Airaalin paced the observation deck on board *Sword-of-the-Dawn*, waiting for the reports from the fleet. Coming out of hyper was always dangerous, and doing so this time—with the Gyfferans already patrolling farther out than he'd anticipated—would be even more dangerous than usual. And so much, now, was at stake.

This is the most important battle, he thought. *Not the taking of Galcen, or the penetration of the Gap Between . . . those were bold strokes against a blinded enemy. If we can defeat Gyffer—a forewarned and aggressive Gyffer, with its fleet still intact—then we are truly the victors, and the other systems will give in to us one by one.*

But this time it will not be quick. The knowledge came to him bearing the weight of certainty; he could see the weave of the universe too clearly to delude himself any longer. *Gyffer will make us bleed.*

Blastproof doors opened and slid shut as Mid-

Commander Taleion entered the observation deck. "Messages coming in, my lord. All units secure; the fleet maneuver was successful."

"Excellent," sus-Airaalin said. "Any mention of General Metadi's whereabouts in the planetary message traffic?"

"Not in any of the material we've been able to pick up and decode," said Taleion. "The Gyfferans are keeping fairly tight control of their communications."

"Keep watching for it, Mael. If Metadi is not dead—and his death seems more and more unlikely as time goes on— then I am convinced he must be here."

If Taleion had doubts, he was too loyal to show them. "Yes, my lord."

The deck's voicelink sounded its alarm. sus-Airaalin went over to the flashing yellow light and activated the pickup.

"Admiral," he said. "What do you have?"

"A courier, my lord," replied the voice on the other end of the link. "Incoming to the *Sword*'s main docking bay."

"One of ours, I presume?"

"Yes, my lord. From Galcen via the original dropout point."

sus-Airaalin frowned slightly. *We have hi-comms with Galcen. Why are they sending a courier when even a fast ship is the slow way to pass messages?*

"What about the courier's message?" he asked. "Do we have that yet?"

"No, my lord. The pilot says that his orders were to report to you in person."

"Send him up here to me as soon as he docks."

"Yes, my lord."

The voicelink clicked off, and the yellow light over the pickup quit flashing.

sus-Airaalin gave a sigh. "We have trouble on Galcen. The question is, how much trouble, and how serious is it?"

"That's two questions, my lord," said Taleion, with a faint smile. "Shall I begin readying pull-back orders?"

"No," he said. "We stand or fall on Gyffer, and we will not leave here until the issue is settled—one way or the other."

The blastproof doors to the deck opened again before Taleion could answer. The courier pilot hurried in and went on one knee to the Grand Admiral.

"My lord sus-Airaalin," he said. "We have word of Metadi's location."

sus-Airaalin stiffened. "Where?"

"Galcen, my lord."

Impossible! thought the Grand Admiral. But he knew all too well that "impossible" was not a wise thing to say when Jos Metadi was involved.

"In what strength, Underlieutenant?" he asked.

The courier pilot, still kneeling, shook his head. "I don't know for sure. Dozens of ships, maybe over a hundred by the sound of the comms chatter during the attack."

"Stop," said sus-Airaalin. "You're telling the story backward. Metadi has attacked Galcen?"

"Yes. After the Adept-worlders took out the hi-comms links, I was ordered to leave the fighting and bring you word."

"I see. And how do you know it was Metadi?"

"The attacking vessels used his name in their transmission."

sus-Airaalin's doubt vanished.

"It was a trap," he said—partly to Taleion and the underlieutenant, but mostly to himself. "An attempt to make us split up our forces. But it isn't going to work, Mael. I will not return to Galcen for the same reason I did not detach anyone for the relief of the homeworlds, or leave a garrison behind. We cannot dilute our strength even for that."

He looked out the windows of the observation deck at the stars of Gyfferan space. This far out, Gyffer's sun was only one bright star among many, and the planets themselves were invisible, swallowed up by the velvet darkness.

"No," he said again. "We will wait here. The Gyfferans will investigate their initial contact, perhaps in force, and find nothing. As time goes by, after the first excitement, their guard will be lowered. The crews at their stations will grow tired—complacent—and become careless. And then—"

He paused. "*Then* we will press the attack."

PART THREE

1. Innish-Kyl: *Warhammer*; RSF *Karipavo* Gyfferan Sector: LDF Cruiser #97; *Sword-of-the-Dawn*; RSF *Veratina*

"**D**ROPPING OUT . . . now."

Reality flickered as *Warhammer* experienced the translation from hyperspace. All the shifting, pearly greyness outside the viewscreens went away in an instant, replaced by deep black and a sparkling web of stars.

Innish-Kyl, thought Beka. *It's been a long time since the last time.*

She glanced over at Nyls Jessan in the copilot's seat. The run to Innish-Kyl hadn't been a particularly long one, as such things went, but she'd grown used to having the ship—and Nyls—to herself. Adding first Ignac' LeSoit and then her brother and his apprentice had made the place seem overcrowded, even after Captain Yevil had gone back aboard RSF *Lekinusa* at the rendezvous. The unseen presence of Tarveet of Pleyver, locked in a cabin and tended by LeSoit, didn't improve her outlook. Still, it was Klea whom Beka found herself brooding about.

"What do you think?" she asked Jessan. "Is that girl really Owen's apprentice?"

"Klea Santreny? I don't see why not. Would your brother lie about it?"

"In a heartbeat," said Beka, "if he thought he had to." She frowned at the control panel. "The question is, though—if she's his apprentice, is she anything else?"

"I don't think so," Jessan said. "And let's face it, she's not the only member of the *'Hammer*'s crew who's a bit closemouthed about the past."

She looked at him again. "You're talking about Ignac'."

"Well . . . yes." Jessan paused. "That story of Captain Yevil's, about the repairs—"

Beka sighed. "If you're trying to tell me that Ignaceu LeSoit didn't exactly spend the last ten years upholding law and order in the civilized galaxy, I already knew that. I've wandered through the edges of that life myself, remember. And I'm not asking Ignac' for names."

"You will, however, allow me to worry about it sometimes?"

"Don't see how I can stop you." She picked up the external comm and keyed it on. "Waycross Inspace Control. This is Freetrader *Warhammer*. Over."

A clicking and beeping came over the link. Then the flat metallic-sounding voice of Waycross Inspace Control came on through the cockpit audio: "Roger, *Warhammer*, go."

Hi-comms, Beka thought with relief. *At least locally.* Having to wait long minutes for lightspeed communications to travel back and forth would have been a sign of other, worse problems. She keyed on the link again.

"Inspace, *Warhammer*. Request permission to orbit with eight ships."

Not to land; not until she had some of the information that she'd come here for. Most of Captain Yevil's Suivan detachment couldn't go into atmosphere, anyhow; orbit would be as close as they'd get. And the armed merchantmen—*Claw Hard, Calthrop,* and *Noonday Sun*—wouldn't be setting down either. Not without some kind of word on just who was running the port of Waycross these days, and in whose interest.

The pause at Inspace's end was longer this time.

"I wonder what's keeping them?" Jessan said.

"Eight ships coming in at once," said Beka promptly. "They're probably trying to figure out whether it means a Mageworlds invasion or party time on the Strip."

The external link clicked and beeped again. "*Warhammer*, Inspace. Who vouches for you?"

Beka stared at Jessan. "Vouches?" Her voice rose in outrage—but she was careful not to key on the link. Later, if necessary, there would be plenty of time to put the fear of hell, damnation, and Beka Rosselin-Metadi into Waycross Inspace Control. "*Vouches? What is this nonsense. . . . Nyls, are you getting anything on the sensors that might explain what the hell is going on down there?*"

"Not yet, Captain." Jessan was already calling up the sensor readouts and running matches against main ship's memory. "It looks like our friends in Waycross have their own way of doing things these days. We've got IDs coming up now on some of the ships in the area—ah, here we are."

"What have you got?"

The Khesatan tapped a line of data on the flatscreen with his index fingernail. "Republic cruiser *Karipavo* is in high orbit over Waycross."

"I remember the *'Pavo*," Beka said. "She was patrolling the Net when we went through on that hell-run to Galcen. Commodore Gil had her then."

"She was the flagship of the whole Net Patrol Fleet," said Jessan. "If the *'Pavo* survived—"

"—then maybe some other ships in the fleet survived," Beka finished. "And Dadda's little girl may have a chance of winning this thing after all."

She keyed on the link. "Inspace, this is *Warhammer*. Commodore Gil aboard RSF *Karipavo* will vouch for us."

"*Warhammer*, Inspace. No officer by that name listed."

Beka clamped her lips down hard on a curse—*later, later*—and looked over at Jessan. "What now?" she asked, with the link still off. "If the *'Pavo*'s gone renegade or been captured, we might as well jump out of here and head for the neutral worlds."

Jessan was looking thoughtful. "Wait one. Let me try

something first. You're not the only person in the galaxy who went to space under something other than your full set of names."

"Go ahead," she said, handing over the link. "But I'm figuring a jump route away from here just in case."

"Good idea. Never hurts to be careful." Jessan keyed on the link. "Inspace, *Warhammer*. Check Jervas, Baronet D'Rugier. If he's in your database, tell him *Warhammer*, same CO, is here and requests conference."

"Roger, wait, out."

The pause this time was several minutes long, enough for more than one message to shuttle back and forth over the inspace comms. Beka drummed her fingernails on the arm of the pilot's chair and waited.

Another click-beep from the link. "*Warhammer*, this is Inspace," came the comm call. "Baronet D'Rugier vouches for you. He requests that you join him on his vessel soonest."

Beka closed her eyes and drew a long breath. *I hate playing these games. I really, really hate it.*

"Negative, Inspace. Inform Baronet D'Rugier that if calls are to be made, he shall call on the Domina of Entibor aboard her vessel. Over."

"Roger. Permission granted *Warhammer* to orbit with eight ships. Out."

Beka leaned back in her seat, stretching. "Well, well. Jervas Gil and *Karipavo*. Things are starting to look up."

RSF *Veratina* and other ships formerly of the Infabede sector fleet, now under the command of General Jos Metadi, were lying in wait—spread out in a loose formation orbiting a gas giant in the Gyfferan system. This close in, the planet's huge presence dominated the *'Tina*'s external viewscreens, filling them with constantly changing swirls and bands of color, visible tracks of the eternal storms below.

The planet's wild beauty, however, had nothing to do with Metadi's choice of a hiding place. That decision had been based on the gas giant's fluctuating electromagnetic discharges, now effectively masking the presence of the General's fleet. All the "noise" also made it harder to collect information; fortunately, RSF *Selsyn-bilai* had carried among its stores a number of sensor drones, small enough to escape all but the most careful search.

The drones had been turned loose in-system immediately after the fleet emerged from hyper. So far, however, they hadn't given Metadi anything particularly useful. If the Mage warfleet was attacking Gyffer, it wasn't doing it anywhere that the drones were looking.

Metadi was getting restless. Even in the old days, he'd preferred taking the offensive, and patience had never been his strongest point. He'd learned a bit of it since then, however—or so he kept reminding himself. The reminders didn't stop him from pacing about the *'Tina*'s passageways, always returning to the Combat Information Center to frown irritably at the empty battle tank.

He was there again for the third time in an hour when the technician monitoring the sensor readouts sat up as if she'd been stung. "New data coming in from the farspace drones."

"Evaluation?"

"Working . . . working . . . sir, massive energy discharges in patterns associated with ship-to-ship combat in realspace, sir. Insufficient data for positive location."

"Well, that's it," said Metadi, with a certain grim satisfaction. "Here we go. Any activity coming up from Gyffer?"

The sensor tech shook her head. "Nothing, sir. Nearspace drones report no significant deviation from previous activity."

Commander Quetaya moved up to look at the screen over the technician's shoulder. "This doesn't look like the main action, though . . . we got two really big bursts, and now nothing."

"Sounds like a skirmish to me," said Metadi. "The Mages are here, all right; the LDF just hasn't run into the main force yet. But they know the fleet's out here, and I'll bet the Mages' head man wants it that way."

The General paused. "You have to admire a man who can

think like that, Commander. He almost deserves to pull this one off."

"Yes, sir," said Quetaya. "In the meantime, do we offer our services to the Gyfferan LDF, or do we keep on lurking out here in the midsystem?"

"We lurk," said the General. "And we monitor the drones for signs of major fleet action. Given the small size of our force, we can do more by keeping ourselves in reserve than we can by adding our strength outright."

"You're thinking of waiting for the main battle and joining it in progress." Quetaya looked doubtful. "With respect, sir—again—that's a dangerous move."

"Of course it's dangerous," Metadi said. "If we wanted to be safe, we'd be sitting on Ophel at a beachfront bar, sucking down large, colorful drinks with fruit garnishes in them and watching the war on the holovid news."

Commodore Jervas Gil—these days, for civilian purposes, the Baronet D'Rugier—had been hard at work in his pocket-sized office aboard RSF *Karipavo* when the messages came in.

Lieutenant Jhunnei brought the first one in person. "The courier you sent to monitor Galcen just showed up. In one piece, no less."

"Excellent," Gil said. He didn't bother to hide his relief. The assignment he'd given the courier ship had been a dangerous one, but with hi-comms down or sketchy all over the civilized galaxy, personal reconnaissance was the only accurate source of information left. "What word has he got for us?"

Jhunnei laid a clipboard full of message flimsies on his desk. "Lots of stuff—he kept his eyes and ears open all the time like a good boy. The big news, though, is that, one, the main Mageworlds warfleet has departed Galcenian space—"

"Did he get a line on them?"

"It looks like they're heading for Gyffer, sir."

Gil wasn't surprised. Gyffer was an industrial power-house with its own highly trained defense forces, and the whole sector had been staunchly pro-Republic—and anti-

Mage—since the days of the last war. It wasn't a target that anyone could afford to ignore.

"Do we have any current information on how Gyffer's been doing?" he asked.

"Current, no," Jhunnei said. "Admiral Vallant in Infabede is screwing around with the hi-comms nodes. But old stuff, backdoored through Perpayne, yes."

"Go on, Lieutenant."

Jhunnei smiled a little. "The Citizen-Assembly told Vallant to go play with himself. Then they seized all the ships that were in port and started fitting them out with shields and guns."

"Good for them," said Gil. "But you said something about two pieces of news—"

"Yes." Jhunnei was smiling broadly now. "It doesn't look like General Metadi's dead after all."

Gil forced himself to stay calm. "Is this just a rumor, or is it a confirmed sighting?"

"Not a sighting, exactly," Jhunnei said. "But *somebody* showed up over Galcen with a mixed bag of Space Force vessels right after the Mages left, and the courier says they were using Metadi's name all over the comm frequencies."

"Mmm," said Gil. "Did they send anyone dirtside?"

His aide shook her head. "Just shot up all the hi-comms nodes, plus everything on the surface that looked like it might have a Mage ID. Then they jumped."

"That sounds like the General, all right." Gil found that he was smiling as well. "Our courier didn't happen to pick up the General's next port of call out of the bridge-to-bridge chatter, did he?"

"Sorry, no."

"That's like Metadi. He's a cagey one—knows that the Mages probably got all our codes when they took Prime Base. How about his jump path?"

Jhunnei was grinning outright. "Gyffer. Just like the Mages."

"You know," Gil said after a moment, "deciding where we should go next just got a whole lot easier."

"Head where the fighting is, eh, Commodore?"

"That's what we joined up for, Lieutenant. And Gyffer's arming ships—if we can beat the Mages into the system, maybe we can sell off those weapons and engine parts we brought back from this last cruise. Never hurts to make a little money."

The comm link on Gil's desk beeped at him. He keyed it on. "Commodore Gil here."

"Message from Waycross Inspace Control."

Gil tensed. The duty officer was supposed to handle any messages from Inspace as long as the 'Pavo was maintaining orbit. *Either the CDO is slacking off, or we've got something serious.*

In either case, though, it wasn't the fault of the comms tech on the other end of the link. The CDO could be dealt with later; meanwhile, it was Inspace's turn.

"What's their problem?" Gil asked.

"A starpilot claiming to be Beka Rosselin-Metadi just entered the system with eight ships," said the comms tech. "Inspace wants to know if you'll vouch for her."

"Eight ships," said Gil thoughtfully. "I wonder where she picked them up. . . . Is the lead vessel in the formation an old *Libra*-class armed freighter?"

A pause on the comm link, and then, "Sensor profile of lead vessel makes it a *Libra*-class."

"Tell Inspace I'll vouch for her, and ask her to call on me as soon as possible. We need to talk."

"Aye, aye, sir."

There was another, longer pause. Then the comms tech came back on, sounding apologetic this time. "Inspace says that the Domina told them quote inform Baronet D'Rugier that if calls are to be made, he shall call on the Domina of Entibor aboard her vessel unquote."

Gil closed his eyes and sighed. "That's her, all right. Tell Inspace not to worry, I'll contact her again later. Gil out." He keyed off the link and turned around in his chair to look at his aide. "Jhunnei, we have a problem, and I don't have anyone to blame but myself for setting it up."

"What kind of problem, sir?"

"The worst kind," said Gil. "Protocol. As planetary nobility goes, the Domina of Entibor outranks an Ovredisan baronet any day of the week. But Entibor gave up its direct authority over the Space Force back in the last war, when Jos Metadi was bringing all the planetary fleets under one command."

"Ah," Jhunnei said. "And neither one of you can afford to take second place, either—not so long as people like Captain Merro are watching and figuring the odds."

The scraps of broken metal drifted in the cold of space, each piece in its separate direction, as the fury of the Gyfferan energy guns had sundered them. To the sensors of Gyfferan Local Defense Force Cruiser #97, they barely registered at all.

The 97's tactical action officer glanced at the cruiser's main battle tank—now empty except for the eight blue dots of the Fast-Response Task Force, arrayed in an open lozenge with the 97 at its center. Then he double-checked the sensor screen.

"The area seems to be clear of hostile units, sir," he reported to the captain. "Two non-Gyfferan units engaged; two destroyed. No messages sent from either ship—none that we intercepted, anyway."

The captain nodded. "Quick and easy. Too damned quick and easy. Their main force is still out here somewhere."

The TAO pulled thoughtfully at his earlobe and stared at the dots in the battle tank.

"Maybe the warfleet hasn't shown up yet," he said. "What if our scoutship read the sensors wrong, and there were only those two ships to start with?"

"Doing reconnaissance work ahead of the main force? No, I don't think so. I'd say our scout picked up the whole fleet, but they spotted him on his way through. So now they've gone and jumped elsewhere."

The TAO looked glum. "This sector's got an awful lot of elsewhere to hide in, sir."

"That's why we're here," said the captain. "Put more scouts out. Expanding-globe search pattern. If there's an uncharted blob of space dust out here I want it listed. Meanwhile, prepare recon in force—in cylinder of columns, form up."

Inside the 97's main battle tank, the blue dots shifted their positions.

"Where are we heading?" asked the TAO.

"Look," said the captain.

He left the command chair and stepped over to the tank. A few quick commands through the keyboard, and the image in the tank changed. One at a time the sun, the planets, and the larger moons of the Gyfferan system—actually, the yellow, orange, and brown dots that represented them— winked into view inside the tank. The ships of the task force dwindled to a single blue dot. At the bottom of the tank, out of the way of the glowing dots, a row of small letters read, DISPLAY NOT TO SCALE.

The captain pointed to the blue dot that was the Task Force. "As you can see here, this spot is aligned with Gyffer's equator." He indicated another spot inside the tank. "Now I want to check what might be waiting at this distance out, aligned with Gyffer's north and south poles."

The TAO frowned at the diagram. "You really think that the Mages would pick someplace that obvious to hide in?"

"Why not? It's easy to find and easy to remember. If they don't want to keep losing people, that's important. Thanks to the Republic, whatever the Mages may or may not have, they don't have a hell of a lot of experience working warfleets in vacuum. They'll make mistakes that anyone who went to the first year at the war college would instinctively avoid. That's our advantage, and it's a big one."

"Understood, sir." The TAO paused. "Will we be leaving a ship here to guard this point? The Mages may come back to look for stragglers."

"Let them," said the captain. "We aren't going to win this war by picking off ships one by one, not as long as Gyffer has a fleet big enough to take on the whole Mage force."

He turned to the 97's communications tech. "Pass a signal to the fleet: form on me, string-of-pearls operations, two-second dropouts, on line from here to coordinates six-twenty-three, five-niner-seven, zero, zero, four."

"Signal being passed now," said the comms tech.

"Very well," the captain said. "Commence operations. All units, synchronize, on my mark, commence run-to-jump. Mark."

"Commencing run-to-jump," the TAO said.

"Roger," said the sensor tech, as the 97 blipped into hyperspace for a two-second count. "Full scan on dropout."

"Dropout," said the TAO. "Sensors?"

"Empty."

"Commencing run-to-jump."

"Roger. Full scan on dropout."

The 97 and the rest of the Fast-Response Task Force continued on their way, searching through Gyfferan space in a skein of tiny jumps and drops—the interminable, nausea-inducing microjumps that made scouting and reconnaissance such an exhausting, mind-deadening task.

Grand Admiral sus-Airaalin laid the message tablet down on his desk. "Whatever happened to our ships at the dropout point," he said to Mid-Commander Taleion, "it happened before they could send out a second message. But I don't think we need to speculate very long concerning their fate."

"No, my lord," Taleion said. "It appears that the Gyfferans have begun conducting reconnaissance in force."

"Yes. But we can't keep on finding their units the hard way, Mael. Send to all units: deploy scoutship detachments in expanding-globe formation."

"Yes, my lord." Taleion made a note on his own tablet. "Anything else?"

The Grand Admiral considered for a moment. "Yes. Also to all units: maintain tetrahedral attack formation; set jump coordinates to halve our distance in to Gyffer. Prepare to jump on my command."

"It's risky," said Taleion. "We may get caught between two parts of the Gyfferan fleet."

"I don't think we've seen their main force yet, Mael. But no matter. Send a courier to Infabede. Tell Vallant that payday is here, and it's time for him to earn his promotion."

Taleion's brow wrinkled. "I don't quite take your meaning."

"Let Vallant's renegades hunt down the Local Defense Forces operating in Gyfferan farspace," sus-Airaalin said. "It was not for amusement's sake that the Resurgency bought and paid for him, after all."

The Grand Admiral contemplated his desk top for a moment, then went on. "Purely between us, Mael, it would not displease me if the Gyfferans proved clever enough to take Vallant down with them. He was a traitor once, and such a man is likely to be a traitor again if it serves his need. In the long run, we are better off without him."

II. Innish-Kyl: RSF *Karipavo*; *Warhammer*
   Gyffer: Local Defense Force
      Headquarters
   Gyfferan Farspace: *Sword-of-the-Dawn*
   Infabede Sector: UDC *Fezrisond*

"I think," said Gil, "that I've figured it out."

Lieutenant Jhunnei glanced up from the cargo inventory they'd been working on over mugs of cha'a in the *'Pavo*'s wardroom. "Figured what out, Commodore?"

"The solution to our current impasse."

"You mean with the Domina?"

"As opposed to all our other problems," Gil said. "Yes. What we need here is neutral ground—some place that isn't either my ship or hers, and some kind of arrangement that won't let either one of us claim all the prestige."

Jhunnei looked interested. "What kind of arrangement?"

"A party," said Gil. "As formal a one as possible."

"A party, sir? In the middle of a war?"

"No better time for it," Gil said. "I learned that particular lesson from the Republic's ambassador to Ophel—you were there that night, remember? The best way to get word out to the bad guys that you think you're going to win is to show them that you don't even care. A party."

Jhunnei cleared the inventory from her clipboard with a

stroke of her stylus and started a new page. "A party it is, then, Commodore. Whom do we invite?"

Gil thought for a moment. "The Domina of Lost Entibor will be the guest of honor, of course; we'll be presenting all the other guests to her. That should balance out the prestige equation well enough to keep everybody satisfied. And all the others: the Domina's entourage, for starters, and the captains or designated representatives of all her ships plus all of ours, plus all their guests and escorts—"

Jhunnei had been plying her stylus vigorously as he spoke. Now she paused. "We're looking at a couple of hundred warm bodies already, Commodore. I don't believe the 'Pavo's got any space big enough that isn't already full of cargo."

"I was thinking of holding it dirtside," Gil said. "Neutral ground, like I said. Find us a place, Lieutenant, and make the arrangements."

"I'll give you the final guest list for approval as soon as I've got it drawn up," his aide said imperturbably. "Anything special I need to know before I start?"

Gil pondered briefly. "I'm fond of little cakes with nut toppings . . . if there's anybody in Waycross who can make them, see that they make enough. And be certain the punch is fairly weak; I don't want anybody to get drunk and start looking for trouble. We've got enough of it out there looking for us."

"Yes, sir. I'll get right on it."

"Thank you, Lieutenant. That will be all."

Gil sat back in his chair and sighed. He'd done his best to do a Jos Metadi imitation, from back in the days when he'd been the aide who was expected to do the impossible flawlessly on short notice. Well, Jhunnei would make out fine. Good training for a good officer.

He turned back to studying the cargo manifests of the vessels in his informal flotilla, showing exactly what they'd collected on their first Mageworlds sortie. The list was fairly grim to look upon—very little of high resale value outside of a few specialized areas. He could probably unload some of the weapons and hyperdrive parts at Gyffer, but it was looking more and more like he'd have to fight his way into the system first.

One problem at a time, he told himself. *Beka Rosselin-Metadi first, because she's right here. Then Gyffer, and the General, and that damned cargo. Then the Mages.*

One problem at a time.

Several days after the Gyfferan Local Defense Force's first abortive contact with the Mage warfleet, the summons came. Llannat Hyfid once again found herself walking with Lieutenant Vinhalyn into a shielded basement room at the LDF headquarters.

The headquarters building was a massive block of grey stone, with a stepped and columned façade in the same Late Archaic style as the nearby State House. Llannat found it almost physically oppressive. Its weight bore down on her in a way that the even older and heavier architecture of the Adepts' Retreat never had. She wondered if the difference lay in the natures of the two buildings, or in the mutability of the universe—or in her.

I am not the person I was. Anyone can see it.

That was part of the problem right there. The meeting she was heading into, at the insistence of both Vinhalyn and the High Command, was going to include at least one Adept from the Gyfferan Guildhouse.

I'll be lucky if nobody runs out of the room screaming.

Nobody did, of course. Most of the people in the low, windowless room were LDF officers, anyway—one or two she didn't know, and a couple more from the first conference with the LDF back when *Night's-Beautiful-Daughter* came into port, and at least one woman she remembered from the crowd at the officers' club on the night of her wedding. The Adept was nobody she'd ever seen before, an ordinary-looking man with a Gyfferan accent, somewhere between her age and Lieutenant Vinhalyn's. His name, according to the senior LDF officer's hasty round of introductions, was Master Something-or-other Kemni, and he was the best the local Guildhouse had at doing location fixes.

"Only in circumscribed areas," Kemni explained to

Llannat. From his voice and expression, he'd been explaining it to the LDF officer for quite a while without much effect. "A few square kilometers, at most. Security assistance and rescue work."

"You helped find those mountain climbers," the LDF officer said. "That was more than just a few square kilometers."

Kemni shook his head. "It wasn't anything like this."

"They used Adepts for location fixes in the last war. If it worked then, it'll work now."

"I wasn't around for the last war," said Kemni. "And I've never done any space-rescue work either."

"Master Kemni has a point," said Lieutenant Vinhalyn. "That's why I proposed that Mistress Hyfid join us as well—she has, in fact, done space-rescue work under combat conditions."

Llannat felt her skin growing warm; she was glad that no one would see the blush of embarrassment. *I pointed at a dot on a monitor screen that I couldn't even interpret, and I said, 'Go that way.' I never expected it to work.*

But if I hadn't done it, Tammas Cantrel and his people would still be floating out there somewhere.

"Even better," the LDF officer said. "She and Master Kemni can check each other's work, as it were."

He turned to the big battle tank that dominated the center of the basement room with its multicolored display—the Gyfferan system, this time, in enough detail to include the major asteroids and artificial objects as well as all ten planets and their moons.

"Somewhere in all this," he said, "there's a fleet. Our first report, from a scoutship on microjump patrol, put the entire body of the Mageworlds force *here.*"

He touched a control. Far out beyond normal system space, at a position parallel to Gyffer's equator and some twenty degrees above the plane of the ecliptic, a dot of red-for-hostile light flashed on.

"Reconnaissance in force by one of the Fast-Response groups," he went on, "found and destroyed no more than two Mage units at the reported coordinates. Our question: where are the rest of the Mages?"

Llannat could see the point of the LDF officer's question. Space—even the relatively small and circumscribed space of a single star system—was big, and keeping out of sight in it was easy, if keeping out of sight was all that you wanted to do. Beka Rosselin-Metadi had brought not one but two ships down onto the very surface of Darvell, in the face of planetary defenses as thorough as Gyffer's. As long as the commander of the Mageworlds force didn't intend to be spotted, no ship out of Gyffer was likely to find him.

He doesn't want us to see his fleet until it's right on top of us, Llannat thought. *He wants Gyffer to be like Galcen, and fold up without a fight.*

She looked from Master Kemni to the glowing red dot in the battle tank, and back again. "Should we try it one at a time, or both together?" she asked.

"Together," Kemni said. "Not linked—it's too dangerous—but working in parallel."

Llannat nodded. "Sounds good. Let's go."

Master Kemni walked to the opposite side of the holotank. Llannat stayed where she was. After a few awkward seconds, when nobody seemed to be doing anything, she decided that she ought to try closing her eyes and relaxing, the way she had done aboard the courier ship *Naversey* when she located Tammas Cantrel. She took a series of deep breaths and let her eyelids drift shut.

Even with her eyes closed, the display in the battle tank filled her awareness. Time passed, marked by the in-and-out of her own breathing and the slow beat of her pulse, and began to slip. Between one breath and the next, she was floating in a kind of no-space that contained at once the display in the tank before her, and the vast empty reaches of the system itself.

Here in this place, the two were one. She reached out further toward the points of light—the orbital docks and the satellite weapons platforms, the moons and planets and the dark places in between—feeling for those places where the currents of the universe moved with the eddies and

surges of active life. The search had gone like this before,
the time she had probed the drifting wreckage of the battle
at the Net.

But this time . . . this time she could see the hint, the barest hint, of silver cords winding through the tank.

If I had a mask, she thought, *I could see them better.
Then I could . . . no. Don't think like that; not with an Adept
standing across from you!*

Llannat forced her attention back to the double entity that
was the Gyfferan system and the holographic model. She
could feel different temperatures in the model, correspond-
ing to something—she didn't know what—in the star system itself.

*But the silver cords—the broken pattern there, all the
twists and knots—I've seen those before. I saw them on*
Night's-Beautiful-Daughter, *when I was watching what the
Professor did, five hundred years ago.*

She heard herself telling the LDF officers, "Search here,"
and felt her hand rise to point at something in the tank. The
cords, the important ones, the ones she had seen before,
drifted farther apart. She heard herself saying, "Search
here," and pointing to a different place, and saw them twist.
Over and over she pointed to different places, telling the
LDF officers where to search, while currents of warmth and
freezing cold washed over her, and she watched the cords
move.

One last time she spoke and pointed; the warm currents
that flowed around her rose and burned like fire; and the silver cords twisted, caught, and wove themselves back into
the pattern as she had seen it before, when it reached completion.

So few threads to mend the universe, she thought. *But
enough, if they are willing.*

She opened her eyes. The last "search here" had barely
left her mouth—she could still feel the breath of it moving
past her lips—and her hand was pointing at the holotank.
Master Kemni looked disgruntled; Lieutenant Vinhalyn and
the LDF officers looked pleased; and nobody was regarding

her with any more suspicion than Adepts got in the normal course of things.

I'm safe, she thought. *I hope.*

"Is this the first time I spoke?" she asked.

"Yes, Mistress," one of the LDF officers replied. Already they were busy working with the tactical computers and the navicomps and the bright new lights glowing in the holovid tank.

"Ah," she said.

Then she staggered, and had to catch herself on a chair before she fell, because the silver cords were back—not just in the tank this time, but in the room around her, like a net, even though her eyes were wide open. Someone else was pulling on the cords, ripping apart the pattern she had mended by her words and actions.

Magework.

The indictment echoed in her mind—but it was not Llannat Hyfid who pronounced it; it was the adversary, the one who kept and guarded the ships on the other side.

Magework and the hand of a Magelord.

"I'll be damned."

Slip of printout flimsy in hand, Beka left the *'Hammer'*s empty cockpit behind her and headed for the common room. She was looking for Nyls Jessan—failing him, LeSoit would do—but she didn't find either one. Instead she almost ran into her brother and Klea Santreny, who were practicing with their staves in the small bit of open space between the dining table and the acceleration couches.

She waved the flimsy at her brother.

"Put that thing down, Owen, and listen to this: 'To Beka Rosselin-Metadi, Domina of Lost Entibor and so forth and so forth, the Right Honorable Jervas, Baronet D'Rugier, requests the favor of your presence as guest of honor and so forth and so forth'. . . do you know what this is?"

Owen grounded his staff and reached out a hand for the flimsy. "It sounds straightforward enough," he said after looking it over. "Somebody wants you to attend a party."

"The commodore of the Mageworlds Patrol Fleet—

what's left of the Mageworlds Patrol Fleet—wants me to attend a party." Beka flung herself down into one of the chairs by the common-room table and frowned at the toes of her boots. "Wants me to be guest of honor at a party, which is worse. And I need to talk to him, so I can't wiggle out of it. Damn, but I hate social occasions!"

Her brother ignored her complaints. He'd always been able to keep his thoughts to himself when she was in a bad mood—unlike Ari, who never could resist the opportunity to scold her for unseemly behavior.

This time, Owen merely raised a curious eyebrow and asked, "When is this affair of the commodore's?"

"Tomorrow afternoon. He isn't wasting any time." She lifted her eyes again and glanced from Owen to Klea. "You're invited too, you know. It says, 'and entourage,' which as far as I can tell means everybody on board the 'Hammer except Tarveet, and I'm not telling the commodore about him."

Klea looked nervous. "I don't—we didn't have Baronets or anything like that on Nammerin. I wouldn't fit in."

"Yes, you would," said Owen firmly. "An apprentice in the Guild is anybody's equal, by definition. And the apprentice of the Master of the Guild is somewhat more than that."

Beka couldn't tell whether Klea believed the exhortation or not. She was too busy staring at her brother to notice.

"You told me she was your apprentice, not Master Ransome's. So what's this 'Master of the Guild' nonsense?"

"I was going to tell you, Bee." His hazel eyes took on a shadowed expression. "When I . . . call it 'found' . . . Master Ransome, I was hoping to claim my staff and end my apprenticeship. He gave me the staff and mastery for the asking. He gave me the Guild as well, though I didn't ask for that."

"You've got to be kidding. Master Ransome loves the Guild so much he practically takes it into bed with him at night. Why the hell would he give it away to you?"

"For safety," Owen said. His voice was low, almost a whisper. "When I found him, he was a prisoner somewhere among the Mages."

"Hell. I always thought he was like Dadda—too damned sneaky for anybody to catch." Beka felt her eyes stinging, and made haste to change the subject. "If you're going to be convincing as the Master of the Guild, you'll have to wear something a bit better than spacer's coveralls."

Owen shrugged. "We do what we can with what we've got."

"Waycross has plenty of custom tailors," she said. "They aren't cheap, though; if you need money, take some out of *Warhammer*'s petty cash box."

He shook his head. "I don't need—"

"Yes, you do," she said. "Trick yourselves out in the fanciest Adept rigs you can put together. This is Waycross, remember—there's no telling who you might wind up having to impress."

It had been too long, sus-Airaalin reflected, since he had last put on the mask and robes of his Circle. He had spent too much time, of late, in playing the Grand Admiral, and too little in the vision and meditation that were a Magelord's proper occupation. Today, at least, would see him working to redress the oversight.

He settled the mask into position over his face, the better to free his inner sight from peripheral distractions, and strode out of his quarters. When he reached the flagship's meditation chamber, he found three of his fellow-Mages gathered there already, kneeling around the white tiled circle in the middle of the black floor, facing inward and unmoving. He didn't disturb them, though as First of the Circle he had the right to call upon their combined strength in time of need. Their task was too important: they labored now in the steady work of binding up the ragged traces of the present universe, in order to provide luck and guidance to the fleet.

Instead, he took a place on the periphery of the circle, closed his eyes, and sought the inner peace which came from a meditation brought to completion. The warm feeling came upon him, and he opened his mind to the flow and movement of power in the universe.

This part of space was wild and untamed; power here

flowed in unruly disorder, untended by the careful Magework that made the homeworlds into places of beauty to the inner eye. The Adepts liked it so, as if the chaotic movement mirrored—or perhaps nourished—something essential that lay within their cold and solitary nature. He could feel them at work here, in this system, not so many as at Galcen, but a nest of them just the same, a danger to the pattern he and his Circle had been weaving so painstakingly and so long.

He looked for the silver threads, and found them. They were knotted and threatened by the strain, like a tangle-flower hedge that had gone too long without the care of a gardener.

Seek deeper, urged the inner voice that had always guided his visions—sometimes it sounded to him like the voice of his old teacher, who had died in the time of the Breaking of Circles. *Seek the true knowledge.*

He sank further into the visionary state, letting his mind shift and turn until he saw things from a different angle, one that showed him the snarled threads as a tangle-flower hedge in sober truth, a thicket of vines taller than his head, bristling in all directions with wicked black thorns. But instead of the riotous overgrowth of red and white blossoms that should have clothed the tangle-flower's prickly skeleton with living beauty, there was nothing except a few withered buds.

No light, he thought, *no air. The flowers smothered before they were ever properly alive.*

Without the correct tools, the task of making this place right would be long and hard—and doomed to failure. He needed to find a billhook to prune away the old growth and make room for the new. Still, in the presence of such maimed beauty there was nothing for it but to do what he could. Gently, sus-Airaalin began to untwist and straighten the thorns so that they no longer choked each other in their upward search for light.

The work was daunting and slow, and there were so many thorns, extending beyond his reach into the tangle and above his head. He labored without ceasing for a long time,

with the sweat trickling down his back and the tangle-
flower vines pricking and stabbing at his palms with their
subtle poison, until he came without warning upon a place
where someone had already been at work among the
thorns—first putting them in order, then overlaying another
pattern, so that a casual glance would see only random disarray.

He stopped.

Magework, he thought. *Magework, and the hand of a
Magelord.*

The pattern was a deep one, extending back beyond his
reach into the hedge. He looked deeper. There in the midst
of the vines and stalks was a scarlet bird of an unfamiliar
species, staring at him with an unblinking gaze. He stared
back. There seemed to be no way that the bird could have
come there, no way in or out among the long thorns.

I must grasp what I would have.

He pushed his arm into the tangle, toward the bird. The
thorns tore his sleeve and pierced his skin, the scratches
burning like fire. He touched the feathered creature, grasped
it, and pulled it forth. But when he opened his hand, there
was no bird, only the desiccated body of one. It crumbled
as he held it, and the bright feathers drifted to the ground at
his feet.

He looked again where the bird had been, and saw what
it had hidden: a tangle-flower, blooming and fragrant, dew-
sparkled.

Exhaustion claimed him, and weakness from the poison
of the thorns. His eyes drifted shut on the vision of the
white flower. When they opened again, he was in the meditation chamber, and Mael Taleion was waiting respectfully
only a few paces away.

"My lord," said Taleion. "Do you need my aid?"

He shook his head. "No, Mael—though the offer does me
great honor."

The Grand Admiral rose to his feet. He felt tired and
weakened after the struggle with the thorns; the refreshment
he had counted on finding in his meditations still eluded
him.

"Something troubles me, Mael."

"Tell me, my lord."

"I felt an adversary at work in the GYfferan system. Not an Adept, but one of our own, and it is one whom I do not know."

On board UDC (ex-RSF) *Fezrisond*, Admiral Vallant frowned irritably at the brown-uniformed officer who stood beside his desk. He'd never liked the idea of having an Eraasian liaison stationed permanently aboard his ship, but his arrangement with Grand Admiral sus-Airaalin and the Mageworlds Resurgency had been specific on the matter.

He liked even less the fact that his unwelcome liaison officer had what he did not—a direct comm link through Ophel to the Mageworlds warfleet. Up to now, however, with hi-comms throughout the rest of the galaxy either down or spotty, the link had been more useful than not.

That situation, Vallant reflected, was beginning to change.

He laid down the clipboard and its slip of printout flimsy. "Suppose," he said, "that this message never reached Infabede."

"Admiral, Lord sus-Airaalin charged me with delivering all his messages—nothing more. I am unable to speculate." The Eraasian paused. "The link through Ophel remains open, however."

It would, Vallant thought sourly. *I should have taken care of you* and *the link when I had the chance.*

But the time for that would have been at the start of the grand operation, while the Mageworlders were still making their push toward Galcen, and he'd been busy then with problems of his own. An unexpected mutiny by the fighter pilots aboard his own flagship had been easily quashed, but it had taken away his attention at a crucial moment.

"Tell your admiral," he said to the liaison, "that since the Gyfferans are proving too much for him, and since he has asked me, as one ally to another, to provide assistance, I will be glad to do so."

The Eraasian bowed. "Admiral, I will convey your message to Lord sus-Airaalin with all dispatch," he said, and left the office. Admiral Vallant, still frowning, watched him go, then signaled for his aide.

"Did you get all that?" Vallant asked the aide as soon as that officer appeared.

"The whole thing. Per your instructions."

"Good. Then you know where we're going next."

"The timing's not so good," the aide said. "But the target's a good one—Gyffer was on the list anyway."

"I don't like having to tackle it with the damned Mages already there. Let sus-Airaalin get one good look at the Gyfferan system and he'll decide that it's exactly what he needs to complete his own collection."

"We could get lucky," the aide said. "The Magish commander wants us to do the farspace work, and something like that isn't too strenuous if it's done right. Our people will still be fresh when Gyffer and the Eraasians have finished mauling each other into a state of exhaustion."

"Luck's damned undependable," said Vallant. "If we want everything to work out in our favor, it's going to take something more than that."

III. Innish-Kyl: Country House of Adelfe Aneverian
Gyffer: Night's-Beautiful-Daughter

COMMODORE GIL had to admit that this time, Lieutenant Jhunnei had outdone herself. He'd always known that Adelfe Aneverian, Hereditary Chairman of Perpayne, had a vacation estate on the seacoast of Innish-Kyl's southern temperate zone. But he'd never thought that the Hereditary Chairman—in his role as one of the silent partners in Gil's privateering enterprise—might lend the fleet his summertime getaway in order to impress Domina Beka Rosselin-Metadi.

Jhunnei had not only thought about it, she'd asked; and as a result the vast acres of manicured lawns and artfully natural woods and thickets were decked out as if for a summer fair. The thick, greenish-blue ground cover crunched faintly underneath Gil's booted feet, and its bruised leaves gave out a subtle spicy odor. Ornamental lanterns, some in colored paper and others in glass and metal, hung from the wide-spreading tree limbs that overshadowed the garden paths.

The glow cubes inside the lanterns gave, as yet, only enough illumination to point up the delicate structures that contained them. The sun had not yet sunk below the seaward horizon, and the sky beyond the force field was a smooth, powdery blue.

Gil had seen the controls for that force field, housed in one of the gardener's sheds along with the pruning shears and the soil-testing kits. He'd recognized the model as a civilian version of one of the Space Force's heavy-duty set-ups, capable of going within a nanosecond from a screen against light rain and small annoying insects to the functional equivalent of a starship's shields. Adelfe Aneverian, it was clear, believed in safety even more fervently than he believed in gracious living.

The guests had been arriving since late afternoon. All of them wore formal dress—although given Lieutenant Jhunnei's final guest list, "formal" tonight meant anything from Space Force full dress blues to a Waycross free-spacer's gaudiest spidersilk and velvet. Or no clothing at all: Merrolakk the Selvaur had shown up wearing a total-body paint job, its multicolored loops and whorls accented with glittering faceted stones and patches of gold and silver leaf.

Gil, for his part, wore his Ovredisan court-formal garb, with the live-steel sword and dagger made for him by the 'Pavo's machine shop. The original set, of light metal without a functional edge, seemed inappropriate these days. After all, some of his more distant ancestors had been robber barons in truth, back before Ovredis had grown up and turned respectable.

He'd given the other live-steel pair—along with an outfit of best-quality free-spacer's gear from one of the local custom tailors—to his guest for the evening, Doctor Inesi syn-Tavaite. Lieutenant Jhunnei and the 'Pavo's chief master-at-arms had made nervous noises about security, but Gil had silenced them both, saying, "I told her she had a place here, and I want her to believe it. Besides—where the hell is she going to run to, half a hemisphere away from the spaceport?"

Not that Doctor syn-Tavaite showed any sign of trying to run. She kept close to Gil, taking an occasional sip from her long-stemmed glass of weak punch and watching the other guests with wide, nervous eyes.

"There are *Adepts* here," she muttered over the rim of her glass. "You didn't say anything about Adepts."

Gil followed her gaze across the expanse of blue-green lawn to the young man and woman in unadorned formal black.

"The Master of the Guild and his apprentice," he said. "They're with the Domina."

And how she *got them,* he added mentally, *is an interesting question. Especially since the last time I saw Owen Rosselin-Metadi he was still an apprentice on Galcen.*

syn-Tavaite didn't seem calmed by the information. "You don't think this is a coincidence, do you, my lord?"

"Call me Commodore," said Gil absently. "Or Jervas. It's my name. . . . No, I don't think it's a coincidence. I have an aide who keeps on telling me there's no such thing as luck or coincidence, and I'm starting to believe her."

"Do you mind if I stay away from them?"

"Whatever you like, Doctor. You're here to enjoy yourself—though I wouldn't mind hearing your impression of this affair after it's over. A fresh perspective can be useful sometimes."

"Thank you, Commodore." syn-Tavaite looked about the crowded grounds. "But where is the Domina? I don't see her."

Gil craned his neck a little. "There. By that big tree with the silver-gilt lanterns. She's the one with the tiara."

He wasn't surprised that syn-Tavaite had missed Beka Rosselin-Metadi the first time she'd looked in that direction. For reasons that Gil couldn't begin to figure out, the Domina had come to the party dressed in simple if exquisitely tailored free-spacer's gear—shirt, jacket, trousers, and boots—combined with formal braids and Entibor's Iron Crown. The two men with her also wore free-spacer's garb, though Nyls Jessan had chosen to replace the usual jacket with a wide-sleeved Khesatan dinner robe of coppery brocade lined in cream-colored satin. All three of them, after the free-spacer fashion, had shown up armed with blasters.

"That man," said syn-Tavaite. "Next to the Domina. Who is he?"

"The tall blond? That, believe it or not, is the General of the Armies of Entibor—Consort to the Domina. And trust me, Doctor, he's not nearly as harmless as it pleases him to look."

Tavaite was shaking her head. "No, no, Commodore. The other one."

Gil looked again at the dark, muscular man in the plain clothes. "Ah. According to the guest list, he's the acting captain of *Warhammer*. Ignaceu LeSoit."

"LeSoit," said syn-Tavaite, pronouncing the word as if it didn't fit her mouth properly. Her accent, with the strange diphthongs and elongated vowels, seemed stronger than ever. "Ignaceu LeSoit."

Owen Rosselin-Metadi, Master of the Adepts' Guild, stood under the cool leaves of a spreading gnarlybark tree, his apprentice by his side, looking out over the grounds of Adelfe Aneverian's vacation estate and the people gathered there. No one had walked up to them to make introductions, and Owen had not approached anyone on his own.

They fear the Adepts, Owen thought bitterly, *and they blame us, too. "We trusted you to protect us from the Mages, and see, now the Mages are come."* He looked at the glass of pale pink liquid in his hand as if someone else were holding it. *They're right about that. I did everything I could to save them, for almost ten years of my life, but everything wasn't quite enough.*

Then, through the crowd, Owen saw someone at last moving toward them: a young man, his plain clothing oddly conspicuous among the glitter and braid of Space Force dress uniforms and the free-spacers' high-spirited finery. He wore the drab coverall of a working spacer, and carried an Adept's staff in his hand.

"Do you see him?" Owen asked Klea.

"Yes," she said. Like Owen, she was dressed in formal blacks, the best that the custom tailors of Waycross could fabricate on short notice. The formal garments weren't often given to an apprentice—so many never finished the full path—but Klea was progressing well, and Owen expected

that he would be giving her the choice of mastery soon
enough.

That's wartime for you, he thought. *Training that should
take years given months, and the new-made master left on
her own to live or die.*

The stranger approached closer, and Owen felt a shock of
recognition: the face, the eyes; this was himself, only younger, as he had been when he worked for Master Ransome.
But he'd kept himself an apprentice all that time, for the
Guild's sake, and this one plainly had not; whatever else the
stranger might be, he was also a full Adept and his own
master.

"Owen Rosselin-Metadi," the stranger said. "Come with
me. You've wasted too much time."

"Klea—" Owen began.

"Yes," she said. "I hear him too."

"Both of you," the other said. "Come on. We have to find
a quiet place."

Together the three walked apart from the main crush of
the party, into the wilder depths of the vast garden, away
from the sight of the manor house and the noise of the sea.

"What shall I call you?" Owen said.

"My name isn't important," the other man said. He
seemed amused by the question. "Call me one who wishes
you well. My home's long gone, and I travel about."

"All right," Owen said. "Where are we going?"

"Just a little farther, to where there is peace. Tell me, apprentice," the stranger said to Klea, "can you guard us?"

"I'll try."

"Not given to prophecy, eh? But you have the gift of seeing, I can tell." He halted. "Here's a good spot, I think."

They had removed to a small glade, away from the gravel
paths, where the ground cover was thick and soft. The
noises of the party faded away into the background.

"Lie here beside me," the stranger said. He stretched
himself out on the plushy blue-green lawn. Owen hesitated
briefly, then lay down next to him, still holding his staff. No
sooner had he done so, it seemed to Owen, than the stranger
was standing above him and offering a hand up. Owen

looked down, and saw both himself and the other man still lying on the ground side by side. A few feet away, Klea stood guard, her staff grounded on the springy turf.

"Where are we going?" Owen asked.

"Where you went once before."

"Where I—?"

"Think!" snapped the other, sounding almost angry. "You went out of body, once, seeking across the galaxy for Master Ransome, and you came to a place you did not expect. Come there again."

"So much," Beka muttered under her breath, "for the idea of having a small private conference. I haven't been at a party with this many people since the first time we saw Ebenra D'Caer."

"Smile," advised Jessan. "Dazzle them with your charisma and convince them that you're really alive."

"I am smiling," Beka said. "And who the hell besides the Domina of Entibor would want to wear this damned tiara? It's giving me a headache again."

"There's a lesson in that, as the Professor would have said, if you care to dig it out," Jessan commented. He snagged a glass of punch from a passing waiter and presented it to her with a flourish. "Here. Try this."

"It's good for headaches?"

"No, but it'll help make you feel at home."

Beka tasted the punch, and smiled—properly, no canine teeth showing—at a passing Selvaur in flamboyant scale-paint and body-enamel. "I ran away from home. Parties like this were part of the reason why."

"I can see your point," put in LeSoit. "I think I'll go check out some of the buffet tables and listen to what D'Rugier's free-spacers have to say."

"Good idea," Beka said. "Have fun. Anything interesting comes up, let me know."

She felt a twinge of envy as *Warhammer*'s number-two gunner strolled off into the crowd of guests. "If there's any fun going on here tonight," she commented to Jessan,

"Ignac's heading to where it's going to be. Free-spacers know how to enjoy life while they've got it."

"Not, alas, one of the luxuries afforded to royalty," said Jessan. "I found the Space Force more to my liking ... speaking of which, it's time to circulate, and hope that eventually we come, as if by accident, to our host."

"Duty before pleasure," Beka said. "Let's wander."

They started across the lawn toward the area where Commodore Gil walked next to a stocky, dark-haired woman. There were more lanterns hanging from the trees along the way, and dense bushes clipped into fantastic shapes at once wild and artificial.

"This is certainly a spectacular piece of real estate," Beka commented in an undertone. "It's a long way from Waycross."

"In several senses of the word," said Jessan. "Generally speaking, the sort of people who can afford to live like this don't much care for rough company."

"I wonder where the commodore got the use of it from, then."

"Diplomatic connections, probably. Wealth on Ovredis migrated out of the old nobility generations ago."

Beka raised her eyebrows. "You mean he joined the Space Force to get a regular paycheck, just like everybody else?"

"That's my guess."

"Good," she said. "I hate public-spirited dilettantes."

Jessan put his hand over his heart in a theatrical gesture. "My lady, you wound me to the quick!"

She stopped and looked at him with a sober expression. "Sorry, Nyls ... what was it, the 'public-spirited' bit?"

He shrugged. "People say that Khesat's the only planet in the civilized galaxy where the natives don't have secret vices. But if they did, 'public spirit' would probably be one of them."

"Mmm. And is it yours?"

"Not even a little," he said, with transparent insincerity. "I'm doing this for the simpleminded amusement it affords

me—and for Baronet D'Rugier's excellent buffet tables.
Lots of spun-sugar fripperies: always a good sign."

"Simpleminded, hah." She smiled at him in spite of herself. "You're as naturally twisty as a back road, and you've
been eyeing Jervas Gil ever since we got here. I'll bet you
five Mandeynan marks you've got something on your mind
right now besides canapes and small talk."

"Caught in my little white lies," Jessan said. "Is there no
end to the shame I bring on my family? I want to get a
closer look at the lady who's standing there with him."

"The nervous-looking one?"

"That's her. She's the only person here who doesn't look
like either a Space Forcer or an interstellar hard case."

"Oh. And what does that make me, then?"

"Domina of Entibor," he said. "And excellent company."

They live well in the Adept-worlds, Ignaceu LeSoit
thought. He surveyed the buffet table and selected two
slices of chilled winemelon and a cup of berries and cream.
Even when they're losing.

The winemelon was crisp and purple-fleshed. Its heady
fragrance and tart-sweet taste reminded him of summer
neiath fruit, back home on Eraasi. LeSoit ate it slowly, sa-
voring the memories as much as the present flavor. The year
before sus-Airaalin and the Resurgency had claimed him, he
and his cousins had picked *neiath* in a highland orchard all
during the long, hazy hot-weather days—eating the ripest
ones, the ones too heavy with juice to survive even a little
while in the close quarters of a woven basket, and packing
up the rest for market.

"Captain LeSoit?"

He came back from the daydream in an unsettling rush,
and looked up to see a woman in Space Force uniform
standing a foot or so away. She wore a lieutenant's insignia,
plus a loop of gold braid around one shoulder—she was
somebody's aide, then, and probably more important than
she looked. There was a speculative expression in her mild
grey eyes that made LeSoit uneasy; he thought that she

must have been watching him for some time before she spoke.

"Lieutenant—?" he said.

"Jhunnei. Flag Aide to Commodore Gil. That's Baronet D'Rugier, as you civilians say." She paused. "Captain LeSoit, I have a favor to ask of you."

"If I can help," he said. The mention of favors put him on edge, but there was no graceful way out—and his own need for information was strong enough to keep him talking.

"You speak Eraasian."

Her statement came unexpectedly, sounding flat enough by itself to compel belief. LeSoit blinked and tried hard to look monolingual.

"I don't think—" he began.

"Our records on you are sketchy," she said, "especially with the Central DataNet down hard and bleeding after the fall of Galcen. But I've managed to correlate a few bits and pieces. For one thing, you *weren't* part of the *Warhammer*'s crew when she passed through the Net. You were, it seems, gainfully employed on the other side of the border. On Eraasi."

"Legal stuff," he said. "Bodyguard work. I got homesick, though, so when *Warhammer* came into port I picked up a free-spacer's berth."

"You do speak Eraasian, then." She didn't wait for him to explain that he'd gotten along by using sign language. She wouldn't have believed him, anyway. "Can you read it as well?"

No point in lying any longer, he thought. *If I say yes, I've at least got a chance at seeing whatever's making her look for an interpreter.*

"Some," he admitted. "What have you got?"

"Captured documents." She glanced over at the shorter, darker-haired woman who was standing by Commodore Gil. "We've got a native speaker on tap already, but I'd like to get a cross-check from another party. Safety first and all that."

"And all that," he said. "Are you saying you want me to look at them right now?"

"I have copies waiting," she said. "In Aneverian's library. If you could come with me?"

Magework and the hand of a Magelord.

The accusation lingered in Llannat's mind all the way back from LDF main headquarters to Telabryk Field, making her silent and restless. When she got out of the hovercar, she didn't go into the Space Force building, but stood outside, undecided, for several minutes.

I need to talk with Ari about this, she thought.

But Ari was on duty right now—well, so was she, technically, but nobody on Gyffer seemed to know what to do with an Adept outside of the occasions when they were asking for miracles on short notice. She couldn't very well haul Ari away from whatever he was working on, just because she needed something solid to lean against until her legs quit shaking.

He's a human being, not some kind of stone wall. He deserves a better job in life than spending all his time propping up the rest of us.

She hesitated a moment longer. Then she wandered off along the perimeter of the Space Force installation, skirting the still mostly deserted buildings until she came to where *Night's-Beautiful-Daughter* rested on the field. She went up the *Daughter*'s ramp and through the passageways to the cockpit. As usual, all the Deathwing's locks and security checkpoints answered to Llannat's ID without question. She and the Space Force might not consider the vessel hers, but the *Daughter* clearly had its own opinion.

When she reached the cockpit she sat down in the pilot's seat. The bodies of the pilot and the copilot had long since been removed from the compartment, of course, and the message on the viewscreen—alien characters inscribed in blood—had been scrubbed away without a trace. The images, though, remained fixed in her mind, as did the words themselves:

" 'Find the Domina,' " she quoted. " 'Tell her what thou

hast seen.' Good idea. Really good idea. Except everybody knows that the Domina is dead."

She'd thought so, too—for her, as for most citizens of the Republic, "the Domina" had meant Perada Rosselin, the last ruler of living Entibor. She'd forgotten that the title was a hereditary one, passed down from antiquity in the maternal line. And in spite of what most of the galaxy had for a long time believed, Perada's only daughter was a long way from being dead.

But Beka wasn't using the title . . . I didn't see how "the Domina" could possibly mean her, but now she's turned up on the holovid news using the title, Iron Crown and all.

So what am I supposed to do? Easy, right: find her and tell her—I don't know what I'm supposed to tell her. The Professor never said.

Thinking about the problem made Llannat's head ache. Trying to solve it was too much like what she'd done with the silver threads, back at LDF headquarters: so many things to be pulled together and tied up properly before the pattern could be completed and the universe made whole.

"Damn the Professor, anyway," she muttered aloud. "It was his project. Let *him* come back and fix it."

Not even the Professor, however, could manage something like that. Instead, he'd done the best that anyone could, and found a student who could carry on the work.

Which means you. Llannat Hyfid, Adept. Or whatever it is that you currently are.

Llannat sighed and pushed back tendrils of loose hair from around her forehead with the heels of her hands. She'd wasted too much time already on chewing her fingernails and wondering what to do. It was time to act. Find the Domina first—go to Suivi Point herself if need be—then see what other surprises had been left to her in the Professor's unwritten will.

She stood up; but before she could leave the cockpit to go in search of Lieutenant Vinhalyn, Vinhalyn found her instead.

"Ah, Mistress Hyfid," he said. "There you are. I was

about to send out search parties. We have orders. We're going to be part of a task force out in Gyfferan farspace."

"I was about to go looking for you, too. We need to leave here before the fighting gets any worse: I have to find the Domina on Suivi Point."

Vinhalyn shook his head regretfully. "I'm afraid not. We're all under oath to the LDF, and we'll be launching as soon as we've gotten the crew together and been briefed. But don't think your work today wasn't useful, or that it wasn't appreciated. It was through your location that we've gotten our primary search zone."

Llannat didn't say anything. She was waiting for the sensation of overriding urgency that more than once in the past had impelled her to leave one place for another without waiting for formal orders.

Nothing, so far. Maybe the universe wants me in Gyffer farspace after all.

At least for a while.

Beka and Jessan ran into Captain Yevil before they could—accidentally, of course—encounter Commodore Gil. The Space Force captain was standing near the buffet tables, finishing a glass of the sparkling pink punch and gazing intently across the lawn at Adelfe Aneverian's manor house. As the others approached, she shrugged and turned to face them instead.

"I don't know where they get this stuff," she said, indicating the glass of punch. "But everybody from one side of the galaxy to the other serves it at parties. If I'd wanted to drink water I'd have brought some of my own."

"Treat yourself to a night in the port after this is over," Beka advised. "What you can't buy over the counter in Waycross probably can't be drunk." She glanced toward the manor house. "What's going on in there? Ghosts at the upstairs windows?"

Yevil shook her head. "Not that I can see. But the commodore's aide went inside with Captain LeSoit about half an hour ago."

"Damnation," said Beka. "He knows better than that. How did she manage to reel him in?"

"I didn't catch most of it," Yevil said. "But there was something about him joining *Warhammer*'s crew on Eraasi, and helping her out with something or other. Ignac' didn't look all that pleased with the idea, but he went along anyway."

"*Hell* and damnation. If the bitch thinks she can get away with blackmailing my people—"

"Gently," murmured Nyls Jessan. "Gently, all. She's probably just fishing for local intelligence about what ships he saw in port before he left, the political sentiments of the average Eraasian working stiff, and so forth and so on."

Beka's lips tightened. "If she wants to debrief anybody off one of my ships, she can damned well go through me."

"We can take it up with the commodore later," Jessan said. "In the meantime, since she already has Gentlesir LeSoit—"

"No she doesn't," Yevil cut in. "There they come back out."

Beka looked over at the manor house in time to see LeSoit and Jhunnei stepping down from the portico onto the graveled drive. Jhunnei's manner, as she abandoned LeSoit and faded away into the crowd, was bland and unreadable. LeSoit stood looking after her and frowning.

He was still frowning a minute or two later, when he approached the trio waiting by the buffet tables.

"Captain," he said to Beka. "If I could speak with you in private for a moment—?"

"No problem," she said, and allowed herself to be drawn away out of earshot. "What's up, Ignac'?"

"There is something you must know. Before the war began, the Mages used replicant technology to put at least one hidden agent in place in the Republic."

"Go on."

"The agent was your father's aide."

"Gil?"

"No. His successor."

"Son of a bitch. If I find him—"

"Her."

"—her, she's dead meat. But I can't do anything about it now. What else?"

"I need you and your friend Jessan to go have a little chat with Baronet D'Rugier."

"We were moving that way anyhow," Beka said. "Tell me what you're up to and I'll think about heading there a little faster."

"I don't know if—"

"*Tell*, Ignac'."

He sighed. "All right. Lieutenant Jhunnei asked me to come with her because she thought I might be able to help with some captured documents written in Eraasian. I can read the language, more or less—I lived there quite a while when I was working for D'Caer—and now I want to see if I speak it well enough to ask Commodore Gil's lady friend a couple of questions."

"Why her?" Beka demanded. "And why do you need Eraasian to do it?"

"Because she's the technician who made the replicant."

IV. Innish-Kyl: Country House of Adelfe Aneverian; *Warhammer*

So FAR, so good, Gil thought as he looked out across the formal garden at the motley assortment of people brought together in one place by Lieutenant Jhunnei's guest list. Doctor syn-Tavaite was still sticking close by him—probably because he represented the security of a familiar face in a noisy and variegated crowd, and one where she was very much a stranger.

It's a fine party, just the same. Nobody's drunk, and nobody's gotten into a fight with anybody else, and the food is holding out.

You still have to talk with the Domina, though, he reminded himself. *That was your whole reason for throwing this party in the first place.*

Gil straightened his shoulders and altered course slightly, so that his apparently casual stroll about the grounds would bring him into the Domina's orbit. He wasn't looking forward to this conversation, or to the task of convincing the Domina that she ought to hand over the flotilla she'd gathered—by whatever means—during her sojourn on Suivi Point. Nothing in Gil's previous encounters with Beka

Rosselin-Metadi, either directly or at a distance, had given him cause to expect a smooth and rational discussion on that particular subject.

When he came a little closer to where Beka stood, he saw that she was already halfway to losing her temper over something. Her mouth was closed hard, and her blue eyes had a dangerous glint in them. When she spoke, however, her words were unexceptional.

"D'Rugier—how pleasant to run into you. The gardens are beautiful at this time of year."

Gil made a half-bow. "My lady. You provide, as always, an ornament to nature's beauty."

"Thank you," said Beka. "But we have to talk, and not just about the herbaceous borders."

"As it pleases you." Gil turned to syn-Tavaite. "I'm afraid I'll have to abandon you for a few minutes, Doctor. The Domina and I have some private matters which require discussion."

He drew Beka aside. *Might as well go for the direct approach,* he decided after a moment of intense consideration. *She's in that kind of mood anyway.*

"My lady," he said. "I was happy to learn you were still alive and free; and when you arrived, not alone but with a small flotilla—"

She cut him off with a sharp gesture of one hand. "Later. What's this I hear about your tame Mageworlder switching a replicant agent for my father's personal aide?"

"Doctor syn-Tavaite," Gil said, "is a prisoner of war. And to the best of my knowledge, her role in replicating Commander Quetaya was limited to the creation of a duplicate body."

"The story's true, then?"

He sighed. "The information I have—it would seem so."

"Hell, death, and damnation . . . no wonder my warning message to Galcen got held up for so long that it didn't do any good."

Her voice was light, almost flippant, but Gil had seen that expression on her face before, and it promised trouble. Violent, large-scale trouble, if the past was any indication.

"There's also some good news, my lady," he said, before the pause could draw out too long. "Or at least, a strong rumor of good news."

"I could use some good news right now. What is it?"

"Your father is quite possibly alive and fighting. A fleet of Space Force vessels using his name in their bridge-to-bridge chatter attacked Mageworlds units on Galcen, then made a run-to-jump for somewhere in the Gyfferan sector."

"Now *that*," said Beka, "changes everything considerably. Are you planning to link up with him?"

"The situation remains fluid, my lady." Gil had first learned the virtues of that particular phrase during his tour as the General's aide; with the right shade of inflection, it could be extended to cover anything from imminent military action to next week's menu in the officers' mess. "But since it also appears that the Mageworlders have decided to make Gyffer their next target—"

"I can read the answer if it's printed large enough. You're heading for Gyffer and you want my ships."

"I wish you to place them under my command . . . yes."

She looked at him for a long moment without saying anything. Then she sighed. "Commodore, I have a headache. Parties give them to me, official parties give them to me even worse, and I am in no state to discuss who's going to give what to whom and still be polite about it."

"My lady," said Gil, "I deeply regret the necessity—"

"I deeply regret your regret. Look, I have to get out of here before the Iron Crown pinches the top of my skull off. Let me make a nice official guest-of-honor-type departure and then slip back in again incognito. It'll make talking business a whole lot easier."

LeSoit waited until Beka and Commodore Gil were out of earshot before turning to the Eraasian woman Gil had addressed as Doctor syn-Tavaite.

"They'll be talking for a while," he said. "Let me show you around the buffet tables. Some of the stuff is a bit strange-looking if you haven't traveled much on this side of the Net. But the winemelon is very good."

She accompanied him without protest. Nyls Jessan raised a curious eyebrow at being thus abandoned—*How much, Lesoit wondered, does our Khesatan friend suspect?*—but said nothing. LeSoit and syn-Tavaite made their way over to the buffet tables.

"Doctor," LeSoit said, as soon as talking became safe. He spoke in Eraasian. "Are you being treated well?"

"The baronet treats me with all honor," she replied in the same language. "But you—who are you, and why do you ask?"

"Iekkenat Lisaiet. A friend, and one of those who wish for peace."

syn-Tavaite laughed; a bit regretfully, LeSoit thought. "Then you're a man in the wrong time and the wrong place, Lisaiet. There's no peace left in the galaxy."

"The pattern may not be finished yet," he said. "Do you know Lord sus-Airaalin?"

"The Grand Admiral? I've heard of him. Everyone has."

"Some of us are bound to him." LeSoit paused. "Where do you stand, Doctor syn-Tavaite?"

She seemed to draw away a little. "It doesn't matter any longer," she said. "I am combat-sworn to Baronet D'Rugier."

"Damn," said LeSoit, in Galcenian. He'd lost the knack of profanity in his birth-tongue years ago, from lack of practice. "Somebody gave *him* some good advice, then."

"I do not know," she said, in the same language. "But we fought in the old style, and I was defeated."

LeSoit frowned. *That's the nobility for you, right down to the bone. She and the baronet must get along like a pair of long-lost cousins.* He switched back to Eraasian. "Couldn't you at least manage to get yourself honorably killed?"

"No," she replied. "I couldn't."

"You went out of body across the galaxy, seeking Master Ransome, and you came to a place you did not expect. Go there again."

Owen Rosselin-Metadi stood looking at the stranger. Not far away, his physical body lay outstretched on the ground beside that of the other, and Klea Santreny kept watch over them both.

"How?" Owen asked. He understood all too well what the other man was talking about: his out-of-body search for the master of the Guild. He'd found Errec Ransome before he was done, but not before going astray in time as well as space. "It was an accident the first time."

"This time it will not be. You were there before; seek yourself, and the others."

"Will you come with me?"

"As far as I may," said the other. "In ways that I can."

"Then I'll try it."

Owen allowed his mind to go blank and still, as he had done that night on Nammerin—a long time ago, it felt like, though he knew better—and plucked from out of the still-ness the point of light that had called to him once before. He took the dot of light and added another to it, and another and another, until a picture emerged, and from the picture, a whole world, and a single place in that world.

Home.

He stood on a flat surface open to the stars, full of shad-owy leaves and pale waxy flowers giving up their fragrance to the night: the rooftop terrace of his family's house in the Galcenian Uplands. Only his own point of vantage had changed, putting him at the south end of the terrace near the herbs and salad greens of the kitchen garden. The Domina, his mother, stood waiting among the flowers as before. And in a moment, her patience was rewarded.

At the other end of the garden, near the low parapet look-ing out to the north, the darkness thickened and seemed for a moment to become solid. A figure stepped forward out of the darkness, a muscular man somewhat under the medium height, with curly dark hair going to grey.

"My lady," he said. His Galcenian was fluent, but strongly accented. "It is good of you to meet with me."

Owen's mother smiled. "I gave up hoping for goodness long ago," she said. "I thought that justice would serve me well enough instead. But since it hasn't—my lord sus-Airaalin, let us talk."

"We're being watched."

"No, this place is secure."

"I think not."

The stranger began to walk away from where Owen stood watching, toward another spot. He looked down, then suddenly laughed. He reached and pulled up the furry shape of a tiny long-nosed kwoufer. *Uncle Hairy,* Owen thought with relief and amusement as he recognized the family pet. He'd lived so long away from his childhood home—first at the Retreat, and then all over the galaxy—that he'd forgotten the little creature's fondness for nocturnal wanderings.

A moment later, Perada laughed as well. "You don't need to worry about Uncle Hairy. He'll keep our secrets."

"So he shall," sus-Airaalin replied, still chuckling as he set the kwoufer loose again. "So he shall."

"To business, then," Perada said. "I will speak frankly, my lord sus-Airaalin: my foremost desire is to avoid another war. The last one was bad enough."

"There, we are in agreement," sus-Airaalin said. "But I want something other than a lack of war. We have had that for too long already. Now I want peace."

"Peace comes in many forms."

"And well I know it, my lady!" sus-Airaalin paused, seemingly to master his temper, then went on. "If your Adepts have their way, the only peace they will grant to my people is the peace of the grave."

Perada nodded gravely. "That thought has occurred to me as well. And if it had pleased me, I would not be talking with you now. Explain, then, my lord: what is this peace you want?"

"I want my people to live their own lives, free of occupation and alien governors," sus-Airaalin said at once. "I want the Mage-Circles to practice according to the old ways. And I want the merchants on the Eraasian side of the Gap Between to join as full partners in the commerce of the galaxy."

"That much seems reasonable," Perada said. "More to the point, enough time has passed that it may even be possible."

"I hope you are right, my lady," said sus-Airaalin. "Al-

ready, there are divisions—factions, if you will—among my
people. Advocates of peace, as I have described it to you,
and others whose despair has already led them elsewhere. In
essence, a war party. They have a great deal of power in the
homeworlds, since their goal is one that even the unsophis-
ticated can see and understand."

"You want my help to keep them at bay, then."

"Yes. I ask you to use your influence to lift the sanctions
on the homeworlds, so that a ruinous war won't be our only
choice. Give us by vote what we would otherwise take by
force."

Perada looked at him—her expression at that moment reminded Owen very much of his sister Beka. "Threats, my
lord?"

sus-Airaalin spread out empty hands. "Not from me. I tell
only what I fear to be true."

"I have to act in the best interest of the Republic," Perada
said. "My own preferences come, if anything, a distant second."

"Nothing I ask will do your worlds any harm. Only let
the vanquished in this last great war become members of
the Republic. We will live by your law if we can live as
your equals."

There was a long pause; then the Domina seemed to let
out a long sigh. "I will do it, my lord sus-Airaalin. On one
condition: I want you to swear yourself to me, personally. I
want the assurance that you are my man."

sus-Airaalin laughed briefly. "We have common goals.
There's no need for an oath."

"Nevertheless," said the Domina. "Swear to me."

"I come as a beggar to the rich man's door," sus-Airaalin
said. "I have no choice but to swear. But if I swear, you
must swear also. Among my people, such oaths go both
ways."

"Among mine also," said Perada. "Let us begin."

sus-Airaalin knelt and raised his hands palm to palm before him. Perada took his hands between her own.

"Do you swear," she said, "to be my man in all things,

to obey my orders and do my bidding, with your life, your fortune, and your hope?"

"My lady, do *you* swear to defend me in honor, to raise me up or cast me down according to merit, and to save my people?"

"I so swear," Perada said.

"I so swear," sus-Airaalin echoed.

Their voices filled Owen's mind ... *I so swear—I so swear—I so swear* ... reverberating while the night grew blacker and thicker around him, until he fell back into his body and opened his eyes under the force-dome of the party on Innish-Kyl.

Beka Rosselin-Metadi dropped the Iron Crown onto her bunk to put away later. Nobody was going to break into her cabin aboard *Warhammer* and carry anything off. The private landing field on Adelfe Aneverian's country estate was almost as safe as high orbit, and a good deal more convenient to the commodore's party.

She stripped off her clothes and let them lie on the cabin deckplates. All that stuff could wait for later, too. Next the formal braids came free, and after that, a brisk session with the colorbrush changed her hair from its natural pale yellow to a rather ordinary brown. She pulled the hair into a loose queue at the nape of her neck, tied with a black velvet ribbon.

Incognito, she reflected, was a handy thing. Taking on another persona might not fool anybody, but it did allow for more open and honest discussion—especially since custom demanded that no one admit to having penetrated the disguise. If she went back to Commodore Gil's party as Tarnekep Portree, then "Captain Portree" she would remain throughout the rest of the evening, even among those who knew the truth.

Beka went over to a section of her wardrobe that hadn't been touched since the outbreak of war. Item by item she pulled out the new garments: the ruffles and lace and red optical-plastic eye patch that changed her from the Domina of Lost Entibor into a Mandeynan gentleman of dubious ancestry and a taste for violence and low company.

She'd lived for a long time as Captain Portree. Some of his habits were probably going to be hers forever, like carrying a knife in a sheath up her sleeve and wearing a blaster in a tied-down holster on her hip. How much of the Mandeynan's personality had been hers to start with was something she preferred not to think about for very long—but even that had its uses.

Not a pleasant person, is Tarnekep Portree, she thought. *Makes a lot of people nervous. Maybe he'll keep the commodore far enough off balance that he won't ask for too much, or brace me enough that I don't end up handing over everything.*

Beka paused in placing the eye patch.

It never hurts, though, to get in a little practice first. And I've got just the person to try it on.

She put the patch in the pocket of her long-coat and drew the blaster. She left the captain's cabin and went to the berthing compartment that had been, since lifting from Suivi, a cell for Councillor Tarveet of Pleyver. The lock was keyed to her ID; she palmed it, and the door slid aside.

Tarveet was sitting on the bottom bunk. His clothes were torn and dirty—they'd been prime examples of fashionable tailoring, Beka remembered, when he wore them to grace her execution—and he'd gone long enough without a depilatory that his loose jaw was thick with stubble. Blaster in hand, she walked in and keyed open the binders that held his wrists.

"Come on out, you," she said. "I've let you slide for long enough. We're going to have a talk."

Without waiting for an answer, she slammed her weapon back into the holster, turned her back on him, and walked away. *If he jumps me, I can kill him. If I'm lucky, he'll jump me.* But nothing happened except that she heard, after a few seconds, the sounds of Tarveet's footsteps on the deckplates behind her as she made her way back to the *'Hammer*'s common room.

She took a seat there on one side of the scarred table, the

same place she'd sat on the night in Waycross when Errec Ransome gave her the news of her mother's death. She pointed at the chair opposite.

"Sit," she said. "Or not, your choice. There's cha'a over there in the galley if you're thirsty, but I'm damned if I'll get it for you."

Tarveet moved to stand by the chair, but he didn't sit down.

"To what do I owe the honor?"

"I want to talk to you," Beka replied, gazing at him steadily.

"Why?" He raised one hand in a tired-looking gesture, and let it fall. "We're past the point where either of us has anything to offer the other."

"Maybe. Maybe not. But you can tell me one thing right now for starters: why did you want me dead?"

"Don't flatter yourself." Tarveet sounded as weary as he looked. "I didn't want you dead. I wanted Pleyver to live. You, as a person, an individual, you're nothing. I wouldn't spend a half-ducat on you if you weren't a threat to Pleyver." He turned fully toward her and leaned forward. "Do you know what a war looks like? It isn't all pretty explosions and clean energy beams in space. It's stinking mud and starvation and pain and blood, and it's visited on the common people, the people who sit on the ground and try to get through one day at a time. They don't care who they pay taxes to—they just want to be alive to pay them. Look at you, Domina of Entibor. Where is Entibor now? Where are its people? Dead and damned. All through pride. Because your mother didn't want to lose her power. Power's what this is all about.

"I suppose you're going to kill me. No matter to me; everyone dies. But hundreds, thousands, millions dead before their time, all so some spoiled bitch can keep her power twenty minutes longer? That's too high a price. And you, with your silly broadcasts and disguises, you'll prolong a war and kill who knows how many more. A bad peace is better than a good war, my lady.

"Now if you'll excuse me, I'll find that cha'a that you talked about."

Tarveet turned and walked into the galley. Beka watched him go with a skeptical expression.

"You know," she said after he'd come back, "a few weeks ago I might have believed in your sincere desire for peace. You give a good speech, and I'll grant you that not everybody out there thinks that standing up to the Mages is a good idea. But feeding me to the beaky-boys—you can't tell me that idea was just good old Pleyveran boosterism at work."

"Perhaps not, then." There was, finally, a glint of malice in his expression as he added, "Perhaps I should have spent a little more money and taken your Consort first. With certain knowledge of his death you might have been open to reason and called off your charade."

"Not likely. The people who killed my mother—and tried to kill my brother Ari and tried to kill me—used Pleyver for a base of operations. That's when the war started. You must have known something was up. And you never let out a peep."

"Does that still bother you?"

"Three guesses. The first two don't count."

"So," he said. "Now we come to what I have that you want. You want to know what I know."

"That's right. Who else on the Republic side of things was part of the plan? There was Nivolm the Rolny and Ebenra d'Caer—but they were from the neutral worlds. There must have been people inside the Republic involved. I think you're one of them. I want to know the names of the rest."

"For what? Revenge? With the galaxy coming apart all around you?"

She said nothing. Suddenly Tarveet leaned back and smiled.

"If you must have answers," he said, and paused to take a sip of cha'a, "go find the Master of the Adepts' Guild. Ask Errec Ransome to tell you what happened to the Domina Perada."

V. Innish-Kyl: Country Estate of Adelfe Aneverian
Gyfferan Nearspace: *RSF Veratina*

"**O**H, DEAR," murmured Nyls Jessan under his breath. "I seem to have been abandoned."

The other members of *Warhammer*'s crew were scattered by now all over the crowded lawn of Adelfe Aneverian's country estate. Beka and Commodore Gil had gone off to discuss something; Ignaceu LeSoit had escorted the commodore's Eraasian prisoner of war over to the buffet tables for refreshment and animated conversation; Owen Rosselin-Metadi and his apprentice had drifted away from the main area some time ago for reasons that Jessan didn't feel qualified to guess.

He shrugged and began to stroll about the grounds in search of some temporary diversion. The diversion found him, instead, in the form of a Space Force lieutenant with an aide's gold aiguillette and a nametag that read JHUNNEI.

"Lieutenant Commander Jessan," she said. "I've been hoping for a chance to talk with you."

"Oh, dear," said Jessan again. "I suppose it was inevitable. . . . Exactly how much of my disgraceful past are you familiar with, anyway?"

"All of it, Commander. And I know who rewrote your records."

Jessan looked at her with renewed respect. "You wouldn't happen to be working for our friends in Intelligence?"

"Of course not," she said promptly. "Given their success rate these days, who'd want to?"

"You have a point there, I'm afraid. In that case, you must be the commodore's aide. My compliments on an excellent party."

She accepted the praise without any blushing or false modesty. "Thank you, Commander. I notice you showed up in civilian persona yourself."

"Not civilian," he corrected her. "General of the Armies of Entibor. Since the public record still has me down as cashiered from the Space Force, I really didn't have any choice."

"Probably not. But we both know the truth; and you *are* still under oath and under orders."

"Mmmh," said Jessan. He accepted a glass of the sparkling punch from a passing waiter and turned back toward Jhunnei. "This wouldn't have anything to do with those ships, would it?"

Jhunnei didn't blink. "The commodore needs them. You're staff corps, not a line officer; and the Domina isn't space-command qualified any more than you are."

"True enough," he said. "But there are some things that it's a good idea to ask for politely rather than to demand. The ships are, after all, hers—to give you or not as she pleases."

"Not exactly a realistic position."

"Oh, I don't know about that." Jessan sipped at his punch. "The commodore's not running a pure Space Force operation here. A lot of his people haven't sworn oaths to anybody—they're a bunch of heavily armed civilians who've thrown in with him based on a little sentiment and a lot of self-interest. If the Baronet D'Rugier starts commandeering people's ships and claiming to outrank the Domina of Lost Entibor, he's going to lose them."

"You approve of that idea, Commander?"

He shook his head. "Nobody, I think, is going to deny that the Space Force can make more use of the Domina's flotilla than she can, acting alone."

"Then what was that speech in honor of?"

"It's advice, Lieutenant," he said. "From somebody who knows Beka Rosselin-Metadi rather well. If the commodore wants those ships, he'll need to go about it carefully—and if the Domina asks him for something in exchange, he'd better be ready to give it to her."

Klea Santreny stood leaning on her staff and waiting. At her feet lay Owen Rosselin-Metadi—that part of him not traveling out of the body somewhere in the vastness of space and time—and beside Owen the shadowy form of the other. Or at least, shadowy to her eyes, as if he were somehow both visible and obscured. How Owen had perceived the stranger she couldn't begin to guess.

"You have good eyes," said a voice beside her.

She turned her head, and saw the stranger standing there. *If I look back around,* she wondered, *will I see him where he was before?* She didn't look.

"Tell me who you really are," she said. "He thinks you look like him—I could feel him thinking it—but you don't."

"Names aren't important. I gave mine away long ago."

The stranger's accent wasn't like Owen's, either; wherever he came from, it wasn't Galcen. Wherever he came from—she shivered. Her grandmother had told her about creatures who looked like men, who didn't have names and weren't there when you looked at them, creatures who arrived after sunset and departed before dawn, taking *things* with them.

She clutched her staff so tightly that her knuckles hurt. "What do you want?"

"Only to help. There was something else, once . . . but I lost it when I lost my name, and it doesn't matter any longer."

"I don't care," she said. "If this is helping, I don't see much use for it."

"There are some things that no one can tell the Master of the Guild. Some things he can only learn for himself. Or never learn."

I don't know what you are, Klea thought. *But you sound crazy.*

She didn't say it, and by the time she'd thought of something else to say instead, he was gone. She went back to watching over Owen's motionless body. The twilight deepened; the garden was lit by the warm yellow glow of the lanterns hanging in the trees. She kept on watching.

I like it better here anyway. There's too many people out there, and they think too loudly. And that aide person, Lieutenant Jhunnei . . . I could feel her listening to me think.

Footsteps crunched on the turf, breaking into her reverie. She looked toward the noise, half-expecting to see the stranger coming back again, but this time the newcomer was clearly real and fully present. With his elegant ruffled shirt and glittering red eye patch, and the black velvet long-coat over it all, he looked like one of Baronet D'Rugier's freespacers—half merchant, half pirate, and completely dangerous.

Klea held herself stiffly, hoping that the privateer wasn't in a mood to cause trouble. He stopped a few feet away, and glanced from her face down to Owen's motionless body.

"Taking good care of him, are you?"

The voice was familiar and the accent unmistakable. Klea risked looking deeper, and caught her breath.

"Domina Beka?"

The young man's mouth quirked up in a tight smile. "So much for trying to fool the Adepts around here."

"I don't understand," said Klea. She supposed she ought to be more formal—this was, after all, the first time she'd spoken with the Domina alone—but it didn't seem to matter.

The privateer shrugged. "Why would anybody want to be the Domina of Entibor for one second longer than they had to?"

Klea recognized sincerity when she heard it, even in disguise. *I didn't think it was possible for somebody else to hate anything as much as I hated working for Freling . . . but this comes close.* "What should I call you, then?"

"Tarnekep Portree. Merchant captain. And other things."

"Captain Portree."

"That's right." He looked down again at Owen. "How long has he been out like that?"

"Since dark."

"I hope he knows what the hell he's doing."

Klea weighed her answers, and decided that honesty was the best after all. "So do I."

"I want him with me when I talk to the commodore," Portree said. "I'll stay here until he comes back."

Klea didn't say anything. They waited: Klea leaning on her staff, Portree with his back to a tree and his arms folded across his chest. At last Owen stirred, opened his eyes, and sat up.

"Where—?" he muttered. Then his gaze landed on Tarnekep Portree, still watching impassively. Recognition was instant. *"Bee?"*

"Tarnekep Portree."

Owen looked at the privateer and shook his head. "You're not planning to talk to the commodore like that, are you?"

"As a matter of fact, I am." Portree glanced from Owen's face to Klea's. "Let's go collect the rest of *Warhammer*'s merry band of misfits, so we can corner the baronet and have ourselves a serious discussion."

Aboard RSF *Veratina*, a dull midwatch was half-over. In the Combat Information Center, the sensor technicians on duty watched their screens while the comptechs ran internal maintenance checks. The Tactical Action Officer leaned back in his chair, watching the empty battle tank and sipping at a cup of lukewarm cha'a that had steeped far too long in the pot.

One of the sensor techs bent forward to look more closely at her screen. "Wait a minute. I'm tracking some motion out here. New stuff."

"Put it up in the tank," the TAO ordered.

The tank lit up with the by now familiar diagram of the Gyfferan system. A mass of blue dots was expanding outward from the home planet like bubbles in sparkling wine.

"Ships rising," said the sensor tech. "Too many for an accurate count at this range without going active."

"Shrink it for the display."

"Shrinking it, aye."

The blue effervescence coalesced into a single bright blue dot, still moving outward from Gyffer.

"That's better," said the TAO. "Looks like we've got everyone who can boost leaving orbit there. Things could get interesting."

"Shall I inform the General, sir?"

"The General already knows," said Metadi, from near the entrance to the CIC.

"Ah, there you are, sir. I didn't see you come in."

Metadi came farther into the CIC. Commander Quetaya, trim and efficient as usual, was with him, ever-present clipboard in hand. "Learn to keep your eyes open," Metadi said to the TAO. "You won't always find your enemies on the other side of a glass screen."

The TAO looked abashed. "Yes, sir."

"Right, then." Metadi gazed at the display in the battle tank. "Looks like the LDF's gone out hunting for Mages. I'll need a set of contingency battle plans based on the assumption that they find what they're looking for—and at least one other set assuming that the Mages start their attack before the LDF can make contact. Records from the last Space Force/Local Defense joint exercise are probably in the *'Tina*'s main memory somewhere; use them for an idea of how a big fleet would go about attacking Gyffer and what kind of resistance the Gyfferans would put up."

"When do you need them, sir?"

"Yesterday," said Metadi, "but as soon as possible will do."

Quetaya stepped forward and proffered her clipboard. "I have a set of preliminary plans prepared, General. Would you care to review them?"

Metadi took the clipboard. "Just out of idle curiosity, Commander, when did you start drawing these up?"

"When you announced our destination, sir," she said. "Given two knowns, our strength and our location, there weren't a whole lot of branches on the decision tree."

He looked at her. "And where do you see those branches taking us?"

"Frankly, sir—barring wild luck or divine intervention— they fall into two main groups: either we run like hell or we all die."

"Wild luck is nobody's friend," said Metadi. "And we aren't so all-around virtuous that some deity is going to pull us out of the soup from sheer admiration. And running isn't an option."

Quetaya looked resigned. "That leaves us with the plans in the 'we all die' subgroup, then."

"Right. Tell me more about that one. Do you have any branches where we accomplish our mission before we all die?"

"Without being a mind reader or a fortune-teller? Nothing's certain. But some of them have a better shot than others."

"Very well, Commander," Metadi said. "I want two of your sets of plans for review at the head of the queue. The branches in which we gain victory, any way at all—and the ones where we lose the quickest. I'll be looking for the gambits of both of them."

"Yes sir," said Quetaya.

"I'm commandeering the TAO's chair for this one." Metadi suited the action to the words. The displaced officer moved over to stand near the bulkhead, while Metadi turned back to Commander Quetaya. "You can start your presentation any time you want. Plug your clipboard into the tank console and display it up there."

The commander looked dubious. "Sir, a lot of this material is classified at quite a high level—"

"Anyone in this compartment might become the senior survivor at almost any time, and have to carry out the remnants of whatever plan we're using. Start your presentation."

"Sir," called out a sensor tech, "farspace probes show energy releases. Possibly more than one location. Attenuation medium."

"Closer than the last group," Metadi said. "Things are heating up. Commander, let's get the briefing started—we may need those battle plans sooner than we thought."

The library of Adelfe Aneverian's country estate was a spacious, well-appointed room, its walls paneled in polished ocherwood, its windows curtained in thick, sound-muffling velvet. The books in the tall, glass-fronted shelves were all printed antiques, leather-bound and paper-paged; if Aneverian or any of his guests ever indulged in textchips or holovids, the evidence was tucked well away out of sight.

A vast ocherwood desk filled up one end of the room, but nobody was sitting behind it. There was a library staircase—a masterpiece of the woodworker's art, done in yet more polished ocherwood—at the other end of the room, and Tarnekep Portree was sitting on the top step. If Commodore Gil wanted to make eye contact with the Mandeynan, he'd either have to crane his neck awkwardly upward, or stand well back.

If the situation weren't so serious, Jessan reflected, it would have been amusing. Beka's choice of incognito hadn't really taken him by surprise. Captain Portree was considerably plainer spoken than the Domina of Entibor could afford to be, and the one-eyed starpilot had the further advantage of making respectable people like the commodore distinctly nervous.

The rest of the 'Hammer's crew were scattered about the room. Ignaceu LeSoit stood warily with his back to the paneled wall. Owen Rosselin-Metadi sat motionless and black-clad in one of the big, high-backed chairs, with his staff across his lap; his apprentice, equally immobile, stood at his right hand. Jessan himself, his legs stretched out before him, lounged in a wing chair near the library staircase, where he could get a good view.

Commodore Gil stood gazing at Tarnekep Portree for a moment, then chose for himself a comfortable armchair a carpet's width away from the library staircase. His Eraasian prisoner of war, silent and nervous-looking, sat rigidly upright on one of the uncushioned ocherwood side chairs a foot or so away. The commodore's aide, Jhunnei, had taken a stance near the door—like Ignac' LeSoit, and like Jessan himself, she'd picked a position affording both a good view and a clear line of fire.

I couldn't have set it up better if we'd been playing at Living Pictures, Jessan thought. *Subject of tableau, "The Three Pillars of the Republic"—the Space Force and the Adepts and the Old Nobility, all of us armed and dangerous and watching each other like cardsharps. And this, Fortune save the galaxy, is supposed to be a* friendly *gathering!*

Nobody said anything for some time. Finally Commodore Gil closed his eyes briefly—praying, Jessan suspected, for patience—then opened them and said, "Captain Portree."

The Mandeynan nodded. "That's me."

"Can I assume that you're empowered to speak on the Domina's behalf?"

"You can."

"Very well. Captain Portree, I will be honest with you: I need the Domina's ships. I would rather have them with her good wishes than without, but I *will* have them."

Tarnekep leaned back against the staircase railings. "I figured that out already," he said. "You've got to be careful, though, if you're doing this as Baronet D'Rugier."

"A necessary role, though it has its limits," Gil said. "Would you be more impressed if I changed into my dress whites?"

"No—your aide in the glittering wonder of her uniform is more than enough to impress me." Tarnekep paused. "But ships aren't the only item on the agenda tonight. The Domina has to know what's in this deal for her."

I hope, Jessan thought, *that the good lieutenant passed on the advice I gave her. Otherwise, this is where the discussion gets sticky.*

But before Gil could say anything, there was movement

at last from the other side of the room. Owen Rosselin-Metadi halted Captain Portree with a gesture, turned to Gil, and said, "A moment, Commodore."

Gil turned away from Captain Portree with what Jessan read as barely disguised relief. "Master Rosselin-Metadi?"

"Commodore," Owen said, "I must object to the presence of your—guest. If you're inviting Mages to our councils we have no hope of success at all."

The Eraasian woman didn't move, but seemed all the same to draw herself closer together. Her grey eyes, which she'd kept on Commodore Gil all this time, had gone wide and dark. The commodore regarded Owen coldly.

"Master Rosselin-Metadi," he said, "Doctor syn-Tavaite is neither Mage nor Magelord. She is a medical technician from Eraasi, and as a prisoner of war she is under my personal protection. If you have any problems with that—"

"He doesn't," Tarnekep cut in. "Lay off the nice man, Owen. Gil's prisoner doesn't bother me. Besides, the gentlelady may have some important information for us—considering that she replicated General Metadi's aide some time back before the war."

If that information startled Beka's brother, he didn't show it. He only said, "Did she, then?" and continued looking at Gil. "Commodore, I've heard reports of mutinies all over the galaxy—and now I hear that your personal prisoner was responsible for planting a spy on my father's staff. The question is: Who are you loyal to?"

"A good question," Tarnekep said, before Gil could draw breath. "But the Master of the Adepts' Guild isn't the one who ought to be asking it."

"What do you mean?" Owen asked. He'd relaxed a little, Jessan noticed, as he turned his attention from Gil to Tarnekep Portree. Not the usual reaction people had to the Mandeynan starpilot—but then, Adepts weren't the usual sort of people. Tarnekep, though, wasn't looking particularly amused.

"I mean I heard something strange and interesting a little while ago," the starpilot said. "Someone told me, 'If you want to know what happened to the Domina Perada, go ask the Master of the Adepts' Guild.' He was talking about the old Master and not the new one—but you were Errec Ransome's confidential agent as much as his apprentice, and you're the Master now. So I'm asking you: how much *does* the Guild know about what happened to Perada Rosselin?"

"I don't—"

"Gentles, I must insist," Gil said. "The first order of business is those ships."

Ignaceu LeSoit moved slightly away from the paneled wall—drawing all eyes to him by the unexpected motion. "No," he said. "I want to hear what happened to the Domina Perada."

There was a long pause, with Owen Rosselin-Metadi caught between Tarnekep Portree's challenging, oddly piebald gaze—one blue eye, one red patch—and LeSoit's tense regard.

"Odd that you should ask," Owen said finally. Nothing in his voice or manner implied that he was yielding to pressure. "Perada Rosselin came to my attention earlier this evening. I went looking for something, but what I found was something other than what I expected."

He looked again at syn-Tavaite and—with the air of someone who has arrived at a desired destination—turned back to Gil. "Tell me, Commodore, can your 'guest' explain to us who a certain lord sus-Airaalin is?"

But it wasn't syn-Tavaite who answered. Lieutenant Jhunnei spoke up instead from her place near the door.

"The 'sus' prefix would put this person in the Eraasian equivalent of the upper nobility."

Owen looked at her directly for the first time. The lieutenant met his gaze straight on. There seemed to be some kind of communication taking place between them, but Jessan couldn't begin to guess at its nature.

"Thank you," said Owen finally. "Lieutenant." He looked back at Gil. "Commodore—please ask your guest to respond."

syn-Tavaite looked at Gil. *Damn it,* Jessan thought, *the poor creature's white as a sheet. There's probably something in the regs about not scaring prisoners to death. . . .*

"It's all right, Doctor," said Gil.

syn-Tavaite knotted her hands together in her lap, and began to speak. "I have heard the name. There is a Grand Admiral sus-Airaalin who commands the fleet of the Resurgency."

Odd, Jessan thought, *why's LeSoit tensing up?* He noticed that LeSoit's weapon was loosened in its holster. *I wish I could remember whether it was that way when we came in here.*

"Now, that is fascinating," Tarnekep said. "But I don't think it has anything to do with either the Domina Perada or those seven ships."

"Bear with me," Owen said. "I won't ask Doctor syn-Tavaite for a description of the man. Let's just assume that the Grand Admiral heading our opposition is a middling-sized gentleman—shorter than me, but taller than, for example, Gentlesir LeSoit over there. Lean, wiry, with curly black hair going to grey."

Now Jessan was sure that LeSoit was holding his hand just above the grip of his blaster. *This will present an interesting choice. If etiquette requires that I shoot someone, where should I aim first?* Still thinking, he withdrew a lace handkerchief from his shirt cuff and flicked at a speck of lint on his over-robe. When he replaced the handkerchief, his hand came away concealing the miniature blaster that lived in the grav-clip up his sleeve.

"Yes," syn-Tavaite said. She kept her eyes fixed on her hands; just looking at Owen seemed to frighten her. "That could be him."

"Indeed," Owen said. "I want to get back to this sus-Airaalin. I have it on excellent authority that he was at some point oath-sworn to my mother Perada Rosselin." He glanced over at Tarnekep. "I don't know what tale your source of information thought the Master of the Guild was going to give you—if the source is who I think it is, any truth that escaped his lips was purely by coincidence—but I'm the Master of the Guild and that's all I've got."

"Wonderful," said Tarnekep. "Wonderfully useless, too, since the Domina Perada's been dead for these two years and more." He turned back to Gil. "Let me see if I can keep all this straight. One, General Metadi is at Gyffer."

"An assumption," Gil said. "But—probably, yes. Another assumption I'm working with is that this Grand Admiral Whatever is at Gyffer as well."

"That's two, then. And three, Metadi's very own aide is a Magebuilt replicant. One created by your guest, in fact."

"Yes," said Gil. "So far, though, the General appears to have escaped from any Magish plot against him."

"That's a hell of a big assumption, Commodore. How do we know what the plot was, or how many replicants there were?" Tarnekep turned his gaze on syn-Tavaite. "You replicated the aide. Did you replicate anyone else?"

"Answer the question, Inesi," Gil said in a quiet voice. "It's okay."

"Yes," syn-Tavaite said, her voice so low that it could hardly be heard. "Replication is slow and difficult, and few have the knowledge to perform it. The risk ... for everybody involved, getting the needful things from this side of the Gap Between ... but I was able to create another successful replicant."

"Well, who?"

"One whom you all know." She looked up and straight at Tarnekep. "I replicated the Domina."

VI. Gyfferan Farspace: LDF #97
Gyfferan Nearspace: *Night's-Beautiful-Daughter*
Innish-Kyl: Country Estate of Adelfe Aneverian
Gyfferan Farspace: *Sword-of-the-Dawn*

AT THE far limits of the Gyfferan system, in an area roughly in line with the home planet's north polar region, LDF Cruiser #97 and the rest of the Fast Response Task Force came out of hyper.

"Dropout," said the 97's TAO. He stifled a yawn. They'd been running the string-of-pearls reconnaissance pattern—drop, scan, jump; drop, scan, jump—all through the watch, and for over a Standard day before that. Like everyone else aboard #97, he'd been fighting off the combined assault of boredom and jump-sickness for almost that long. "Sensors?"

"Empty," said the duty sensor tech.

The TAO wondered if another cup of cha'a would help, or a bit of food. The pastries in the 97's galley had been stale since yesterday morning. "Commencing run-to-jump."

"Roger," said the sensor tech. "Full scan on dropout."

The cruiser blipped into hyperspace, and back out again. The TAO swallowed hard. Food would be a bad idea.

"Dropout," he said. "Sensors?"

"Empty."

"Reports coming in, sir," the comms tech broke in. "Scouts in grid two zero tack five seven report enemy scoutcraft spotted at extreme sensor range."

"Maintain present realspace course and speed," the TAO ordered. "Put the contacts up in the tank and pass the word to the captain."

The 97's captain showed up a minute or two later, holding one of the stale pastries in his hand. "What's the situation?"

The TAO indicated the display in the tank. "Enemy scoutcraft, extreme range."

"Do you have backtracks on them?" the captain asked.

"Working," said the duty comptech. "Looks like they're doing an expanding-globe search of their own, Captain."

"Find the main mass of the formation. Find it now."

"Working."

The comms tech broke in again. "Message from Central—Gyffer is sending out additional units, this time with Adepts aboard for searching.

"Adepts." The captain frowned. "I never did like the spooks. We're going to find the Mages on our own, the old-fashioned way."

The silence in Aneverian's library thickened and congealed. Beka became aware, as though from a great distance, that she had Tarnekep Portree's blaster out of its holster and ready in her hand. On the other side of the room, the Eraasian medic was so pale she looked grey.

"I wouldn't, Captain Portree." The commodore also had a small hand-blaster out and aimed.

Jessan cleared his throat. Beka saw that the hand which had brought out his handkerchief earlier now held a miniature blaster much like Gil's.

"Neither would I, Baronet, if I were you." He smiled at Doctor syn-Tavaite—*Nyls, you're amazing,* Beka thought dizzily; *I didn't know there was anybody alive in the galaxy who could manage to look reassuring and hold someone at gunpoint at the same time*—and said, "You can relax, gentlelady. The good captain means no harm, I assure you."

"I can take a hint when I hear one," Beka said, and slammed the weapon back into its holster. "But indulge my curiosity, Doctor syn-Tavaite: *which* Domina?"

"Not y— Not the young Domina, Captain. The one who was dead."

"Perada Rosselin." Owen was almost as pale as syn-Tavaite; Beka couldn't tell if it was with anger or with fear. "You made a replicant of Perada Rosselin. *When?*"

"Before now, three . . . I think . . . of your Standard years."

"That doesn't make sense." It was Lieutenant Jhunnei who spoke. "The timing is all wrong. Why would they replicate her just before they killed her?"

syn-Tavaite shook her head violently. "No, no . . . not before. I remember—even on our side of the Gap Between, we heard that news. After."

"Tell the story," Gil said. He put his blaster away. "From the beginning. Who asked you to replicate the Domina?"

"One of the Masked Ones," syn-Tavaite said. "He came to me at my place of work and said he had a task for me elsewhere, on another world. I went with him—there was a fine house where he stayed, like this one but much bigger, and all empty except for machines that moved and spoke—and he gave me the . . . the laboratory, I think you call it . . . and the tissue samples for seeding the replicant. When I had done, he left the replicant empty and returned me to my home. That was all."

Jessan was looking curious; it was the medic in him coming out, Beka supposed.

" 'Empty'?" he asked syn-Tavaite.

"Yes . . . a person must give up the old body and fill the replicant, or the new body is nothing, a shell. But this man had no living person to fill the Domina. At least, not while I was there."

"This guy who fetched you," Beka said. She was beginning to feel the first stirrings of an uneasy suspicion. "Did you ever see his face without the mask?"

"Yes, my l—Captain."

Beka leaned forward. "Tell me what he looked like."

"An old man," syn-Tavaite said. "Not tall . . . and thin, with grey hair. He had kind eyes, but sad. He spoke with a strange accent, in old-fashioned terms, but always very politely. He carried a Great Lord's staff, made with silver ornaments after the antique style."

"The Professor," Beka said. "My old copilot. It has to be."

Owen leaned forward. He'd gotten his color back, and his hazel eyes were full of anger and surprise. "Mistress Hyfid's report to Master Ransome never mentioned any of that!"

"Maybe she thought it wasn't any of Master Ransome's business," Beka said. "The Prof was dead by then anyhow, and Llannat had his staff—I gave it to her, if you want to know how she got it. I was there when he died."

Commodore Gil had been whispering rapidly to Jhunnei. The lieutenant nodded, then pulled a comm link out of her uniform pocket and began talking over it in a low voice.

Gil turned back to the room at large. "Records are scattered," he said, cutting off whatever anyone else might have said next, "but in my private files I have a copy of a report I prepared for General Metadi some time ago. I've asked my aide to call up a part of it."

He walked over to the library fireplace and took down a controller from the mantelpiece, where it had lain in the shadow of a heavy brass candlestick. A touch of the keypad, and one of the glass-fronted bookshelves vanished: it had been a projection concealing a holovid tank.

"There, if you please," he said to Jhunnei.

"Yes sir," she said. "Patching through from *Karipavo.*"

A moment later a flatpic appeared in the rear of the tank—a shot marked as being from a security camera on High Station Pleyver. The picture showed Tarnekep Portree, complete with eye patch, and behind him a slight, grey-haired man in a Mandeynan long-coat with silver buttons.

"Him?" Gil asked syn-Tavaite.

She nodded.

"There you are, Captain Portree," Gil said. "Positive identification, for whatever it's worth."

Beka smiled at him—one of Tarnekep Portree's better smiles, the kind that tended to make law-abiding citizens suddenly remember urgent business elsewhere.

"Whatever it's worth," she said. "I'll tell you what it's worth, Commodore. It's worth a fleet. Domina Beka Rosselin-Metadi will give you all of her ships, except for *Warhammer*. In exchange, the Domina wants a hostage against their safe return."

She pointed at syn-Tavaite. "Her."

Married life would be ideal, Ari reflected, if only there didn't happen to be a war going on.

The task force to which *Night's-Beautiful-Daughter* had been assigned took formation in the outer orbits above Gyffer. The TF lifted as a group and headed in column for a jump point marked by a temporary beacon. They accelerated at the rate of the slowest vessel in the formation, then jumped in sequence, vanishing one by one into the grey swirling mists of hyperspace.

"Short transit," Lieutenant Vinhalyn said to Ari. They were in the *Daughter*'s cockpit with the Deathwing's pilot and copilot, waiting for the dropout. "Action close to Gyffer."

Ari watched the navicomp's timer—a Gyfferan model, recently installed—tick down toward zero. "What's our tasking, exactly?"

"We're a 'special application unit,'" Vinhalyn said. "And communications relay."

"In other words, we have to stay out of the fighting."

"It's just as well," Vinhalyn said. "With an antique configuration like this, the comps on both sides are going to evaluate our sensor profile as 'probable enemy.' The *Daughter* needs to be preserved for study as an orbital museum, not refitted and sent out into combat—if the Mageworlders kept any such relics from the early days, the Republic destroyed them long ago."

He sighed. "But we all do what we must, and at least the reports of my preliminary investigations are on file with the faculty of history at Telabryk University."

The navicomp beeped. "Stand by," Vinhalyn said over the general announcing system. "Dropout."

The stars came back, bright and glorious.

"Report navigation fix," Vinhalyn said.

"Working," the pilot replied. "Working. Complete. In position; in formation; on track, course, and speed."

"Very well. Send to TF leader, 'Alpha Station.' "

"Making the signal now."

"And now," Vinhalyn said to Ari, "we stand by and await orders."

They walked back from the cockpit to the sensor area. The Magebuilt Deathwing didn't have a common room as such, and nothing else was where a Republic-trained spacer would have expected it to be. Still, both men had spent enough time aboard the *Daughter* to be comfortable with the odd architecture.

A speaker in the bulkhead clicked on. The voice of the pilot came over the Deathwing's general announcement system. "Captain, we've got new position orders."

"Very well," said Vinhalyn. "Maneuver to comply."

"Roger." The speaker clicked off.

Vinhalyn turned to Ari. "Do you want to check on Mistress Hyfid?"

"Because she's the 'special application'?" Ari shook his head. "No. Let her rest."

Doctor syn-Tavaite looked at Gil. "My lord baronet—no. You cannot send me out among the Adepts. You promised me a place amid your crew, and I hold you to your word."

"Captain Portree," Gil said. "Please ask the Domina—"

"No," said Beka. "Those are the terms. You're heading into battle; she'll be safer with me."

syn-Tavaite shook her head. "My lord baronet, the danger is no matter. I am combat-sworn to you, not this other."

Beka sighed. "Gentlelady, I promise I won't let the Adepts hurt you."

"And how exactly are you planning to enforce that?" Owen was still angry; his usually calm face was flushed with the emotion. "You're planning to bring a Mageworlder onto the 'Hammer—somebody who admits to working in forbidden technology and doing the bidding of the Magelords!"

"Knock it off, Owen," Beka said wearily. "Your own mother wasn't too proud to talk with a Great Magelord, so you can damned well put yourself out to be polite to a medical technician. And if you don't like it you can *walk* home from Innish-Kyl."

She turned back to syn-Tavaite. "Don't worry about the Adepts, Doctor syn-Tavaite. I own the ship, and what I say, goes. A regular place in the ship's crew, and if I ever get around to paying them you'll get the same cut as everybody else."

"Good but not sufficient," Gil said. "She is still a member of my complement. As such she would be on detached duty on your ship, and answerable only to me, should I choose to assign her there. Further, she will travel armed and under arms, and will not be assigned any duties without her consent."

"Done," Beka said. "My word as the 'Hammer's captain. Friend Jessan over there is a medic—he'll swear it on the healer's oath for you, if that'll help."

"That's right." Jessan, bless him, spoke up without needing any more prompting. "No danger to you that isn't also danger to all of us."

syn-Tavaite looked at Jessan. "As a healer you swear it?"

"Yes," said Jessan. "I swear."

"If this is what my lord baronet requires of me—"

"I ask it of you," said Gil. "Because it's needed. And when the fighting is over, if I'm still alive to do it, I'll take you back to Eraasi myself."

"Then I will go."

In the observation deck of *Sword-of-the-Dawn*, Grand Admiral sus-Airaalin was pacing again. The armor-glass of the viewports on all sides of him glowed now with the amber and violet glyphs that provided a visual dimension to the reports from the great ship's array of sensors. All about the amethyst sigil that marked the center of the formation, the glass shimmered with purple flashes: more vessels dropping out of hyper in a spherical screen around the flagship. The display was a thing of beauty and grace, a fragment of the old technology saved from the time of destruction—though sus-Airaalin found himself wishing, sometimes, for one of the Adept-worlders' holographic battle tanks, to look inward as if from a distance, rather than outward, inescapably part of the scene. He supposed that using a battle tank allowed the Adept-worlders to give without a second thought those orders which otherwise would be unbearably painful.

Mid-Commander Taleion entered the observation deck, message tablet in hand. "My lord, scouts in sector five report enemy scoutcraft."

sus-Airaalin halted his restless movement. "Good," he said. "They have come out at last. From their scouts we can find the main body. It won't be far."

"Shall I instruct the Circles to begin searching?"

"I fear it would do us little good, Mael. The web of power is tangled here; I can't see the patterns clearly enough to search them for the enemy."

At the edge of sus-Airaalin's vision, the armor-glass window lit up with a shimmering aurora of yellow-amber light as more glyphs appeared. He turned, and Mid-Commander Taleion approached closer, in order to read the display.

"It looks like the Gyfferan scouts have found us first, my lord," Taleion said.

"Not their scouts," said sus-Airaalin.

One of the amethyst glyphs changed intensity and configuration, and then another.

Our ships, sus-Airaalin read the changes; *under attack.*

"A message, Mael: sections five and seven, swing to encircle. Launch Vengeance missiles against the Gyfferan drop point. Section four, get a count and a point of origin on the Gyfferans. Send out scouts along their backtrail. Deploy fighters. All units, maintain formation, hold your fire until enemy vessels are at half-range."

Taleion scribbled madly on his message tablet and jabbed at the Transmit button with his stylus. "Fighters out."

sus-Airaalin let out a long exhalation of relief. "Now we will see the true mettle of the fleet."

"We will prevail," asserted Taleion. "We must."

"In this encounter, yes. But the real battle has not even begun."

Another violet glyph changed its shape and position, and glowed brilliantly for a few seconds before darkening to nothing but a trace of grey—*An explosion,* sus-Airaalin read it, *one of ours.* But the instant one of the orange sigils flared and darkened as well, and yet another reconfigured itself. *One Gyfferan destroyed; one with its mobility damaged.*

The Grand Admiral shook his head. "This would almost be pretty," he murmured, "if people weren't dying out there."

"Yes, my lord." Taleion consulted his message tablet again. "Report from Section four, my lord. The enemy is in range—a small force, seemingly. We have a tentative point of origin on them."

"Destroy them. Direct Captain Iekkon's task force to reconnoiter their presumed origin point in force."

On the display window, more amber sigils flared and went to grey. At the same time other, different sigils appeared.

Transports carrying fighters, thought sus-Airaalin. *Small craft. No matter. Our fighters will handle them. Our shields can take the rest. It's time to act boldly, or lose all.*

"Mid-Commander Taleion," he said. "Instruct the fleet to make course for Gyffer. Transit in realspace."

Some hours after *Night's-Beautiful-Daughter* had taken her assigned position, a new message came in—this one for the *Daughter*'s own action rather than for relay to other, farther, units. Vinhalyn turned to Ari.

"We're directed to take station farther out," he said, "and requested to determine 'by special means' the Mages' location and intentions. Rosselin-Metadi, will you request Mistress Hyfid to prognosticate for us?"

Ari sighed. "She'll love this," he said, but he headed aft anyway, to the cabin he and Llannat shared. She was there, as she usually was during her waking hours—working on the ShadowDance, this time. She stopped when he came in, and walked over to lean her head against his chest. He could see beads of sweat on the back of her neck, even in the chill shipboard air.

"Hello, Ari," she said. Her voice was muffled by the fabric of his tunic. "What's the news?"

"No news," he said. "But the high command wants you to perform another miracle for them."

She muttered something that sounded like one of his sister Beka's favorite oaths. "All right, give me a mo—"

The ship jerked violently, throwing them against the bulkhead. No sooner had they recovered their balance than the Mechanical Breakdown alarm began sounding over the speakers in the room and in the corridor outside. Ari dropped a kiss on Llannat's forehead before he let her go, and headed off at a run for his station in the Deathwing's engineering spaces.

"We've lost a tube on starboard-ventral," Chief Yance, the engineering watchstander, said as Ari entered the compartment. "Bridge has been informed."

"Engineering, bridge," came a call over the bulkhead speaker. "Interrogative status?"

"Shutting down all engines preparatory to damage assessment," said the chief.

"Roger," said the pilot. "Standing by."

Ari busied himself with checking the readout logs, correlating the levels on the antique Mage-calibrated gauges against his knowledge of how similar Republic-built engines ran. What he saw didn't look good.

What he heard next didn't sound better.

"Engineering, bridge. Stand by to provide maximum power."

"Negative, bridge," Yance called back. "We require repair."

"Give me what you've got. Maximum thrust on all available tubes," came the response. "We're under orders to fall back."

"I'll give you what I can," the engineer said. Ari was already helping him cut out the damaged tube and shut off its opposite number, so that thrust would be balanced on both sides of the Deathwing's axis—but the throttle call for power came in even faster and harder than they had expected. Ari watched the readouts all over the board start to flash at him in bright yellow instead of the usual violet.

"Ease back! Ease back!" the engineer called to the pilot over the internal comm. "We're going to lose it down here."

"We are under pursuit," the pilot replied, voice tense. "I need jump speed *now*."

More lights flashed yellow, and an alarm started hooting. Two more of the tube linings blew out, and *Night's-Beautiful-Daughter* started to tumble.

"Goddamn piece of junk antique Mageborn son of a bitch!" the engineer said, shutting down systems.

The speaker clicked on. "Lieutenant Commander Rosselin-Metadi, bridge."

Ari left the engineer cursing behind him as he sprinted forward. Vinhalyn and Llannat were both in the cockpit, along with the pilot and copilot.

"We're in trouble," Vinhalyn said as Ari entered. "No engines. Guns unreliable, assuming they work at all."

"We have cloaking," Llannat said.

Vinhalyn looked dubious, and the pilot said, "Untested."

"You wanted advice from an Adept," Llannat said. "I have some. Test it now."

"I'll have to see what we can do with it," said Vinhalyn. "Give me a few minutes to find the manuals. . . . I hope I can translate the technical jargon. . . ."

He headed back aft, still muttering under his breath. Ari and Llannat looked at each other.

"I don't like this," Llannat said. "I felt something—something's looking for me."

"Who?"

"I don't know. It isn't an Adept. And it isn't a friend. But it knows who I am."

"I'm shutting down and going passive," the pilot said. "Make 'em slow down and look hard if they want to find us."

"They'll find us," Llannat said. "They're close. And they want me."

VII. WARHAMMER: HYPERSPACE TRANSIT

ASTEROID BASE

GYFFERAN FARSPACE: NIGHT'S-BEAUTIFUL-DAUGHTER; LDF #97

BEKA ROSSELIN-METADI looked around the *'Hammer's* common room and suppressed a sigh. *This isn't going to be easy.*

Even allowing for the fact that Councillor Tarveet was locked back up in number-one crew berthing and likely to stay there for the duration, the compartment felt hot and crowded. It wasn't so much the number of people gathered around the table—after all, her father had run *Warhammer* with a full crew back in the old days—as the way they spread out to take up the space.

With the exception of Nyls Jessan, who'd slid without comment into his usual place beside her at the table, nobody seemed to want to come within arm's length of anybody else. The two Adepts, Master and apprentice, made a single black-clad unit sitting as far away as possible from Inesi syn-Tavaite, who looked, for her part, as though she didn't think the distance was far enough. Ignaceu LeSoit hadn't sat down at the table at all, but stood leaning against the partition between the common room and the galley.

Beka drew a deep breath, then put her fingertips together and leaned back in her chair. The lace cuffs of her Mandeynan-style shirt fell back from her wrists. She'd taken off Tarnekep Portree's eye patch and changed her hair back to yellow as a gesture toward resuming her proper identity, but she hadn't felt inclined to go any farther.

"All right," she said. "We're on course for the Prof's old base. *My* base, now. And I intend to use it."

"Oh, dear," murmured Jessan.

Beka suppressed a smile. "Exactly."

She looked at the others one by one, and continued. "It's like this. We know that the Professor had a replicant made, not long after the Domina Perada was killed. He didn't use it for anything that I know of—if I've got the timing figured right he joined up with me immediately afterward—so he had to keep it someplace. And I don't think he put it in a safe-deposit box on Suivi Point."

Jessan looked at Beka. "You think there's an unawakened—"

"Empty," syn-Tavaite corrected quietly. She looked down at the tabletop as if trying to hide the fact that she'd spoken.

"—an empty replicant hidden on the base."

"That's right," Beka said. She turned to Klea Santreny. "Owen said a while back that you had a vision or something like that, about a grey-haired man who was defending someone." When the young woman nodded, Beka went on. "How did the guy in your vision compare with that picture the commodore showed us, back on Innish-Kyl?"

"It was the same man." Klea paused. "He looked older, though. And tired. I think he'd been fighting the shadows for a long, long time."

"Maybe he had been," said Beka. She hesitated before going on—the next question would settle whether she really did have a plan, however crazy. *If I'm wrong, then I made a fool of myself in front of the commodore and everybody.*

Worse than that—if I'm wrong, the civilized galaxy doesn't have a prayer.

"Gentlelady Santreny," she said at last, "what did the woman with him look like?"

"Like you," Klea said. "But she wasn't you."

"Glad to hear it," said Beka under her breath. "Sometimes I've wondered." Then, to Klea: "Close enough for kin?"

Klea nodded. "Oh, yes."

"Good," Beka said, feeling more relief than she dared to show. "Owen, you're the full-fledged Adept here. Could that mean the Professor is keeping Mother safe in some place ... some place like what Doctor syn-Tavaite called 'out-of-the-body' ... until someone comes to help him bring her back?"

"It's been a long time," Jessan protested. "Three years. Even if someone could."

Owen passed a hand over his face and sighed. For the first time since the start of the commodore's garden party, he looked tired and uncertain.

"All times and all places meet in the Void," he said. "And the Void is where Klea saw them. It's no place for the living to venture. I've been there. I know."

" 'No place for the living,' " said Beka. "But Mother's dead, and so is the Prof; he knew all along he was going to die in the raid on Darvell. Hell, I wouldn't put it past him to have arranged things that way."

syn-Tavaite looked up from the table and spoke directly to Ignaceu LeSoit—in Eraasian, Beka supposed; it certainly wasn't any language she'd ever heard on the Republic side of the Net.

"Nemeis-dai oach?"

"Nemeis-de," LeSoit replied curtly in the same language. "Yes. Tell."

syn-Tavaite knotted her hands together and looked down at the tabletop again. "This man you speak of ... the Great Lords are hard to keep in the grave, and in stories have been known to pass through the death of the body for no more reason than that they wished to travel where the living cannot go. To protect someone weaker from the shadows of what you call the Void—one of the Great Lords might find that a good enough reason to die."

"All right," said Beka. "Another question, then: how, exactly, would someone go about 'filling' a replicant?"

syn-Tavaite shook her head. "That is a thing for the Masked Ones, not for such as me. I have watched, only."

Beka looked at Owen. "Sounds like your line of work."

"You're talking about Magecraft." Owen was looking pale again. "Sorcery. No Adept has ever . . . Bee, even if I wanted to do it, I wouldn't know how."

"Then you'd better figure it out in a hurry," she told him. "Because if Grand Admiral sus-Airaalin was oath-sworn to the Domina Perada, then the Domina Perada is the only person in the civilized galaxy who can make him call off his attack."

In the Combat Information Center of Gyfferan Local Defense Cruiser #97, the situation grew tenser as the watch continued.

"Lost contact with scouting parties one and two," said the communications tech. "Negative comms with task force reserve."

"Hell," said the captain. "Do you have a track on any of the Mage units?"

"Negative location, negative track."

"Report contact data to Central," the CO said. "Estimated Mage strength, estimated armament—"

"Sir! We've lost contact with cruiser #22," broke in the sensor tech. "Pulse data consistent with engine failure."

"Very well. Where are the goddamned Mages?"

"Unknown, sir."

"Get me tentative marks. Hell, get me guesses."

"Aye, aye, s—"

He never finished. The walls of the Combat Information Center buckled inward, as the compression from an explosive hit heated the air instantly to over a thousand degrees.

A moment later the fires ignited by the superheated blast went out like snuffed candles—the oxygen that should have fed them dispersed into vacuum through a massive hole in the metal skin of the ship. One by one, the 97's bulkheads exploded outward as the weakened areas lost structural integrity.

Far aft, in the engineering spaces, the surviving crew members could hear the crunching sounds as the damage progressed toward them. As they had done a hundred times before during loss-of-pressure drills, some donned p-suits while others waited their turn and still others began the orderly shutdown of the cruiser's power plant.

Moments later, as the hull damage reached them, the engines released their energy in a catastrophic second blast. Cruiser #97 continued on, maintaining course and speed, dark and lifeless among the glittering stars.

Warhammer's hyperspace transit continued as the ship fell into the usual routine of watches and maintenance checks. The days consisted of the thousand tiny details, mixed with boredom, that filled a spacer's time. On the twelfth day, Beka passed through the common room, where Jessan and LeSoit were playing double tammani and trying to teach syn-Tavaite the rules, while Owen and Klea looked on. It wasn't the easy camaraderie of a close-knit crew, but at least it was an improvement.

"Expect dropout in a few minutes," Beka said. "I'm going to be dodging asteroids when it happens. So don't bother me."

She went on forward into the cockpit, the airtight doors snicking shut behind her, and toggled on the intraship comm.

"Strap down, people—I'll be doing some heavy braking on dropout. That means you, too, Owen."

She clicked off the comm and sat watching the navicomp chronometer reel down the numbers to dropout.

When the 0:00 flashed red, the automatic dropout sequence started. Beka switched on the realspace engines. As soon as the stars reappeared, she threw the *'Hammer* into a skew-flip—putting the engines on the starship's leading edge—and pushed the throttles up to maximum. Inertia pressed her back in her seat as the vessel lost velocity.

As soon as speed got reasonable, she flipped again to bring the cockpit forward, and started searching for the recognition signals and beacons hidden in the asteroid field to bring her to the base. At last there it was, on visual. Beka felt both exultation and dread as it came into view. The base was safety and comfort. But what was waiting for her there, and what would she do if she was wrong?

Wrong's easy. We aren't any worse off than we were before.

The big question is, what do I do if I'm right? Everybody thinks I've got this figured out down to the last move—even Owen believes that I know what I'm doing, and he damned well ought to know better, considering how Mother grounded us both for a month after that time with the slug. . . .

The crater appeared that marked the entrance to the asteroid's hidden landing bay. She brought the *'Hammer* into it slowly, working the nullgravs as much as the realspace engines. The walls turned from rough stone to smooth, then to polished metal, before opening out into the huge, cavernous bay filled with its assortment of spacecraft. Beka brought *Warhammer* down onto her landing legs and cut all exterior power.

She leaned back in her chair and closed her eyes.

Home.

After a few moments she stood up and went back to the common room. Klea and Doctor syn-Tavaite—neither one of them accustomed to high-g braking maneuvers—still looked a bit greenish, but nobody seemed to have suffered any actual harm.

"Warm clothing, everyone," she said. "It's chilly outside."

Back in her own cabin she pulled a quilted jacket out of the locker—and recognized, with a start, the garment she'd

292 ■ Debra Doyle & James D. Macdonald

worn the first time she'd come here, when she'd thought at first that the Professor intended to replicate her.

Odd that I thought of something like that. He must have had syn-Tavaite's brand-new replicant Domina tucked away somewhere in a stasis box the whole time we were talking.

What had he said, exactly, when she'd accused him of planning her own replication?

"A Mageworld biochemist with a full laboratory setup could . . . but I can't."

Not a lie. The Professor had never lied if he could possibly avoid it; she'd never figured out whether his reasons were aesthetic or moral. And that time he'd told her the literal truth.

"Stupid," she muttered. "If I were looking for the one place in the civilized galaxy most likely to have that kind of lab setup, where's the first place that I should have looked?"

She hurried back through the common room—"Wait here," she said to the others as she passed by—and went outside into the echoing bay. A walkaround told her that *Warhammer* had made the trip in fine form, though the bay itself was chillier than she'd remembered. She shivered inside her jacket and went back up the ramp.

"All right, everyone, come on," Beka said when she reentered the ship. "You don't need to pack—anything you could possibly need is inside."

Beka led the way through the entrance door into the sickbay and through there into the Entibor room. A touch on the switch brought up the holographic illusions. The plain, undecorated chamber became a room from the Summer Palace of House Rosselin, as it had looked before the Mageworlders' attacks had turned the whole planet into broken, poisoned rock. Beyond the high, arched windows, the sun was just setting over the trees and the mountains beyond.

"I remember this place," syn-Tavaite said. "We dined here."

One of the black-enameled household robots floated up

on silent nullgravs. A crimson light flashed inside its ovoid sensor pod.

"Welcome back, my lady," it said to Beka. "Lieutenant Commander Jessan, Gentlesir LeSoit, Doctor syn-Tavaite. Will you be wishing the same quarters as before?"

"Yes," said Beka. "All of us. The two new guests are Owen Rosselin-Metadi, Master of the Adepts' Guild, a native of Galcen, and his apprentice Klea Santreny of Nammerin. See that their accommodations are suitable as well. Aboard *Warhammer*, in number-one crew berthing, there is another person, whose name is not important. Make certain that he has adequate food and water, and that the cabin door stays locked with him behind it."

"Yes, my lady," the robot said.

"One more thing," Beka said. "Is there a stasis box containing a replicant on board this station?"

"Not to my knowledge, my lady," the robot replied. "Shall I query my series mates?"

"Yes," Beka said. "Please do."

The red light inside the robot's sensor pod flickered for a moment before it spoke again. "I'm sorry, my lady. None of us have any information concerning stasis boxes or replicants, in any combination."

"Thank you," Beka said. "You may go."

She turned back to the others. "Now that the formalities are out of the way, let's figure out what we're going to do next. First is finding the replicant. I'm certain that it exists, and that it's here."

"You do realize," Jessan said, "that searching the whole base is not going to be like playing a game of find-the-slipper. This place is huge."

"If she's here, she's in a stasis box, and something like that can't just have been shoved out of the way at random," Beka said. "There's got to be a record somewhere. The Prof would have wanted it to be found."

"The Prof didn't need a record if he already knew where the replicant was," said Jessan.

"He left the base to me, and he knew he wasn't coming back. So there has to be a record—maybe in the main comp system. I wasn't looking for anything like that the last time I was here, so I wouldn't necessarily have spotted it. You can all look different places; the robots will help if you ask."

"How about Tarveet?" LeSoit cut in. "I don't like leaving him alone on the ship."

"You heard," said Beka. "The robots will take care of him."

LeSoit looked dubious. "Like they did with D'Caer?"

"That's something else I have to look into," Beka said. "When I was here that time when we found he'd vanished, the Prof had just died and I was fresh out of a healing pod on Gyffer. We didn't spend a lot of time on meticulous records checks."

"We'll see," Jessan said. "Meantime, I'm going to check out the sickbay for anything that looks like a stasis box."

He turned to syn-Tavaite with a flourish and a courtly bow. "Doctor, will you accompany me?"

The others had all gone, and Klea Santreny was alone with Owen in the strange, illusion-filled room. The sun had gone down beyond the distant mountains, and the first stars glimmered in the night sky.

"I didn't know you could get holographic projections this good," she said. "Even that place we went to on Innish-Kyl wasn't this pretty."

"That's because Aneverian's country house was real," Owen said. "Reality has lumps in it; fantasy doesn't. And this is all fantasy."

"There must have been a real place a lot like this, though," Klea said, "because I can feel the memories here if I try hard enough. I think ... I think somebody very lonely made this room to remember something by."

"Memories like that can be dangerous," said Owen. "Don't get to liking this place too much. I'm not comfortable with the thought that Magelords can come and go here as they please."

"The air is cold here," Klea said. "And dry. Not like home."

"The sooner we find that stasis box, the sooner we can leave. And I'll be glad to go."

Klea looked at him curiously. "You think there really is a stasis box with a replicant in it?"

"My sister does. And if I were a gambler, I wouldn't put money on her hunch being wrong."

"You said there wasn't any such thing as luck."

"There isn't. But some people don't have to be Adepts to see which way the universe is flowing. They have the knack of throwing themselves into the stream at the moment when it's heading the way they want to go."

"Owen," Klea said, "what happens after we find the box? Does your sister—"

"Expect me to do sorcery, or work a miracle, or jump into the Void blindfolded carrying a life preserver?" Owen shrugged. "Something like that. But what she's contemplating—it goes against everything my own Master taught me."

"So what are we going to do?"

"Watch to see which way the stream is running," he said. "And in the meantime, search."

Llannat Hyfid was in the *Daughter*'s meditation room when the Mages broke through.

She had been in a high state of nerves ever since Ari had given her another hasty kiss and hurried down to the engine room to help attempt repairs. He hadn't come back. After a while all feeling of ship's motion had ceased, only to be replaced by an uneasy vibration, then by a high-pitched sound more felt through the deckplates than heard.

She had run, then, to the black-walled chamber where the door opened only to her, and had knelt there gripping her staff in her hand, trying to find and trace the currents of the universe. Somewhere, somehow, there had to be a trickle of power that she could follow, some loose thread in the weaving that she could catch hold of to pull them all out of the Magelords' grip—but there was nothing that she could see or do, and the universe held itself aloof.

"Patience," she muttered, and was silent. The ship had not been destroyed. Did they want prisoners? A moment of hand-to-hand fighting seemed the best she could hope for, and not even that if the Mages pumped some kind of gas into *Night's-Beautiful-Daughter* and waited to let it do its work.

Llannat wished she could be with Ari one last time. The brief while that they'd been married . . . she pushed the memories behind her.

Uneasy motion returned to the ship, followed by a short period of weightlessness. Then gravity returned. Llannat became aware that a stranger was approaching the meditation room.

The door slid open. A dark figure stood in the opening, dressed in the robes and mask of a Mage—similar in color to an Adept's garb, but different in cut and style. But the staff this person carried was very similar indeed to the staff that Llannat clenched in her own sweating hand.

The newcomer spoke. *"Ekkat aredenei, etaze."*

He bowed, then knelt before her, laying his staff on the deck, and spoke again in slow, heavily accented Galcenian:

"Welcome home, Mistress."

Jessan stood in the gleaming, well-appointed sickbay of the asteroid base, with Doctor syn-Tavaite beside him. He remembered the first time that Ari and Llannat Hyfid had seen the sickbay, when they were fresh from the Med Station on Nammerin—Llannat had pointed out, with awed appreciation, that the equipment was state-of-the-art, nothing older than two Standard years.

And now, he thought, *we all know why.*

"Look around," he said to syn-Tavaite. "Do you remember this room?"

"No," the Eraasian said. She seemed confused. "I remember the room we were in before. But the door that opens into here—didn't, when the Masked One brought me to this place."

"Damn," said Jessan. "Another brilliant idea shot to hell. Any other differences you've noticed so far?"

"We didn't come through here to find that other room," she said. "And the entrance was different . . . not a door in bare rock . . . I saw a great house on a mountainside, and everything green and growing."

"How odd," Jessan said. "But considering the person who used to own this place, not really surprising."

"You knew the Masked One?"

"Oh, yes," said Jessan. "Someday, Doctor, I'll tell you about the night he and the captain showed up in *my* work-room. In the meantime, let's try going at our problem the other way around. That door in the other room—the one that opens into this sickbay now—where did it lead to be-fore?"

"A big room," syn-Tavaite replied at once. "With more high windows, and other doors leading from it, and a stone floor, and a fire on the hearth."

"Doesn't sound like a sickbay to me," Jessan said. "Maybe it was another holoprojection." A quick scan of the immaculate walls, however, failed to reveal any unexplained switches or toggles. "Damn."

He fell silent for a while, thinking. Finally he looked up. "That bay outside has disguised itself as a landing field at least once before. Let's head back to *Warhammer*. I need to get a comm link."

"A . . . link? You're going to leave me alone someplace?"

"Yes. But we'll be able to talk." He gave her what he hoped was a reassuring smile. "Don't worry, you'll be safe."

"Safe among the Adepts," syn-Tavaite muttered. She added something else in a language Jessan didn't under-stand.

Probably just as well, he thought. *It didn't sound partic-ularly flattering.*

However, she followed him without protest out into the main docking area, where he ducked briefly into

Warhammer and came out with one of the pocket comm links. He handed her the link.

"Here," he said. "I'll be in touch with you over this. If you want to say something to me, push that button there and talk. As soon as you see something that looks like the place you came to before, give me the word."

She gave him an uncertain nod. "Yes. If I see mountains and sky here inside a cave in the rock, I will surely tell you."

"Good. Now stay right here."

Jessan went back inside, and made his way through the base's maze of passageways to a room filled with holoprojectors and comp consoles—and memories. The last time he'd been in here, Beka had been trying to get the truth about Perada's assassination out of Ebenra D'Caer. The Professor had used an elaborate illusion-making setup to turn the base's landing bay into a spaceport on Ovredis.

He frowned as he remembered further. The Prof had drawn that particular sequence extempore, playing over the keys on the projector console to create a rolling panorama. What if he'd done the same thing for Doctor syn-Tavaite?

No. He came in with her. He couldn't have been up in the booth making the scenery.

He looked up at the overhead. "I need a robot in here."

A few seconds later, one of the robots floated into the projection room. "What can I do for you, Commander?"

"Can you work the controls in here?"

"Of course, Commander," the robot said. "The base comps are provided with any number of pleasing sequences, all of which I am able to access."

"Do any of those sequences show the landing field at Entibor?"

"Which field, Commander? There are several."

"The one at the Summer Palace," Jessan said.

"An excellent choice," said the robot. "That sequence is one of the most extensive in the entire library. The real-time links to the continuing display in the informal dining room are particularly—"

"Thank you," said Jessan. "Run it, please."

The robot floated over to the holoprojector console. Jessan keyed on his comm link.

"Stand by, Doctor," he said. "Take a look at this."

VIII. Asteroid Base
Gyfferan Farspace: *Sword-of-the-Dawn*

BEKA STOOD in the control center of the asteroid base, the circular chamber that housed the base's hyperspace communications links, its internal security monitors, and the access terminals for main base memory. She hadn't been in here since taking the *'Hammer* to Suivi Point; nor—absent the necessary specific instructions about this most secure of the base's areas—had any of the robots entered the room to clean. The Professor's last, handwritten note still lay crumpled on the console where she had dropped it.

The door behind her slid open to let in Ignaceu LeSoit. Beka nodded a greeting.

"Ignac'," she said. "How are the others doing?"

"All right, I suppose. Jessan knows his way around; Doctor syn-Tavaite is safe with him. The Adepts—I don't know what they're doing, but they can probably take care of themselves."

"I hope so," Beka said. "I'm going to need Owen if this is going to work. If it doesn't . . ."

"If it doesn't, we're still in a good position to wait out the rest of the war quite comfortably." ·

Beka gave him a curious look. "Are you putting that forward as a serious suggestion?"

"I didn't think you'd want to overlook anything."

She shook her head. "The base isn't secure—not from the Mageworlders, anyhow. They know right where this place is, and can come and go undetected. They didn't have any trouble pulling out Ebenra D'Caer."

"He never mentioned a rescue," LeSoit said. "At least not to me. And I was as close to him as anyone."

"There's no record of him leaving," Beka said. "Watch."

She sat down at the main security console. "This is the log from D'Caer's cell," she said, bringing up the sequences on a flatvid screen. "He was being tended by the Professor's robots, and the record shows that he was in place right up to the moment when I opened his door. Then he was gone."

"That's what the record shows, all right," LeSoit said. "But you know, comps and robots aren't people. You may not be authorized to ask them those particular questions."

"I damned well ought to be authorized," she said. "And they know it. Look at this."

She picked up the Professor's note and shoved it at LeSoit. He smoothed out the wadded-up paper and began reading it—at first aloud, then onward silently to the end.

" 'My lady: I write this on the night before our leavetaking for Darvell; I do not know when you shall read it. . . . The robots will have told you long since that the base and all its contents are yours. . . .' "

"That's it," Beka said when he finished and looked up. "He never came back from Darvell, but the rest of us did— and when we got here, D'Caer was gone. I searched everything in the files, from the moment when he arrived and was definitely present until the moment when I checked for myself and he was definitely gone. Nothing."

"He signed the note," LeSoit said.

"Who?"

"The Professor. He signed the note. 'Arekhon Khreseio sus-Khalgaeth sus-Peledaen.' It's his name."

"He never told me," Beka said. She felt an irrational jealousy toward LeSoit, that he should have read the signature when she could not. " 'Names change and the universe has forgotten mine,' he said when I asked."

"If the universe forgets a name like that, it's because the owner wants it forgotten," said LeSoit. "We're looking at high nobility there, on both sides."

Beka stared at the square of paper without speaking until the graceful characters quit showing a tendency to blur.

"All right," she said finally. "I've called up the actions of Ebenra D'Caer, and I've called up the actions of the Professor and all the rest of us for that time period. You think I should call up the actions of one Arekhon sus-Peledaen?"

LeSoit shrugged. "Would it hurt?"

"I suppose not." She turned back to the console and searched the security records under the new terms. New sequences began to play in the flatscreen. "I'll be damned," she said.

The records showed the cell of Ebenra D'Caer, unconscious as he had been in all the sequences before, and this time they also showed the Professor—*sus-Peledaen*, Beka reminded herself—entering D'Caer's cell in the company of one of the household robots. At a command from the Professor, the robot carried D'Caer away. The Professor locked the cell behind them.

The next sequence showed the base's landing bay, with *Warhammer* in its customary place among the vast collection of ships. The Professor accompanied the robot carrying D'Caer aboard one of the smaller spacecraft. A few minutes later both man and robot exited the craft unencumbered. The Professor walked into the base, not looking back.

"Identify craft," Beka said.

FREETRADER MAIN CHANCE, came a small box on-screen.

"Is *Main Chance* currently on board this station?"

NEGATIVE.

"What is the current location and status of *Main Chance*?"

UNKNOWN, came the response. LAST KNOWN DESTINATION ERAASI VIA THE NET.

"Damnation," Beka said, and turned back to the recording. "Continue playback of actions of sus-Peledaen."

The security records followed the Professor back through the sickbay and into the Entibor room, where the tall windows looked out across the wooded hills. The long chamber was flooded with illusory starlight. Removing his tunic, the Professor hung it on the back of a chair and sat in his shirtsleeves. Another household robot brought him a crystal decanter filled with dark liquid, and matching glasses.

He poured a drink for himself and sat with his fingers upon the delicate stem, gazing out across the landscape he had created. The moon rose, casting shadows across his white shirt and touching his grey hair with silver. He sat there for a long time, while Beka watched the record, before he looked up in the direction of the archway that led farther into the station, and spoke to the one who had come.

"You're awake late, Mistress Hyfid," he said.

"Damnation," Beka said again, and froze the picture. "The Professor was the Magelord who released D'Caer. And here I thought he was a friend."

"He was," said LeSoit. "You went to the far side of the Net to get D'Caer, and a lot of other things followed from that."

"Nothing that matters anymore," Beka said sourly. "We're still losing." She spoke again to the log recorder. "Call up all records of sus-Peledaen prior to arrival of Ebenra D'Caer on this station."

A moment passed, then another.

NO BASE RECORDS OF ACTIVITIES OF SUS-PELEDAEN PRIOR TO ARRIVAL OF EBENRA D'CAER EXIST.

"The hell they don't. Call up all base records of Doctor Inesi syn-Tavaite prior to today."

NO BASE RECORDS OF DOCTOR SYN-TAVAITE PRIOR TO TODAY EXIST.

"'No base records exist' ... what the hell is that supposed to mean?"

"Wait a minute," LeSoit said. "Let's try something else. Call up all records of a visit by General Metadi to this station."

GENERAL METADI HAS NEVER VISITED THIS STATION.

"You see?" he said. "The message is different."

Beka frowned at the console. "So Doctor syn-Tavaite was here, but this machine won't tell us. And something happened, but it won't tell us that, either. Wonderful."

"I think that Arekhon sus-Peledaen wanted to make sure the truth was well hidden."

"Hidden from me?"

"No," said LeSoit. "Hidden from those who knew his true name. The Professor was up to something he didn't want the rest of the Magelords to find out."

"All right, Doctor," Jessan said over the comm link. "Now what do you see?"

syn-Tavaite's voice came back to him, sounding awed and nervous. "This is the place. How did you do it?"

"I didn't," said Jessan. "The Professor—your Masked One—did it, a long time ago. Stay right there and I'll join you."

He clicked off the link, said to the robot, "Continue the sequence as instructed," and made his way through the base to the docking bay. Seeming night had fallen outside the windows of the Entibor room, where more household robots were setting the long table for dinner as he passed through. He left the robots at work behind him and continued out through the sickbay to the docking area where syn-Tavaite stood waiting.

Jessan had to admit that the change was spectacular. Everything around him was silvery-grey with moonlight, while the mountains that bordered the landing field loomed like dark shoulders against a paler sky. He could almost feel the night wind and smell the dew-moistened earth.

He looked back at the door he'd come through and found that it had vanished, hidden beneath the Professor's complex illusions. But syn-Tavaite remained visible before him, as did *Warhammer*, poised behind the Eraasian woman for all the world as if this were someone's private landing area in an upcountry field.

"Well, Doctor," he said. "Here we are. Does this look a

bit more like the place where you went to create the replicant?"

"Yes," she said. "It was day when we came, but the mountains are the same."

"Which way did you go next?"

She pointed—not back at the sickbay door, but in the other direction. Jessan followed the gesture and saw a wide, high structure rising over the treetops on the hillside above, its white walls pale and ghostlike beneath the moon, its windows aglow with yellow light. A road wound up toward the great house through the trees.

"The Summer Palace of House Rosselin," he said quietly. "How did you get there last time?"

"We took a car that floated," syn-Tavaite told him. "A marvelous thing."

"I suppose it would seem that way," murmured Jessan, recalling the noisy, bad-smelling groundhuggers that he'd ridden on the Mageworlds side of the Net. "Well, we're going to walk it this evening, so let's go."

They set out on foot. He wasn't surprised when the great house approached more rapidly than seemed possible—though all the same, the effect was distinctly unsettling. They soon arrived under the front gates, where the moonlight threw the patterns on the carved stone into sharp relief.

With a faint start, Jessan recognized the gate as the main base door in the landing bay, the door that Beka had long ago warned him was a false entrance and booby-trapped against intrusion. He regarded it uneasily.

"Are you sure this was the way you came?" he asked.

"Oh, yes."

"Mmm." He thought for a moment. "Did the Masked One do or say anything in particular to make the gate open?"

syn-Tavaite shook her head. "No. He only touched the gate, and we entered."

Positive interlock with the landing-field illusions, Jessan thought. *I hope.*

He put his hand against the stone, half-expecting to be

felled by an energy bolt or dropped into a pit or any one of a dozen other holovid-style demises.

The gate swung open.

The more time Klea Santreny spent in the Domina's asteroid base, the less she liked it.

"It's too big, it's too empty, and I'm never certain what's real and what isn't." She gestured toward the dead-end wall that currently confronted them. They'd come a long way from the holographically enhanced upper regions, into an area of dim passageways and empty rooms. She hoped that Owen knew the way back. "At least down here in the basement I can be fairly sure that a blank wall isn't really something else in disguise."

"Maybe," said Owen. He stood leaning on his staff and looking at the wall. "And maybe not. This is a strange place, and full of Magery. Old workings, but very strong."

He put out a hand and touched the wall. For a moment he said nothing—then, carefully, he drew his hand away.

"Yes," he said. "You spoke more truth than you knew—close your eyes and look at the wall again."

She'd spent enough time around Owen by now to know that in spite of the apparent contradiction, he meant exactly what he'd said. She closed her eyes and laid the palm of her hand against the cool stone blocks in front of her.

"All right," Owen said. "What do you see?"

She concentrated, trying to sort out the impressions. "There's something in here that doesn't belong. Bright pebbles in the rock . . . or stars, burning and burning . . . I can't tell whether everything I'm feeling is big or little."

"Anything else?"

"I don't think . . . yes. It *is* a door. The stars light the way through."

"Can you follow them?"

"Yes."

"Then we'll open the door. Ready . . . with me . . . now."

She didn't have time to argue; she could sense him moving away, along the path marked out by the bright places in the rock, and knew that he expected her to follow.

It's just like going from one light to another on a dark street, she told herself, and took a step forward.

The first step was the hardest—like forcing herself to leave a safe place for the long walk home, and not daring to look back over her shoulder. After that the lights came closer and closer together, until she passed the final marker and knew that she was through.

Klea opened her eyes.

Walls of rough stone pressed in close on either side, and she could feel cold rock against her back. A faint white light shone nearby, pale at first but growing brighter, illuminating the long, tunnel-like passage that stretched out ahead of her into the dark.

She looked over to her right. Owen was there—the white light was coming from his staff.

"Where are we?" she asked.

"Still inside the base somewhere, I hope."

"You mean you don't know for sure?"

He sighed. "Omniscience was never part of the job description. This base is full of doors and passages, and not all of them lead to places that I want to think about right now."

"Oh." Klea thought about the solid wall at her back. She couldn't feel the lights anymore—maybe they only worked in one direction. "What do we do?"

"We go on," said Owen. "And look for more doors."

They followed the narrow passage for some time. Klea couldn't tell if they were rising, descending, or keeping to a level path somewhere far beneath the surface of the asteroid. Doors—some of dull metal, some of wood—led away from the sides of the tunnel from time to time, but none of them opened to a physical touch, and none had the interior markers that would allow passage.

She lost track of time long before they reached the final door. This one, unlike all the others, stood ajar. Whatever lay beyond it was hidden in darkness.

"It looks like this is it," Klea said. "If we end up right where we started—"

"I don't think so."

The door opened onto another passageway at right angles

to the first. They followed the new passage for some time
before coming to an open archway with a pale light beyond
it. When they passed through the archway, they were once
again in the long room with arched windows where they
had begun their search.

"I told you," said Klea. "Right where we started."

"No," Owen said. He glanced about the shadowy room
with an abstracted expression. "Not really. It's a mirror image of the room above."

He crossed the room to the far door, the one that should
have opened into the base's sickbay, and touched the
lockplate. The door slid open—but instead of medical
equipment and storage cabinets, Klea saw a paneled room
with a great fireplace of rough stone. A polished slab of
the same pale grey rock had been set into the back of the
hearth, and there were pictures carved into the stone.

Owen was already kneeling by the empty hearth, his
hands tracing the carvings, by the time Klea got up the
courage to enter. She hurried to join him.

"What is it?" she asked.

He glanced up at her, then turned his attention back to
the hearth. "The carvings are the royal arms of Entibor and
the personal arms of House Rosselin. And this is another
door."

Klea hesitated for a moment, then bent and touched the
carved slab. Owen was right; she could feel the way-
markers glowing inside the rock.

"Do we go through?" she asked.

"I think we have to," he said. "This is the other side of
reality here. If we don't go through, we can't get back."

She closed her eyes, the way she had before, and stepped
forward. When she opened them again, she and Owen were
standing in the memory-room, with the first rays of moonlight coming in through the row of tall windows, and tall
candles in twisted silver holders burning on the long table.
There was a white cloth on the table as well; and porcelain
plates flanked by silver cutlery; and Beka Rosselin-Metadi
sitting at the head of the table and Ignaceu LeSoit at its
foot.

"Just in time for dinner," Owen's sister said.

Llannat stared at the Mage kneeling on the deck before her, and fought against a rising sense of panic. Of all the things she'd expected to happen, this was perhaps the last.

Now what am I supposed to do? she thought. *Kill him while he's kneeling there, and try to escape?*

To where? answered the voice of reason inside her head. And another, colder voice said, *What use would it be to run? They already know what you really are—and you do, too.*

What I really am. I should have known a long time ago: if the student of an Adept is an Adept, the student of a Magelord is surely a Mage.

Revulsion came over her like a dark wave, blurring her vision and threatening to beat her down onto the deck. So strong was the feeling that she contemplated asking the kneeling Mage to kill her now and put an end to everything—but the moment passed. The dark tide went out again, and she knew that, Mage or Adept, she was still Llannat Hyfid of Maraghai, and she was not alone. She would have known it, if she were alone.

She said aloud, "What has become of the others who were in this ship with me?"

"They have been taken away, Mistress," the Mage replied. "Those who were hurt are being tended."

"Were any killed?"

"No, Mistress. The First of my Circle forbade it."

"I want to speak with them. Come, take me to them."

"Yes, Mistress."

The Mage retrieved his staff, stood, and began to walk away. Llannat followed.

"Whose ship is this, Mistress?" the Mage asked as they walked through the passageways of *Night's-Beautiful-Daughter*.

"Mine," Llannat said, without thinking. Then she paused. She'd given a false answer this time—at least, false as the Gyfferan Local Defense Force would have understood the matter—but only because in her own mind she knew the answer to be true. The *Daughter* was hers by right of inheritance. She would have to be more careful what she said from now on.

But the Mage asked no more questions. He merely said, "Ah," and continued to lead the way to the *Daughter*'s main hatch. The Deathwing hung suspended above the brightly lit deck of a landing bay, gripped in metal claws extending from the overhead. They climbed down a temporary stairway to the deck, then went via white-painted passageways to a cabin much like the one she had left behind on the Deathwing.

The Mage ushered her in, bowing, and said, "If it pleases you, Mistress, wait here. My First shall attend you shortly."

"And if it doesn't please me?"

Her host looked startled, or at least as startled as anyone who wore a full-face mask of black plastic could manage to look. "You are free to come and go as you will, Mistress. If you require anything, it shall be provided."

"I want to see the others from my ship," Llannat said. "Now."

"Yes, Mistress," the Mage said. "Pray accompany me."

He led the way again, this time to another level, and from there to a series of rooms. He slid open the first door and stepped back. A force field shimmered across the opening. Llannat looked in—there were Lieutenant Vinhalyn, Chief Yance, and all the rest of the *Daughter*'s crew, but not Ari.

"Is this everyone?" Llannat asked.

"There was another," the Mage responded. "A big man. He was hurt in the fighting. But he will be well."

"What will you do with these?"

"What you command, Mistress."

"Llannat Hyfid!" Lieutenant Vinhalyn called out through the force field. "Whose side are you on?"

"The right one, I hope," Llannat called back. "I'm playing all this by ear." To the Mage she said, "Show these the honor you show me."

"As you wish," the Mage responded.

He flipped a panel control and the force field vanished.

"Now," Llannat said, "take me to the other man. I wish to see him. Then I will speak with your First."

The Mage bowed his head. "So it shall be. Do you wish your *geaerith* for the interview?"

"Geaerith?" Llannat asked.

"Your . . . ah, your mask," the Mage replied, and tapped his plastic face covering.

"Yes," Llannat said. "I suppose so. Yes, fetch me one."

Klea had taken a seat at the long table, as had Owen, but nobody, so far, had done so much as lift the covers off the serving dishes. There was red wine in crystal goblets, which nobody was drinking. Klea had taken a sip of hers, enough to determine that it was a long way from purple aqua vitae or Tree Frog beer, and had let the goblet stand untouched thereafter.

Jessan and Doctor syn-Tavaite were still missing and the Domina was getting restless. Finally Beka shoved back her chair and stood up.

"I could have sworn Nyls was too practical to miss dinner," she said. "I'll have to send the robots—"

Before she could finish, the far wall of the dining room shimmered as the holoprojection rearranged itself into a carved wooden doorway. The door opened, and Jessan and syn-Tavaite entered the room.

"I thought you were lost," Beka said.

"Not exactly." The Khesatan moved to stand by the table at the Domina's left hand, but he didn't sit down. Instead, he picked up a glass of wine and drank off almost half of it without stopping. "We found another way into the base— that false door is a real one if you've got the Summer Palace landing field illusion up and running in the docking bay. And after *that*, Doctor syn-Tavaite showed me her laboratory."

"For making replicants?"

The Domina's voice sounded brittle, almost uncertain— Klea wondered if she was, after all, afraid of what she hoped to do. *Funny—the way Owen talks, his sister isn't afraid of anything.*

Jessan drained the rest of his wine. "Yes."

"Was there—"

"A replicant in a stasis box? No."

"You're sure you looked everywhere?"

Klea thought she saw Jessan shudder. "Oh, yes."

All this time, Owen had been looking at the new doorway with a curious expression. "Which room is on the other side of that wall?" he asked. "Is it the laboratory?"

Jessan shook his head. "No—it's another room from the Summer Palace. The Great Hall, if I remember my art history correctly. Allegorical frescoes on the ceiling, armorial carvings on the hearth. . . ."

"The hearth." Owen stood up. "I wonder—"

The door opened for him when he touched it. Through the gap, Klea saw the paneled room with the great fireplace, brightly lit by glow-globes in wrought-metal sconces along the walls.

"Well, well, well," said the Domina. "Today has been just *full* of pleasant surprises."

Owen was already standing by the hearth when Klea and the others joined him. "Here," he said, pointing to the carved patterns that he had called the arms of Entibor and House Rosselin. "Look behind here."

"I don't think so," Jessan replied. "It's all illusion, remember?"

The Khesatan extended both hands into the projection that made up the wooden overmantel. "There's nothing back here but smooth wall." He moved his hands over to the right, and they sank into the embroidered tapestry that overlaid the rich wooden panels. "Nothing here either. No cloth, no wood, just metal."

"We'll see," said Beka. She raised her voice. "Base: switch off the holoprojections."

The illusion vanished. Klea saw that the entire room was a featureless cube of polished steel. The only relief from the stark blankness was provided by sliding doors at either end and recessed light panels in the ceiling. The steel walls were all of one piece, unmarked and unmarred.

"All right, Owen," Beka said. "Do you still say this is it?"

"It has to be."

The Domina frowned at the steel walls for a moment, then reached inside her jacket and pulled out a marking stylus. "Base: turn the projections back on."

The fireplace, the hangings, the leaded-glass windows all reappeared. "Here we go," Beka said. "Let's see what happens."

With the stylus, she outlined the carved slab. The top of the scribing tool appeared to sink into the stone and vanish without leaving a mark, but she kept on working. When she'd finished, she took a step backward.

"Base: projections off."

Once again the fireplace disappeared. On the wall where it had been, a square black outline remained.

"Right," Beka said. She raised her voice again. "Robots, fetch me a mask and a cutting torch."

Owen looked at her. "Bee, you aren't going to—"

"Quit sounding like Ari," she replied. "I own this place; I can do what I want with it. And I'm fully qualified in hull repair."

One of the maintenance robots trundled up, carrying a cutting outfit. "Your tools, my lady."

"Thank you." Beka picked up the mask and fitted it over her face, then pulled on the thick gloves. "Don't look, people, if you don't want flash burns."

The Domina picked up the torch and keyed the self-starter. A brilliant flame sprang from the nozzle, and Klea had to look away. For a few minutes the steel room was full of the hissing sound of the torch and the smell of hot metal. Then the hissing stopped, followed by a metallic clang.

Klea looked up. A square opening loomed in the wall, an opening the same size as the carved hearthstone had been. And beyond the opening, revealed by the action of the cutting torch, was an empty, gaping hole.

The Domina flipped up her mask. "There," she said. "Be careful how you look inside—the edges are still hot."

"I've done as much work around the spacedocks as you,"

314 • DEbRA DoyLE & JAMES D. MACdoNALd

Owen replied. Carefully, he extended his staff into the gap in the wall. A few seconds later, the same pale white light Klea had seen come out of the staff earlier lit up the opening.

Owen bent forward. The uncanny light fell onto his face, making him look suddenly older.

"You were right," he said. "There's a stasis box in here. It has a transparent top."

The Domina seemed to stop breathing for a moment. Her features were pale and tense. "Anything inside it?"

"Yes." Owen paused. When he went on, it was in a voice Klea had never heard from him before. "It's got Mother."

PART FOUR

I. Gyfferan System Space: RFS *Veratina*; UDC *Fezrisond*; RSF *Karipavo* Asteroid Base
Gyfferan Farspace: *Sword-of-the-Dawn*

"**T**HIS IS how it's going to work," Metadi said.

With Tyche and Quetaya, he was standing at the *'Tina*'s main battle tank. The infantry colonel was already in his armored p-suit, with the helmet cradled underneath one arm.

The General illuminated an area inside the tank. "There's our axis of attack: the place the main Gyfferan fleet is heading toward, and the damaged units are limping away from. We'll make our first dropout over here, and listen on the passive detection gear for electronic combat noise—lightspeed and hypercomm signals, fire control and ranging beams, energy flares, you know the drill. When we find some, we'll take another line of bearing, then jump at right angles to it. Do it a second time, get another bearing, and where those three lines cross we'll have our fix on the action."

Quetaya frowned at the display. "Even based on the sketchy info we've got, it looks like a bad time is being had by all in that little corner of the universe. Driving straight in could get us fired on by both sides instead of just the Mages."

"It's a risk I'm willing to accept," Metadi said. "I want to find the Mages' flagship and take it out, not just cause random damage."

"If the flagship goes and we go with it," she said, "what's that going to gain us?"

"Us personally? Nothing but a starpilot's grave out here in the dark. And some glory, maybe, but glory's cold. The important thing is, we'll have bought the rest of the Space Force a bit more time."

"You do have a way with words, General," said Tyche. "Nobody could make an attack like this one sound like fun, but at least you make it sound worth the trouble."

"Years of practice, Colonel. Years of practice."

"I'm off to join my recons, then," said Tyche. "See you again when the dust settles."

"There's a pub on Gyffer," said Metadi, "or at least there used to be. The Seven Orbs. I'll buy you a drink when all this is over."

"Drinks, aye."

The colonel saluted and left CIC. Metadi resumed his seat at the TAO's station.

"All units stand by for hyperspace translation on my signal," he said. "Ready to jump . . . go."

The stylized planetary system in the main battle tank suddenly boiled with activity in the region of the system's gas giant. The blue dots that signified the warships of Metadi's task force broke out of orbit, streaked up to jump speed, and vanished from the realspace diagram.

"So you still won't do it," Beka said to Owen.

They were back at their evening meal in the Entibor room, dining by candlelight around the long table. Nobody had much appetite, it seemed, even after a prolonged stretch on the 'Hammer's space rations. The knowledge of the stasis box waiting for them in the next room, and the memory of what it contained, were too much with them for anyone's comfort.

"I didn't say I wouldn't do it," Owen said. "I said that I couldn't. I don't know how to reach the Void on my own—even assuming that's how the work is done. An Adept's no good for this, Bee. You want a Mage."

Down at the far end of the table, next to LeSoit, Doctor syn-Tavaite met Beka's glance straight on for the first time, and shook her head. "Not I. My part was done already. The Masked One would have kept me longer, if more was needed."

Beka frowned. Moodily, she began drawing lines on the tablecloth with the tip of her dagger. If the fabric gave way under the pressure, the Prof's robots would know how to mend it. He'd always thought of things like that, and had prepared for them well in advance. . . . She looked up.

"The Prof knew he was going to buy it on Darvell; he'd already told the robots that the base was mine by the time we left. Back before that, he had Doctor syn-Tavaite make a replicant for him, and the first thing he did with it was seal it away and go looking for me. He must have wanted me to have the replicant. And if he wanted me to have it, he must have seen a way for someone else to—to finish the process."

Jessan smiled faintly. "I'd hate to count the amazing leaps of logic in that statement. Just the same, you're right; if we don't work on those assumptions we might as well retire from the fight and take up flower arranging."

"Thanks for the vote of confidence," Beka said. "I think." She tested the point of her dagger on the pad of one finger, and watched the yellow candlelight flow up and down the blade. "All right. Owen says we need a Mage, and Doctor syn-Tavaite says that she isn't one. Fine: if there's one thing the civilized galaxy has too many of right now, it's Mages. All we have to do is borrow one of them for a while."

Ignaceu LeSoit set down his wineglass. "And convince him to bring about the defeat of his own side, of his own free will and out of the kindness of his heart? Good luck."

"Frankly, Ignac'," Beka said, "I don't care how the Mage in question feels about it—if we have him, I can convince him. The hard part is going to be catching him." She looked about the table. "Anybody have an idea where to go hunting?"

"There were Mages on Nammerin," Klea said.

"And on Pleyver," said Owen, "and on Ophel and Artat and probably any other world you'd care to name. There were even deep-cover agents on Galcen—sometimes their workings would disturb me there."

"You said Pleyver?" Beka broke in.

"Yes. I met some there, if you remember—including at least one Great Lord. And Pleyver is in open rebellion against the Republic. There are almost certainly Mages on Pleyver."

"Yes . . ." Beka thought for a moment, then smiled. "I wonder if Pleyver would trade me the use of one Magelord for the safe return of their councillor?"

"If I were running the show on Pleyver," LeSoit said, "I know what I'd say to a proposal like that. I'd tell you to keep the councillor and welcome to him."

"Well, you aren't running the show out there," Beka told him, "and we won't know until we try." She looked around the table. "Ladies and gentlemen, I've made up my mind. We leave for Pleyver first thing tomorrow morning."

"Admiral—we're approaching the Gyfferan system."

"Very well, Salagrie." Admiral Vallant turned to face his aide. "We've done what our allies requested by coming here. Now we act on our own."

Vallant was in his office aboard *Fezrisond*. The map-cube on the corner of his desk held a holographic representation—vastly shrunk—of former Republic space. The diagram, in white dots within a black matrix, showed the Infabede sector highlighted as an irregular turquoise blob. Gyffer and its assorted dependencies, occupying a portion of space between Infabede and the rest of the galaxy, were currently highlighted in pale green. Other points of interest were picked out in red.

The admiral regarded all of this with satisfaction. On the whole, things were going quite well: Mandeyn and Artat were nearly surrounded and should soon come under his control, and as soon as the Gyfferans saw reason, his reach would extend to within striking range of Galcen itself.

After that, no matter what the Mages had gained, he would control even more. They would have to negotiate with him.

The comm link on his desktop beeped. "Gyfferan scouts approaching, Admiral. We're being hailed."

"Tell them that we're here to defend them against the Mages," Vallant said. "And get our ships within range of all of their units. I want to capture as many as I can. We'll need them later."

There was a pause. Then, over the link: "Gyffer requests to know the reason we had units hiding in their system, Admiral."

"Find out what they're talking about." Vallant looked at his aide. "If our intelligence section sent anybody out here without clearing it first . . ."

"If they did," said Salagrie, "they didn't run it past me."

The comms tech on the other end of the link came on again: "Gyfferan scouts report that RSF *Veratina* was spotted on sensors earlier today, making a jump run. They know she was assigned to your fleet. They demand to know why you were spying."

"Tell them they'll get their explanation." He paused, and addressed Salagrie again. "But I wasn't spying. At least not that way." He leaned toward his aide. "Find out where *Veratina* is right now. Captain Faramon is going to have some serious explaining to do."

Llannat's masked guide took her through more white-painted passageways to a large room that was, plainly, the sickbay of the ship. Some of the equipment was unfamiliar; most of it, though, looked like ordinary Republic technology, several decades out of date. She went over to the bed where Ari lay.

He looked pale and uncomfortable—the bed was even less adapted to his huge frame than the standard-issue Space Force models had been—but he was awake, and the change in his expression when he saw her did much to ease her own inner pain. His left arm lay unbandaged outside the sheet; she smiled at him and took his hand.

"You look like hell," she said. "What happened?"

"I got shot," he replied. "Nothing too bad. They have me patched up with gauze and tape—first-aid stuff, really, but I don't see any healing pods in here, so I can't complain."

"Well, I can," said Llannat. She turned to her guide. "Is this the best treatment your medics have to offer?"

Her guide made an apologetic gesture. "I'm sorry, Mistress, but we have only a limited supply of *eibriyu* on board."

"*Eibriyu?*"

The guide seemed to grope for the proper words in Galcenian. "Ah . . . material? For rebuilding the body . . . it takes purpose quickly as needed."

"Fetch some," Llannat said. "I want this man beside me when I speak with the First."

"Perhaps I can be of help," said another voice close by. The new speaker's Galcenian, while accented, was far more fluent than the guide's had been.

Llannat turned, and saw a person—a man, by the voice—in the black robes and mask of a Mage, carrying another, identical mask in his hand.

"I am the First of the Circle aboard this vessel," he said, and offered the mask to Llannat.

She hesitated for a moment, then took the mask and slipped it on. She found that the portion over the eyes was partially transparent, leaving the room darkened and misty—but now, when she stretched out her senses around her, she could see quite clearly the nets and patterns woven by the silver cords.

"If you are the First aboard this ship," Llannat said, "then tell your medics to give this man the same treatment that your own crew members would receive."

"So it shall be," the First said, and spoke rapidly to the other in his own tongue before turning back to her. "Is there more that you require?"

"I need information," Llannat said. "I need to know purposes."

During the whole time she was speaking she had not taken her eyes away from the silver cords. *Another reason for the mask,* she thought. *No one can tell whether a Mage is looking at things, or looking* into *them.* As she was looking now, still seeking the pattern she had seen aboard *Night's-Beautiful-Daughter* what seemed like a lifetime ago, the pattern that the Professor had left behind him for her to finish.

She found it. Closer than ever before, but distorted. Large patches of the fabric no longer held the design that the Professor had so laboriously created. The First was speaking to her, but Llannat no longer heard what he said. She was concentrating on grasping the loosened cords and weaving them again into the fabric, bringing the design together. One of the cords moved closer to its position. . . .

New movement in the room brought Llannat out of her almost-trance. She saw a man in a brown uniform, carrying a metal tablet not unlike the clipboards used on the Republic side of the Net. He spoke in his own tongue to the First.

"Your pardon, my lady," said the First. "This has the highest priority identifiers. You see how minor duties interfere with the most important matters?"

He looked at the pad and apparently read whatever was there.

"Your pardon again," he said to Llannat. "I must leave you for a moment."

He turned at once and departed, with the messenger following behind. Shortly afterward Llannat felt the disorientation that signaled a jump into hyper.

The silver cords floating in her peripheral vision knotted and slid into place.

"Ready," Beka said. "Moving out."

Warhammer rose from the deckplates on nullgravs, turned, and headed out of the bay. Beka took the freighter at low speed into the asteroid field, and carefully through—getting out was easier than getting in, but it still wasn't a job for an amateur. Several minutes of finicky piloting later, Beka flipped on the intraship comms.

"Stand by for run-to-jump," she said. "If you're not strapped in, time to get that way. Next stop, Pleyver."

"Wait a minute," Jessan said from the copilot's seat beside her. "Contact up ahead. Big one."

"Oh, lovely," Beka said. "Absolutely lovely." She fed more power to the realspace engines. "What's the ID?"

"Warship," Jessan said. "Lighting us up with frequencies in the fire-control range. But nothing Republic in the signature."

"Mages?"

"Looks like."

"Just what I goddamn needed." She switched on the shields at full, kicked in the override to give more-than-maximum power to the engines, and pushed the throttles all the way forward. "Where *is* the son of a bitch?"

"Moving, he's moving."

"Tell me he isn't covering my jump point for Pleyver."

"He's heading that way."

"Get there before me?"

"It'll be close."

"I'm going to jump if I have to leave my engines behind." Beka cut the shields in half and fed the power that she'd freed to the 'Hammer's realspace engines.

"They're launching fighters."

"Let's see 'em outrun me." Beka flipped on the internal comm. "Gunners, take your stations."

Jessan unstrapped and headed aft.

Beka kept on flipping switches. "Gravity, off; life support, off; all nonessentials off-line."

She pushed the newly freed power to the realspace engines as well, then checked the navicomp and the sensor screen. "Come on, you bastard, where are you?"

A few more seconds, and she didn't need to ask: she had the Mage warship on visual. She watched it swelling from a bright star to something the size of an asteroid in its own right—as if High Station Pleyver had sprouted guns and engines and dropped out of hyperspace on top of her.

"Hell," she said. The warship was sitting on her jump

point, all right. She put in some up vector. "Sorry about that, big boy—I'll see you later. Guns?"

"Number One gun on station," came Jessan's reply; and LeSoit, echoing: "Number Two gun on station."

"Anything in range, kill it," Beka said. "But don't just shoot for the sake of shooting—I want every ounce of juice I have for speed."

"Roger," she heard her gunners echo. Then she was passing above the other vessel, watching the huge bulk of the warship slide by on the 'Hammer's ventral side. She had clear stars in front of her; she was running—

A wrenching shudder ran through the ship. The 'Hammer bucked and pulled against the grip of a heavy tractor beam.

"Hold your fire!" Beka called out the gunners. She fed more power to the realspace engines. "I'll need everything we've got just to pull away!"

The engines roared; the freighter's hull sang and moaned with the vibration that tore at it in every direction; but slowly, slowly, Warhammer began to make forward progress and pull away from the beam.

"Come on, baby, you can do it," Beka murmured. "You can do it. Fastest pair of legs in the galaxy . . ."

She heard Jessan swear in Khesatan over the earphones and heard a bolt of energy fire from Number One gun bubble. Then both guns were firing—continuously now—and Jessan cursed again as something struck the freighter's after portion with a deafening, bone-jarring impact. Damage-control lights flared red all over the main console, and the numbers on the engine power readout ran down toward zero. The rear sensor screens went blank. Loss-of-pressure alarms shrieked.

"What the *hell*—!"

Jessan's voice came to her over the internal comm. "One of their fighters rammed us."

"Damn and blast." She switched off the engines. After a few seconds, she flipped on the comm. "Everyone, stand by. We've got a problem. We appear to have been captured by a Mage warship."

* * *

"Dropout in five minutes, Commodore," Jhunnei said.

"Very well," Commodore Gil said, "I'll be in CIC in four."

He poured himself one last cup of cha'a and left his office for the *Pavo*'s Combat Information Center.

"We're set for general quarters on translation," the tactical action officer told Gil as he entered. "No telling what'll be waiting for us. Ops officer is on the bridge, overseeing navigation personally."

"Get positive identification on all targets before launching any attacks," Gil said. He took a seat near the main battle tank. The tank's display area was darkened while the *'Tina* ran in hyper. "We may be attacked by friendlies who aren't sure of our allegiance and intentions."

"Condition red, weapons tight," the TAO said to the gun talker, and the message was passed through the weapons spaces.

"Stand by for dropout," came a voice over the ship's internal comm system. "Five, four, three, two, one, mark."

The hyperspace transition wave swept through the ship. "Full sensor scan," the TAO said. "Light up the tank."

The holographic display winked into life. This time it showed the Gyfferan system, with the view in the tank centering on Gyffer itself. Blue dots appeared, marking the body of Gil's task force: *Karipavo* and her sisters from the Net Patrol Fleet; Merrolakk the Selvaur's privateer flotilla; and the odd collection of armed merchantmen and Space Force vessels from the Suivi Detachment that had been the reluctant contribution of Domina Beka Rosselin-Metadi.

"Unknown units detected," the comptech on the main tank said. "Bringing them up now."

"At least this time we have hi-comms," Gil commented to the TAO. "Locally, anyway. Fighting blind and deaf isn't an experience I plan to repeat just for the pleasure of it."

A yellow dot appeared in the tank close to Gyffer. "Energy release in Gyfferan system space," called out a sensor tech.

"Rotate that over here," the TAO said. "Magnify. What parameters are you reading?"

"Task Force D'Rugier dropping out in sequence, in place," reported the tech in charge of fleet communications. "Comms normal."

"Deploy fighters in diamond formation," Gil said. "Scouts out to Gyffer."

"Picking up transmissions in the clear from Gyffer Inspace Control," said the local-comms operator.

"What do you have?" TAO asked.

"All units in the Gyfferan Local Defense Forces are being directed to save themselves if they can . . . more traffic from Gyffer, transmission from the surface, Gyfferan Citizen-Assembly requests immediate aid from Republic Space Force or any planetary government capable of responding."

"Can't get more immediate than us," Gil said. "Reply to the Citizen-Assembly, tell them that the Space Force is here."

"IDs coming in on vessels in Gyfferan system space," the tank comptech said. "Gyfferan units displayed in green, task force units in blue. Unknowns yellow. We have a bunch of ID'ed vessels marked as Space Force, not from this task force."

"Get names on them," Gil ordered. "Correlate with last assignment prior to the war."

"Working. The Space Force units are from the Infabede Sector Fleet."

"Infabede units appear to be attacking Gyfferan units," the TAO said, looking at the data running up the sensor tech's screen.

"That would be Vallant, damn his eyes," Gil said, remembering the news he'd picked up on Innish-Kyl. "Designate Infabede units hostile. Put a screen around Gyffer. Protect their spacedocks and their communications nodes for as long as possible. And send a signal to the Infabede units, message as follows: 'To Infabede Sector Fleet, this is Net Patrol Fleet. Interrogative what the hell do you think you're doing, over.' And while we're waiting for a reply to *that*," Gil remarked to the TAO, "if anyone out there shoots at a Gyfferan unit, that someone is a designated target."

"Yes, sir."

"You know, Jhunnei," Gil remarked to his aide, leaning back and taking a sip from his cha'a, "I used to worry that because I'd joined up after the last war was over, I'd never do anything more important than write reports and assign other people to write reports for me to read."

"Who knows, Commodore?" Jhunnei replied. "Maybe you'll get to write the report after we finish this one."

Gil shook his head. "Until you said that, Lieutenant, I was almost ready to enjoy myself."

Beka flipped off the link and sagged back in the pilot's seat. She gazed wearily out the *'Hammer*'s viewscreen as the Magebuilt battleship drew closer and closer.

How the hell did they find me? Was it Tarveet—did I tell him the coordinates when he had me drugged on Suivi?

Beka sat up straight again. *Tarveet.* She could at least make sure that he didn't live long enough to enjoy a Mageworlds victory. She left the cockpit and ran back through the common room—where Doctor syn-Tavaite looked somewhere between pleased and in despair—and onward to the crew berthing compartment that had been Tarveet's prison ever since Suivi Point.

The door refused to open for her. *Jammed. On purpose.* She slammed her fist against the bulkhead.

"Damn, damn, damn . . ."

"No, Captain." Ignaceu LeSoit had appeared at her elbow while she was still working at the lock. "Tarveet didn't reveal the site of your base to the Mages."

Beka snarled at him. "How the hell do *you* know, Ignac'?"

He shook his head. Any further reply he might have made was cut short by the sound of magnetic grapnels striking on the hull. Then Jessan came, and Doctor syn-Tavaite with him.

"I can't find Owen or Klea anywhere," Jessan said. "The inner door to the main lock is closed. The outer door is open, and there are two p-suits missing. I believe they've gone outside."

Beka pounded on the bulkhead again. "Damn, damn, damn it to hell ... what do they think they're doing?"

"They said that there would be Mages aboard this ship," syn-Tavaite said. "They said that they were going to find one for you."

Beka went back to the 'Hammer's cockpit—she didn't want to deal with anybody else right now, and especially not with Inesi syn-Tavaite or Ignaceu LeSoit. Instead, she watched the Mage battleship grow larger and closer as its magnetic grapnels pulled the freighter in. More beams, tractors and pressors working together, drew the 'Hammer down to rest on blocks inside a huge docking bay. Bright worklights washed over the freighter's hull, glaring into the cockpit windows; the outer bay doors closed down like jaws; blast-armored and pressure-suited workers came out of their airlocks and into the bay.

"No point in waiting," she said aloud, and headed aft.

She didn't know what Owen and Klea were up to, beyond the information that Doctor syn-Tavaite had passed along, but anything that served to distract the Mages from possible intruders could only help. As long as the two Adepts—and the replicant—were safe, her long-shot plan still had a chance.

In the common room, Jessan and Lesoit and syn-Tavaite were sitting at the mess table in an uneasy silence. They all looked up when Beka entered.

"I'm going out," she said. "They want a prisoner, I'll give them one. The rest of you, stay inside and stay quiet."

Jessan looked unhappy. "I wish you'd let me go instead."

"Sorry," she said. "You're not notorious enough."

"Be careful, then."

"For as long as I can." She looked at syn-Tavaite. "Remember, Doctor: you're combat-sworn to D'Rugier, and he gave you to me. Betray me now, and you're breaking your word to him. As for you, Ignac'—"

"Captain?"

"This makes three times now that I haven't killed you, for old times' sake. Remember that. All of you: nobody mentions my brother and his apprentice, or what we've got in the hold. If Owen makes it back here, you do whatever he says."

"Understood, Captain," said Jessan. He had grown steadily more pale and drawn as she spoke. "Bee—"

"Goodbye, Nyls. I've got to leave now."

She left the common room without looking back. In the *'Hammer*'s airlock, she donned her p-suit with practiced haste, sealing her blaster into the suit's cargo pocket. Maybe she'd need it. Maybe she'd even have a chance to use it.

Right. And maybe I'll sprout wings and fly home to Galcen. But as long as I'm planning to jump off the roof, I might as well try flapping my arms all the way down.

She closed the inner door and set the lock to cycle. The joints of her p-suit stiffened around her. When the cycle had finished, she hit the bulkhead controls to open the outer door and lower the ramp. The foot of the ramp clanged down onto metal deckplates, and Beka stepped out of the lock.

A cluster of p-suited workers had gathered at the edge of what looked like a safety circle painted around the landing blocks. She approached halfway to the circle's perimeter, then stopped and waited for the workers to come the rest of the way.

The stark worklights glinted from the workers' helmets, and they seemed to move in slow motion. A voice sounded in Beka's ears—an all-frequency transmission, most likely, coming over her helmet's comm link—saying words that she didn't understand. She kept on waiting.

332 • Debra Doyle & James D. Macdonald

After the voice fell silent, the workers in their white pressure suits came up and surrounded her. She saw that they carried blasters of unfamiliar design, made with oversized trigger studs for use with gauntleted hands. Not workers, then, but an armed guard. Except for the visible presence of the weapons, however, none of the Mageworlders had so much as offered a threatening gesture.

The troopers formed two ranks, a column on each side of her, and started back toward the airlock from which they had emerged. Beka, now surrounded, had no choice but to go with them. The airlock, twice as tall as she was and wide enough for a skipsled to pass through with ease, held the entire formation without crowding. The outer door slid shut behind them. The lock was huge, taking so long to traverse that Beka felt the changing pressure make the joints of her suit grow looser as she walked.

The inner doors of the lock slid open and the troopers around her stopped. They removed their helmets to reveal disconcertingly ordinary men and women—a bit on the short side, most of them, by Republic standards—with the collars of brown uniforms peeking from the necks of their suits.

The ranks in front of her parted and she saw that another man had been waiting on the far side of the lock. His plain brown uniform was the same color as the troopers' collars, but instead of a blaster he carried a short rod of dark wood bound in silver: a Mage's staff. He nodded at the troopers to either side of her and gave an order she couldn't hear.

She felt hands fumbling at her own helmet, lifting it away. Then the man spoke again, this time in Galcenian. "Happy meeting, gentlelady. I will escort you to your quarters."

Beka drew herself up to her full height. "I am Domina Beka Rosselin-Metadi," she said. "Domina of Lost Entibor, of Entibor-in-Exile, and of the Colonies Beyond. And I wish to speak with your commander."

"You shall," the man said. "Come and refresh yourself first. You will meet with the Grand Admiral soon."

Beka nodded.

"Come," the man said again, and walked away.

After a moment, she followed. The squad of troopers remained behind—apparently a single Mage was considered as roughly equivalent for escort purposes. This one didn't look dangerous, but Beka knew better than to believe in appearances.

"You are our guest," the man said, without turning his head. "While you remain our guest, no harm shall come to you if we can prevent it."

"I see. What happens if someone decides I'm not your guest any longer?"

"The Grand Admiral can tell you more than I."

They turned right down a narrow passageway. The Mage faced her and pushed a lockplate. A door slid open.

"Here are your quarters. When you are ready, the Grand Admiral will see you. He waits on your pleasure."

"I suppose the door will be locked from the outside?"

"With regret—yes," the man said. "It is for your own safety aboard ship, my lady, that you will need an escort at all times. Should you desire anything, I am Mid-Commander Mael Taleion. Speak my name, and I shall appear."

"Very well. I'll take the opportunity to rest for a moment, but I still want to speak with your admiral as soon as possible."

"So it shall be."

The man bowed. Beka turned and walked into the room. The door slid shut behind her.

She looked about her new quarters. *I don't know where they've put me,* she thought, *but it sure isn't the detention level. Looks more like officer's country, in fact.*

The room was large for a ship's cabin, brightly lit and well ventilated, but with a distinct alien flavor to it, as if all the dimensions and angles differed subtly from those that were standard on the Republic side of the Net. Water poured down one wall and vanished into a hole in the floor after running diagonally across the space in a small watercourse filled with rounded stones. When Beka checked, she found that the stones were permanently fastened in place.

No accounting for taste, she thought. *I wonder if the personal waterfall is standard equipment in all the cabins, or a special treat for important guests and honored prisoners?*

Beka pulled off the gauntlets of her p-suit and threw them onto the low, flat bed that filled one corner of the room. With her hands free, it was easy to strip off the rest of the bulky garment. She pulled her blaster from the cargo pocket and belted it around her waist. That was one advantage to "guest" status, she reflected; no search and seizure.

She pulled up a double handful of water from the waterfall—the temperature was just on the cold side of lukewarm, another reminder that these quarters had been designed according to an alien aesthetic—and splashed it onto her face. She shook the excess water from her hands and started back toward the door.

Time to see about calling for the mid-commander, she thought. *The more of the Mages' attention I can take up, the more of a chance Owen and Klea will have.*

She found what looked like a comm speaker set into the bulkhead near the door, with a button beside it. She lifted a hand, thinking to push the button and await results—but she never got the chance. Instead, a strong arm came from behind to grab her shoulders and pull her away to one side.

Her hand fell to her blaster. Before she could pull it free another hand pressed down on hers, keeping the weapon holstered.

"Silence," a voice whispered in Galcenian. "Be still."

In the *'Hammer*'s common room, after Beka had left, the silence stretched out for some time.

"When my people come here," syn-Tavaite said finally, "my position will be very, very bad."

Jessan looked up from his contemplation of the tabletop. "Remember what the Domina said."

"How can I forget? But what is there we can do?"

LeSoit shrugged. "I've always said that when my time came I'd like it to find me playing at cards."

"If you don't stop dealing off the bottom," Jessan said, "it probably will."

LeSoit pulled a deck of cards out of his jacket pocket. "If that's an invitation, I accept."

"I must be insane to agree to play with your deck," Jessan said. "But any diversion is preferable to terrorized monotony. Let's see, you're up three thousand at the moment, right?"

"Three thousand, two hundred and nine," LeSoit said. "Want to continue, or start a new series?"

"Continue, I think." Jessan took some chips from their storage space under the table.

"It is unbelievable," syn-Tavaite said. "To play cards at such a time—"

"Reconcile yourself to it," Jessan said. "My deal."

"Want to join?" LeSoit asked.

syn-Tavaite stood up. "I will go now and check on the stasis box. That, at least, will make me of some use."

She left the common room. At the table, Jessan dealt out the hands and picked up his cards.

"Something I've wondered," he said, laying down the three of trefoils. "Where did a Magebuilt warship come from, out this far from anywhere?"

"There's a war on," LeSoit said, covering the three with a three of forges. He drew a new card from the pack and nodded to Jessan. "Over to you."

"Sure, but this is an out-of-the-way place for a major unit to be patrolling. And having a battleship show up on the direct jump run from the middle of nowhere to Pleyver snaps the suspenders of my disbelief." Jessan laid down a five of forges and replenished his hand from the deck.

"We're dealing with Mages," LeSoit said. He covered the five of forges with a two of forges from his hand.

"That's an all-purpose explanation which I find rather unsatisfactory," Jessan said. "Got any forges?"

"It's true as far as it goes," Ignac' said. "Draw one."

"Beka thought that Tarveet did it," Jessan said, reaching out to Ignac's fan of cards. "She said he must have gotten the base coordinates out of her under drugs, then told the Mages about it. You say he didn't. Why?"

"Common sense," LeSoit said, as Jessan took one of his

cards. The former gunfighter took another card from his hand, the two of tors this time, and added it to the pile growing on the table. "Tarveet's the sort who'd keep that info himself in case he could turn it to his own advantage later. Sell it to the Mages, maybe. Tell them flat out? I doubt it."

Jessan laid down the two of flasks on the two of forges. "All right, I can go with that," he said. "I suppose it's also unlikely—even if the Mages did learn about the coordinates—that they'd assign a unit here just on the off chance that we might someday decide to show up. Nevertheless, here they are."

"Here they are," LeSoit agreed. "But Tarveet isn't the one you're looking for." He laid down the scepter of flasks on the two. "I'm the one who sent them the message to come. Last night."

"You son of a bitch," Jessan said. He had his blaster out and aimed. "I told Beka months ago that we ought to shoot you, but she said no."

"Maybe she'll change her mind after she comes back," LeSoit said. "You'll have plenty of time to shoot me then. Meanwhile, it's your turn."

From the outer skin of the Magebuilt battleship, the stars looked bright and cold. Klea had never seen so many, all glowing steadily without any atmosphere around her to blur them, and seeming to hang over her like a suspended waterfall of light.

They're not going to fall down on me, she told herself, and clutched with pressure-gauntleted hands at the ringbolt on the metal hull beneath her. *They're not.*

She touched her p-suit's helmet against Owen's—*"Don't use the comm link,"* he'd told her, back in the airlock; *"somebody might be listening"*—and said, "They've shut the bay doors. How are we going to get in?"

"Don't worry. A warship this size always has small craft coming and going—fighters, couriers, whatever. All we have to do is be there when one of them heads out."

"Someone will see us."

"People see what they expect to see. Even Mages."

"Right," said Klea. She fell silent again. The stars were *not* going to fall on her ... they were *not* moving ... they *were* moving ..."Owen!"

"We're accelerating," he said. "Snap the safety line of your p-suit around that bolt and hold on."

"Owen ..."

Klea felt inertia pulling her backward. Her staff tugged at the clip on her belt. Then, all at once, the stars blazed up and went out.

A swirling greyness surrounded the battleship, relieved only where the exterior of the hull showed before Klea's face when she pressed her helmet against it. She squirmed over until her helmet once more touched Owen's.

"What *is* this?"

"This," Owen replied, "is what hyperspace looks like. We're in it."

Beka said nothing and let herself be dragged farther aside into a cubicle off the main cabin—a cleaning-gear locker of some kind, from the racks and shelves. The locker extended back into darkness down a service tunnel. Up front near the overhead, an incandescent globe cast a yellow glare down on the two men facing her.

"Hello, Beka," said the one who had demanded silence. He was dirty, ragged, and unshaven, but the clothes he wore were an Adept's formal blacks. In one hand, for a staff, he held a piece of plastic pipe as tall as he was. The other man, also thin and ragged, wore what had clearly once been a Space Force general's uniform; he was unarmed.

Beka stared at the Adept. "Master Ransome. Owen said you were—"

"Captured. Yes. But no longer."

"If you're trying to escape, I can't help you. They gave me the guest bedroom, but I'm still a prisoner."

"I had another kind of help in mind," Ransome said. "The Mages will be coming back for you soon. They'll be taking you to Lord sus-Airaalin."

"How did you know that?"

Ransome's haggard features took on a distant expression. "I have been . . . watching, for a long while. The currents of power flow strongly here, and there is strong Magework pulling and corrupting them. Someone who is patient, and has the time to wait and watch, can see many things. And I have had a great deal of time, since Galcen fell."

"I see," said Beka. "What is it that you want me to do?"

"You need to kill the Mage commander," the man in the general's uniform said.

She eyed him suspiciously. "Why haven't the two of you done the deed yourselves?"

"sus-Airaalin is a Great Magelord," Ransome said. "He protects himself constantly against me—even though he believes that I am no longer aboard his ship, he never lets down his guard. But you are still armed. sus-Airaalin himself wishes to speak with you; his death is necessary for the civilized galaxy to have peace."

"You're sure about that? Or is it just wishful thinking?"

Ransome smiled thinly. "Wishful thinking isn't something I've been indulging in much lately. I have seen it, and it is so. Any other path leads to a Mage victory. Kill him."

With that the man in the general's uniform opened the closet door and nodded Beka through it. The closet door shut again, its outline vanishing into the wall as soon as it had closed. Beka went back to the comm speaker and pushed the button. A few seconds later the main door to the compartment opened to admit Mid-Commander Taleion.

"Domina, I have come to escort you to the commander of *Sword-of-the-Dawn*, Grand Admiral Theio syn-Ricte sus-Airaalin."

III. Gyfferan System Space: RSF Karipavo
Deep Space: Sword-of-the-Dawn

"MESSAGE COMING in, Commodore," said *Karipavo*'s communications tech. "From the Infabede Fleet. Text follows: 'You are entering Infabede Hegemony Area. This planet is under the protection of Admiral Vallant. Prepare to turn over your vessels to Infabede Command. Come dead in space, go dark. Prepare to be boarded.' "

"My, my," Gil said. "Personal message to Admiral Vallant: 'From Commodore Gil, RSF. You are in a state of rebellion and mutiny. Order your vessels to depart Gyfferan space at once. You are under arrest. Transfer yourself to my flagship to be placed in custody pending trial.' "

"That doesn't leave much negotiating room," the TAO said.

"I don't have much time for negotiations," Gil said. "There's a war with the Mages going on. Get me a location on Vallant's flagship."

"Fezrisond?"

"That's the one."

"One of our vessels under attack," the comptech at the

main tank called out. The red dot of a hostile unit in orbit over Gyffer showed the location. "Identify attacker as RSF *Wraynim*. Attacking *Claw Hard*, armed merchant."

"Return fire," Gil said. He highlighted two other units in the TF nearby to come to assist, then looked up. "Where's the *Fezzy*?"

"Got her located," the comptech said, rotating the display in the tank to show it to Gil.

"He's kept himself well out of harm's way," the TAO said.

"Let's bring some harm over to him, then," Gil said. "Get me eight ships, cruisers or better—Captain Lingor's division would do it, I think. Get them to an intercept point and a blocking ring. I'm going to go in there myself."

Gil turned to his aide. "Jhunnei, what do you think? Give him a chance to surrender?"

"Why bother?" she replied. "Save the Republic the trouble, and make him an example to his troops."

"I thought so," Gil said. "Put a fighter group on top of the *Fezzy*. And plot a minimum-time course to kinetic range on him."

"Captain Lingor reports her division en route," the comms tech called out. "Requests instructions."

"Tell her to take the *Fezzy* under fire with missiles. Break off the attack when I get there."

"RSF *Wraynim* has been hit," the comptech said. "Appears to be unable to maneuver, no longer firing. Shields flickering."

"Pass to *Claw Hard*, weapons tight."

"*Fezrisond* under attack with missiles," the comptech said. "Appears to be putting on speed and turning. Reports of attacks by Infabede vessels all over the system."

"Stay with *Fezrisond*," Gil said. "I want to pass under his stern in kinetic range. Pass to all units, condition red, weapons free. Designate Infabede units hostile. Increase main battle display magnification."

The picture in the battle tank grew in size until it showed Captain Lingor's group as blue shapes at the outer edges, surrounding the red triangle that represented Admiral Vallant's flagship.

"Send to Captain Lingor: 'Cease-fire missiles,' " Gil said. "That son of a bitch is mine."

"Cease-fire aye," the comm talkers tech said. "Captain Lingor rogers for cease-fire."

"Get me under his tubes," Gil said, "and we'll shoot straight up his rear. I want all the kinetic weapons ganged to my control panel."

In the main battle tank, the blue triangle that was *Karipavo* drove inward toward the red triangle that was *Fezrisond*, closer and closer until the shapes appeared to merge. The comptech increased magnification again so that the two triangles were alone in the tank, with the fighter squadrons flickering in and out of the display like tiny motes of luminescent dust.

"Fire." Gil closed the contact on his master panel. The great ship shuddered, the lights dimmed, and the CIC was full of the silence of tense, suspended breath.

"Fire." Again the ship shuddered.

"Fire."

"Registering hits to *Fezrisond*," called out the sensor tech. "Damage is light."

"Prepare to come around," Gil ordered. "We're going to do it again."

"Wait a minute, Commodore," said Jhunnei, from where she'd been watching the sensor readouts over the technician's shoulder. "Movement on *Fezrisond*. Appears to be a shuttle."

"Tell the fighters to bring it in," Gil said.

"Message receipt," reported the comms tech. "From *Fezrisond*. They request we cease attack. Claim Admiral Vallant has departed."

"That shuttle," said Gil. "Is it headed in our direction?"

"Negative, sir. Heading away."

"Belay my last," Gil said. "Destroy that shuttle. I say again, destroy it. Make a general broadcast to all units, Infabede Fleet: 'Come dead in space, go dark, prepare to be boarded.' Give them twenty seconds to comply."

"Shuttle destroyed, sir," reported the sensor tech. "More units dropping out of hyper, just above the system, edge of active sensor range. Not SF or Gyfferan. Tentative ID Mage."

"Commodore, we're losing hi-comms again," said the comms tech, just before the main battle tank flickered and went dark.

"It's the Mages, all right," Jhunnei said. "They're here."

Mid-Commander Taleion escorted Beka through the passageways of *Sword-of-the-Dawn*. Most of them looked like ship's passageways anywhere, narrow and labyrinthine, but with the same alien twist to everything that she'd noted back in the cabin. After walking for some time they came to a sealed door guarded by a pair of black-robed Mages.

Just like the holovids, thought Beka nervously. *Remember, they're not immortal. You saw the Prof kill one back on Darvell.*

The door opened, admitting Beka and Taleion to what she could only think of as an audience chamber: a huge room, as large as the docking bay had been, with a raised portion at one end where a crowd of people stood clustered together.

Don't be too impressed; for all you know they could have rigged this place out of a cargo hold for your benefit.

Beka scanned the platform for someone who looked important enough to be Grand Admiral sus-Airaalin, architect of the Republic's destruction. He wasn't obvious. The most sinister thing in the whole place was a group of Mages in black robes and masks—not that Mages weren't worrisome, but these weren't doing anything, any more than the pair at the door had been.

A soft voice from beside her interrupted her thoughts. "My lady Domina Beka Rosselin of Entibor? I am Grand Admiral sus-Airaalin. At your service and your family's."

Beka turned. The man who had addressed her wore the same sort of brown uniform as most of the others on this ship. She supposed that if she could read the insignia on his collar she'd be impressed. Far more impressive, however, was the black-and-silver staff that hung by a clip from his belt.

I won't get any closer than this, she thought.

Pulling her blaster from its holster, she fired three full-power bolts in quick succession, straight at the Grand Admiral. None of them seemed to have any effect. With a cry of frustration she threw the blaster at his head and launched herself at him, dagger in hand.

He was fast—as fast as the Prof had been. The short staff was in his hand, and a moment later she was on her back on the deck, with her dagger gone and her wrist stinging.

The Grand Admiral stood looking down at her. "Your pardon, my lady, for the indignity. Please be assured, I hold you in as high regard as before."

"Damnation," Beka said, rolling to her feet. Mid-Commander Taleion handed her back her dagger, grip first, and her blaster as well a moment later. She sheathed the blade and, as always, checked the charge and safety on the blaster before holstering it. The thing showed normal readouts, the charge almost full.

"Damnation," Beka repeated. "My lord Grand Admiral, I'm delighted to make your acquaintance."

"The pleasure is mine," sus-Airaalin said. "Believe me, my lady, though you are my prisoner, I desire nothing from you that you cannot in all honor perform. When all is said and done, we both seek a just and lasting peace."

"If you want peace, why not take your whole damned fleet back the way you came?"

"It's too late for that, my lady. All our reward for staying on our side of the Gap Between was slavery and destruction."

"So you decided to come over here and spread the happiness around. Never mind—for reasons of your own, you went to a lot of trouble to find and capture me. Why?"

"As I said, for peace."

"And that's why you had my mother killed, and why you had assassins tracking me and my brothers all over the galaxy?"

sus-Airaalin shook his head with what looked oddly like

genuine puzzlement. "I fear that the assassins you allude to were none of my doing. More likely, they proceeded from the machinations of other groups within the Resurgency, factions which saw only a military solution to our woes. My own hopes were . . . otherwise . . . but when that hope ended—there's a saying on Eraasi, that once blood has covered your boot tops you might as well wade in it up to your neck."

He bowed briefly to Beka. "We shall speak again. My apologies for leaving you so abruptly, but I have a battle to conduct. And while we stand here talking, the peace we both pursue has run a little way farther off."

Grand Admiral sus-Airaalin turned his back on the young Domina and walked steadily out of the observation room, Mid-Commander Taleion following a pace or so behind. As the door slid closed behind them, sus-Airaalin collapsed heavily against the nearest bulkhead. Through a haze of pain, he heard Taleion calling for a physician.

"That was foolish of you, my lord," Taleion said. "I told you when Lisaiet made contact that the woman was dangerous and shouldn't be allowed to go armed."

"And I told you it was necessary," sus-Airaalin said. "She is important to the weave of the future. I have willed it."

Gritting his teeth, he fumbled at the fasteners of his tunic and pulled it partway open, revealing the edges of a piece of blast armor. One of the hits had partially penetrated. The other had just missed the edge of the plate, and an ugly burn marred the Grand Admiral's shoulder.

The *Sword*'s chief physician arrived at a run. When she saw the burn, she pulled open her emergency pack and began swabbing the open flesh.

"Good thing the prisoner didn't try for a head shot," she remarked. "Get yourself killed, my lord, and what will all the rest of us do?"

"The prisoner did try," sus-Airaalin said. He gasped as the antiseptic bit into the open wound. "She's a strong-minded one, and a luck-maker on top of it. I barely managed to deflect her aim and still present a convincing illusion afterward."

"Thank your own luck, then," the physician said. She reached into her pack again. "There's nothing wrong with you that a bit of *eibriyu* can't cure. But next time be careful, would you?"

"The time for being careful is over, I think." sus-Airaalin felt the synthetic tissue going onto the burn—first a cool sensation, easing the pain, then a pleasant warmth. A night's rest and the burn would be gone without a scar; but for the next few hours, while the undifferentiated tissue conformed to his own body and took on purpose, he would be vulnerable.

So be it, he thought. *If the Circle needs a death for this battle, let it be mine.*

More hasty footsteps in the passageway heralded the arrival of one of the *Sword*'s troopers, a runner from the flagship's Combat Information Center. "The Adept-worlders have changed their tactics, my lord, and appear to have new units available. The watch officer tells me that he suspects them of bringing in a new commander, one far more competent than the last. Your presence is requested."

"Tell Captain syn-Athekh that I trust his judgment," sus-Airaalin said. "We are approaching the crisis, and our Circles need me more. I will be in the meditation room, working to bring luck for the fleet."

The physician was finished with her work; sus-Airaalin refastened his tunic and turned to Mid-Commander Taleion. "Mael, escort the Domina back to her quarters, then join me."

Owen had been right as usual, Klea reflected. When the Mage battleship dropped out of hyperspace, a squadron of fighters issued from the docking bay like mud-hornets from the bank of an irrigation ditch. In all the haste and activity, nobody seemed to notice a pair of Adepts in pressure-suits entering through the open doors.

The Adepts in the holovids used to turn themselves invis-

ible all the time, she thought. *Maybe if I'd believed in it then I wouldn't be scared now.*

The bay was huge, divided with force fields into pressurized sections. It still contained a squadron or more of empty fighter craft awaiting refueling or repair. In the shadow of one such, Owen and Klea shed their p-suits and retrieved their staves from the carrying clips.

"Somebody is going to find the suits," Klea said. "And when they do, they'll know they've got intruders on board."

"Someone will find the suits," agreed Owen. "A pilot who's too busy planning her next sortie, or a maintenance tech with his hands full of gear, or a trooper who's more worried about the sergeant than about the enemy. Maybe they'll report it, or maybe not. If they do report it, it'll still take a while to go up the chain of command to someone who not only knows enough to look for Adepts, but knows how to find the Adepts he's looking for. By then we'll be gone."

He took his staff in hand and began strolling toward the entrance of the bay. Klea glanced about nervously and followed.

"I still don't like it," she said. "Why isn't anybody pointing their fingers at us and yelling?"

"Because they aren't looking where we happen to be walking," Owen said. "Self-effacement is a useful talent; most Adepts come by it naturally. I'm sure you've met people yourself from time to time whose gaze you wished to avoid, and who somehow didn't happen to see you."

Klea thought back to some of the customers at Freling's Bar. "Yes," she said. "Thanks for reminding me. Whatever happens, this is better."

"I'm glad you still think so. In the meantime, just work on making yourself not-noticed—tell yourself nobody's going to pick you out when they can have somebody else. It'll work."

"But these are Mages—"

"Not exactly. Mageworlders. The first real Mage we run into is going back with us to *Warhammer.*"

"If we can find it," said Klea.

"Don't be a pessimist. Finding the 'Hammer isn't going to be a problem. We never got more than one bay over while we were crawling around outside on the hull."

"What makes you so certain we can find a Mage without getting lost ourselves?"

"A feeling," said Owen. "A familiar pattern in the currents of the universe. One of the Mages on this ship is someone I have dealt with before."

They had reached the door of the bay by now, and passed through it into a narrow, white-painted passageway. Not far beyond, the passage came to a four-way branch. Ladders ran up and down from the intersection, leading to what Klea supposed were other decks in the huge battleship. A black-clad figure stepped out from around the left-hand turning: a small, dark-skinned woman who carried a mask in one hand and wore a black-and-silver staff at her belt.

"Hello, Owen," she said. "I've been waiting for you."

"Llannat Hyfid," Owen said. "I've been hunting for you—though I didn't know it. I thought I was on the track of a Mage. And it looks like I was right."

Klea stared at both of them. "You *know* each other?"

"Oh, yes," Owen said. "This is a woman I've met. I even helped to train her."

"You trained Mages?"

"Apparently so," Owen replied. Then, without taking his eyes off Llannat, he said, "Look behind you, Klea."

She turned, and bit back an outcry that would surely have betrayed them. A giant of a man had come up behind her— big as one of the Selvaurs that she'd sometimes met back on Nammerin, with a blaster at the ready in one massive hand.

I've had it, she thought as she brought her staff up into the guard position. *Even if he doesn't shoot me, he's big enough to take away my staff and use it for a toothpick if he wants to.*

But the big man was putting up the blaster and bowing, as smoothly as a holovid hero. "My apologies, gentlelady. Owen, if I were you I'd speak politely to Mistress Hyfid."

"Ari," Owen said. He looked impatient. "I don't know

what you think you're doing, but you'd be well advised to stay away from her. She's a Magelord now, or the next thing to it."

The big man didn't back down. "She's also my wife, baby brother, so treat her with respect."

Klea stared at Owen. "*This* is the brother you talked about back on Nammerin? How many other siblings do you have?"

"Beka and Ari are the only two I'm aware of," Owen said. "I think you'll agree they're more than enough." He turned back to the dark woman. "Now—sister-in-law—it's time you told me what you're doing here."

The woman shrugged. "We were captured. The Eraasians don't know what I am, exactly, so they've apparently decided to treat me as a Mage until further notice. I've got the freedom of the ship, at least until somebody decides to take it away from me, and when I insisted on Ari as part of the deal, nobody squawked."

"That's all very well," said Owen. "The question is, which side are you on these days?"

"I haven't broken my oath," she said. " '. . . To seek always the greater good,' remember? I'm still looking for it. I had a feeling I might find a piece of it down here by the docking bays, and I found you instead. What are *you* doing here?"

Owen laughed quietly, without much humor. "Looking for a Mage, as it happens. Beka's here, and she needs one."

"You mean the everlasting apprentice has found a task that he can't perform?" said Ari. "I won't allow you to use my wife as your tool, Owen."

"Why don't you let your wife tell me what she'll do or not do?" Owen demanded. "I don't see a sign that says 'Keeper' tacked to your forehead. Llannat—come with us back to *Warhammer* and I'll tell you what this is all about."

"Bee brought the '*Hammer* aboard a Mage warship?" Ari asked. "I knew she was crazy, but I never thought she was that crazy—and I sure didn't think that the Mages were crazy."

"We got captured, same as you," Owen said. "And I

don't think anybody's going to give me the freedom of the ship if they happen to catch me. Let's get moving."

"All right," said Llannat. She nodded toward one of the passages. "The main bay entrance is back this way. Come on."

They started off, four together, in the direction she'd indicated. Owen spoke quietly as they walked.

"The first thing you should know is that there's a replicant aboard *Warhammer* that needs wakening—'filling,' the technician says. The technician also says that it takes a Magelord to do that part of the work. So I told her I'd find one."

The dark woman looked at him doubtfully. "I don't know how to do anything like that."

"You have a teacher," Owen said. "Ask him."

"Had. My teacher is dead."

"Dead is such a relative word," Owen replied. "We know where he is. Klea's seen him, waiting in the Void. And our mother with him."

"Don't say things like that, Owen." The big man's voice was gentle, but the warning note in it was unmistakable. "The joke isn't funny."

"If there's a joke here," said Owen, "it's on all of us, for thinking her truly gone and despairing accordingly. The man we called the Professor was your teacher, wasn't he, Llannat? Before he died, he prepared a replicant body for his liege lady Perada. He's with her now, waiting for a Mage to come and put her life into the empty body."

Llannat Hyfid made a choking noise that might have been either laughter or disgust. "And you're calling *me* a Mage! This is—is—what will Master Ransome say when he finds out what you're planning to do?"

"He has nothing to say," Owen said. "I am the Master of the Guild now, and my word is final."

"Fortune save the galaxy," muttered Ari.

"There is no fortune," said Owen. "Only what we do for ourselves. And that's the true cream of the joke—I don't just need a Mage for the final stage of the replication process, I need a Mage if I'm going to find Mother at all. Because if I'm going to find her, I have to go walking in the Void."

"I've been to the Void," Llannat said. "I didn't like it."

"Neither did I, the little I saw of it," Owen said. "I've only been brought there, never gone there on my own. But the Mages—I've seen them go in and out of the Void like starships dropping in and out of hyper, so I know that it can be done."

"You want me to go back there?"

"Yes. And take me with you."

Llannat nodded. Her eyes were dark with some emotion that Klea couldn't identify. "I saw you in the Void once, when I was cast into it by the Mage I fought on Darvell. I saw myself, too, and a stranger with us." She paused. "I don't think I have any choice except to help you. If I can."

The woman put the mask over her face. The black plastic hid any fear or uncertainty she might have been feeling. All Klea could see was the featureless, unmoving surface.

"Yes," Llannat said. Coming from behind the mask, her voice had all its warm overtones suppressed and distorted, making Klea think suddenly of the Mages she had fought on Nammerin. "Yes. I *can* help you. If I look between the patterns, I can see the way clearly. We go . . . here."

On the last word, both she and Owen vanished, leaving Ari and Klea alone in the passageway.

IV. WARHAMMER: Captured Gyfferan Space: RSF *Veratina* The Void

ABOARD THE *'Hammer*, Nyls Jessan was rummaging in the toys and entertainment drawer in the captain's cabin. He found what he was seeking—the miniature holoprojector he'd picked up on his first visit to the asteroid base. He dug up the recording of one of his favorite plays and walked out again.

All the fighting and scheming to save the civilized galaxy had come down to looking for a way to pass the time. Somehow, though, playing cards with Ignaceu LeSoit had lost its savor when he'd learned that the former gunfighter was in fact a Mageworlds agent.

"If you're inviting Mages to our councils we have no hope of success at all." Owen Rosselin-Metadi had said that at the conference on Innish-Kyl—but the Adept had been looking the wrong way. *So that's why LeSoit was so nervous. Afraid someone would find him out.*

Jessan walked back through the common room, pointedly ignoring the man who sat at the table shuffling and dealing himself random hands of cards. Instead the Khesatan walked over to the starboard passageway and the hatch leading to number-one cargo bay.

He climbed down the ladder into the echoing hold. The light there was harsh white, casting black shadows as featureless as space itself. The stasis box containing the replicant of Perada Rosselin was griped down against the far bulkhead—the same kind of traveling stasis box that Beka had lain in as the seemingly dead Tarnekep Portree, back on Eraasi in the last moments before the war began.

Doctor syn-Tavaite was there too, sitting on the deck beside the box, her eyes closed. She looked up when Jessan's feet hit the deckplates.

"What's going on up above?" she asked.

"Nothing of any importance," Jessan said. "I grew tired of the card game and decided to watch a play instead. Would you like to join me?"

"If you wish," syn-Tavaite said.

She didn't sound too enthusiastic, but neither did she object. Jessan set the holoprojector beside the stasis box, aimed its projection surface into the bay, and flipped it on. He sat down beside syn-Tavaite, leaning back against the side of the box, and watched the other end of the bay vanish, replaced by a brightly lit stage. An actor in an elaborate costume of rich brocade entered from one side and began to speak.

"Please, what is this?" syn-Tavaite asked.

"One of my favorite dramas," Jessan said. "A classic among my people. I was delighted to find that the Professor—your Masked One, that is—had this recording among his effects."

"My Galcenian isn't that good; I don't understand what they're saying."

"They aren't speaking Galcenian," Jessan said. "That's Khesatan. Here . . ."

He stood and checked the settings on the top of the projector. He found the options key to select language—as he'd suspected, the Professor had been as thorough with that as with everything else. Eraasian was on the list.

Who knows, Jessan thought. *Maybe the Prof wanted to hear voices speaking in his own tongue once in a while.*

He changed the setting and sat back down.

"I know the words by heart," he said. "You can follow the story now."

They watched the players come and go for some time. "What is this play called?" syn-Tavaite asked.

"It's called *By Honor Betray'd*," Jessan replied. "It's one of what are called on Khesat the revenge dramas. That man there"—he pointed at an actor in a cloth-of-gold doublet and a waxed and gilded beard—"is the Duke. He doesn't know that his three sons are planning to kill him and divide his lands among them. Now listen . . . I don't know how good the translation is, but in the original the language is magnificent."

The actors moved about the stage in their finery among the clearly artificial scenes. The director of this production had been a purist, and had chosen to abandon holographic naturalism in favor of historical authenticity of presentation. Then someone walked through one of the painted flats as if it wasn't there—someone in modern dress.

"Gentlesir LeSoit," Jessan said. "Was it truly necessary for you to ruin this, too?"

"Save your disapproval for later," LeSoit said. "We have visitors."

"Your friends, I suppose."

"No," said LeSoit. "Yours."

The Mage agent gestured at the scenery behind him as two more people walked through the illusory stage play: the apprentice Adept Klea Santreny; and, following close after and looming above the frail-seeming young woman, Ari Rosselin-Metadi.

"Nothing in range that looks or acts like a Mage flagship," reported the comptech at RSF *Veratina*'s main battle tank.

"Plague take it," said General Metadi. "He has to be out here somewhere. Message traffic analysis?"

"Negative correlation, sir," the comms tech on the intercept board said. "Random patterns in Mage comms."

"Probe data coming in," said the sensor tech. "Energy releases in Gyfferan system space. Signatures consistent with Gyfferan units and Space Force units. Negative Mage correlation."

"Send to all units," Metadi said to the TAO. "Break contact. Regroup at point Tango Five One."

The crew in CIC felt the acceleration of a run-to-jump then the momentary sense of dislocation as the cruiser underwent hyperspace translation.

"All right," General Metadi said. "Relax, everyone. Let's see if we can get some sandwiches passed around. I have to do some thinking."

Commander Quetaya approached, looking worried "More trouble, General?"

"I have a sinking feeling," Metadi said, "that I know what's going on at Gyffer." He nodded toward her clipboard. "Bring up the plans which have Admiral Vallant allied with the Mages, acting under their direction, and hitting Gyffer first."

"You sure expect a lot of me, General."

"I know you'll deliver. Now, where are the summaries?" Another brief wave of dislocation passed through the compartment as the *'Tina* dropped out of hyper.

"Clean in this area," the TAO said. A moment later, he added, "Task force is present. Lost two units—*Grenfyl* and *Tarpifex*."

"Lost two aye," Metadi said. "Log their last known position. We'll look for survivors later."

"New data from Gyfferan system," said a sensor tech "Signature match on EM pulses. Space Force units currently operating in Gyfferan space belong to Infabede sector."

"You were right, General," Rosel said.

"I usually am—except when I'm wrong," Metadi said "Now, if Vallant is at Gyffer, where is the Mage commande going to linger?"

Quetaya proffered her clipboard. "Three areas of highes probability are marked, sir."

Metadi studied the diagrams on her clipboard. "I don't like any of these. Get me some better ones."

"Sir?"

"Whoever's running the Mages is a clever bastard. He knows we'll be running probability checks. So I want you to find the inverse of the most likely places. I want to look there."

"Message coming from Gyffer," said a comms tech. "Citizen-Assembly is requesting aid from anyone capable of rendering it."

"I'm way ahead of them," Metadi said. "No one shoots up my home planet without ticking me off a bit."

"I never thought the LDF would fold this easily," the TAO said.

"They haven't folded," Metadi said sharply. "Remember, they've already spent the last two weeks holding off the same fleet that took Galcen and the Net without even breathing hard."

"Sir," said the comms tech. "Same frequency as the Gyfferan request for aid: reply from Net Patrol Fleet. Net Patrol is standing by to render assistance."

"Who's in command of that fleet?" Quetaya asked, checking ship's memory as she spoke.

"Depends on what losses they took in the Mage breakthrough," Metadi said. "Could be anyone by now."

"Says here the boss used to be a Captain Gil."

"That's him. Good man. Bit of a romantic, but he hides it well—and he knows how to keep a cool head in a crisis. I hope whoever's running the show now is as smart as he was."

Metadi reached over for a stylus and drew a circle on one of Rosel's charts. "Given the changing situation, I think we should look for our Mage right about there. TAO, make the signal."

"Signal to the task force—make course for new coordinates, one-five-three-three-one-niner," said the TAO.

"Stand by, jump."

Again the ship entered hyper. The trip wasn't very long

this time. As soon as they dropped out the comptechs began to put up red Mage-ID'ed contacts in the main tank.

"Looks like you were right about people being here," Quetaya said, "but I don't see anything that looks like a flagship."

"Message coming in, Infabede crypto," the hyperspace comms tech said. "Personal for Captain Faramon."

"Very well," Metadi replied. He called the message to the screen by his control seat. "Let's see . . ." He inserted Faramon's personal cipher key. " . . . and there it is. 'From UDC *Fezrisond* To UDC *Veratina*, Personal For Captain Faramon. Make hyper transit of Gyffer, rendezvous with this unit. I intend to transfer my flag to you. Admiral Vallant sends.' "

General Metadi sat back and thought for a moment. "A thing like this requires some kind of response. Let's see . . . Faramon's personal cipher; message follows: 'From RSF *Veratina* to UDC *Fezrisond*, Personal for Mutineer Vallant. I intend to capture or kill you, whichever is easier. General Metadi sends.' "

"Message sent," said the hyperspace communications tech.

"Any response?"

"Just a minute," said the tech. "Hi-comms losing integrity." She pulled off her headset. "No good, General Metadi, sir. Hi-comms are down hard."

"Switch to lightspeed comms," Metadi ordered. "And work off of probabilities. The Mages are about to strike. If they get us with the same trick twice in a row, we deserve to lose."

The main tank display was showing probability bubbles again, hollow spheres that changed volume and position as the possible location of each contact changed with time.

"Hang on," said the main tank comptech. "Here's something. Vessel dropping out of hyper. You were right, sir—it looks like a Mage."

"Big one, too," said another comptech. "Check out the emissions on that son of a bitch!"

"He's in location for the center of a screen," said the

TAO. "Appears to be dropping off fighters. You were hunting for a large, well-protected unit, General? That one fits the bill."

"Assume that vessel to be the Mage flagship," Metadi said. "Keep a close watch on it. Constant track, with extrapolation."

"Messenger arriving, docking bay two. Courier from Colonel Tyche's recon group."

"Send him up."

Shortly afterward, a young infantry trooper came into the CIC. "Message from Colonel Tyche," he said. "He requests permission to board and capture the large Mage target."

"Wait," Metadi said. "I'll send him a reply shortly."

"Sir," Commander Quetaya said. "Since hi-comms are down, I'd like permission to take a shuttle and make contact with the CO of the Net Patrol forces. Inform him of our presence. Point out the Mage flagship and try to coordinate an attack."

"I need you here," Metadi said. "You're the only one of my officers completely familiar with all our plans."

"That's why I have to go, sir," she replied. "Without hi-comms, how else can we coordinate with Net Patrol?"

Metadi sighed. "You have a point, unfortunately. Permission granted to make contact with Net Patrol Fleet in Gyfferan space."

"Thank you, sir."

"Don't thank me yet." He turned to the PI trooper. "Message to the colonel: 'Permission granted to board Mage flagship. Do not, I say again do not, commence operations without positive signal from me to begin.' "

"Yes, sir, understood."

"Trouble," said the TAO suddenly. He pointed toward the large Mage unit. The sphere of probability was stretching into an oval spheroid. The bubbles of the screening vessels around the Mage flagship were also elongating and distorting. "Looks like he's putting on speed. Possible run-to-jump."

"What's on his path?"

"Gyfferan system space."

"Match his velocity," Metadi said. "Break EMCON.
Signal to the fleet: when he jumps, we jump. Drop out close
over Gyffer."

The Void was cold grey fog—no sky, no land, no horizon.
Light came from everywhere and nowhere at once. Llannat
could feel the fog drawing the strength out of her as she
stood. The silver cords were gone. She pulled off her mask
and clipped it onto her belt, but the featureless grey non-
place around her remained the same.

Owen was standing beside her. In his plain spacer's coverall he seemed an unlikely figure to be Errec Ransome's
successor and Master of the Guild. But his strength was unmistakable, and so was the steady, uncompromising thread
of his presence in the weave of the universe. She wondered
what had persuaded him to give up the apprenticeship he'd
always preferred, and claim mastery at last.

There was no time now to ask, however. Not with the
Void leaching the power out of them with every breath they
took.

"The Domina," she said to Owen. "If Perada's here, she's
been here for years. There'll be nothing left to bring back."

"Your teacher is guarding her. And for those not in-body,
time means nothing. We're the ones who need to worry."

Llannat shivered. "How do you find somebody, though,
when all places are the same place?"

"If all places are the same place," Owen said, "then to
make a journey is to arrive." He pointed into the greyness
seemingly at random. "There. See?"

She followed the gesture, and saw what looked like a
black speck in the distance. "I didn't see that before."

"We weren't going there before."

They started moving through the mist toward the speck of
darkness. As they approached, the speck turned from a dot
level with their eyes to a flat black disk, and then to an orb
hovering far up above them, like a black sun in a sky that
never was. Another dark speck appeared before them: first
a line, then a tower, jutting up like a black and broken tooth.

Llannat put out her hand to call a halt. The dark tower

rose up from the mist before them, with more dark shapes in the mist hinting at walls to either side and a looming citadel behind. High in the air came a keening sound, as of some massive and hungry animal crying its need.

"I never saw this place," she said. "And I'm not going in."

"It's the only place here," Owen said. "It must be where we need to go."

"No," Llannat said. "It's wrong; I can see the ugliness of it without needing a mask to make the patterns clearer. Whatever lives in there is dead beyond helping. You showed me doors, the times I saw you in trances and visions. Show us doors now."

"I don't know what you mean," Owen said.

"You do know," Llannat said. "You have to know. Because if you can't find us a way, we'll die. And the Domina will never live."

"Dropping out of hyper over the Gyfferan system," reported the tactical action officer on RSF *Veratina*.

"Launch permission from dock one," said the small-craft controller. "Shuttle away."

"Very well," General Metadi said. "Now where's the Mage?"

"Getting sensor data," the TAO said. "We're in Gyfferan system space, all right. Hi-comms still down."

"Find the bastard."

"We've been spotted," said the sensor tech. "Fire-control frequencies."

"Evasive steering," Metadi said. "Signal to all units, take loose line of bearing, two-four-zero on me. Fire independently. Target is Mage flagship. Make every shot count."

"We've got EM flares up five," said the sensor tech. "They evaluate as Space Force units attacking Mages."

"ID units," the TAO said.

"This is odd," said the sensor tech. "Space Force units ID as members of Infabede Sector Fleet."

"Don't worry about it," Metadi said. "All Mage units are hostile. All Infabede units are presumed hostile. Net Patrol, task force, and Gyffer units are friendlies. We have one target: the Mage flagship."

"Mage flagship aye," said the TAO. "*Forpin* reports under fire." A pause. "Lost comms with *Forpin*."

"Get me some speed," Metadi said.

"We're already pushing it, sir."

"If we aren't spattering tubes all over system space we aren't pushing it hard enough."

"Lost comms with *Darmyn*. Lost comms with *Aleys*."

"Get an intercept course on that Mage," Metadi said, leaning forward and pointing at the sphere of probability marking the unit he'd identified as the Mage flagship. "Take us up to jump speed, but do not jump. Run in realspace."

"We can't go at jump speed for that long," the TAO protested. "We'll start losing the engines."

"Follow my orders," Metadi replied. "I want to get this ship over there."

"Jump speed aye."

"Very well," Metadi said. "Signal to Colonel Tyche: Commence boarding action. Execute."

"Message to Colonel Tyche, aye," the comms tech on the lightspeed board echoed.

"Now, this is the way to go," Metadi said, leaning back again. "Just me and him, and all I need is one shot at him."

"One shot's all that we're going to get," the TAO said. "Mages are inbound Gyffer: tentative count on friendlies and unknowns show Mage numerical superiority."

"That doesn't concern me," Metadi said. "This is what I drew my pay for from the Republic, all those years. I want to give them their money's worth."

"Show me a door," repeated Llannat. "Show me a door now."

"I don't know what you mean," Owen said.

"You know," Llannat said. "You have to know, because if you don't know, we'll die." She paused. "You said you'd been in the Void before. Tell me what you saw."

"I saw the dead, and I killed a Mage, and I went away

hurt and bleeding. An Adept's skills count for nothing in the Void."

"That's what they always told us, anyway," Llannat said. "But even if you were pulled in here against your will, you found your own way out. How?"

"I followed the man I killed."

"You followed him? Then we'll follow you."

Llannat concentrated on the man before her, in his worn grey spacer's coverall with his staff in his hands. She remembered how the Mage she had fought in the Void had formed an ally out of the swirling mist, and how the dark tower had come when Owen looked for it.

It can be done, she reassured herself. *I've seen it done.*

Out of the mist beside them rose an image of Owen Rosselin-Metadi, sculpted of fog-smoke and the chilling vapor that was the substance of the Void. The phantom turned, running away into the mist.

It can be done. I did it.

There was no time left for thought—already the phantom Owen was lost in the swirling greyness. But his staff was blazing with white light, making a beacon for them in the shadows.

"Come on," Llannat said. "We have to follow him."

They started off again, running, following the bobbing white light in the mist. For a long, mind-deadening time the pursuit continued, while the cold and the mist burned away Llannat's strength even further.

How does he do it? Llannat wondered, casting a glance aside at Owen. He was moving in a steady, ground-eating stride, not even breathing hard. The light ahead grew neither nearer nor farther as they ran along. Llannat felt a pain growing in her side. She wasn't sure how long she could keep on.

Then the light ahead vanished.

Owen halted. "Where—?"

Before he could finish the question, a shadow appeared in the greyness before them, an opening in the non-substance of this non-place. She hesitated, but Owen didn't. Without

breaking stride he entered the dark place and vanished, and
rather than lose him she followed.

They were in a stone corridor, a deep passageway like
those beneath the Adepts' Retreat on Galcen. Doors of
rough-finished wood opened from one side or another. The
staff in Owen's hands blazed white, illuminating the way.

"Only one of the doors is the right one," Llannat said,
and was sure that it was true. "Which one . . . we should
know it when we get there."

"I hope so. I doubt we'll have a second chance."

They went on. The corridor seemed to stretch out forever,
far beyond the light cast by Owen's staff. At last they came
to a blank wall—a dead end, more of the same grey stone
as the rest of the corridor.

"We missed it," Owen said. "One of the doors we
passed."

"No," Llannat said. She reached out with her
noncorporeal senses, and felt *inside* the substance of the
wall. And there they were—the markers to allow someone
trained in the use of power to pass through the solid substance, as she had done long ago in the strange maze beneath the Professor's asteroid.

"Here," she told Owen. "Pass through here."

"There's no Power in the Void," Owen said. "I can't."

"You have to. Do you want to rescue the Domina, or
not?"

His face was pale in the light of his staff, and he shook
his head in frustration. "I tell you, I can't."

"Then grab hold and let me take you," Llannat said.

Own hesitated for a moment, then took hold of her wrist.
She pressed her other hand against the stone and willed herself to sink inward, to become one with the material of the
wall. She felt a brief instant of vertigo, oddly reminiscent of
the discontinuity of a hyperspace jump. Then she passed
through the wall and into the space beyond.

Bright light dazzled her eyes. She stood before the fireplace in the Summer Palace on Entibor, with the arms of
Entibor and of House Rosselin carved in the stone behind
her. Owen stood beside her in the sunlit room.

"Through this way," she said, pointing. A note gonged through the air—a sound she recognized from her vision on board *Night's-Beautiful-Daughter*. "That's the alert. We don't have much time."

Together they passed from the fireplace room and into another just as luxurious, with high arched windows facing green-forested hills. A red bird flitted from tree to tree. . . . In the next instant there came a tremendous glare of blue-white light, and the room dissolved into dazzle before her eyes. There was a smell of smoke; the openwork carving of the table was smoldering where the light had struck. A moment later came a roar of sound as the windows blew in, showering glass splinters everywhere. Llannat felt them touch her body and pass harmlessly through, though each left a trail of pain in its wake, like the pain of the mist in the Void.

"Come on!" she screamed at Owen, pulling him by the arm. "This way!"

Out through the broken embrasures of the windows they went, down to the hillside below, where a swirl of red flame mixed with choking smoke. The smoke was grey, the grey mist of the Void. And the flame was the red glare of a staff, a Mage's staff, held by a slightly-built, grey-haired man in dark trousers and a white, bloodstained shirt.

He bowed, and sketched a salute in the mist with his staff.

"Mistress Hyfid, you've arrived."

"Yes," she said. "I'm here, Professor."

V. Gyfferan space: *Sword-of-the-Dawn*; RSF *Karipavo*
The Void

I N THE quiet of his quarters, Theio syn-Ricte sus-Airaalin carefully belted on his robes as arch-Mage. Not for him today the uniform of a Grand Admiral. When he joined his Circle in the meditation room, he would wear the proper garments of his rank, with every piece in place and each tie correctly tied.

Carefully he settled the black mask over his face and tightened the drawstrings of his hood to hold it closely in place. This was no time for the *geaerith* to slip askew. He would need to see the patterns as they developed.

Already they were there, teasing at the sides of his vision, coming unbidden—the pattern was shaping up well. Unless . . .

There was one tiny discordance far away from the center of the pattern, winking in and out of his peripheral vision, as if it weren't real at all. If that interference spread—like the rings that followed a dropped stone spreading across a pond—if it spread, it could endanger everything, the careful plans of years and the fragile pattern just beginning to emerge.

The interference wasn't coming from the strange Mage, nor yet from the young Domina. Those two were threads, powerful threads, in the weaving of the true pattern. The interference came from elsewhere—there seemed to be a flavor of Adeptry in it, but it was shadowed and obscure.

The source of the interference was moving about, somewhere on the ship. . . . sus-Airaalin extended his senses, but could not pin it down. Something else caught at his attention, absorbed it: a Mageworking, powerful but untutored, drawing the threads of the universe into a pattern of its own—a pattern that was, in fact, the missing part of the design he had struggled from the beginning to create. True peace, the goal so long desired and so long worked for.

But the working was not yet right—the strange Mage was doing everything by instinct, and not all the proper threads were in place. Without the last threads, the pattern could never be completed. Its fabric would fray and destroy the rest.

It will *be completed,* sus-Airaalin thought. *As I told Lisaiet before, I have desired it, and it will be so.*

He left his quarters and went, not to the meditation room after all, but to the cabin of the young Domina.

Llannat held out her arms to the Professor. "I've missed you," she said.

"You've done all that was needful, and more," the Professor said in his courtly voice. "But the end and the beginning of your duty is near."

He clasped her briefly by the shoulders, then released her and stepped aside. The mist parted to reveal a fair woman dressed in white, wrapped in a hooded cloak of thick white wool, like a shroud.

"This is the one you've come to find," the Professor said. "The game was nearly lost—but now there is a chance to win it for good and all."

Llannat knelt before the woman. "Domina," she said. "I have to tell you what I've seen: the Mages have come with ships of war against the Republic. You are needed."

"Mother," Owen said. His voice was low and uncertain—

Llannat had never heard him sound that way before. "We're here to bring you back to the living world, if you will come."

"I will come," the woman said.

Llannat turned back to the older man. "Professor, are you coming too?"

"No, Mistress. My work is finished."

"Will I ever see you again?"

" 'Yes' and 'no' are both such limiting words," the Professor said. "So I'll say 'I don't know,' and leave it at that."

He bowed, and stepped away into the mist.

Owen was holding his mother in a tight embrace. He lowered his arms. "Let's pick a direction and go in it. The way out isn't going to come to us—at least, it isn't right now."

Llannat shook her head, and gestured at a darkening on one part of what would be the horizon, if there were a horizon in this place.

"There," she said. "That's the door. I can see the pattern for it now . . . it's a matter of adjusting your eyes to look for where things aren't, instead of where they are. Let's go."

"Wait," Owen said. "There's something moving in the Void that needs our help. Over there."

He pointed to his right. Now Llannat could see it too—there, not far away, stood a black-robed and black-masked Mage, his staff in one hand, his other hand hanging motionless from a wounded arm. Beside him floated a creature of mist, darker than the greyness of the Void, a nightmare thing with ropy tendrils lashing out at someone half-hidden in the knee-high, swirling fog.

"Come," Owen said, and the three of them approached the fight—for it was a fight, even if badly one-sided.

A young woman with an Adept's staff struck out repeatedly at the creature of mist, but her blows were ineffective. The body of the mist-creature thinned a little where she struck it, but it coalesced again after the staff had passed through.

Llannat recognized the girl; she recognized the mist-creature. The girl was her own younger self—the Llannat who had been cast into the Void during the 'Hammer's raid on Darvell, the raid where the Professor had been killed, and his staff had come to Llannat at Beka Rosselin-Metadi's hands. That time, she had fought a Mage and his creature of mist, and she had nearly died—until a pair of Adepts came and sent her back to the world of reality.

Now Llannat saw that struggle again, from the vantage point of her older self. The younger Llannat was overmatched in her fight against the Void-creature; even now, a pseudopod of grey mist was curling down over the girl's shoulder. When she dropped and rolled away, two more ropes of living mist whipped out and caught her by the ankle and waist as she came up.

The girl lashed out, but Llannat could tell that she was hurting. Her breath came in gasps; sweat rolled down her dark face. Another rope whipped out from the creature, catching her by the wrist. Her staff fell into the mists of the Void. She staggered and fell to one knee.

"Get back!" Owen shouted to the woman on the ground. His staff blazed up again into blinding white light.

The girl staggered away, and fell again.

But by then Llannat had other things to concern her. She let Owen handle the Mage—she had business of her own with the creature of mist. *All times and places meet in the Void,* she thought. *The last time we fought, this creature had the best of me. But not any longer.*

She struck, her Magestaff glowing brightly as she channeled her power through it. When she touched one of the creature's pseudopods, the limb fell away from the indistinct trunk. Again she struck, and again the wound on the thing did not heal, but instead bled pale steam from within its dark-mist covering. Then, without warning, the creature dissolved entirely.

She turned to see Owen standing at guard. The Mage collapsed slowly before him, clutching his belly where bright blood spurted out between his fingers. The black-robed man fell down into the fog and was gone.

Owen turned back to Perada. "What happened to the Adept?"

"Gone," the older woman said. "I sent her back to Ari—he needs her."

"Good," Llannat said. "She needs him, too. But now we have to go."

"This way," Owen said, guiding them both back toward the dark opening in the mist. Away off to the right, the dark tower still stood.

Aboard *Karipavo*, Gil leaned forward in his command chair, the better to see the main battle tank.

"They're flat kicking us to pieces," the TAO said.

Gil had no choice but to agree. "Whatever they have, it has longer range than anything we've got, higher accuracy, and more hitting power. So we deal with that. We have to get in among 'em, where they don't dare use their big stuff without endangering themselves, and where our weapons have an equal chance against them."

"Yeah," said the TAO, "but the run-in is going to be hell."

"Jump behind 'em, then jump back into the thick," Gil said. "That's the way it has to be. Make that up as a signal—all units, jump to beyond system space, then immediately jump back in-system; put your drop point in the center of the sphere of probability for the nearest Mage concentration."

"Report coming in from Fighter Det 32," said the lightspeed comms technician. "Odd contact."

"Report."

"Small vessel squawking identifiers as Republic shuttle located inbound near Mage main body."

"Punch it up on the screen," said Gil.

"Identifier shows it's from *Veratina*."

"One of Vallant's cruisers," said the TAO. "Evaluate part of mutineer force attached to the Mages."

"Negate that," said Gil. "*Veratina* was part of the force reported over Galcen with Metadi."

"Metadi's flag?"

"Could be," Gil said. "Pass to 32: Take *Veratina* shuttle. Transfer all crew to *Karipavo*."

"Report from 32—*Veratina* shuttle contains one person, Republic officer in uniform, requesting conference with commander, Republic forces."

"Roger that," Gil said. "Come aboard *Karipavo*." He turned to Lieutenant Jhunnei. "What do you think?"

"A message from Metadi that he doesn't trust to lightspeed comms?"

"Could be," Gil said. "Stand by to receive them, and bring the officer to me soonest."

It was some time before the fighter, an Eldan two-seater from Fighter Detachment 32, came into the '*Pavo*'s docking bay. The pilot brought his passenger up to the CIC: a Space Force commander with a loop of gold braid on her uniform shoulder.

The pilot saluted. "Lieutenant Tirbat reporting, sir, with person removed from *Veratina*'s shuttle."

Gil looked at the woman whose picture he had last seen tucked in among the pages of Inesi syn-Tavaite's careful, meticulous notes.

"Rosel Quetaya," Gil said. "You're a damned Mage replicant."

"I'm no such thing, Commodore." Her cheeks were red and her voice was indignant—indignant enough to be convincing, if Gil hadn't seen those notebooks, and hadn't heard Doctor syn-Tavaite talking on Innish-Kyl about Magelords and their works.

"I have information for you," the woman continued. "I know where General Metadi is located."

"You do, do you?"

"Yes," She passed across a datachip. "Over in sector one-five green, we've got a major Mage unit. General Metadi intends to do a firing pass and destroy it if possible. He requests you to stand clear, and provide diversion in other sectors."

"Mark that unit in the tank, and pass to all units, '*Enemy flagship located. Target and destroy at all costs.*'"

The woman wasn't red-faced any longer, but pale with anger. "Damn you, Jervas! General Metadi ordered you to stand clear!"

"You mean the Mage commander did. Lieutenant Jhunnei!"

"Yes, sir?"

"Take this—person—and put her in the brig. We'll deal with her later when we have more time."

"I don't like this," said Beka.

But the protest was mostly pro forma. She didn't think that resisting the Grand Admiral would do any good—not when he was wearing his full Magelord's getup, and not when shooting straight at him hadn't done anything before. And besides, he was taking her back where she wanted to go—to *Warhammer*, and the replicant that waited there.

One way or another, we've got ourselves a Mage. I just wish I knew what he was up to.

sus-Airaalin said only, "Please make haste, my lady. The patterns are drawing close."

They reached the docking bay that held *Warhammer*. The door to the bay lay open, and the dock had been pressurized. Beyond the force field at the end of the bay, the cold stars shone. *Warhammer*'s ramp was still down.

They entered an eerily silent ship. No one was in the common room, or in the cockpit. A hand of cards lay spread out on the common-room table.

"Damnation," she muttered, and pulled the blaster. sus-Airaalin made no move to stop her.

She walked quickly down the passageway to the crewside berthing compartments. The seal on Tarveet's quarters was in place. The other compartment was empty.

"Below," she said to the Grand Admiral. "You want anybody, they're likely in the hold."

They went down the starboard passage to bay one. Down the ladder to the large and echoing cargo space they went, and there, against an incongruous backdrop of holographic Khesatan stage scenery, Beka found the rest of her crew—Llannat Hyfid (*Where the hell,* Beka wondered, *did she come from?*) standing with Owen by the head of the stasis box, with Nyls Jessan kneeling beside it monitoring the readouts on the power levels. Doctor syn-Tavaite was hovering over the box and speaking rapidly to Ignac' in her own language while the two of them worked with quick hand motions on the figure inside. After recognizing Mistress Hyfid, Beka wasn't surprised to see Ari standing there as well—a massive, calm figure, with his arms crossed over his chest and an emergency medical kit lying by his feet.

"What the hell are they doing?" she whispered—half to herself, and half to the dark and silent figure beside her.

"Something at which they will fail, if they are not assisted," the Grand Admiral said quietly. "This is the working I saw in my quarters . . . and I see now what I must do."

Beka watched, mesmerized, as sus-Airaalin moved forward, unnoticed by those who labored over the crystal coffin. He halted behind Mistress Hyfid, overshadowing her, and placed his hands on her shoulders. She didn't seem to notice his presence; her concentration was too intense.

After a moment, Beka too stepped into the cluster of people around the stasis box. She looked down. The lid was off, and she could see the—body?—resting inside. As Beka watched the face grew firmer, changing from a youthful oval to a more sharply planed and defined state.

Then, with a gasp and a jerk, the figure started to breathe.

Llannat Hyfid opened her eyes. "It's happened."

syn-Tavaite said something sharp in Eraasian, and Ignac' twisted a dial attached to a meter with a tube running beneath the covering sheets.

"We made it," Owen said softly. He seemed to notice Beka for the first time. "Bee, you were right. We made it."

Then, suddenly, syn-Tavaite picked up a pair of shears, a common set of shears, and began rapidly cutting away the sheets of foil.

"Up, up, get her up," syn-Tavaite said in Galcenian. "She needs to walk around. Get the blood flowing. Help her remember the body."

Ari stepped forward and raised the Domina from the stasis box.

"Here, Mother," he said, lifting her and helping her step out onto the metal deckplates. "We're all here."

Doctor syn-Tavaite came forward with a robe—one of

Jessan's, from the looks of it. It was deep green with a gold satin lining.

"Are you feeling well, my lady?" she asked, carefully helping the Domina into the loose garment.

"I feel weak," came the reply. Beka recognized her mother's voice. "This place—"

"You're on board *Warhammer*, Mother," Ari said. "You're home."

"In the cargo bay?" The Domina was weak, but the note of amusement in her voice sounded real. "Surely not even Jos—"

"Your husband is not here, my lady." It was the first time the Grand Admiral had spoken since leaving Beka's side. "But I also welcome you back to the life of the body. I had not thought to speak with you again."

Doctor syn-Tavaite drew a frightened breath. "A Masked One," she whispered. "My lord, I am acting as honor demands."

"So are we all," sus-Airaalin replied.

Nyls Jessan reached for his blaster. "And who the hell do you think you are?"

The Grand Admiral bowed. "I am Lord sus-Airaalin."

"Ah," said Perada. "Now I remember." She stepped away from Ari's support and stood facing the Magelord. "You swore to me, sus-Airaalin. 'Let me be raised up or cast down according to my merit,' you said. Now you have come with war against my people and my worlds. How are you to escape judgment?"

To Beka's unspoken surprise, the Grand Admiral knelt. "My lady," he said. "I have never broken oath to any, nor do I break it now."

"Then call off your fleet and your attack, and return to the worlds you came from."

"My lady, I cannot. I am sworn to the lords of the Resurgency by oaths from which I am not free—oaths into which I entered after I was released from yours by your death."

Perada looked at him. "Is this true?"

"My lady, I do not lie."

The Domina of Entibor turned away her face. "Then what is there to do? We have tried, and failed."

"Damn it all to hell," said Beka. "I didn't go through all this just to listen to a room full of people explaining why there isn't anything that they can do. There must be *something*—"

"There is," said Llannat Hyfid. She looked terrified but resolute as she stepped forward to face sus-Airaalin where he knelt. "I call upon you, my lord, to honor your ancient customs. I challenge you for your Circle."

"You have neither the skill nor the standing to challenge me," the Grand Admiral said.

"My lord sus-Airaalin," Perada said, "by your oath of service, I command you to accept."

The Grand Admiral rose to his feet. "As you will, Domina. Mistress Hyfid: Will you fight me for the mastery of my Circle and all that I hold?"

"I will fight you," Llannat said.

"To the death," sus-Airaalin said, and raised his staff.

Llannat raised hers. "To the death."

VI. Gyfferan System Space: RSF *Karipavo*; *Sword-of-the-Dawn* *Warhammer*: Captured

In *Karipavo*'s main battle tank, the glowing dot that represented the Mage flagship was expanding into an amorphous blob as time passed and the uncertainty of the flagship's real-time location increased.

"Turn toward, target marked," the TAO said.

"Vector the fighters into position," Gil said. "Get hard data on location as soon as possible."

Light flared on the *'Pavo*'s sensor screens as he spoke, and a shudder ran through the deckplates.

"Hit Alfa, hit Alfa," came a voice over the intraship comms, sent from Damage Control Central. "Supply from Repair Two."

A series of shudders ran through the ship. The messages from Damage Control kept on coming. "Hit Bravo. Hit Charlie. Hit Delta. Hit . . ."

The announcement cut off. At the same time lights and gravity went away in the Combat Information Center. A moment later they came back, but with half-values, and the main battle tank was empty. Either its accumulated data had been lost, or there wasn't enough power to bring up a full display.

Either way, thought Gil, *we're in trouble.* "Damage report?"

"Serious engineering hit," said the TAO. "No response via interior communications from Damage Control Central."

"Weapons and ship control?"

"Self-powered missiles only, fire control marginal. Shields low and flickering. Negative ability to accelerate or maneuver."

"We took some hits, all right," Gil said. "Will our current course intercept the last known posit for the Mage commander?"

"Unknown. We'd begun our turn, but may not have—"

"I don't want 'may.' Get me an answer."

"Working."

Gil turned to the fighter-control talker. "Any comms with the fighter det?"

"Patchy. We've been losing units out there."

"Runner reports Damage Control Central took a direct hit," said Lieutenant Jhunnei. "Rerouting IC, secondary control on-line. One more hit like that, sir, and we're going to be a nice bright cloud of glowing dust."

Gil nodded, slowly. "The same thought had crossed my own mind, Lieutenant."

The tech at the exterior comms panel leaned back and took off the headset. "That's it, Commodore. We're blind and deaf. Progressive damage has reached the comms spaces."

At the same moment, ship's gravity clicked off entirely, then began to cycle from zero to a multiple of standard—Gil guessed that it was about a three. *Damned uncomfortable, at any rate.* The half-power lights died, to be replaced by the self-powered red battle glows.

Gil took a deep breath. "Give the order to abandon ship."

In *Warhammer*'s cargo bay, the magnificent lines of *By Honor Betray'd* were still continuing, in Eraasian, within a hold transformed into a theater by lifelike holoprojection. In among the moving illusions, Llannat Hyfid and sus-Airaalin faced each other, motionless.

Neither one wants to make the first move, Beka thought. Nobody else had moved either. Everyone in the cargo bay was watching the combat, as if they were in fact one of the Circles for which Llannat and sus-Airaalin contended.

Llannat held her short staff one-handed, angled out before her. Slowly, a nimbus of green fire appeared near her hand and crept out along its length. sus-Airaalin didn't wait for her to be ready; he struck out, whipping his staff down toward Llannat in a blaze of crimson light. She raised her staff in time and deflected the force of the blow.

Beka looked across the bay to where Ari was again cradling the Domina Perada in his arms. He didn't seem to notice his burden; all his attention was given to watching the fight. His eyes were fixed on sus-Airaalin, and the red of the blazing power on the Magelord's staff was reflected in his eyes.

If Llannat buys it, Beka thought, *there's going to be hell to pay.*

All around the duel, the play ran on. The Duke and his friend Lucet were disguised as beggars in the lanes of Mesara. Lucet was speaking, showing the diamond watch that Alona had given him, the one with the miniature of the house in Favinzi on the lid.

Abruptly, Lucet warped and deformed as someone else entered through him.

"Master Ransome!" Beka said.

For all they seemed to notice the newcomer, Llannat and sus-Airaalin might have been sealed away from the rest of the cargo bay by walls of glass. Still caught up in their deadly play, the Adept and the Magelord circled one another, striking and parrying.

"Come along," Ransome said to Beka. He continued walking toward the group clustered by the holoprojector. "We have tasks to complete, you and I. The war has reached a critical phase, and we have only one chance to avoid defeat."

"I tried taking your advice once already," Beka said. "I

shot the Grand Admiral for you, but it didn't do us any good."

The Domina Perada pulled herself up out of Ari's supporting arms. "Master Ransome," she said. "You're too late. The last chance is here and now."

"What are you talking about?" another voice said. The man who had been with Ransome before came out of the holoprojection as well. "Come on!"

"No," Perada said. "Leave us. If you have a ship waiting, go to it now."

The man stared at Perada for a second, then turned toward Beka. "Don't listen to her! She's a replicant—a Magebuilt construct!"

"No," said Owen. He had kept silent all this time, watching the duel with a steady, intent concentration, as if he could lend energy to Mistress Hyfid just by willing it. Now he turned to address Ransome and his companion. "She's real. I ought to know—I helped bring her back."

"Sorcery!" Ransome cried, and swung at Owen with his makeshift staff. "Traitor! You, of all people!"

To Beka's surprise, Owen didn't try to block the blow. He took it full force, staggering back under the impact.

"I deserved that much, Master," he said, "but no more. Put up your staff."

The *Pavo*'s CIC was all but deserted now, a dark and ghostly place in the light of the red battle-glows. The faint whisper of circulating air had ceased some time ago, when the life-support systems had shut down. Gravity was still cycling erratically.

"Sir, come on," Lieutenant Jhunnei said. "You need to get to a lifepod."

"I think I'll stay for a while," Gil said. He sat back in his chair, gripping the arms to keep in place as gravity dropped to zero, then came back up heavy.

His aide looked distressed. "Sir, will you at least come down to the docking bay and see if that shuttle from the *Tina* is still operative?"

Gil shook his head. "You may if you want to. I'm where I want to be right now."

"Commodore," Jhunnei said, "if you're staying, I request permission to remain with you."

"Denied," Gil said. "No sense both of us getting killed."

"Sir."

"I mean it. Get to your abandon-ship station."

"Yes, sir."

She turned and left.

At length the red-lit compartment was silent and still. Gil stood and walked without undue haste to his in-space cabin, located midway between CIC and the bridge. His pressure suit waited in its locker. He put it on, leaving the faceplate open. No sense in using the bottled air until he had to—he'd breathe the ship's air as long as possible. He clipped a light amplifier to his belt and headed out again, walking carefully as the deck seemed to go from one angle to another under his feet with the cycling gravity. He braced or balanced himself with his hands as he walked aft.

"Let's see," he muttered, as his light picked out the compartment numbers. "Weapons spaces, skin nacelles."

One path was blocked by collapsed bulkheads jamming the door—he turned and took another way. There was no ship's gravity here, which was a good thing. A little farther on, he had to leap across a pit extending downward through at least two decks.

Half a trooper was wedged into the broken frames near the top of the hole.

"Poor bastard," Gil muttered, and went on.

The ship's air grew chilly and thin as Gil worked his way outward: time to seal up, switch to the air in his p-suit and clip the light amplifier onto his faceplate. He continued through levels of increasing destruction until he drew close to the skin of the ship. There he entered a self-powered lock, used in better times for maintenance checks and safety inspections, and made his way through onto the 'Pavo's exterior surface.

Gil attached his lifeline to a ringbolt beside the hatch, then set out on foot toward the location of the self-powered missiles—the close-in and medium-range stuff. Stars big and bright as glowbulbs swam through space over his head as the ship rotated around its longitudinal axis. The magnifiers and light amplifiers attached to his helmet showed the planets of the Gyfferan system as pale, flattened disks.

When he reached the missile battery, he pulled open its diagnostic pod and set the checks. Working by hand, he keyed in search parameters: the EM signatures of the Mage flagship, or as many of them as he could recall from watching the readouts over the comptech's shoulder. He set the unit to alert on a 0.9 match. That done, he allowed himself to relax a little. The missiles were in place and powered up. A good set of weapons.

Not too far away, energy beams flowed through space. Off in what passed for the middle distance, an explosion blossomed. The missile pod beeped. The target was nearby—a grey disk, at the center of a swarm of fighters.

That'll be the Mage flagship.

Gil opened the viewscreen of the diagnostic and set the warhead on one of the missiles to Seek. The missile recorded its lock-on. He paused, then started the lock and launch sequence from the local control board. He turned the final key to the Fire position and closed the panel's cover.

"Well, that's that," he said, and leaned back against the diagnostic pod to watch the show. The missiles went in sequence—the testing and maintenance board wasn't sophisticated enough to handle volley or simultaneous fire—arching out in a trail of flame, then going dark as the first launch phase ended.

Gil waited a while longer. Nothing remained on visual above him except the stars. His air supply was getting into the critical zone.

"I wonder if there's any cha'a left inside?" he said, and headed back toward the lock.

On *Sword-of-the-Dawn*'s fighting bridge, a technician looked up from her scope. "Missiles, incoming. Bearing three-four-two close."

"Where'd those come from?" wondered Captain syn-

Athekh, the *Sword*'s commander. "Raise shields to take impact."

"Shields in threatened quadrant damaged," the technician called out. "Stand by for impact. Three. Two. One . . ."

"Where's the Grand Admiral?" syn-Athekh demanded. "We need him in here."

"I'll go find him," Mid-Commander Taleion said. "I believe he wants me to locate him now."

The docking bay of the Mage flagship rocked with a missile hit. *Warhammer* swayed on the blocks holding her in place. In the captive freighter's number-one cargo hold, a muffled thud vibrated through the silent air. The holoprojector fell on its side and went off.

Jessan would probably claim there was something symbolic about that, thought Beka. *But I don't want to think about it right now.*

More impacts sounded, growing nearer. Mistress Hyfid and the Grand Admiral never paused in their duel—not for the noise and the vibration of the missile hits, nor for the changes in the appearance of the hold after the holoprojection died—and not for the presence of Master Ransome. Owen was still off-balance from the Adept Master's blow, a trickle of blood running down his sleeve from the first blow he had taken, when Errec Ransome spun around and lifted his staff to strike again.

For a moment Beka thought that Ransome meant to aid Mistress Hyfid in her struggle with sus-Airaalin. She drew breath to warn him off—*That won't work; it has to be single combat!*—but the words caught in her throat as she realized the Adept Master's true purpose. Llannat Hyfid was intent on her struggle with the Eraasian Grand Admiral: she would never notice the treacherous attack coming against her from behind.

Beka didn't dare cry out a warning; the moment of divided attention might give sus-Airaalin the opening he was looking for. She lifted her blaster—still set on Full—and took aim.

I'm sorry, Master Ransome. Dadda may never forgive me, but I can't let you stop us now.

She never had a chance to fire. A dark-clad figure, moving quickly, stepped between Mistress Hyfid and the threatened blow.

Goddammit, Ignac', Beka thought. Her teeth drew back from her lips in a frustrated snarl. *This isn't your fight. Get the hell out of the way before somebody shoots you!*

But Ignaceu LeSoit, blaster drawn, was already blocking Beka's line of fire. "I tell you, old man, let the matter take its course."

LeSoit fired, but Master Ransome never altered expression. Beka saw the bolt connect, but Ransome did not fall. LeSoit didn't seem surprised.

"You endanger everything," he said to Ransome, and raised his blaster to fire again.

Ransome struck out with his staff—LeSoit's second bolt went wild as Ransome caught him across the throat with a killing blow. Beka watched her shipmate crumple under the impact.

Dead, she thought, as he fell and her line of fire came clear at last. She shot Errec Ransome twice before LeSoit hit the metal deckplates, but it did no more good than shooting sus-Airaalin had done. LeSoit lay motionless, blood pooling under his face. *Dead. Damn you, Ignac', why couldn't you stay away from all this?*

She fired again—*Damn all these Mages and Adepts, you can't get a clear shot at any of them!*—and heard the buzz of another weapon as somebody else—*Jessan, it has to be; what the hell took him so long?*—joined in. One, at least, of the bolts connected; Ransome jerked and fell.

"Errec!"

It was the Domina Perada who had cried out. Beka turned involuntarily toward the sound of her mother's voice—only to see, at the boundaries of her vision, that Ransome was not yet dead, but pushing up again onto his feet. Beka pivoted—*What does it take to kill one of these sons of bitches, anyway?*—but it was too late. The Adept Master had Ignac' LeSoit's blaster in one hand, and the other arm wrapped around the neck of the Nammerinish girl, Klea Santreny.

Why her? Beka wondered. *Is it because she was the closest, or because she was the weakest—or is it because she's Owen's apprentice, the way Owen was his?*

For a moment, all movement in the cargo bay froze, except for the dark, twinned figures of Llannnat Hyfid and Grand Admiral sus-Airaalin, still striking and turning in their private and deadly dance. Not even the sound of blaster fire had broken into their concentration.

"This is madness, Errec," said Perada. "The girl is nothing to you. Let her go."

The Adept Master turned his eyes toward her and shook his head.

"No," he said. "I haven't finished yet."

In the next instant, Ransome and Klea vanished together—as cleanly as if they had taken a step away from realspace and gone into hyper. Beka fired again, sending a half-dozen shots into the empty air where Ransome had stood only a fraction of a second before. In the middle of the cargo bay, Llannat and sus-Airaalin never paused in their duel.

"It's no use," said Owen. His face was pale under its thin film of sweat, and his voice was bleak. "He's taken her into the Void."

And from there, Beka thought, *who the hell knows where he might go and how much more harm he might be able to do? Somebody has to stop him before he screws up everything.*

"Figure out how to go after him, dammit," she snarled at her brother. "You were messing around in the Void just a few minutes ago. Can't you find the way back without a road map?"

"Adepts don't—"

"Ransome just did. Do it." She paused, then lowered her blaster and spoke again in a quieter voice. "As a favor, Owen"—*and you've never refused me a favor yet*—"take *me* there. The son of a bitch killed my friend, and if I can catch him, he's dead meat."

Owen looked at her for a long moment. For an instant Beka thought that he was going to refuse her after all. Then she felt the room go dark and twist around her. She was going down, falling away. . . .

Panic caught at her throat: *This is unnatural; nobody should do something like this without a starship around them!* She reached out blindly for support and stability as the twisting continued and the universe tried to move sideways. She caught what she needed, and the random twisting steadied into a kind of steady progress, like a starship settling onto its proper course. *Pick the jump point—make the run-up—*

And we're through.

Nyls Jessan let his blaster hand sag down to his side. The sound of weapons fire had died away in the cargo hold, and the compartment, which had seemed crowded before, was nearly empty. Captain Rosselin-Metadi was gone—vanished—with her brother—no, with *both* her brothers, and the Domina Perada as well.

Gone after Master Ransome, he thought wearily. *It's only right; he was their friend, so they should be the ones to deal with him. I suppose I'm still here because someone has to keep an eye on this end of things.*

And there aren't very many of us left.

Not many at all. Only Llannat and the Magelord, caught up in their single combat to the exclusion of all else; a ragged man in a general's uniform, who regarded everything with dismay; and Doctor Inesi syn-Tavaite, on her knees beside LeSoit's crumpled form.

The Eraasian shook her head and stood up. "Iekkenat Lisaiet is dead," she said.

"I'm sorry," Jessan said. The words sounded flat and inadequate. "I never thought that Errec Ransome, of all people, would turn and betray us."

The man in uniform made a vague gesture toward the duel still continuing in the middle of the hold. "Aren't you going to do something?"

"I am doing something," Jessan told him. "I'm staying

here and watching what happens between Mistress Hyfid and the Grand Admiral. Regardless of what comes next, there have to be witnesses."

Back inside *Karipavo*, Gil made his way forward through the dark passageways. Lights and gravity had failed entirely now, though the pressure gauge on his suit indicated that the atmosphere was holding out in the inner compartments. He opened the faceplate. Might as well breathe ship's air for as long as he could.

Strange. He wasn't alone aboard the *'Pavo* after all. With the helmet open, he could hear a voice, a woman singing. He couldn't make out the words.

Gil followed the sound—it was coming from the detention area. Soon he could hear the verses clearly enough to recognize the tune. The last time he'd heard that song, the free-spacers of Galcen Prime had been singing it at Beka Rosselin-Metadi's wake:

> *"Forgot by the planets that bore us,*
> *Forsaken by all we hold dear,*
> *The good ones have all gone before us*
> *And only the evil are here."*

He flashed his light inside the compartments one at a time, until he came to one that had a prisoner in it. Gil assumed that the crew member assigned to open the brig during abandon-ship must have been one of the casualties.

> *"Assemble my spaceship around me*
> *And fuel it with beer when you're done,*
> *I don't need a life-support system*
> *If only the engines will run."*

"Then strap me again in—" Rosel Quetaya stopped her song and looked up at him. "Going down with the ship, Commodore?"

"I had some work to do," he said. "And leaving someone

else to die alone in the dark isn't my style. Come with me and let's see if we can't find something to eat."

Together they made their way forward toward the wardroom. Gil was reasonably certain that there'd be a cha'a dispenser nearby, and with luck it would be undamaged. Some of the red-glows were working in this part of the ship. Gravity seemed to have stabilized at a small fraction of normal—or perhaps it was the centrifugal force of the ship's rotation that gave the illusion.

They turned the last corner into the wardroom pantry, and found that Lieutenant Jhunnei had gotten there before them. The commodore's aide was sitting on a table, sipping a cup of hot cha'a. Two more steaming cups sat on the table beside her.

"Hello, Commodore," she said. "I was expecting you."

"I ordered you to abandon ship," Gil said.

"If ship's power were still up, I'd already have the court-martial forms filled out for your signature, sir," Jhunnei said. "But I guess you'll just have to mark down another count of neglect of duty on your mental list and leave it at that."

"I didn't want you to get killed due to my incompetence."

"Not to worry," Jhunnei said. "The way things happened, by the time I got to the launch bay everyone had gone. There was only one *Myrkit*-class shuttle left behind." She definitely looked pleased with herself, Gil thought; and she was smiling broadly as she continued, "I really don't know why nobody noticed it before I got there."

Llannat gasped for breath and dragged her arm back into position. She was tired, tired in mind and body. Her muscles were aching, and she was having a hard time focusing her eyes.

The power of the universe—which she had drawn upon freely so many times before—wasn't responding to her calls for help any longer. Only her own efforts protected her from the black-clad figure who came on and on against her like a force of nature.

She felt the deck heave under her feet and lost her balance. Falling, she felt the staff the other was wielding against her smash down across her back. She rolled away. Light was fading around her. Her eyes growing dim? No, the lights in the compartment were going out. They flared back up again. She opened herself again to the universe, but it failed to come.

Now she looked elsewhere for power—perhaps it was in the tangle of silver cords she could see around her. They had come back to her more strongly when the light had faded. Maybe she could bend them to her will?

No. It was impossible to concentrate on moving the cords and still pay enough attention to the staff in her hand. She was lost. More blows kept on coming in at her, their force great enough to make her hand sting when she caught them on her staff, and her counterstrokes were always turned.

"No," she muttered. She threw a series of blows, but they were turned as well. Her own defenses came more and more slowly. But she wouldn't give up. Wouldn't go down.

Llannat opened herself to the Adepts' power, to the bright oneness with the universe that accepted the flow of power as it was, without trying to change it. She choked up on her staff, shortening it, holding it in both hands, and swung it flat, putting her shoulders behind the blow. It slid beneath her opponent's arm, taking him in the ribs. She could feel bone break under the impact as she followed through. He fell heavily onto his side, then rolled on his back, breathing with difficulty.

Casting aside her staff, she tore off her mask and dropped to her knees beside him. "Come on," she said. "You aren't hurt that bad. I'm a medic. Let me help you."

She removed his mask. The man was pale, too pale, beneath the layer of sweat.

He's going into shock.

She looked about the cargo bay for help, and saw Nyls Jessan, and the Eraasian woman who had created the replicant.

"Jessan," she said. "Get over here. I've got a casualty."

"No, Mistress," the man before her said. He spoke with

difficulty, each word a prodigy of effort. "I am dying. It is as it must be. Take my energy, make it yours."

"I don't want your energy. I can help you. Your wound isn't fatal, if we hurry."

"No help," the man said. At last Llannat recognized his voice—he was the First she had spoken with before, in the Mages' sickbay. "This is as it must be. You have defeated me. You are the First of all the Mage-Circles—and you are not bound to the Resurgency on Eraasi by any oaths whatsoever. For the sake of the galaxy, Mistress, you must hold your power and use it well."

His breath failed him then; he closed his eyes. Llannat felt for a pulse. Nothing. The Grand Admiral was dead.

A man walked forward from the shadows, a short man in a brown uniform. He wore a staff at his belt.

"I am Mid-Commander Taleion," he said. "The Second of your Circle. Command me."

VII. The Void

WARHAMMER: NUMBER-ONE CARGO BAY

SWORD-of-THE-DAWN: OBSERVATION DECK

RSF VERATINA: COMBAT INFORMATION CENTER

B EKA FELL several feet, hit the ground, and rolled as the Professor had taught her, coming up with her blaster gripped in both hands, pointing straight out from her center of gravity.

Grey mist was everywhere, swirling about like the pseudosubstance of hyperspace—but hyperspace was the starpilot's friend, promising rest from labor and safety from pursuit, and this place, she could tell from the feel of it, was no friend to anybody. The air was neither hot nor cold, and the fog burned wherever it touched her.

Ransome. I want Errec Ransome. Where the hell is that son of a bitch?

She didn't see the former Master of the Adepts' Guild anywhere. She did see Owen, standing a little way off and leaning on his staff. He looked pale and tired. He was frowning a little—not at her, but at the other two who had come with her. Ari and—leaning against Ari's massive frame with her face turned away from the sight of the Void—the Domina Perada.

Beka rounded on Ari. Her nerves were frayed, and it felt

good to lose her temper in this flat and sterile place. "What the hell are *you* doing here?"

Ari, for once, didn't rise to the bait. "I don't know," he said. "You're the one who had to go asking our brother for a favor. This is no time to argue about the results."

She bit her lip in frustration. "Owen," she said. "What happened? I told you just me, not the whole damned family."

"It wasn't my idea," Owen said. "You must have done something to make it happen that way."

"*Me?* I'm just a starship pilot, remember. You're the one who walks through walls."

"Children." The Domina's quiet voice cut through their rising tones, just as it had when they were young. "You're wasting time."

Beka let out her breath in a long sigh. "I know, Mother, I know. Owen—where the hell are we, anyway?"

"This is the Void," Owen said. "You asked me to bring you here, and I have. I hope we don't all come to regret it."

"Not if I can get hold of Master Ransome," Beka said. "What the hell is *wrong* with him anyway? You told me that he'd been captured, not that he'd gone insane."

"I don't know what happened to him," Owen said. "He's here, though. I can feel it."

Beka waved her blaster at the endless, undifferentiated fog. "What the hell does *here* mean in a place like this? That bastard killed my friend, and I want him dead."

"*Here* is here," Owen said. "Where what you will, becomes real."

"What I—"

"Be quiet," said Ari. "Look."

She looked.

As if Owen's words had called it forth, a dense mass had begun to coalesce out of the formless grey expanse above and ahead of them. It grew darker and colder, like a black sun burning through the fog, and brought with it the moaning sound of wind around bare stone. The mist-covered non-surface upon which they stood began to sway and shudder.

A black monolith thrust itself up through the fog, high and wide, like a stone dagger piercing a length of fabric from beneath. The monolith became a tower, built of rock and bound with iron, with narrow windows set in its walls—and at its base, where it stood fixed and firm, a massive wooden door.

"Damn," said Beka quietly. She tightened her grip on her blaster. "What brought *that* thing here?"

"Things bring themselves here," said Perada. Her voice was tight, as if she thought about subjects best not remembered. "This is a place where it doesn't pay to think too long about something, or it may come looking for you."

Beka looked at her mother. The Domina was pale to the lips, and her eyes were full of a fear that she didn't express.

I used to think that Mother wasn't afraid of anything, Beka thought. *I wish I hadn't found out I was wrong.*

She straightened her shoulders. "Good," she said. "Then I'm thinking real hard about Master Ransome."

Ari looked upward at the looming tower. "Could be it worked, baby sister. *Something* sure came looking for us."

"We came after it," Owen corrected him. "Which amounts to the same thing. Here, at least."

"If you say so," said Ari. "You're the Adept." He pointed at the heavy wooden door. Beka saw for the first time that it hung splintered and askew on its wrought-iron hinges. "There's a way in," he said. "If you want to go hunting for someone."

"That's why I'm here," she said. "Damned if I know about you and Mother, though."

Ari shrugged. "I know how to hunt things."

"I was part of this from the beginning," said Perada. Her voice was stronger now, and she stepped away from Ari's support. "Now it's time to finish it for good. Owen—"

"Yes, Mother?"

"Show us the way."

Owen led them inside, holding his staff up before him. It gave off a pale and dingy light. *A two-credit glowstick could do a better job,* Beka thought irritably. She dwelt on her discontent, keeping it alive—it was a distraction, like a pebble in a shoe, to keep her from thinking too hard about where she was and what she was doing.

Within the great keep, the light of Owen's staff shone into halls and corners, illuminating broken doorways and stone floors covered with decaying sticks of furniture. Beka went up to one of the doorways and looked into the room. Inside, jagged edges of milk-colored glass still clung to the frames of shattered windows, in walls lined with empty, broken bookshelves. A golden goblet lay amid the dirt, partly covered with dust and grime. A splash of rubies from the goblet spread across the floor like a puddle of spilled wine.

"Nobody here," Beka said. "Wherever this is."

"A symbol," said Owen. "A construct, called up out of the Void to mirror a person's mind."

"Wonderful," she said. "I hope it isn't the inside of your head that looks like this, because I'm damned sure it isn't me."

"Don't look at me, either," Ari said, his voice a deep rumble. "I wouldn't visit a place like this on a holiday."

"Children," said Perada again. She sounded weary, Beka thought, and full of all the sorrow in the galaxy. "Can't you tell? This is Errec Ransome's last stronghold. This is the Retreat on Galcen, as his mind builds it here for him."

At length they came to a room with a single door on its far side, and behind that door a stone wall. The wall was cracked and marred, but not broken. The four of them looked at the wall for a while in silence. It stood there, firm and unyielding, defying them to pass.

Then Ari put his hands against it and pushed. The wall remained solid. "No good. It's not going anywhere."

Owen drew a deep breath, and struck at the wall with his staff. "Listen to me, Errec Ransome. The Retreat isn't yours any longer. It never was yours. It belongs to the Adepts' Guild, and you gave away the Mastery of the Guild to me."

Silence, from the halls and the empty rooms. Far off, Beka heard the keening of the wind.

"Let me try," Perada said. She laid a hand against the blank masonry. "Let me in, Errec. In the name of what we shared."

The stones and mortar crumbled and fell away.

"Come," said Perada, and stepped through the gap.

Beka followed, with Ari and Owen close after her. They entered a part of the tower where destruction and decay had not taken root: a long room full of deep carpets and rich wood, where the polished windows blazed with colored glass, and bright sunlight shone through them onto tapestries, rugs, and books. Only one thing marred the perfection of the place: from all around the eerie howling sounded louder than ever before.

Errec Ransome was waiting there for them, with Klea beside him. She looked broken-spirited and weak; her head was bent and her eyes downcast. Beka couldn't see her expression. She held her staff awkwardly, as if it were no more than a broomstick.

"Welcome," Ransome said. "More came than I expected. But I'm happy to see you, Perada. It can be lonely in the Void."

"That's true, at least," the Domina said. "As I have reason to know."

"Master Ransome," Owen broke in, before his mother could say anything more. "I can see how you might have wanted no part of a future that would include peace with the Mageworlds. I can see how you couldn't endure watching Mistress Hyfid betray her training. I would have let you go into the Void unhindered." He paused. "But you had no right to take my apprentice with you. Give her back."

Ransome laughed. "The Nammerinish tart? No. You failed me, and I have need of her. I have a great deal of work before me to undo all the damage that you have done, and she will be *my* apprentice here."

"You've done quite enough," Perada said. Her voice was cold now, cold as the Void outside—as cold, Beka thought, as the Domina herself must have felt after she had resolved to lose Entibor rather than surrender the civilized galaxy to the Magelords. "You weren't satisfied with winning the last war and humbling the Mages; you were the Breaker of Circles, and you wanted the Mages destroyed. You wanted to stop any movement toward unity, any chance that someone might persuade the Republic to bring in the Mageworlds as equals rather than keeping them locked away on the far side of the Net. And to do that, you needed to kill me."

Beka's grip tightened on her blaster; only shock and a momentary disbelief kept her from firing. But the stricken expression on Errec Ransome's face convinced her that Perada had spoken the truth.

"You were committing treason," Ransome said. "You were sworn to a Mage. You *were* a Mage. You had to die."

You bastard, thought Beka. *After everything we did—after everywhere we looked—after I damn-near took the civilized galaxy to pieces with my bare hands—it was all done in the name of your precious Guild after all. And Dadda was blind enough to call you his best and oldest friend!*

But Perada didn't look surprised. "Do you believe in vengeful ghosts?" she asked Ransome.

"No."

"Believe in them," Perada said. "We exist."

"Then believe in this also," Ransome said. "I will bear no interference in my work. The war can still be won, if only I have the time—and here in the Void, I will have all the time I need."

There was a blur of movement beside him.

" 'Nammerinish tart,' " Klea said, as her staff came down on him, her posture suddenly no longer awkward, her form in the Dance perfect. "I'm my own, not yours, and I'm *not* a tart."

Now, thought Beka, as Ransome staggered forward. She leveled her blaster and fired twice in rapid succession.

The bolts flashed through Ransome without apparent effect. They slammed through the furnishings behind him without leaving holes. Their passage through the air left none of the usual acrid smell. But as their sound and light died, the stones of the tower began to waver and turn into smoke.

The walls fell and the floor dissolved, and once more there was nothing, anywhere, but the swirling grey fog that was the mark and substance of the Void.

Owen stepped forward, his staff a blazing bar of white light. "Now, Master Ransome—fight me."

Ransome smiled, and there was a bitterness in it that hurt Beka to look at. "The final, true contest for Mastery, after the way of the Mages? So be it, and let the apprentice here stand witness."

"Apprentice no longer," said Owen. "She said it herself. She is her own. Mistress Santreny?"

The girl took a step nearer. "Owen?"

"Whatever happens, see that the others get home."

If the command—and the unexpected elevation in rank— were too much for Klea, Beka thought, she didn't show it. Her eyes were clear, and she nodded gravely. "I will."

"Good." Owen turned back to Master Ransome. "Let us begin."

The two Adepts faced one another, and their staves lashed out in swirling blazes of light, a basketwork of glowing lines surrounding them, swift and deadly.

Ari stood looking at them with the same intent regard he had given to Llannat Hyfid's duel in the cargo bay. "Master Ransome is the one who killed you, Mother?"

"He gave the order," Perada said. "He laid the track. He set hired assassins on you and on your sister, so that the Mages would be blamed."

"Then he's mine."

With that, Ari walked into the fight.

Beka watched him go, her useless blaster still gripped tightly in her hand. "It's no good," she said, half to herself and half to Perada. "Ari's just going to get himself killed."

Perada laid a hand on Beka's wrist. "No," she said. "Errec has always been one to hide away his wounds, from friend and enemy alike. He was hurt when he came here, and now he lacks the strength to hold the citadel together around us. All he can do is keep up an illusion of soundness. That, and fight."

"And hope for a fair duel," said Beka. Her lips curled back in a silent snarl. "He doesn't deserve one."

"Perhaps; perhaps not," said the Domina. "But the choice isn't his any longer."

Beka turned her attention back to the fight. Ari had stepped into the midst of it, ignoring the random strokes that came his way, and Owen had seen him. Beka, watching them, was sure of it—she saw Owen's gaze shift away from Ransome for an instant, and focus on his brother.

Then Owen turned his attention back to Ransome, and began a flurry of fast, light attacks to the older Adept's head—strikes not meant to hurt or slow him, Beka realized, but to distract him from the other man who was approaching from behind. Owen wasn't even defending himself, even though more than one of Ransome's blows fell solidly against his body. He didn't stop weaving his elaborate web of feints and distractions until his brother had come within arm's reach.

Owen faltered, leaving himself open. Ransome lifted up his staff for the killing stroke. And Ari seized the onetime Master of the Adept's Guild from behind, lifted him, and slammed him down across his knee. Ransome's spine broke with a loud crack.

"Hunters kill their own prey," Ari said, dropping the broken body into the fog-smoke. "Murderers hire others to do their killing for them."

The howling in the air faded and died. Only the chilling fog remained.

"Now what?" Beka asked, holstering her blaster. "Ari, Owen—are you hurt?"

"Maybe," said Ari. "Nothing serious." He turned to his brother, and his brother's former apprentice. "Owen—Mistress Santreny—take us home."

"Hold back," Beka said, and snatched out her blaster again. Another form was rising from the mist—Errec Ransome, but not as she had ever seen him.

This Ransome was younger, and fanatic hatred had not yet cast its shadow over his face. He ignored all of them, except for the Domina. To her, he held out a hand.

"Perada?" The voice was younger too, with a note of confusion in it. "What are you doing in this place? You should be home, and safe."

The Domina ignored his outstretched hand. "*Now* believe

in ghosts, Errec Ransome. You died before your time, and didn't have the grace to know it."

The young Errec lowered his hand and looked ashamed. "Have I wronged you, Perada? What can I do to make it right?"

"You have wronged me grievously, Errec," the Domina said. "Give me your name and reputation. This bloodstained disaster of a war needs a villain, if I'm going to have a chance at peacemaking afterward—and I will make that villain you."

Ransome bowed his head. "If I have wronged you, that is only just. Take my name and reputation; use them as you will."

"I already have them," Perada said. "Now you are a wanderer. Go repair what you can. I give you leave."

The Domina of Entibor turned her back on Errec Ransome and faced her children. "Let's go home."

"Mistress," said Mid-Commander Taleion, "you have your duties to attend to."

"Yes, of course," Llannat said. Her body ached, and her spirit was numb with fatigue, but the Eraasian stood waiting, patiently, for her to take the fealty that he offered. She groped in her mind for the proper orders. "Please have the people here seen to. Heal those who are wounded. Treat them as your honored guests—as you would treat me."

"Yes, Mistress," Taleion said. "Come now to the control area. We have been hit by missiles and boarded by Adeptworld troops. You are needed."

Llannat allowed herself to be drawn away, up through *Warhammer* and deep into *Sword-of-the-Dawn*. She went up to the *Sword*'s fighting bridge, with Mid-Commander Taleion beside her, and sat in the Grand Admiral's command chair. None of the brown-uniformed officers protested, or even appeared surprised. She wondered if they had been expecting something like this—a duel for mastery, and the changes it might bring—ever since *Night's-Beautiful-Daughter* had brought a strange Magelord to join them.

"Your Circle is gathered," Taleion said. "Command us."

Llannat took a deep breath. *I'm a medic. What in heaven's name am I doing here?* But the Second of her Circle was waiting, and sus-Airaalin's last command lay heavy upon her. She drew upon what knowledge she had, and spoke. "How stands the battle?"

"At the cusp of victory," said Taleion. "Or of defeat."

"You said that we had been boarded?"

"Yes."

"Have you captured any of the boarding parties?"

"Some have been overpowered. The rest fight on."

"Then bring the prisoners to me."

"There were only a few," Taleion protested, "and fewer of those unwounded. Are you sure?"

Llannat caught her Second's gaze, and held it with her own. "Do you intend to question my orders, or to obey?"

"I obey," the mid-commander said, and departed.

Llannat looked at the colored glyphs on the viewscreens around her. She could see the silver cords that surrounded her. They were straight, and overlaid in a pleasing pattern that while itself unmoving, nevertheless suggested movement. She turned her attention to it.

"Mistress, the prisoners."

Llannat looked at the scene in front of her, with the cords still in her peripheral vision. The cords overlaid the young man in partial blast armor, bleeding heavily from a cut across his forehead. One of his eyes was swollen shut. She recognized his collar insignia—a Republic colonel.

"What is your name?" she asked.

"Natanel Tyche, Colonel, Space Force Planetary Infantry," he responded. "Who the hell are you?"

That was the question. And she knew the answer, fully and completely. "I am the commander of the Mageworlds warfleet, and the First of all the Circles."

The pattern was finished, perfect, and the power of the universe flowed through it without break or disturbance.

"I am the First of all the Circles," she repeated. "Now we stand at the Unification of the Galaxy, as was foretold."

* * *

Beka felt the shock of passage take her as Owen brought them out of the Void—*Exactly like making a hyperspace jump without benefit of engines,* she thought dizzily; *I think I'll pass on doing it again any time soon*—and they were back inside the familiar, comfortable starkness of *Warhammer*'s number-one cargo hold.

Nyls Jessan was there, bless him, catching her as she stumbled and letting her lean against his shoulder until her shaking stopped. She didn't see what the others were doing and she didn't care; it felt too good to be touching someone warm and real for a change.

Finally, she looked up. "At least *that*'s over," she said.

"Oh, I don't know about that," said another voice.

Councillor Tarveet stood in the shadows of the bay— newly shaven, freshly dressed in what Beka recognized as yet another of Jessan's better robes, with a blaster from *Warhammer*'s weapons locker in his hand.

Beka pulled away from Jessan. "Who the hell let you go?"

Tarveet gestured idly with his blaster. "Our mutual friend General Ochemet was so kind as to shoot open the locked door. His final folly, I'm afraid. Stand over there with the rest, if you please."

"You slimy, slug-eating bastard," Beka said. "You're only alive because I didn't bother to kill you back on Suivi Point. I tell you what—I'll let you keep on living, and I'll let you leave."

"That's out of your power, my lady," Tarveet said. "The decision is mine, now. Maybe I won't tell your secrets; maybe I will. You told me a lot of secrets, on Suivi Point. And I know some other secrets—like yours, Domina Perada. Shall I tell those, too?"

"Do you think you can buy the Mages with your secrets?" Perada asked. "I tell you, they aren't interested."

"Maybe not, my lady," Tarveet said, "but I'm enjoying this. No matter who wins, I'll be free. And you'll be dead."

Beka drew and fired. Faster than she ever had before, with a speed that only Tarnekep Portree might have equaled. Before Tarveet could push his trigger stud.

For a moment, there was silence in number-one cargo hold, except for the scrabbling noise of Tarveet trying to pull his dropped blaster to him. Lying on the deck with his guts shot out, he wasn't making much progress.

Beka walked over and set her boot on his wrist just as his fingers touched the weapon's grip.

He looked up at her, his eyes dimmed with pain.

"I'll tell you a secret if you'll let me live. You want to know my secret, don't you?"

"Not particularly," said Beka, and shot him in the head.

RSF *Veratina* drove in toward the gigantic Mage flagship. The other members of General Metadi's small task force were out of comms—destroyed, or adrift, or too battered even to respond to hailing—and the *'Tina* herself was damaged. But the Mage flagship had been damaged too, taking missile hits at close range from some unknown ship. Metadi currently felt a vast sense of gratitude toward the commander of the unknown. Thanks to that vessel, the Mage flagship was now vulnerable, with parts of its sensor suite gone and a good portion of its shielding down.

Metadi maneuvered to remain in the flagship's sensor gaps. Soon he would be in range for a doubled attack: close enough to his target that none of his missiles would go astray; and close enough that he could time the *'Tina*'s energy guns to hammer a fraction of a second later against the points where the missiles had hit. Missiles and energy guns together would strike inward, destroying the heart of the ship before the Mageworlders' damage-control system could begin its work.

"Status of the rest of the task force?" Metadi asked.

"No comms with anyone," said the TAO.

"Net Patrol?"

"Based on what we saw, they were getting shot up pretty badly too. *Karipavo* was hit, went dark and launched lifepods before we lost her."

"Right. Concentrate on the target."

"Ten seconds to designated range. Six. Five. Four . . ."

The sensor tech stiffened abruptly. "Mage ship is dropping all shields!"

"Missiles away."

"Message coming from Mage, all frequencies, in Galcenian." The voice of the external comms tech was almost unnaturally calm, as if an excited stammer were only a few syllables away. "They surrender."

"Check fire!" Metadi half-rose from his command seat. "Check fire!"

"Hi-comms are back up," reported the sensor tech. "All Mage vessels have shields down, decelerating."

"Pass to all units, weapons tight, Metadi sends."

The comms tech looked up again. "Message from Mage vessel, marked Personal For General Metadi."

"I don't have any secrets here," Metadi said. "Put it on the speaker."

"On the speaker aye."

The speaker clicked on. "General, this is Colonel Tyche. I'm on board the Mage flagship. The Mages have laid down their arms. I have control here. The Mage commanders want to speak with you."

Metadi sat back again in his chair. "Put them on." Quietly, to the TAO, he said, "Keep their vessel covered with guns. This might be a trap."

Over the speaker came another voice. "Dadda? This is Beka. I found the bastard who ordered Mother killed. Want to go somewhere for a drink? I'll tell you all about it."

"*You're* the Mage commander?"

"No, my sister-in-law is."

"Sister-in-law? I think I need that drink."

"I'm buying the first round. Beka out."

Epilogue
Telabryk: The Seven Orbs

By the time Commodore Jervas Gil could get away from his battered command, the party at the Seven Orbs Tavern had been going on for several days.

The celebration had begun when the first shuttles from General Jos Metadi's task force hit portside. It gathered strength and continued as elements from all the other fleets in the system began to gather and send down liberty parties. At some point along the way—probably about the time that Jos Metadi conferred with Gyffer's Citizen-Assembly and declared that Gyffer and the Space Force between them would pick up the tab—the gathering turned into a full-scale free-spacer's wake and spilled over into a dozen or more taverns, pubs, bars, saloons, and dives.

Now the epicenter of the party at the Seven Orbs was filled with an odd assortment of privateers from Innish-Kyl, Gyfferan LDF officers, Space Force troopers from Suivi, the Net, and Infabede, and free-spacers from everywhere. There were even a few Mageworlders, quiet and courteous in their plain brown uniforms, sampling the local hospitality and looking somewhat incredulous that they should be drinking here at all.

In one of the tavern's back rooms, a mixed bag of revelers were singing one of the traditional songs, one that Gil had last heard in the *'Pavo'*'s detention block, and before that at Beka Rosselin-Metadi's wake on Galcen:

> *"Assemble my spaceship around me*
> *And fuel it with beer when you're done,*
> *I don't need a life-support system*
> *If only the engines will run."*

Of course, the fighting hadn't come to an instant stop everywhere in the galaxy with the cease-fire over Gyffer. The Mageworlds reserve force under sus-Hasaaden had run into the Space Force's Ontimi Sector Fleet a few days later, and each had attempted to surrender to the other before all the signals had been read; and the Pleyveran Sector Fleet was still involved in straightening out the civil war between groundside and High Station Pleyver. Nevertheless, the end of the Battle for Gyffer would probably go down in the history texts as the day the Second Magewar officially ended.

> *"Then strap me again in my cockpit*
> *And toast me in faraway bars.*
> *Just let me fire off into hyper,*
> *I'll make my own way to the stars."*

Gil supposed that he would be telling his hypothetical grandchildren about what everything had been like when peace broke out. He'd found Doctor Inesi syn-Tavaite among the crew of *Warhammer*, looking about her as if she had similar plans for the future and wanted to make certain she had the details properly fixed in her memory. He didn't blame her; in fact, he'd spent the last hour or so soaking up impressions himself, especially the conversations going on in corners between people who under normal circumstances might never have spoken at all.

There was someone who looked like Perada Rosselin in deep incognito, for example, sharing a carafe of red wine with Mid-Commander Mael Taleion and discussing, with a frankness that would have appalled the diplomats, future relations between the Mageworlds and the Republic:

"Nobody's going to give anything away officially at first," Perada had said. "But there will have to be peace negotiations—your fleet is still strong enough that everybody will agree to that."

"I am not sure that negotiations will satisfy some of our people, my lady. They are bitter, still."

Perada laughed and poured him some more wine. "As are some of ours, no doubt. Put all the bitter ones on the negotiating teams and send them to Khesat. Wonderful place to hold diplomatic conferences, Khesat. In my grandmother's day, there was a two-week war in the Wrysten system that took thirty-five years on Khesat to arrive at a settlement. The ambassadors kept breaking off the talks for more study—most of their study, it turned out later, was being done at the pleasure establishments and opera houses."

Taleion smiled in turn. "I begin to understand, my lady. And if your Space Force doesn't bother to enforce the ban at the Gap Between while the negotiations are going on—"

"They won't," said Perada. "They'll be too busy putting themselves back together after some major embarrassments. They've got Captain Faramon and the other mutinous officers to deal with, for example. Besides, the Net costs money, and the money will have more important places to go for quite a while. As for your Mage-Circles ... I think that the new Master of the Adepts' Guild sees matters differently from the way the old one did. Having the First of all your Circles for a sister-in-law seems to have changed his mind."

"All will be well, then, I think," Taleion said. "The blockade in the Gap Between was futile anyway—space is big and ships are small. We were able to move single cargoes through the Gap whenever we wished once we began to have ships. Give us leave to follow our own ways, and to trade openly with your worlds, and the rest will follow. My lord sus-Airaalin would have been content."

"Then I've kept my word to him," Perada said, "and so am I. Let's drink to his memory, Mael—after all, this is a night for toasting absent friends."

They'd drunk the toast in more of the strong red wine; and Gil, observing, had turned his attention to another corner of the room, where Beka Rosselin-Metadi and Nyls Jessan were drinking beer with her brother Ari and Mistress Llannat Hyfid. The young Domina appeared to be teasing her brother about the joys of married life.

"So how are you going to arrange things, big brother, if the Space Force sends you to the back of beyond somewhere and the Mage-Circles call for Llannat on Eraasi or Ninglin? I know that Adepts and Mages are supposed to be good at doing things long distance, but not even they can—"

"Shut up, Bee," Ari said. His ears were bright red. "We'll think of something."

"I already have thought of something," Llannat said. "I'm leaving the Space Force. Having the First of the Mages be a Space Force officer is an embarrassment to both sides. I'm going home to Maraghai. If the Mage-Circles need me they'll know how to find me."

Ari took her hand. "If you put in your papers, I might as well do it too. I'll talk to Ferrdacorr about setting up a clinic somewhere in the High Ridges—they need medics up there." He looked at his sister. "What about you, Bee? I can't exactly see you settling down into dirtside domesticity."

"Hell, no," she said. "As soon as the 'Hammer's fixed, Nyls and I are going back to running cargo through what used to be the Net. It ought to be fun—the outplanets are going to be full of pirates and outlaws and menaces to society."

"You should fit right in," Ari had said.

Gil had been forced to agree. It was just as well, he thought, that Domina Beka Rosselin-Metadi had already announced her intention to dissolve the government of Entibor-in-Exile and let the royal title lapse into oblivion. Perada Rosselin had concurred—there were a number of advantages, or so she claimed, to being officially dead, and she planned to enjoy all of them for some time to come.

Now, with Inesi syn-Tavaite on his arm, Gil made his way through the crush to the back of the pub, where the General was holding forth. Perada, her private talk with Mael Taleion safely concluded, was occupying the seat next to him, and looking smug about it.

"What are my plans for the future?" the General asked rhetorically. He had an interested audience of Space Force officers and merchant-captains, all of them pretending they didn't recognize the blonde, blue-eyed woman beside him. "I'm going to retire from the Space Force and spend my free time touring the galaxy and checking up on old friends." He caught Gil's eye. "And *you*, Commodore, are as far as I can tell the senior surviving officer in the late fiasco. If you aren't the senior survivor now, you will be by the time I'm done. You're going to take over my job."

Gil shook his head. "Oh, no, General. Not until I've used up my accumulated leave. I promised Inesi—Doctor syn-Tavaite, I mean—that I'd take her back home to Eraasi after the war was over, and I intend to keep my promise."

"Do it," said Metadi. "You can relieve me when you get back. Rosel's tour of duty isn't up for another year and a half, so she can show you the ropes."

Gil was beginning to feel trapped. "But didn't you get my message, sir? Commander Quetaya is dead—your aide is a Magebuilt replicant."

The General shook his head. "The Mages tried, but I'm afraid they missed."

"Sir?"

"The last time I saw that replicant, I'd just stuffed her into a garbage hopper at Galcen Prime." Metadi looked regretful. "She'd been well briefed, but not quite well enough, so I managed to get her before she could remove the original and take her place.

"I was right about the replicant," the General continued,

"but wrong about who was responsible. I thought it was the start of a coup by a faction inside the Space Force—I knew there was something funny going on there; I just didn't know what. And I knew that if there was one replicant there might be others, so I decided to keep quiet and take care of the problem myself."

"It worked out," Gil said, "and it put you in position to deal with Vallant."

"No, *you* dealt with Vallant—not to mention the Mage flagship."

"It was pure luck that got my missiles through to *Sword-of-the-Dawn*," Gil protested. "That's all."

"You had luck when you needed it. Those missiles hit at exactly the right time and the right place—and believe me, Commodore, I'm grateful."

"So am I," said Perada. "So am I."

"Under the circumstances," said Gil, "I suppose I should be grateful too." He turned to syn-Tavaite. "The evening is growing late. I think it's time for us to get back."

Wait just a minute, Baronet!

It was Merrolakk the Selvaur, resplendent in a celebratory coat of gold and silver body-paint.

"Ah, yes, Captain?" Gil said. Out of the corner of his eye, he could see Metadi watching him with amusement. "You have a problem?"

They say you're going to take her— Merrolakk nodded at syn-Tavaite. *—back home to Eraasi.*

"Well, yes," said Gil. "I did promise, after all."

You made me a promise too, Merro said. *When I turned her over, you said that if she had any ransom value, it was mine.*

"Yes. And?"

Seven ships, Commodore. You traded her for seven ships. So the way I figure it, that's what she's worth. Pay up.

Gil drew a deep breath. "I won't deny that Inesi syn-Tavaite is worth the ransom under discussion—"

Damned good thing, too.

"—but I will point out that I don't *have* the price of seven ships at the moment."

Merro grunted. *Not my problem. If you can't pay, I'll take my prisoner back.*

"Like hell you will," said Gil. "I'll just give you the ships, instead." He reached into his uniform pocket and pulled out a notepad and stylus.

Merro hooted at him with Selvauran laughter. *You're a pleasure to deal with, for a thin-skin.*

"There," said Gil, handing over the slip of flimsy. "Orders assigning seven vessels from the Net Patrol Fleet to you for administrative and tactical control. My aide will see to the details. Done?"

Done, said the Selvaur, and proferred a green-scaled hand.

They shook hands on the deal. Then, with a sigh of relief, Gil was finally able to start making his way back through the crowded pub toward the door. Beside him, Inesi syn-Tavaite was looking worried.

"Will you get in trouble for giving ships away like that?" she asked. "They belong to the Republic, don't they?"

"They used to," he said. "With the Net being dismantled they wouldn't have a lot to do, anyway. But that isn't my problem. I'm taking you home before I do anything else. If the Space Force is angry with me for giving away those ships, they can cashier me. If I'm lucky, some job for a penniless baronet is bound to turn up."

"My people say, 'Luck belongs to the people who make it,' " syn-Tavaite said.

"I'm planning to make myself quite a lot of it," Gil said. He offered her his arm. "Starting now, I think. My lady, will you do me the honor of traveling aboard my flagship?"

syn-Tavaite took his arm and smiled. "With pleasure, my lord baronet."

THE BEST IN
SCIENCE FICTION